SEE NO EVIL

KENDRA MORENO

Copyright © 2023 by Kendra Moreno

All rights reserved.

No part of this book may be reproduced in any form or by any electronic or mechanical means, including information storage and retrieval systems, without written permission from the author, except for the use of brief quotations in a book review.

Paperback Cover by RJ Creatives
Chapter Header Art by Daz Inks
Proofreading by Turbo Kitten Industries
Formatting by The Nutty Formatter

For every woman who has ever choked on the words in your throat,
Whose first taste of blood was from biting your tongue.
This one's for you.

Always be Lilith, Never Eve

TRIGGER WARNING

This book has mentions of some topics that may affect those with triggers. Please make sure to read below carefully and if further clarification is needed, feel free to email me at <u>kendramorenoauthor@gmail.com</u> to ask. I will be happy to explain the source of the triggers. I want you to read my book, but mental health comes first. Please tread carefully.

Triggers:
Religious Trauma, Drug Use, Drug Overdose, Violence, Slight gore, A scene with knife play and *Death*

First Death

The apple tempts on the branch.
Take me. Taste me. Ruin me.
Eve never stood a chance.
We all eat lies when our hearts are hungry...

1

MENA

Death sticks in your throat like the last bite of cake you could not say no to.

That's the first thought that crosses my mind as my senses slowly come back to me. The second thought is that I can't see. I open my eyes to darkness, the kind of darkness that is so thick, there's not a single detail to be made out of it. Reaching out to find something familiar, perhaps my bed sheets, my hand only finds the hardness of wood. It's close, barely a few inches in front of my face, and when I move around, I realize I'm completely surrounded by it. A box. I'm in a box barely large enough to fit my body, let alone to allow much movement.

Panic seizes me. The last thing I remember is Agatha Abernathy's ball. She'd gone all out again this year, hiring circus performers and dancers to attend and steal the show anytime anyone else thought to dance. Agatha is known for her creativity, but it gets rather ridiculous at a certain point. I felt the circus performers were over the top and unnecessary, but she'll be remembered this year and that's all she cares about.

In addition to the performers, Agatha had brought in one of the best pastry chefs from Paris for her party. There'd been tables laden with cakes and treats that I'd been unable to resist. The pastry chef was money well spent at least, but the last thing I remember is taking a bite that I no longer had the room for in my corset. As a widowed woman, I'm not held to the same standards as the young ladies trying to find a husband. I'm allowed the decorum of eating whatever I wish, as long as my corset allows it. I'd had my corset particularly tight for Agatha's party, determined to show off my figure. After all, there's been talks behind my back about my waist lately. My pride had gotten the better of me, though not enough to dissuade me from the cake that had tasted like sugared caramels.

As if the thought of it brings memories back, the taste floods my mouth again and makes it water despite the panic at not knowing what's going on. For a second, I'm reminded again of the bite, of that savory sweetness I craved almost impulsively. My throat clenches violently and tightens, a cough retching up from deep in my chest.

The last bite of cake clears my throat and I'm able to spit it out to the side of me. The memory of choking, of not being able to breathe fills my mind. Of frantically gesturing for someone to notice that I couldn't breathe at Agatha's ball. Everyone had looked at me in amusement, too owl-eyed to realize just how much trouble I was in. My vision had darkened, and then I remember nothing else. What had happened? Am I in a hospital? No, I wouldn't be in a box if that were the case.

"Hello?" I call, my voice echoing too loud inside the box. The sound doesn't seem to travel very far. When I thump on the walls of my prison, I realize that there's no hollow sound, as if I'm cushioned on every side. My heart drops and some false instinct convinces me I just didn't speak loud enough before. "Can anyone hear me? Hello? I need help! I. . . I can't move! Anyone?"

There's no answer and the harder I listen, the more static fills my ears. No one is coming to help me. I can't even be sure anyone is hearing my calls. Which leaves only one option.

I'll have to get myself out of this situation.

I press my hand against the surface above me, running my fingers along the woodgrain to determine any weaknesses. When I find the fine crack that splits along the edge, I thank God that someone hammered in a nail that split the wood. They are a terrible craftsman, but if not for that, there would be nothing I can do. I'm not particularly strong even though I'd like to think I am. I press against the crack and the wood creaks. Taking a deep breath, I start to hit the crack as hard as I can. It doesn't do much. I can hardly use my body weight in this position and with so little room to draw my hand back, it takes considerable wasted effort, but I do the best I can. I keep my fingers balled into a fist and hit, and hit, and hit, until my knuckles are sore and wet. The blood starts to drip down my arm, but I don't pay attention to it. Instead, I switch back and forth between my hands, trying to space out my hits so I don't get exhausted too fast. Unfortunately, I'm still not that strong. I don't magically get stronger the longer I hit. My panic slows me down, forcing me to stop every few minutes to take deep breaths to calm myself. When one of my hits makes the wood creak and split, something falls from the crack I've made and splatters across my face. I choke and try to shift despite there not being enough room for that, but some of the material still ends up in my mouth. The grit of dirt makes me grimace, but it doesn't affect me nearly as much as the realization that comes with it.

Dirt. I'm in a box.

Someone buried me alive.

The panic threatens to choke me, but again, I'm the only one who's going to come to my rescue, so I take a few deep breaths and continue to hit the box, more dirt starting to funnel into my box, taking up precious room. The wood splits and I'm able to tear a large piece of the wood away, pulling it in and shoving it down, soft dirt following behind. I keep my mouth closed, terrified of suffocating on the dirt falling on top of me. I tear more and more pieces above me away and kick them to the bottom of my... coffin. When it feels large enough to sit up, I start to dig my way up through the dirt. Thankfully, it's as soft as freshly dug earth, so perhaps I haven't been buried for long.

I keep my eyes closed as I claw at the dirt, exhaustion tugging at me despite my desperation. I don't know how much longer I can continue, but I refuse to give up now. Pushing my way up through the dirt is a lot like swimming in molasses. Each stroke comes with far too little progress, but progress all the same. The dirt and mud clings to me viciously, threatening to drag me down again. I push hard, using my damaged hands and my shoulders. Every few minutes I take a moment to breathe. I have to keep my head tilted down so that pockets of air form around my mouth while in the dirt. It's a brutal journey, but finally, after what feels like hours and hours, I reach up to claw away dirt and my hand breaks through. Relief fills me as I shove as hard as I can, desperation coating my rapid breathing. My limbs are weak, but that doesn't stop me from breaking the surface and taking in a great gulp of air.

My head and arms break the surface first. I wipe the dirt from around my eyes and catch sight of the night sky for the first time. Everything in my body sings at the sight that I wasn't sure I'd be able to see again.

"Just a little more strength," I rasp to myself, my voice thick and raw from my prior choking.

With what little strength I have left, I hoist myself up, dragging first my chest from the mud and then my hips. Wiggling back and forth, I claw at the grass and free myself from my grave. I collapse immediately and roll onto my back, taking in the full moon above me. It's almost beautiful despite the circumstances. Carefully, I roll onto my stomach and push myself up on shaking arms to take in the grave in front of me. There's only a wooden sign on the grave right now. No doubt the gravestone is still being carved, so this is temporary.

"Philomena Seagraves," I read out loud. "10 September 1872 to 7 July 1901." The night of Agatha's ball. So what day is it now? Beneath the dates, the words "Beloved wife" are inscribed, and I scowl. Is that all I was? A widower? Is that the only worth I was ever assigned? Bloody bastards. Whoever was in charge of my gravestone was a twat.

"You know, I thought the most shocking part of watching a woman claw her way up from a fresh grave would be the clawing part," a voice says. My heart nearly leaps out of my throat as I spin and take in the man sitting a few feet away on another gravestone. "Instead," he continues, as if this isn't a mad situation, "the most shocking part of you coming out of a grave is that you look completely perturbed by what's on your gravestone."

"Who are you?" I command, trying to sound fierce, but my raspy, damaged throat makes it less authoritative than I'd like. "Did you do this to me?"

He laughs, a throaty sound that makes something inside of me unfurl and pay attention despite this entire situation. It's then that I take him in completely. He's dressed in a black suit that looks out-of-date, as if he hasn't caught onto the current fashions. The material looks expensive though, so perhaps he's some eccentric rich man living in the past. Which might have been more believable had he not appeared close to my own age. No older than thirty-five, he's a dashing man, his facial features struck exactly in the way that makes young eligible women fan themselves in arousal. His eyes are a striking ice blue, so light, they're almost white. His skin is equally as pale as his eyes, even more of a clash with his dark evening suit. When he laughs at my words, he throws his head back in amusement, exposing a regal throat that makes me want to run my tongue along it.

I blink. Here I sit covered in mud, probably before my would-be murderer, and I'm thinking about his throat. What has gotten into me?

The man finally collects himself and meets my eyes. The eye contact is unnerving, like looking into a scene I shouldn't be allowed to see.

"Did I bury you? Of course not. Darling, my job is to lead souls to the Underworld, not to release the soul in the first place."

My weakness is starting to get to me, and I press my hand against my forehead when pain starts to pulse. I'm exhausted and desperate for answers, but my energy is waning.

"You speak in riddles," I grunt, closing my eyes against the sudden pain behind them. "What has happened to me?"

"Your answers are as good as mine," he replies, still highly amused. "Imagine my surprise when I was called to your death to collect a soul only to find I couldn't collect the soul at all because, well, here you are. I didn't know what to expect at first, but watching you burst from the ground like some Penny Dreadful has made my evening, I'll tell you that."

I crack my eyes to glare at him. "You're talking about death," I rasp. "You're clearly delusional. I'm alive, as apparent by my presence before you now."

"Yes," he nods knowingly. "You're very much alive now. There's no question of that. But you were not so only twenty-four hours ago. You were at least dead long enough to be buried."

The pain behind my eyes increases and I grimace at it. "You're mad. I wasn't dead. I'm not dead. Look at me."

He tilts his head in curiosity, his brows furrowing. "Well, clearly you have no more answers than I do, little Dreadful. That's okay. We can—"

But his words fade away from my mind as I get a good look at the world around us. I'm in a graveyard, clearly. I should have expected that all things considering. But with the bite of pain behind my eyes that threatens to split my skull and the sweet sugary taste of cake in my mouth, something else draws my attention and holds it. People are milling about as if it's daytime. They're dressed in strange, outdated clothing, just like the man before me, but that's where the similarities end. These people glow with a faint green light, and when they cross paths with one of the gravestones, I can see it clearly reflected through them. Terror fills me.

I scramble back suddenly, making the man sitting before me pause. He follows my gaze and frowns.

"What's the matter with you now? Are you going to die again?" He shrugs. "At least I'll be able to fulfill my duty. I've got to tell you, you're not the only soul to ferry tonight. The moment you woke, and your soul reentered your body, there's been a call for someone else. I have a schedule to keep you know."

"Do you . . . Do you see them?" I ask frantically, pointing at the nearest person floating around. "Tell me you see them?"

He frowns. "The lost souls? Of course I see them. I'm the Grim Reaper. The real question is why can you see them?"

My eyes jerk to him and take in the matter-of-fact expression on his face. He doesn't look scary. He doesn't even give off an aura of danger to me, but his words filter into my mind.

I'm the Grim Reaper...

Fear and true panic fill me until I find myself scrambling away from him, away from the phantoms around us, my muddy and ripped dress wrapping around my legs and making it difficult to move quickly. I've lost my mind. This has to all be a dream, and if it's not, I'm drugged up in an asylum somewhere. There's no way all of this is true. It can't be.

"What... What... This doesn't..."

The man rolls his eyes. "I can see this will take longer for you to understand. You died, and then you didn't. You—"

But I'm no longer listening. My exhaustion still eating at my bones and threatening to make me drop, I launch to my feet and begin to run on my weak limbs. The gown I wear is difficult to run in with it sticking to me after the mud, but I can't help it. I need to get away. I need to go home.

This is a dream. This is a dream. This is a dream.

Despite that line repeating in my mind over and over again, I still run, just in case it's not.

2
ATHAN

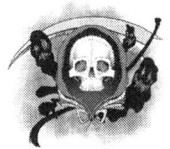

I watch her go with true confusion. What the fuck is going on here? First, I show up to her death only to be blocked from taking her soul, and then she climbs out of the ground like some demonic creature rising from the dead. In all my centuries as the Grim Reaper, I've never seen anything like it. I've certainly never felt the type of power that she exudes. Human? Or something else? Despite my duties, I need to know. I need to figure out this puzzle and learn what exactly happened here. None of it makes sense.

"Does this happen often around here?" I ask the nearest lost soul, an older woman who looks like she used to make a nice stew in her living days.

The woman pauses her haunting to look over at me with hollow, sad eyes. Lost souls don't often linger because they had full and happy lives. Their trauma blocks them from moving on. Some of them don't even understand they're dead, but this one clearly does. The wrinkles in her face show her story of a hard life despite being important enough to be in an aristocratic graveyard. I can't feel her body here, but when she runs her hand along a gravestone of a man, I realize she's not here because of her. The man is buried next to another woman, his wife, but clearly, there was some drama incurred between them.

"Not as often as you'd think," she answers in a heavily accented voice. Ireland, perhaps? "Usually when they pop up, they're clean."

I blink. Ah, so this lost soul believes the woman to have just been another lost soul. I already know that's not the case. The woman, Philomena as her marker says, was flesh and blood, and her soul never left her body. I'd been called here to a death that wasn't a true death. Which is strange. Dead is dead usually.

"Thank you for your help," I tell the woman warmly. I point to the grave. "He's not lost. He went into the light with his wife." I only offer the information in case it makes her change her mind about lingering around, in case she would like to continue on.

She sighs. "I know. I loved that man with every fiber of my being, but he never loved me enough to risk his fortune." She meets my eyes. "Love is both a blessing and a curse."

"I could walk you into the light," I offer. "If you'd like. I'm told it feels a lot like going home."

She shakes her head. "I don't have a home anymore, Reaper. There's nowhere to return. Nowhere to go. My house is a ruin, a cemetery, so in this cemetery is where I'll remain." She sighs so deeply that I can feel her pain. "I don't deserve to go."

Sadness fills me. Lost Souls suffer their guilt for all eternity, and clearly, this woman's guilt is heavy. She's aware of what she is, understands what I am, so she'll always be aware of her failings and her sins. It's a sad existence, a painful one. "If you ever change your mind, you only have to call for me."

She bows her head in thanks and settles on top of the grave of her once lover, her fingers tracing the carved lines there, as if trying to burn them into her fingertips.

I leave her there, along with the other lost souls, and follow the trail of mud left behind by the woman. I may be a busy man, but the souls can wait until I figure out just what's going on with Philomena.

My curiosity needs satiating, and the only way to do so is to follow her and see what she knows. Even if it's nothing.

And it has nothing to do with how beautiful she was even fresh from a grave. Of course it doesn't. I'm only curious.

Besides, curiosity is the lust of the mind, so it only makes sense.

With a heavy sigh, I shift into my Church Grim form and follow.

3
MENA

No one tells you that accidently dying and not really being dead has its immediate downsides.

In my rush to get away from the man in the graveyard, I thought of nothing but getting back home and putting distance between us. By the time I find myself on the cobblestones outside of my home, I've convinced myself it's all a trick, that some arsehole is enjoying playing some silly fool's trick on me. I'm so convinced of this that I forget I also climbed from a grave not even an hour ago and so therefore, I'm still caked in mud and blood from my knuckles. So when I climb the steps to my home and turn the knob to slip inside, I don't think about what I may look like.

Not until Mrs. Kingsley, my head housekeeper, screams and drops the vase she'd been carrying. It shatters across the floor, dancing along the marble and cutting at my bare feet. She covers her mouth as she stares at me, horror flashing in her eyes.

"Mrs. Kingsley," I try, holding out my hands to calm her. "It's me, Mena."

Talking does the opposite of my desired effect. Hearing me speak sends her into a fit of terror and she immediately jerks back. "Demon!" she screams. "Phantom! Help me!"

"No, no, no. I'm not a demon," I reassure her. At least I don't think I am. As if to doublecheck, I press my hand against my forehead, searching for horns, but I find nothing. No, not a demon. Just very confused. "Mrs. Kingsley. I'm not dead. I wasn't dead when they buried me! I don't know what's happened, but it's been a terrible evening and I—" My voice chokes off when the sob fills my throat. "I need help. Please."

Mrs. Kingsley doesn't stop screaming until Mrs. Lily, the chef, and Mr. Kline, my carrier, come running. They freeze when they see me standing in the entryway covered in mud and grime, and the chaos only increases. They all panic at the sight of me, as I stand shivering before them. I'm leaving behind muddy tracks, but I can't be bothered to think about that right now. I'm desperate to get clean and hide from the world.

"Stop! Please," I cry, the sobs starting to spill from my throat truly now. "Please! I don't know what's happening!"

When their panic doesn't dissipate and Mrs. Kingsley faints from being so worked up, I can't take it anymore. I rush toward the stairs, desperate to get away, to hide from all of this mess. It'll go away as long as I ignore it. I can pretend nothing is happening.

I take the stairs two at a time, scrambling up them on legs too weak to do more than support me. I bruise my shins, but I don't care. I just need to hide.

I'm so fully focused on that task as I reach the top of the stairs, that I almost miss the phantom strolling along the top of the staircase, a man I recognize from portraits. My late husband's grandfather. He notices me staring at him in horror and turns toward me curiously, but I don't want anything to do with him. I don't want to see phantoms. I don't want this. Oh God, I don't want this.

Rushing past the phantom, I slam against my bedroom door and slip inside. The furniture is all covered by sheets, and I shriek in panic and terror. I'd died. I'd really died and been buried. What is happening to me? What am I?

Scrambling to the corner of the room, I curl into a ball and cry on my knees, overwhelmed and terrified. Something whistles in my ears, like someone is whistling a tune a long way down the street, and a horn blares faintly, but I curl myself tighter and hide, afraid of what else those sounds might bring.

I'm still covered in mud, still dressed in my burial gown, but I can do nothing but hide from the world. My chest aches with my sobs, my lungs begging for relief. There will be none.

I stay curled up in a ball in the corner and cry until I have no more tears to spill. When the first rays of the sun break the horizon and come in through the window, I'm numb.

But numb is better than afraid.

Numb is better than dead.

4
MENA

I have not moved for three days. I remain in the corner in my dirty burial gown until the mud dries and makes me feel like a long forgotten doll in an attic. If I move, the shell cracks, and I'm not prepared for what will come from the cracks when that happens. I feel foreign, so strange in my own body, that I can't fathom anything besides sitting in this corner. My stomach growls with hunger pains, but still I don't move. I can't. What beast will be released if I decide to play at being human again? What will I have to face?

I know now it was no illusion. I understand that I died at Agatha's party and by some twist of fate, I came back. Death is supposed to be eternal. When you die, you go to Heaven or Hell, if the Church is to be believed. I consider myself religious, but all of that fades into the background in the face of what I'm witnessing. When I'd died, there had only been darkness. There were no great gates into a golden city. There were no angels singing to welcome me home. In the same thought, there was no burning, no fire, no hell. Perhaps it's because my soul never left, but perhaps it's because those two things don't exist. Compared to the rest of the events, I'm least concerned with my religion and my unstable relationship with God. There are bigger problems right now.

Such as on this third day, when the maids begin to knock and call through the door to check on me.

The sheets draped over all the furniture remain where they were when I came rushing into this room. Likely, things had been covered in preparation for whatever heir they had managed to find to take over the business and inheritance. The poor sod would be disappointed when he was informed that I am not in fact dead. The maids, after their initial shock and horror, would have likely uncovered everything outside, but they hadn't been brave enough to come searching until now.

"Miss Seagraves," Mrs. Kingsley calls through the door hesitantly.

I don't move, afraid to. I don't want to know what it feels like to crack this shell of mud around me. I don't know what emotions will come tumbling out.

Mrs. Kingsley has never called me by my surname in private. She's been with me for ten years at this point, so she calls me Mena. She's never allowed me to call her by her first name out of decorum, but in my weakest moments, she allows me to call her Molly. I've never felt weaker and somehow also more strong than I do right now.

"Mena," Mrs. Kingsley murmurs. "May I come in, child?"

Only Mrs. Kingsley could call a nearly thirty-year-old woman a child.

I don't answer her, afraid to lift my head let alone crack my lips. My limbs are stiff from sitting in the same position for so long. My chest aches with the pain of not understanding what's happening to me. Every now and then, I hear that whistle along with this strange ominous clanking and horn that I can't place. It's not constant, so it's easy to ignore until it comes again. My stomach growls in pain. I should be incredibly weak by now without food and water but despite the situation, I don't feel on the verge of death again.

I feel almost... strong.

"I'm coming in, Mena," Mrs. Kingsley calls and then I hear the doorknob turn. When she discovers it locked, there's a shuffle and then the jingle of keys. I'd forgotten the master keys, but clearly Mrs. Kingsley did not. I don't lift my head when the door swings open with a creak. I know she's peering into the darkness, searching for me, and when she finds me huddled in the corner, she pauses.

"Have you crawled up in that corner and died like an injured animal?" she asks. When I don't immediately answer, she takes a halting step inside. "Mena?"

Carefully, I ease my head up. My neck aches in protest at the movement. The mud caked around my body cracks as it shifts, the now dried substance littering the floor as it falls away in chunks. I don't know what I look like, but I know it must not be pretty by the way Mrs. Kingsley gasps. I can tell she wants to leave me here. What a sight I must make as an undead woman. What a horror I must appear.

I open my mouth to reply, and my lips split and bleed. My voice is raw in my throat and the first sound out of my mouth is a croak that doesn't help matters. It takes a few times of clearing my throat before I can whisper, "I'm alive."

Mrs. Kingsley nods as if that settles everything. "Right, well, let us get you cleaned up, dear. We can't have you wearing mud."

Grimacing, I glance down at the sheer amount of dirt that remains caked on my skin. "I must have left a mess behind."

She waves away my words. "It's no trouble, child. You rarely leave a mess. It gave the others something to fill their minds with instead of... well..." She gestures to my appearance, and I frown.

"Circumstances were rather dire, I'm afraid," I offer.

"Come, come. We'll get you in the bath and then you can tell me all about it."

Mrs. Kingsley helps me stand. My limbs groan in protest at being moved after being prone for as long as I was. Small bits of dirt flake off as I move, leaving a trail behind as she helps me to the bathing chamber and starts to fill the tub. I wait until she tells me to get into the warm water and sigh at the feeling. Normally, I bathe myself, but Mrs. Kingsley helps with the motions, and when it comes to my hair, she offers to wash it instead, giving my aching limbs a rest.

"Now that you look more like yourself," she says as she settles to the side of the tub. "Tell me what happened."

"I don't honestly know," I whisper, tucking my chin on top of my knees above the water. "I remember choking and then I woke up in darkness. I was... buried."

Mrs. Kingsley nods her head. "We were informed of your passing a few hours after you left for Mrs. Abernathy's ball. A bellman came and explained you had perished. I'll tell you we were stricken with grief. There's not a single one of us that wished that sort of fate on you, child. There was a funeral held the next day. I was in attendance."

I peer over at her. "Did I look... dead?"

"I wouldn't know, Mena. You were sealed up in that pine box, so we didn't see you." She studies me. "There was no sound coming from it."

Sighing, I meet her eyes. "So I was dead, and now I'm not."

There's nothing said between us for a few minutes as those words weigh heavily. It feels like some profound realization, but it also reminds me that I'm not crazy. Everyone assumed I was dead because I was. I wasn't buried alive. I was buried at a funeral, dead as can be, and then I woke up from whatever strange ailment affected me.

"Yes, well, there was some chap from the country thinking he had inherited everything. We were preparing the house for his arrival, but I've already sent word that circumstances have changed and your death was only a rumor. Some second cousin to the late Mr. Seagraves I believe. I've instructed everyone to return the house to your liking and food is being prepared. You haven't eaten in days."

On cue, my stomach grumbles and she smiles, falling back into the same pattern as before.

"Food would be lovely," I murmur. "Would you mind terribly if I take it in my rooms?"

Her smile is gentle as she pats me on the shoulder and stands. "I'll have it sent in, dear. Do you need anything else?"

Yes. My sanity. But I don't say that out loud. Instead, I carefully shake my head no, and she leaves me to my bathing. I sit there long after my skin prunes and the water cools, and then I drag myself out, dress, and lay down in my bed. I have no desire to go out and find more phantoms or be faced with more evidence of my resurrection.

The horn sounds again in the distance.

5
MENA

Walter Seagraves was a well-established merchant when I met him at one of the balls. I was a young, eligible woman, and he was one of the most eligible bachelors looking for a wife that season. I was twenty-two, a bit old by many men's standards, but still pretty enough that I had options. I'd never much liked the parading around of women like we were pieces of meat at the butcher, but it had been necessary. My mother had taken the utmost time to ensure I stood out in Parisian gowns despite my distaste for the pomp and circumstance. When Walter had taken notice of me, I'd been resentful at first, until I grew to know him.

He was a sweet man, kind and gentle in the ways most men were not. Despite those traits, he was a brilliant businessman and made his family fortune grow exponentially. I'd grown to care for him, though I would not call it love. Everything about him was just nice, perfectly pleasing, even the intimacy. I found that there was no variation in his niceness and grew bored quickly. Walter, however, was smitten with me and we were a good match. I could have done much worse, so I'd settled into a life with him.

And then tragedy struck.

Walter had gone on a business trip to barter a deal with another businessman in Italy. There'd been a storm that the ship had not been able to weather. I received the letter a month after he left informing me of his death and immediately panicked at what was to be done. Women don't inherit estates, so I would be at the whims of whatever family member came to take it away.

But Walter Seagraves was perhaps the nicest man in all of England. Unbeknownst to me, he had a will drawn up after our marriage, sealed and notarized so it could not be contested. There would be no man taking over the estate. It was to be left to me entirely, in my name. The proper avenues had already been taken care of and I would want for nothing. All of his business dealings became my own. All of his assets were bestowed upon me. I would not be at the whims of a man.

And so, at the ripe age of twenty-four, I became a rich widow without a man's control, the most dangerous animal according to the London elite, and also the most interesting.

Life was a whirlwind after that moment, and it hasn't stopped since. I oversee large merchant ships and their business dealings. I must also keep up social appearances. It's exhausting, and I've developed a distaste for social interactions as necessary as they are.

Still, I have no desire to handle any of that now. I've not even left my rooms since I came back from the dead, holed away like some feral, frightened animal. The one time I'd tried to leave the room, I'd been faced with the familiar phantom again and ended up slamming the door in his face. Despite his incorporeal form, he didn't encroach on my privacy which is a relief if I'm being honest. If he'd have followed, I might have run screaming through the house, and I doubt Mrs. Kingsley would be able to smooth over yet another mental break. They'd end up calling the asylum for me. So, in my rooms I remain for now, until I feel brave enough to face whatever insanity I'm currently suffering from.

I'm sitting in my reading nook now, perusing a new book Mrs. Kingsley had brought in for me. The story is interesting enough, but my mind keeps wandering to thoughts of the coffin, to that feeling of darkness and claustrophobia that I have no desire to ever repeat. I'm so lost in thought that I don't realize I'm no longer alone until he clears his throat.

I shriek, the book in my hands going flying as I jerk violently from the surprise. I scramble from the nook and stare with wide eyes at the familiar man standing across from me. He's staring at me in amusement again, as if I'm his favorite theater piece.

"Is that anyway to welcome an old friend?" he chastises, his eyes taking in my state of undress. "I see you've finally cleaned up. Good. I was starting to worry coming back from the dead had warped your mind."

Realizing that I'm trapped in my room with this creature, I grab the closest thing near me to brandish it as a weapon. When it turns out to be a silver candlestick, I hold out in front of me, prepared to hit him as hard as I can, he laughs.

"What's that going to do?" he asks with a grin. "Set me on fire?"

"How did you get in here?" I hiss, holding the candlestick like a club. "What do you want?"

He shrugs. "I'm the Grim Reaper, Little Dreadful. There isn't much that can keep me out." He takes a step toward me, and I tense, prepared to swing the candlestick. "You realize I'm not human, right? I doubt you can hurt me with a true weapon, let alone with a silver candlestick."

I blink, but I don't lower the candlestick. It gives me some sort of comfort to have something held in my hands. Otherwise, I might descend into a fit of terror and panic.

"What do you want?" I ask again, gritting my teeth at the constant amusement he seems to feel around me.

"Well," he replies, moving to take a seat in one of my reading chairs, "I watched you crawl your way from a grave after dying. I'm trying to figure out how."

"I have no answers for you," I growl. "You might as well leave."

He sighs and looks around the room, his eyes taking in the bed and the stack of books I've made my way through since I've been locked in my solitude. "Have you left your room at all?" There's pity in his voice, care, but I shake my head at that. There's no way this creature cares at all for me.

"No," I reply, the candlestick lowering a little. "Can you blame me?"

Shaking his head, he gestures for the window seat. I sit down to humor him, and because my own curiosity is eating at me. He claims to be the Grim Reaper, but I've imagined death to be this scary monster who steals your soul in the night. This man seems kind despite his constant amusement.

"Neither one of us have answers for what you are, Philomena—"

"Just Mena," I correct him, and when his eyes trail along my face, I flush. "My friends call me Mena."

He bows his head. "Yes, well, we have no idea how the events have come to transpire, Mena. I assume you're as curious for answers as I am, so what do you say we work together to figure it out?"

"How do I know I can trust you?" I ask, staring at him. He really is a beautiful man, but if he's what he says he is, then he could be dangerous. "How do I know you're not here to just harvest my soul at the first opportunity?"

The deep husky laughter that spills from him warms me in ways it shouldn't. I straighten, waiting on his answer.

"That's not how it works, Little Dreadful. There are rules even I must follow. I cannot take a soul tethered to a body. Though I'm called to death, I do nothing more than escort the souls to the Underworld. I do not kill. I do not steal." He steeples his fingers together. "As for trusting me, I give you my word that I will cause you no harm and when my curiosity is sated, I will leave you in peace."

"The word of Death," I breathe, studying him. "Does that hold much weight?"

His eyes crinkle, but the smile doesn't quite enter his eyes. "The heaviest."

I take a few seconds to consider his words before sighing and looking out the window. Out on the street, I can see normal people going about their business. Among them, I see more phantoms, lingering, some trailing along after people, some frantically running. I don't know anything about them except that I can suddenly see them after my death. Perhaps this man, this Grim Reaper, can give me the answers I seek. Perhaps, he can help me figure out what's happening to me.

"I accept," I finally say. "Where do we look for answers first?"

"Before any of that," he says. "I think it's time you left your rooms." When I start to shake my head, he stops me. "If we're to research anything, it can't be from inside this room. There are a great many things we must do to discover the source of this... ailment." He tilts his head. "Besides, someone so beautiful as you should never hide away in the shadows."

My chest warms but I don't outwardly react. I don't know if it's a good thing or a dangerous thing that Death thinks I'm beautiful.

"I suppose if we're to discover anything, I must leave," I murmur. "I have business that needs attending to I'm certain. What's first, Reaper?"

He nods. "If we're going to be working together, you can call me Athan."

"Athan," I repeat, and he straightens. "Okay, Athan. What first?"

His pale eyes flash in the low light. "Whatever you are, Mena, you're a mystery. And it's been so long since I've had a good mystery."

The way his eyes linger on me makes me shift in discomfort, but it's not out of fear.

No. Not fear at all.

I've truly gone insane then. That's the only answer that makes sense.

Otherwise, I would not be lusting after the Grim Reaper like a woman overcome with hysteria.

6
ATHAN

After initially following Mena from the cemetery, I'd expected to arrive somewhere far different from the grand estate in the middle of London's richest district. Though she'd been buried in the aristocrat section, I still hadn't expected her to have such a large home. I certainly hadn't expected her to live in it alone save for her staff. Women in this time do not own property, but this one does. When I'd watched her walk inside and cause chaos with her appearance, I decided to leave her to rest and search for my own answers.

I'd looked into any other possible clue mentioned in the Death Codex and there had been nothing, no mention of a soul refusing to leave a body and therefore reanimating it. Seeking out a necromancer had done nothing but cause me annoyance when the idiot had declared me a monster and tried to kill me. I have no doubt he would have then tried to reanimate me. I didn't have the heart to tell him necromancy didn't affect Reapers. That's just the way of things and if he were somehow successful in killing me, it wouldn't make any difference to me. I'd left him to his mumbling and mad ramblings. Necromancers are my least favorite of the magic users.

I came back to the source again seeking my answers, only to find her still hiding away in her rooms. It does me no good to have a scared kitten, so I immediately pressure her to leave, only because it'll foster her health. So she died and came back to life, had to dig her way up from six feet down? I've seen humans handle worse.

Probably.

To my surprise, it doesn't take much prodding, but the first time she steps from the doorway and sees the lost soul, she freezes.

"They can't hurt you," I tell her. "Lost souls are just spirits that refuse to move on for whatever reason they hold. Have you always been able to see them?"

She shakes her head. "No, not until after. . . I dug my way out."

Nodding, I glance at the old lost soul watching us curiously. "Then it's a new development. We should note that down."

"I doubt I can forget it," she grumbles, and the sarcasm in her voice makes me smile. Not a scared kitten at all, just in shock.

Everything about Mena is a wonder. She lives alone in this large house. At the top of the staircase hangs a portrait of her and a slightly older man. She's as beautiful in that painting as she is in person. With her prim stature that tells me she was trained to be a lady from birth and her bone structure, she was meant for a life such as this. She wears her womanly curves well and though she doesn't currently wear a corset in favor of a more comfortable dress, she's built by a loving hand. When she glances at me, her eyes flash from dark blue to ice in the light, as if there's a sheen there. When I frown and peer closer, it's gone, leaving behind the pretty blue. How strange.

This woman is a mystery. From the way she carries herself to the way she'd died. I've never been called to a death where I could not collect the soul. I'd waited there on top of the grave for hours, attempting to figure out what I was doing wrong, when she'd burst her way forth. It's all very odd.

"Your husband isn't here to tend to your recovery?" I ask, gesturing toward the portrait. Many women have husbands who travel the world and leave their wives at home to miss them. Perhaps, this one is no different.

She glances up at the portrait with a frown. "My late husband is none of your concern."

I raise my brows. "It must have been a shock to become a widow at such a young age."

Her lips purse in annoyance, but she still replies. "It was still not nearly as shocking as current events."

The chuckle slips out before I can stop it. Quick wit as well as beauty. What a catch her late husband must have thought he caught before his death.

"As I expected," I offer with a smile. "Well, your company is much appreciated. It's been so long since I've been able to just chat with someone. Though I will have to leave at random moments, I will thoroughly enjoy our time together, Mena."

She glances at me, her pupils dilating at my use of her name. Those eyes flash ice again and return to normal. The mystery calls even harder, and I smile.

"Where shall we start?" she asks, sighing as she looks around the large office and library.

I settle onto the large masculine leather sofa and grin up at her. "Tell me, Mena. Do you perhaps have a copy of the Bible?"

7
MENA

I don't realize how long we've spent in the office parlor until Mrs. Kingsley appears in the doorway with a frown. Her eyes trace over the room, take in my relaxed posture in my chair, before going over to Athan where he sprawls out on the settee. I can tell she wants to ask who he is and how he got in the house, but instead, she focuses back on me.

"I hadn't realized you'd left your rooms, Ms. Seagraves. Will your guest be staying for supper?"

My eyes immediately slide over to Athan and his permanent expression of amusement. Does a Grim Reaper eat? I hadn't ever thought to ask. "Will you be staying for supper, Mr. Reaper?"

His brows raise at my formal title. He'd never offered a surname so I'm using his title. Most would not question it. Mrs. Kingsley studies him closely while I address him, as if confused about him. I don't blame her. Athan is incredibly beautiful for a man, but he also gives off an air of danger that almost doesn't make sense. Such plush lips shouldn't be capable of venom, but I have no doubt that Athan can be as conniving as any man, if not more so.

"If it is no trouble," he finally answers. "I would love to stay for supper."

Mrs. Kingsley nods. "Then it will be served in a few minutes. We'll await your arrival in the dining room."

She sends one last lingering look toward Athan before nodding at me. She leaves without voicing the question in her eyes, but I know she'll ask me later. Her curiosity won't allow her to ignore it.

"Mrs. Kingsley, was it?" Athan asks, watching her curiously. "She cares an awful lot about you."

Shrugging at his prodding, I stand and stretch my limbs. They've ached as of late, as if they're no longer properly aligned inside my body. "Molly has been with me for a decade. She's as fond of me as I am her." Looking toward the doorway, I gesture for Athan to join me. "She will come back in this room with far more ire if we don't head to the dining room. Her decorum is only for your benefit."

The way his lips tip up makes something in my stomach flutter. I expected someone who is the personification of death to be creepy and hollow, but so far, though Athan is very suave and teasing, he's also incredibly kind. Who would have thought that the Grim Reaper would be so filled with kindness?

Athan offers me his elbow like any proper gentleman, so I slide my arm through his and allow him to lead me toward the dining room. I'm certainly not dressed to receive company and Mrs. Kingsley seems to think the same as we step inside, her brow raising.

The dining room features a table large enough for ten, but I've rarely used it for so many. For years, it's only been myself and my staff who take a seat and eat. We're far less formal in my home, but with company, Mrs. Kingsley will refuse to join us. Despite me telling her I don't care for those particular appearances, she refuses to cause me trouble. There's no way for me to tell her that Athan is not a part of the society and that appearances don't matter in front of him without seeming highly out of place, so I just leave it as is. I'll try to explain later when we're alone again.

"I apologize the meal is not up to standards," Mrs. Kingsley begins as plates are set in front of us. "Ms. Seagraves prefers to skip all the extra courses."

"They're useless," I add with a smile. "A tease and nothing more. It's best to get to the main meal as quickly as possible." I lean over to Athan where he sits beside me. "Besides, it means dessert comes faster."

His eyes flash at my words. "I do so enjoy dessert."

The smile that curls his lips makes me think we're not talking about the same thing at all, but I certainly can't ask him what he means. Even if we were alone, I don't think I could be so forward. When his eyes fall to my lips and my neck flushes with heat, I force myself to lean back and focus on the stew before us.

Athan takes a bite and moans in a such a way, I drop my spoon with a clatter. Mrs. Kingsley shoots me a look as she brings in a basket of fresh rolls. I can't tell if it's disapproving or curiosity.

"My apologies," he says with a grin. "I haven't had such a meal in quite some time. I'd forgotten how good food can be."

Mrs. Kingsley preens under the praise and straightens. "Our chef, Mrs. Lily, is a wonderful cook. I think you'll find pleasure in the pudding she's made for dessert as well."

"I have no doubt I will," Athan replies. His eyes dance over to mine, watching as I take a dainty bite.

There's a hum under his breath, as if he likes watching my lips press against the spoon. My body warms at the thought, that he could enjoy my appearance. I haven't felt so studied in years and despite not wanting anything to do with men if I can help it, it seems that the attention of a Grim Reaper is far different from anything else I might have considered. As he looks at me, my body twists and tightens, sitting up at attention despite my focus on my meal. I've never felt such awareness of a man. I've never been so aware of his eyes on me.

I glance over at him to find his eyes already on me. "Is there something on my face, Mr. Reaper?" I ask, suddenly self-conscious of the intense way he watches me.

"No," he murmurs, those eyes tracing along my expression. "No, your face is perfect, Miss Seagraves."

Hearing him speak my name so formally makes me want to ask him to repeat it. Something awakens inside of me and I'm suddenly hungry. I'm famished, but it's not food I desire, though the food we feast on is as lovely as always. I hunger for the Reaper before me, to taste him, to drink my fill of his lips. It's not proper for such notions to pass my mind, but the temptation to speak the words out loud is strong. What would he think of me if I were so forward? Would he curl up his lips in distaste, or would my own hunger be reflected in his eyes. I shift in my chair as Mrs. Kingsley returns to place the dessert on the table. She holds the pudding in her hands, comes to set it on the table, but as she gets close to me, she pauses, her pupils blowing wide. She hovers for a few seconds, and I glance up at her in confusion.

"Mrs. Kingsley, are you alright?" I ask gently.

Athan pauses with his spoon halfway to his mouth, his eyes on my housekeeper.

Mrs. Kingsley doesn't answer, her eyes still wide. Slowly, I watch her trail her gaze down to the pudding in her hands, to the large bowl she'd been about to present us with. She'd placed it in the crystal because of the company. She stares at it for one second. Two.

"Mrs. Kingsley?" I ask, leaning toward her.

As if my movement is what causes it, Mrs. Kingsley suddenly plummets her face into the bowl of pudding and begins to slurp it up. She does so without the manners she has drilled into me, without care of the chocolate pudding getting all over her face and clothing. She simply feasts on the bowl hungrily.

"Mrs. Kingsley!" I shout because I'm so shocked. I've never seen her behave with anything other than class. This is completely out of character.

Athan stands up in confusion, unsure of how to help. "Does she do this often?"

"No, never," I tell him, standing and moving closer to the woman

I consider a friend. I reach out for her, my hand shaking as in fear. Which is strange. I've never been afraid of Mrs. Kingsley. Pushing through the fear, I force myself to lay my hand on her shoulder. She freezes instantly, her face still planted firmly in the bowl. Slowly, she raises her face and I get a good look at the pudding covering her. It stains her cheeks, her nose, all around her mouth. It even spreads to her forehead and around her eyes. Bits of pudding drip from her chin back into the bowl as she blinks up at me.

"Mrs. Kingsley, are you well?" I ask gently. I don't know what's happened, but it can't be anything good.

She blinks again and then looks down at the bowl in horror. "Oh dear, I don't know what's come over me. I'm so sorry—"

"Don't be," I offer, gently taking the bowl and setting it on the table. "I only worry if there's something wrong."

She waves away my words. "I'm perfectly fine, child. I was just overcome so suddenly. . ." She presses a hand to her cheek and seems to realize she's covered in pudding. "I should go clean up. I'm so sorry to ruin dessert—"

"Nonsense. You take care of yourself first," I say, helping her in the direction of her room. I'm afraid to leave her alone in case she loses her senses again and harms herself.

Before we make it three steps, the doorbell rings. Frowning, Athan glances toward the entryway. "Are you expecting company at this hour?"

I shake my head. "No."

Mrs. Kingsley gasps. "I cannot answer the door so. . ."

When neither one of us moves, the ring comes again and a sense of awareness brushes down my spine. I shiver, a sudden chill taking over until I find myself straightening in fear.

Whoever is at the door, danger whispers from their shoulders.

My blood chills despite the warmth around me.

8
OTTO

I'd felt the ricochet of her death from so far away, I knew there must have been others who felt the first awakening the same as I. I had been in the middle of a meeting with the King of China when I'd felt it. Like a death toll ringing and an earthquake beneath my feet, I knew the time had come. Standing from the meeting and cutting off the other King, I'd bowed my head briefly before leaving without an explanation. As a fellow King, I owe no one anything, though our business affairs may suffer due to my rudeness. It doesn't matter to me if they do. After all, now that I've felt the first death, the world will change. It must.

I told no one where I was going. I did not send word to my coven or anyone of import. Instead, I immediately shifted into my raven form and took to the skies. I was frustrated that I'd been so far away from her location when the ricochet echoed. It took me too many days to reach Europe and then another couple to reach the shores of England. It makes sense that she would be in London, a bustling city worthy of my presence. I've always loved London, even a hundred years ago when the streets often smelled of manure and filth. There's always been hope in the streets, a yearning for something more among the humans who call it home.

And now she calls it home, so it will be my home, too.

I've waited centuries for this prophecy to come to pass. Long ago, I'd discovered a scroll among the ruins of a burnt cathedral, a parchment that had somehow survived the heat. It had been so fragile, so easily torn, that I'd had to be extremely careful unrolling it. Within that scroll, I'd read the words that decided my fate for me.

She will rise, Lilith, Mother of Monsters. She will rise, and rise again, seven deaths for each sin, and seven rebirths to claim her crown. Her powers will awaken each time she rises and call her monsters to her side. The world will cower in darkness before her, for Eve may have been given to Adam and told to obey, but Lilith was told she was everything.

I'd read those words, burned them into my heart, and vowed to find her, and now the moment has come.

I find myself standing outside of the large home on the rich streets of London. It doesn't matter where the call brought me. If it would have taken me into the slums, I would have walked into them the same. Straightening my coat and making sure my appearance is up to the standards this street dictates, for I wish to please her, I make my way up the steps and knock on the large wooden door. We'll have to replace that soon, for if other monsters come and harm her, the wooden door will do nothing to stop them.

When there's no answer despite the sounds I can hear inside the home, I decide to knock again despite it being improper and rude. I'm eager to meet her, to rest my eyes on her beauty. For Lilith will be beautiful. She's a goddess, and though she'll take time to grow into her powers, I have no doubt that she'll glow with it.

Finally, someone approaches and the door pulls open. Before me stands a man I recognize well and fury fills me. I'm not first. I knew I was late because of my distance but I'd hoped...

"Reaper," I hiss, baring my fangs at him. "It's been a long time."

The reaper raises his brows at me in amusement, the smug bastard. "I didn't expect to find you here, Your Majesty," he mocks. "What business do you have with Miss Seagraves?"

As if his voice summons her, she appears behind him, and my jaw goes slack as those blue eyes flash like that of an animal's. She wears nothing but an evening gown and I realize I've come at a late hour. Her hair is piled on top of her head, revealing her slender neck. It begs me to bite it, to run my fangs along the vein there, to offer her the ecstasy I know I can.

"I'm afraid I don't know you," she says, and her voice is like warm honey dripping along my skin.

I suck in a rattling desperate breath. "Of course. How improper of me, Miss Seagraves," I rasp, bowing low before her. "My name is King Otto Van Doren and I have travelled far to find you." I look up and meet her eyes from my lowered position. "My Queen."

9
MENA

I stare at the man standing on my doorstep in confusion. "I'm afraid you've mistaken me for someone else... Your Majesty. I, um, I'm not a queen, nor do I have any plans to be."

King Otto glances at Athan with a raised brow. "You haven't told her?"

"Told her what?" Athan asks with a frown, the same time as I ask, "Told me what?"

The man looks between the two of us and settles on me. "Who you are. What's happening to you. Why you feel so strange."

I blink at him, at this perfect stranger who somehow knows things are happening, but still, I play ignorance. "I'm not sure what you mean?"

His eyes flash and the grin that splits his lips reveals the fangs there. My heart flutters in fear, and also curiosity. What has my life become that I'm not running screaming from this man?

"No?" he asks, tilting his head. "So you have not recently perished only to find yourself alive again?"

I freeze, but to my surprise, so does Athan. "How do you know about that?" Athan demands, asking the question on the tip of my own tongue.

King Otto studies me closely, perusing my body, and while I should be offended, I find myself only aroused at the look. He stares at me in hunger, though I don't think he's hungry for only my blood. It's a sexual hunger, one I've found myself experiencing since Athan has appeared, and now I feel it for this man. Perhaps, the death has rattled my brain. That's the only explanation for it.

Of course, it doesn't hurt that both men are excruciatingly handsome.

"I know a great many things about what's happening to our dear Miss Seagraves," he purrs. "If you invite me inside, perhaps we can settle in and discuss these matters."

I could say no. I don't know this man. I can feel the danger he exudes as clearly as if I could see it, but something tells me he won't harm me.

My queen.

Whatever he is, he's not here to hurt me, not in the normal sense. I have no idea if he's dangerous in other ways or not.

I tilt up my chin. "No one in this household is to be harmed," I command, pushed to make the statement in case I'm wrong and he's as dangerous as he feels.

"You have my word that I will not harm anyone you care for, Miss Seagraves," he replies, bowing his head to me. A king showing subservience. I've certainly not seen it so easily done. Judging by the way he's dressed, this king is wealthy beyond compare and bears the highest title, and yet he bows to me, a woman with no true title. It's strange and also endearing.

Stepping back, I gesture for him to come inside. He doesn't move, a grimace stretching his face.

"You have to say the words," Athan tells me. "Vampires can't come inside without being invited formally."

My eyes jerk to his. "Vampires?"

Athan nods. "He's given you his word that no one will be

harmed, so you're safe to invite him in." He glances at King Otto. "He's an asshole, but I doubt he's traveled all this way to make empty promises and play games."

"Indeed," King Otto says. "I mean you no danger, Miss Seagraves. I only intend to help you."

"What do you think?" I ask Athan, needing his advice. He was only a stranger a week ago, but I'll be the first to admit I'm well outside of my depths now. The Grim Reaper? Phantoms? And now a Vampire King? I know nothing about this world, but it makes me nervous. If they're real, what else is real?

Athan shrugs. "I think we don't have any other leads so far, so what harm can it do to let him in?"

Sighing at the turn my life has taken, I nod. "Okay. I formally invite you into my home, Your Majesty, as long as you hold to your promise not to harm anyone within this house. If your promise is broken, the invitation is rescinded."

King Otto's eyes brighten. "Clever, clever," he murmurs and steps over the threshold. "I think you'll do fine in this world, Miss Seagraves."

"Mena, please," I reply, directing him to the office. "I prefer Mena."

"Mena," he repeats, tasting my name in a way that sends shivers along my skin. "You may call me Otto."

He glances at me and an inhuman shine flashes in his eyes. "It's a pleasure to meet you, Otto."

"Yes, yes," Athan grumbles. "Clearly the vampire is as charming as any king should be. Can we get to the information you supposedly know?"

Looking over at Athan, I note his tension. Clearly, he and the vampire king have history of some sort. I don't dare ask, not when there are more important things to decipher. Such as what's happening to me.

Once inside the office, I close the door behind us to avoid prying ears from listening in. I have no doubt Mrs. Kingsley would panic if she caught our conversation and think me insane.

"Let's start with how you knew about my death," I say, pouring a glass of whiskey from the decanter. I hesitate on the second glass, and glance over my shoulders. "Do both of you take whiskey?"

Athan nods, but Otto smiles at me knowingly. The question had mainly been for him. "Vampires are capable of eating and drinking like humans. It just offers no nourishment."

Nodding at his answer, I pour two more glasses and pass them each one. Only once I've settled into my own seat do both of them sit down and face me.

"I knew about your death the same way Athan did, I'm sure." He shrugs. "I felt it."

Athan frowns. "Yes, but I'm a reaper. I was called to her death to collect her soul."

"And could you collect it?" Otto asks eagerly.

"No," Athan admits. "I arrived after her funeral, so she was already buried. Her soul was tucked safely away back in her body by the time I arrived, and I could not guide it no matter what I tried."

Otto's eyes widen. "You were buried?"

I nod, shivering at the memory. "Six feet down."

He glares at Athan. "Please tell me you dug her up."

"Why would I do that?" Athan asks with a laugh. "I thought I was there to guide a soul to the Underworld. Digging up dead bodies doesn't seem very respectful."

"You knew she wasn't dead—"

"It's okay," I interrupt, holding up my glass. "I do not blame Athan for not acting. How could anyone have known I'd come back to life and crawl my way up from my grave?" I shrug. "At this point, it's the least of my worries even if I will now suffer a fear of small spaces."

I say the words nonchalantly, but Otto's eyes flash with regret. "I'm sorry I did not come sooner and that you had to face that trauma alone, my queen. I will endeavor to be by your side for all future troubles."

Blinking at the words that sound too much like a vow, I shake my head. "That's not necessary, but thank you. You said you felt my death?"

"And your rebirth," he nods. "I knew that the prophecy was coming to pass and came as fast as I could. Unfortunately, I was in China at the time of the call, so it took me far too long to reach your location, but I was glad to feel the call all the same."

"Prophecy?" Athan asks, straightening. "Which prophecy?"

"You would not have heard of it," Otto claims, reaching into his coat pocket to bring out a piece of stationery. "The original was damaged in a cathedral fire and is therefore too fragile to travel, but I copied down the words for this occasion."

He passes the paper over to Athan who takes it and traces the symbols written there. "It's in Demonia." At my confusion, he adds, "An old language spoken by higher demons."

"Demons are real?" I ask, leaning in. "That must mean—"

"Angels are real, too," Athan nods. "Pompous, evil bastards, but yes, they're real."

I blink. In what world are angels called evil? "Okay, so what does this prophecy say?"

"I don't speak the language—" Athan begins.

"I do," Otto interrupts. "Allow me to translate, my queen." He doesn't reach for the paper, as if he has the words burned into his memory. *"She will rise, Lilith, Mother of Monsters. She will rise, and rise again, seven deaths for each sin, and seven rebirths to claim her crown. Her powers will awaken each time she rises and call her monsters to her side. The world will cower in darkness before her, for Eve may have been given to Adam and told to obey, but Lilith was told she was everything."* He clears his throat. "There was more, but the scroll was burned after that, and I could no longer decipher the words."

Athan runs a hand through his hair in agitation. "So we have an incomplete prophecy. Do you know how dangerous that is?"

"Hang on," I stop them, even more confused than before. "Those words talk about Lilith. It says nothing about me."

Otto studies me, his head tilting to the side. Everything about him is put together like an artist took extra care. His dark skin only highlights his caramel eyes and plush lips. His sharp cheekbones draw the eyes to his fangs when they flash. As he tilts his head, his long dreads shift with the movement. Vampires are often described as monsters, as horrible creatures of the night, but if this is what they look like, I'm certain most victims simply follow him into the night. He's beautiful, and when he studies me like he does now, I almost can't look away from his eyes.

"You," he declares, "*are* Lilith, Mena. Her reincarnation, but Lilith all the same."

The world comes to a crashing halt around me. I forget everything else except for the words that just came out of his mouth. "*What?*"

"You are the reincarnation of Lilith," he repeats seriously. "This was only the first death, and with each one, you'll grow more powerful, but it's a slow process—"

"The first death?" I repeat. I know I'm just parroting the words, but I can't seem to help myself. This all seems so far-fetched. "More powerful? I don't have any powers."

"Seven deaths and seven rebirths," he nods. "The prophecy is very clear about that. Like I said, with each death you'll grow more powerful—"

"Stop," I growl, holding up my hand. He falls silent immediately. "So you're telling me I have to die again and again and then I rise as some all-powerful demon?"

Otto snorts. "Good God, no. Yes, you must die seven times, but you don't rise a demon. You will be you, just with the powers of Lilith, her reincarnation. The new Lilith if you will."

Standing at his words, I start to pace. "This can't be true. Sure, there was a strange event where I supposedly died and came back.

Let's call that luck or a miracle. Either way, there's a flaw in your idea."

"Which is?" Athan asks curiously. He looks as if he's enjoying all of this the smug bastard.

"I have no powers," I point out, gesturing to my body. "I'm human."

The phantom of the house appears through the wall like a mockery to my words, but I try not to focus on him. Otto still seems to notice my awareness and grins.

"No?" he asks, standing from his seat. He stands taller than me, but he wears boots while I stand in slippers.

"I have no powers," I repeat. "I'm completely normal notwithstanding the strange circumstances of my death."

His tilts his head. "How did you die, Mena?"

I flush. "Choking on a piece of cake I'm told."

"So Gluttony if we're to go by the each sin line. Which means you'll likely have gained a power similar to that sin." He tilts his head. "Tell me, little queen, has anyone been overcome with gluttonous intent in your presence since you returned?"

I freeze, the scene of Mrs. Kingsley's face covered in pudding flashing in my mind. Athan seems to realize the same because his eyes meet mine.

"Ah," Otto hums in amusement. "I thought so."

I need to run. I need to get away from this. I can't handle such words, such profound discovery. But I don't tell Otto and Athan. How does one run from a reaper and a vampire without them knowing?

You play on their expectations of a woman.

I press my hand to my forehead, pretending exhaustion. "It's been a long evening," I rasp, pretending to stumble a little to add belief to my act. "I think I need to ponder all of this in the morning after I've had some rest. Would it be so rude of me to retire?"

"Of course not," Otto coos. "Rest for now, my queen. We will protect the house from any nefarious monsters seeking you out."

I don't have the time to question him about that. More monsters? What on earth have I gotten myself into?

Nodding at his words, I retire from the office, leaving them to deal with their own problems. Likely, Athan will go do whatever Reapers do and Otto will be. . . well, I don't know. I just know I need to escape this house.

"Good evening," I tell them, keeping the exhaustion in my voice as I leave. The moment I get up to my rooms, I take stock of it all and begin to formulate a plan.

10
MENA

I've gone through all my options. There are currently two men who are very much not just men downstairs doing whatever it is they do. I'd left instructions for Mrs. Kingsley to show them to a room and usher them off to bed.

I also instructed her to send for the carriage the moment the sun rises and have it packed with my belongings.

I will not be staying here. Whether Otto is correct or not, I don't wish to find out. If I must die over and over again, I don't want it. The power that comes with it, I don't want it. I've rarely wanted something so little as to be in the reincarnation of the demon mother Lilith. I'd grown up reading the Bible and praying to a God that never answered. In my later years, I've prayed less and less since it feels like I was never heard. I'm certainly not the most devout Christian, and I don't know much about Lilith, but I know enough to know that's not what I wish for. So I'm leaving. I won't be telling Athan or Otto. Only Mrs. Kingsley will know my destination. No one else.

I have dozens of trunks, but I only pack the things I need right away as well as the items worth the most money. My jewels, my silver, that all goes within one trunk. My clothing goes in another. I need everything that will be worth money in case I choose not to come back here. When Mrs. Kingsley brings my deeds and business books, I tuck them into the small bag I'll be carrying with me. Once I'm ready, I force myself to sleep for the few hours until dawn before climbing from my bed.

Staring at myself in the mirror, I take in the smoothness of my skin. Though I had hardly gotten enough sleep, there are no dark circles beneath my eyes. I should look exhausted, but instead, I look as close to perfect as possible. Good genes or the powers I now carry? Does becoming Lilith include perfect skin?

"I will not be dying a hundred times," I tell my reflection. "I refuse."

I wait for the soft knock on the door before I open it and follow Mrs. Kingsley through the house on silent feet. I glance once at the doors Otto and Athan are behind and dismiss the guilt I feel. They'll be well taken care of while here and when they wake to find me gone, they'll simply return to their business. I don't expect them to chase after me. This will be a clear sign that I want nothing to do with this prophecy.

My trunks will be brought after me, but for now, only the smallest trunk holding a few pieces of clothing and riches will come with me until I get settled in. My destination is the house in the country I rarely use. Walter had purchased it before we were wed and that's where we spent our honeymoon. I much prefer the bustle of the city, but to avoid the monsters supposedly coming after me and the trouble of dying, the country seems a safer option.

"I'll be along with your trunks in a few days' time," Mrs. Kingsley whispers as she gives me a tight hug. "Be safe."

She didn't ask questions when I asked for the favor. She didn't protest or ask me to at least let the men in the house know where I'm going. She simply fulfills the favor and loads me onto the carriage with a final goodbye. I don't know when we'll return to the London house. I don't know if I'll ever be able to.

I wave to her as the carriage pulls away and settle back against the cushion. This part of the trip is a short one. The country house is better accessed by train so we're going to the train station where I'll board and ride for a few hours until we reach the stop necessary. There will be a carriage waiting for me there to take me the rest of the way to the country house. Everyone had been alerted of my arrival so it should go smoothly.

And it does until I reach the train station and realize I'm still thirty minutes early. Sighing at the wait and anxious that Otto and Athan will wake up and come searching for me, I stare at the tracks in agitation.

"Pardon me, Sir?" I call to the ticket master as he comes by. "Will the Lexington line by any chance be early?"

"No, Miss. It will be right on time," he replies. "Is there anything else I can help you with?"

Frowning, I shake my head. "That will be all, thank you."

He bows his head just slightly and carries on with his preparations. Though The Lexington Line is my train, there will be other trains that arrive and carry on. Around me stand other passengers waiting for their train. Here, there is a glaring difference between classes, and it unnerves me just as it always has. Families who clearly scraped together their last bit of spare change to afford the tickets sit clustered together, a meager bag filled with their entire belongings sitting at their feet. Rich women off to visit their country homes for one reason or another stand regally along the platform, their chins up in the air when the poorer families brush by. To my left, a father stands with two small children, his eyes hollow and haunted, as if he's been stricken with some sort of terrible news. The children look sad, but confused, as if he hasn't quite told them what's happening.

"Why are we going to live with them again?" the little girl asks. She can't be any older than ten, her blond ringlets circling her face. She's well-kept and clean despite the black coal dust smattering the father's clothing.

"I told you, darling. Mother went on a really long trip and won't be back for a long time. Your grandparents will take good care of you until I can make enough money to follow." Exhaustion fills his voice, and within that exhaustion, I hear his grief. His eyes meet mine briefly, before glancing away, and that's when I see her.

A woman stands off to the side, her face pretty and distinguished like that of the elite. She's transparent, just as all the other phantoms have been, her haziness broken up every now and then by someone passing through her. Sadness fills her eyes, and she longingly moves around the small family, distressed when she can't touch them.

I press my hand to my heart when it aches for them. The children's mother won't be back. I don't think the father will come back into the country to stay. It seems this will be a permanent solution decided by a father too overcome with grief to take care of his children at the loss of his wife. The woman glances over at me and I look away quickly, not wanting to invite her attention, but I'm too slow. She drifts over to me, desperation in her eyes.

"Please, if you can see me, I need your help," she begs, coming close.

I shift, not wanting to accidently touch her. "I can't help you. I'm sorry."

"I don't ask for much," she continues, tears flowing from her eyes. "I just need someone to tell him something. A single line. That's all." She looks back at her family. "My husband, he's lost without me, and I can't let him make this mistake. He'll drink himself to death if he sends the children away."

I hesitate. "I shouldn't—"

"Please," she begs, lurching closer. "I beg of you! My children!"

Wringing my fingers together, I glance at the children and father again, at the way he barely moves, so lost in his grief, he doesn't notice his small son tugging on his pantleg for his attention. "What's the line?" I choke out, focusing back on the woman.

"Tell him. . . tell him that the blackbird never flies alone." She glances over to him. "Will you please tell him that?"

"Just that single line?" I furrow my brows.

"Yes. He'll know what it means."

Sighing, I straighten my clothing and prepare myself to look like an insane woman. Hopefully, no one else notices and decides to send me to the local asylum. Carefully, I pick my way over the tiles and stand before the man and children. The children notice me immediately, the little boy hiding behind his father's pantleg, but the young girl looks up at me with wonder in her eyes. It takes a few seconds for the man to focus and realize I'm there. He startles back when he comes to, his eyes taking in my posture and clothing, noting my class immediately.

"Pardon me, Miss. I didn't see you there," he starts to apologize, but I don't allow him to finish.

"The blackbird never flies alone," I say, making sure his eyes are on mine.

He freezes. "What did you just say?"

"The blackbird never flies alone," I repeat, glancing over at the phantom to see her smiling through her tears. "I apologize if I've come across as crazy, I just. . . Something told me to tell you those words."

He blinks and some of the fog clears. Carefully, he looks down at his children, at their confused faces, and sighs. "Leave it to Vanessa to find a way to reach me," he murmurs. To me, he says, "thank you, Miss."

I nod and return back to my place, the phantom woman waiting for me.

"Thank you," she rasps. "You have no idea how much you've just done for me."

"It was a single line. It couldn't have. . ." My words trail off when I watch the man gather his children and shuffle them away from the train station, back to whatever home they came from. "I don't understand."

Smiling, the phantom woman drifts close enough for me to feel her chill air. "I used to call him my blackbird because he would come home covered in coal," she explains. "My parents didn't agree with our marriage. They said I was marrying below my station, but we were in love, and I decided to give it all up for that chance." Her eyes meet mine. "We were happy. He was my blackbird and I was his dove. We always said the other would never fly alone because we had each other." Her tears flow faster. "And our children were our babies. The thing about blackbirds and doves is they mate for life, so this has been hard on him."

"And what happened to you?" I ask, my chest aching with her story.

"Consumption," she says sadly. "I couldn't even hold my babies for fear of getting them sick. But at least they know I'm with them now thanks to you." She bows her head. "You have my forever gratitude, Mena."

I pause. "How did you know my name?"

Her eyes sparkle. "The world is shaking with your name. Can't you feel it?" She turns to leave, but looks over her shoulder one last time to meet my eyes. "Make sure that when it stops shaking, you're a force to be reckoned with."

I watch her trail after her family, not moving until she disappears completely. Only when she does do I start to pace along the platform, anxiety in every step. I'd just helped a family with this newfound power, yes, but with it came something even more groundbreaking.

The phantoms know who I am.

I look at the clock again and groan in frustration that there is still another twenty minutes to wait. In my annoyance, I trail a little too close to the edge. The whistle blows in the distance, signaling another train's arrival. Not mine. I still must wait for my own. But other people on the platform stand in preparation for their train. A man comes toward the platform, his face buried in the paper, so he doesn't see me. When I realize he's coming right at me, I try to move to the side and immediately bump into yet another person rushing forward to board their train. Mind the gap. It's always been drilled into me, but I have no control as I'm thrown off balance.

"Miss!" someone calls and my arms wave in an attempt to gain my balance again. It's useless. I stumble back, and my foot only finds empty air.

The scream that bursts from my throat is shrill as I fall, my expensive train ticket for first class going flying from my hand as I slam into the tracks with a painful crunch. I gasp, try to stand, and find that I can't seem to get my feet beneath me. Above me, people are screaming. Someone reaches down their arm to help me up just as the whistle of the train sounds closer. I look to my left, see it speeding closer, and panic.

I try to scramble to my feet, but my leg doesn't seem to want to work. The pain that echoes up my thigh tells me I may have broken it, but that's the least of my worries.

I reach for the man, desperate to take his hand. "Help me!" I cry, pushing myself up as much as I'm able. "Please!"

"Take my hand!" he screams. Others beside him reach for me, too, but it's pointless. I won't be able to reach them, and no one will dare jump down to save me. It would be suicide. I won't be saved before the train arrives.

"My leg! I think it's broken."

Panic flickers in his eyes, and I know he knows what I do. No one will be able to help me. No one will save me.

I suppose now is as good of time as any to find out if Otto was right.

Painfully, I settle back onto my tailbone, my dress poofed out around me. Those on the platform scream for me, scream for the train to stop, scream for someone to save me. The train whistle sounds again, and I glance to my left, see I have only seconds left.

Taking a deep breath, I close my eyes and count.

One... two... three... four...

Pain, and then nothing but darkness.

Second Death

The earth claims everything for itself.
Man's mistake is thinking he can pry
what he wants from earth's brutal claws.

Ignorance will always be bliss on borrowed time.

11
MENA

My chest aches. My limbs feel strange. My mouth is dry.

I realize all three feelings at once and blink open my eyes in confusion. I try to curl my fingers, but they're stiff. It takes a few seconds to get the movement right and I can reach up to my face to feel it. Why does my skin feel so tight? Why do my teeth hurt? Why does my hair feel so matted and crusty?

Three strangers are looking down at me as I come to completely, their eyes blown wide in horror. One is as white as the phantoms I see. Oh, wait. There's an actual phantom drifting around them, watching everything eagerly. What is he doing? He looks practically excited at me opening my eyes.

"What happened?" I croak, my dry mouth making words difficult. They come out a little demonic even to my own ears.

The pale stranger screams and stumbles back before slamming against the wall violently. It's only then I realize we're moving, as if we're in a carriage. I only realize because the pale stranger slams against what must be the doors and tumbles right out of them, disappearing onto the ground beyond.

A carriage. I'm in a carriage.

The other two strangers slap the top of the carriage, a thump echoing through, and it rolls to a stop as they jump out after their friend to check on him. One touches their fingers to his neck as I sit up to watch, curious about what's happening. No one has answered my questions yet. He glances at the other solemnly, his fingers falling away.

"Dead," he says, and then they both slowly look over at me where I'm sitting up.

"What exactly is happening?" I rasp, my eyes on the now dead man where a phantom begins to climb from his body, wrenching its way out of the body like it's difficult. I haven't actually seen someone die before and their phantom come out. It's unnerving. "Who are you people, and where are you taking me?"

My head feels like it's splitting, and I press my hand to it only to realize just how much I'm covered in something sticky. I pull my hand away and stare at the bright red on my hand. The memories come crashing back in. The phantom woman and her family. Falling onto the train tracks.

The pain.

"Oh God," I whisper, pressing my hand against my body chest, searching for wounds. I wiggle my leg only to realize it's no longer broken. I know it had been broken. The pain makes it easy to remember. I notice my shoes are missing though, my feet bare as I wiggle them. There's some strange tag tied with string onto my big toe, the words too small to read.

My eyes meet the two living men as they ease forward.

"We're the carriage drivers for Glassberry," one finally grows brave enough to say. "We were transporting you to the morgue."

"The morgue," I repeat foolishly. I know exactly why they were taking me there. This isn't my first time dying. . . strangely enough. But for it to happen twice?

"You were dead," the other man says. "Cold and mangled."

"And yet you're awake and speaking," the other adds, his eyes taking in my body. "Your bones were shattered—"

"I think you were mistaken," I rasp, pressing my hand against my stomach where my corset pushes too tightly into my skin. "I'm alive and well."

They stare at me as if I'm a monster. Perhaps I am. Perhaps I wasn't running from the monsters back in London at all. Perhaps, this entire time, I've been running from myself. My skin crawls at their looks, at the way they glance down at their now dead friend in disbelief. Apparently, they'll still be making a trip to the morgue, just not for their original reason.

"I. . ." What do you say in the face of this? What excuse can you give that doesn't sound absolutely insane. "I should leave you to your business."

Maybe nothing is best to say. I will remain silent and not acknowledge the strangeness of the situation.

"Miss," the one on the right says, his eyes wide and afraid. "You were hit by a train. . ."

"I feel fine," I lie. "Perfectly healthy. I think I'll be fine from here on."

They hesitate, clearly uncertain how to handle this situation.

"You should see a doctor," the second man says, his voice shaky. "You were hit with the full force of the train. I was certain that your neck was broken. . . that your skull was crushed."

That would explain the large amount of blood and gore currently drying in my hair. I resist the urge to reach up and feel along my skull, searching for any cracks. "Did I miss the Lexington Train?"

They both nod. "It went through an hour ago, held up by your. . . accident, but it left."

"Bullocks," I mumble, looking down at the grime and blood covering my dress. Maybe I'm missing an injury. "Perhaps, a doctor is precisely what I need. Would you mind terribly taking me to the hospital?"

They hesitate again, as if not wanting to climb into the carriage with me any longer. I don't blame them. I can't imagine the sight I make right now.

"Please," I add when they say nothing. "I do feel a little strange."

The first man gathers his wits before the other. He nods slowly before glancing at his friend. "We should take Harry to the. . . morgue."

Where they'd been taking me. And now they're taking their friend.

"We'll drop you at the hospital on our way," he tells me. "Can you move?"

I nod and stand before shuffling backward away from the door. He watches me with wide eyes as I move a body that had been crushed by the train only an hour ago. I can't imagine what they've witnessed. I can't imagine what they'll tell people about this.

I press my hand to my forehead as they climb inside. Something is seriously wrong with me. Some part of me had hoped that Otto was wrong, that there's no mystery to me like Athan thinks. Part of me thought it was all foolish myths, but sitting here, rising a second time, I can't help but start to believe in this idiotic prophecy.

I'm sick. I've lost my mind. That has to be it. But those lies don't stick in my brain like they did before. They feel like the lies they are.

Settling back into the carriage as it starts to move, I think that a doctor might help me, after all.

Besides, where else can I go? I'm not going to go crawling back to face Athan and Otto in this state. I couldn't bear to see their amusement.

12
OTTO

"She is running," I lament as I stare out the window after her. The sun is just barely starting to rise so it doesn't yet burn my skin, but I still narrow my eyes to limit the rays. It's always so bright before being quickly covered by the clouds that haunt London. I'm capable of walking the streets in the day under cloud coverage, but it's difficult. I must keep as much of my skin covered as possible and I can't linger. Lingering brings pain. Lingering too long will bring death.

"Of course, she is," the Reaper replies, amusement in his voice. The asshole is always amused. "Wouldn't you if given all that information?" He shakes his head. "You should have done it in small increments."

I shrug at his words, unbothered. "It's necessary. The quicker she accepts her fate, the easier it will be."

"Says the vampire who went on a killing spree when he found out what he was," Athan mocks and I flash my fangs at him. "You're more foolish of a king than the humans. She was already scared before you came along. You just added too much too quickly and now she's running away."

"Let her run," I grunt, rolling my eyes. "It's not like we won't be able to find her."

"That's beside the point. I wish for her to be less afraid of me."

Raising my brows, I meet the reaper's eyes. "Oh?"

"Don't give me that look, vampire," he grumbles. "I'm only curious about her predicament."

I turn fully toward him as her carriage pulls away, off to wherever she has deemed safe. "So your curiosity has nothing to do with her beauty?" I tilt my head. "Nothing to do with the wit she holds at bay because of the ridiculous societal standards?"

"No," he answers, too fast. A lie. A big one. "It's only curiosity."

"Yes, well, I for one am curious about the way her blood will taste rushing across my tongue after I sink my fangs into her slender neck," I reply, watching the reaper carefully. When his pupils flare, I continue. "I wonder what she'll sound like as I sink my cock between her lush thighs and—"

"Enough," Athan snarls, and I grin in victory.

"You like her," I point out. "I'm not the only one who has thought about what she tastes like, am I?"

"It doesn't matter if you are or not," he hisses. "I have a job to do. I can't linger here forever."

I tsk and meet his eyes. "You and I both know how being the reaper works, Athan. You may have a job to do, but you're in control of it. There's nothing holding you back if you choose this option."

The reaper doesn't look at me. Instead, he moves over to the curtain and looks out, uncaring about the small bit of sunshine the day will see. For a moment, jealousy fills me. It's been so long since I could just enjoy the sunshine, but I'm old enough to know this is my life now. So long ago, I found myself dying and at the mercy of my maker. He had given me a choice, and in my cowardice, I'd chosen eternal life. I hadn't realized what came with that, what violence I would be forced to live. Now, as the King of the European Coven, there's nothing I'd like more than excitement.

And Mena is that excitement I've yearned for, that I've waited for. Centuries, and now here we are. I'm all in. I don't care if the reaper decides to do the same. Mena deserves all the protection she can get.

We sit there arguing for hours. Athan insists on going after her right away, but I decide it's much better to wait and give her a chance to come to her senses. She'll realize that no matter where she goes, the prophecy will follow. Now that she knows of it, now that it's begun, there's no going back.

"We go when Mrs. Kingsley leaves," I offer. "Mena will go nowhere without her. I'm willing to bet that woman is planning to join her wherever she ends up."

"Why wait when—" Athan clamps his mouth shut and tilts his head. "There's been another death."

"Someone you need to collect?" I ask, boredom in my tone. "Reapers. You're all the same—"

"No," Athan interrupts. "It's Mena."

I perk up and clap my hands together in excitement. "Marvelous! This may go much faster than I expected." But then I sober at the realization. This is the second death, and a few seconds after Athan feels it, the power washes over me in turn, the echo of it pulsing in my chest. I meet Athan's eyes. "We must hurry, reaper," I rasp.

"Now you want to hurry?" he grunts in annoyance. "Make up your mind."

"No, you don't understand." I rush to grab a coat and something to shield my face. "We will not be the only ones who are called to her death, Athan." I make sure he's looking at me. "I need you to realize that with each death, her power will grow, and with it, more creatures will flock to her side."

"And?" he asks, frowning.

"Not all of them are at peace with her existence."

13
MENA

The London Hospital is full to bursting when the carriage pulls up to the front. The men who'd previously been taking me to the morgue hadn't said a word on the ride there, the air within the carriage somber. The first phantom remains in the carriage, his eyes bright with amusement as the new phantom belonging to the dead man stares in confusion at his body, asking each of us what happened. When he stares at me in horror, afraid, I tense, trying my hardest to ignore his presence. The first chance I could escape, before the carriage even came to a full stop, they were ushering me from the carriage and moving quickly to take their friend to the morgue, leaving me behind.

As if I'm a demon.

If Otto is to be believed, I might be, but I prefer not to think about something like that. I can't fathom the idea, but considering I've died and come back twice now, there must be some truth to his prophecy. Whatever is happening with me, perhaps, I need more help than I care to know. So I'm here, at the hospital, covered in blood and gore and the grime of the train tracks, my dress ripped and bloody.

Plenty of people turn to look at me as I stumble inside the hospital. What a sight I must make, my chin tilted up, my dress ruined. A few people move away from me so I know I must look frightful. There are so many people waiting for care inside, I grow uneasy at the cluster of it. Women, children, and men alike all wait for help, some of them coughing up the blood of consumption, some of them feverish. So many sicknesses have run rampant in London these last few years. The overwhelming sadness within these walls chokes me.

And none of that is from the many phantoms moving among the people. It's all purely living human grief and pain.

I see one of the nurses rushing through and move to intercept her.

"Excuse me?" I call, my throat brutally rough. She pauses at the tone, turns toward me, and freezes. Her eyes widen, the clipboard in her hand momentarily forgotten as she takes in my state. "I'm sorry to bother you, but I must see the doctor."

"Have you signed in?"

I shake my head. "No, but I was hoping to bypass the line due to my extenuating circumstances."

The nurse scowls. "We don't have time for—"

"I was hit by a train," I rush to add. "I was in a carriage to the morgue when I woke up. Please, I just... I need help."

She looks me over, seeing the state I'm in, her eyes absorbing every detail. She notes the blood matted in my hair and covering my body. "I'm sorry, Miss. We don't have the room and you don't appear to be suffering an emergency at this very moment. Train or not, you're standing and walking and speaking. All good signs. If you stay here, I can't promise that you'll be seen before the patients suffering current life-threatening ailments."

Taking a deep breath, I twist my fingers together to stop myself from reacting badly. "Please," I beg of her. "I think... I think I'm losing my mind."

The nurse takes me in again, as if she hadn't gotten enough of a fill before. "You were hit by a train?" she asks again. "Full speed or slow?"

"Full pulling into the station. I don't remember much, only that I was knocked onto the tracks and woke up in the morgue carriage."

The nurse sighs and looks around before stepping closer. "Look, Miss. We really don't have the room here. There's a current epidemic of consumption and we simply don't have enough beds. However, there's a different doctor down the street. Just walk down three blocks and take a left. It'll be on the right." She hesitates, as if not really wanting to send me there, but there's no other choice. "He should have the time to see you."

"Anything is better than nothing," I tell her, taking her hand before I realize how much it's covered in blood. I grimace and release her quickly and she wipes her hand on her uniform. "Thank you. I owe you much."

"Don't thank me yet," she murmurs. "You'll be looking for the Ward House. Good luck."

I leave the sounds of sick people behind in search of the doctor she sent me to. I walk down the street for three blocks like instructed before turning left. I study the address signs carefully until I find Ward House and stare up at the building. Like most structures on this street, this one is old, clearly a couple of hundred years old. It's a bit in disrepair and the whole thing could use a new coat of paint. The yellow it was once painted has long since faded and the only evidence that it was yellow is the small chips left behind. There's nothing that declares it a hospital per se, but across the door, in bold golden letters, are the words: "Dr. Jekyll's Ailments & Curiosities."

I hesitate at the phrasing. She'd said he would have time to take me, but the sign implies he's more of a spiritual type of doctor. This isn't exactly what I wished for, but perhaps this may be precisely what I need.

Taking a deep breath, I lift my fist and knock on the door.

14
MENA

The horn and whistling I've been hearing sounds in the distance and I turn to look over my shoulder, searching for the source. As before, I see nothing, and dismiss it from my mind. Whatever the horn is, it's louder now, more insistent, but I'm convinced it's in my mind. Why would a ship horn sound so close in the center of London?

I wait for a minute without anyone answering the door. The fog off the Thames rolls through the streets behind me, covering the cobblestones in an eerie white shroud. There are decidedly less phantoms here, but they still linger, trailing along the street in silence, perpetual sadness on their faces. When there's still no answer, I raise my hand and knock again, this time a little louder.

Nothing. Maybe he's not here.

I try one more time and call, "Hello?" Nothing. "Doctor? I need your help."

I've come at a bad time. It's only then that I realize the hour has grown far later than I realized. With the fog rolling in, it's difficult to tell the position of the sun, but the sky begins to darken. I must be too late.

Sighing, I turn to leave. I suppose I must go home and face Otto and Athan dressed like this. The thought of Athan's infuriating smirk fills me with annoyance, but before I can move down the steps and brace myself for that look, there's movement behind me. I hear footsteps and then someone unlocks the door from the inside. I turn, expecting an older gentleman as the door swings open.

Instead, I stare into a pair of pretty green eyes on a face not much older than my own.

I've never seen such a young doctor. His face is smooth and pristine, beautiful almost by masculine standards. He holds up a lantern to get a good look at me, the frown on his face stretched into a permanent annoyance. That's when I notice the metal arm at his side, a well-made prosthetic. If not for my study, I might have thought him only wearing a glove.

"I'm not accepting patients," he declares, and starts to shut the door.

"Wait! Please," I cry, pressing my hand against the door. "The nurse at the hospital said you could help."

He grumbles under his breath. "The nurse at the hospital lied. I'm not accepting patients, especially at this hour."

"Please," I beg. "I've nowhere else to turn for help. The hospitals are full with consumption and I just need someone to look me over."

He squints at me, his long lashes accentuating the green in his eyes. With the growing darkness, he doesn't seem to be able to tell just how bad of state I'm in. "What exactly is wrong with you? Hysteria? Bleeding pains? Need a pregnancy gone?" He parrots off the words with condensation in every line.

I straighten, annoyed at his condensation, and purse my lip at him. "No," I hiss. "No, none of that. I was hit by a train."

He pauses before holding up the lantern higher, noting the blood coating me and the grime and tears in my dress. "And you're walking? Was it a slow-moving train?"

Shaking my head, I sigh. "No. It was full speed coming into a station." I hesitate, not sure what all I should say, but if I need help, I should explain further. Especially since he seems reluctant to help. "I was knocked onto the tracks and broke my leg. I couldn't climb out of the way in time."

His frown deepens. "A broken leg, you say?" His eyes trail down to the legs I'm clearly standing on.

"I know what it sounds like," I offer. "I know I sound insane, but I promise I'm not lying. I don't remember the hit, but I woke up inside the morgue carriage after. They were certain I was dead. Broken neck. Cracked chest. Shattered skull. Mangled body."

"You hardly look mangled," he points out.

"Precisely," I declare, lifting my chin. "Which is why I need your help. I don't know if I'm still injured or if I've entirely lost my senses. Something is *wrong*." I gesture to my body. "I just want to make sure there's not anything more serious that I'm missing."

He hesitates for a few seconds longer before stepping back from the doorway and gesturing for me to pass him. "Come inside, Missus..."

"It's Miss," I correct as I move passed him. "And you can call me Mena."

He nods, and once I'm passed, the door closes behind me.

Locking me inside with Doctor Jekyll and his ailments and curiosities.

15
MENA

"I just don't understand," Dr. Jekyll mutters under his breath as he continues to check me over.

We've been at this for the better part of an hour. He has me sitting on a hospital bed, one of three, as he goes over injuries. He's been nothing but professional, and we've gone over the injuries that were suspected of me.

"Your understanding is as good as mine," I offer even though he hadn't expected an answer.

"Broken neck," he says, reaching up to feel along my neck. I lean it to the side to give him better access. His swift fingers fluttering along my bones there makes something flutter low in my stomach, but I push it down. He's doing his job, nothing more. So what if his fingers are soft and strong?

"Every one of your vertebrae in your neck are whole and connected," he declares.

"Yes," I reply. "Or else I'd think I couldn't be walking around. But they were very clear. My neck was broken when they loaded me in the carriage."

"Broken leg," he continues, reaching toward my skirts, but he hesitates and looks up to me. "May I?"

"You may," I reply, reaching down to help hold my skirts out of the way.

"Broken along your thigh or your femur?" he asks, pressing against my shin.

"I don't actually know. I remember pain shooting up from my knee and that I was unable to stand. That's all."

He nods and presses around my knee, feeling for irregularities. "There's nothing amiss here either. Your bones are solid and strong." He stands and helps me adjust my skirts. "You also mentioned your chest."

Carefully, I reach up to press my hand against my neckline. "Yes. They claimed it was shattered, that my ribs were no longer protecting my organs, and that it had been flattened significantly. From my understanding, my organs were. . . outside my body." And true to that word, there is some gore on me that is not blood or grime from the tracks. Some of it has a meat-like consistency I'd prefer not to think about.

"I should like to inspect your ribs," he says. "But I will be unable to while you are dressed." He grabs a dressing gown. "I will procure you some temporary clothing, but for now, could you put this on and allow me to check you over better?"

I hesitate, but take the dressing gown tentatively. "I should need some assistance with the corset if you don't mind."

The doctor pauses before moving around to my back. "Of course. How foolish of me to think you could loosen the ties." His fingers move swiftly along the ties and buttons, making quick work. As soon as he's finished and I'm holding my dress against my front, he backs away and closes the curtain. "Alert me when you're ready, Miss Mena."

The moment the curtain closes, I strip myself from my clothing, tossing the ruined material to the side before pulling on the cotton dressing gown. It goes down to my knees and ties at the back, covering me as modestly as possible while still allowing access to my body for procedures.

"I'm ready," I call, and the curtain swipes back. Dr. Jekyll steps back inside and closes the curtain around us, giving us further privacy and protecting my modesty from any prying eyes even though we're alone. I appreciate the effort.

"First, I'll check over your sternum and abdomen. Internal bleeding can be the silent killer so I shall search for any signs of such as well as cracked ribs." He hesitates, his eyes on me. "Would you mind if I untied the back and checked your spine first?"

"Of course not," I murmur, reaching back to loosen the strings I'd just tied.

His fingers poke and prod along my vertebrae, searching for any evidence besides the blood that I'd been hit by a train. It's clear I'd been bleeding from some wounds. He'd mentioned it with the patterns along my clothing and skin, but where there should be wounds, there's nothing but pink scars, as if they had healed so quickly, they couldn't hide the evidence.

Once he's done inspecting my spine, he presses against my ribs. Then he moves around to my front and meets my eyes. "I'm going to remove your left arm from the dressing gown so that I may check your stomach and ribs. Will that be acceptable?"

I nod and start to pull my arm from the dressing gown. I hold the cotton against me for a moment before I sigh and drop it, revealing my bare chest. Dr. Jekyll doesn't hesitate. Nor do his eyes linger on my assets. Instead, he's incredibly professional and immediately checks over my rib cage. Upon finding nothing, he presses me back to lie down and begins to press into my stomach, searching for his evidence. The moment he's done, he tugs the cotton gown back up, saving my modesty before stepping back.

"Well, Miss Mena—"

"Just Mena," I tell him, tying the dressing gown back closed.

"Mena," he begins again. "As best as I can tell, and despite the clear sign of wounds, you're healthy and whole. There are no cracked bones, no signs of internal bleeding, and you're coherent and walking. If you had not been covered in your blood and grease from the tracks, I'd find it hard to believe your story."

"I understand," I rasp. "I know how I sound."

"And your wounds, they're healed save for a pink scar. The blood coming from said wounds looks fresh as you say. The wounds appear to be at the healing stage weeks old. There are pieces that clearly look like internal bits that are mangled and chopped. This strangeness is why I believe you most," he points out, moving to take a seat on the stool nearby. "I do not know how it's happened, and while I tend to disbelieve most supernatural inclinations, it's hard to dismiss that evidence so clearly smeared on your skin. The head wound alone is proof enough that you were injured recently despite the raised scar that speaks of a past injury."

The breath in my lungs whooshes out. "I appreciate your belief in me, Doctor."

"Henry," he corrects. "You can call me Henry. Now, you were certain the morgue carriers claimed you were dead?"

I nod. "Yes, I'm certain. One of them suffered a fright when I woke up and died from the fear." Sighing, I tuck my feet beneath me. "I'd be lying if I said it's the first time someone thought me dead."

He perks up. "What do you mean?"

"A week ago, I was buried after a choking fit. I'd claim alive, but those who buried me thought me dead and attended a funeral. I'm afraid I awoke in the ground and had to. . . well, it was not a pleasant experience."

"I'd imagine not," he answers, staring at me in surprise. "You're completely serious?"

"Completely," I answer. "I know what I must sound like. Believe me, if I thought I could hide this, I would, but this is the second time now and I'm starting to think I'm destined for the lunatic asylum. Any minute now, I'm going to wake up from this nightmare. And then I will be back to my old life without reapers and vampires and—"

"I'm sorry," Henry interrupts. "Did you just say vampires?"

Before I can answer and brush away my words as nothing but stress, a knock on the door cuts me short and draws the doctor's attention away from me. He frowns and glances at the clock. "There shouldn't be anyone coming at this late hour."

"Perhaps someone needs help?" I ask, hoping to distract further from my raving and fear of lunacy.

"Yes, well it's not uncommon for young women to find me and request elixirs for their unwanted pregnancy. Wait here, Mena. I'll send them away if it's nothing and make it quick if it's someone needing services."

"Don't worry about me," I tell him. "I'll be fine. Do whatever you must."

He disappears for a few minutes. I wait patiently on the bed, listening for any sign of conversation, but he returns with a deeper frown. "There was no one there. Perhaps it was a mistake." He looks me over and sighs. "I'd like to keep you here overnight." At my look, he hurries to clarify. "To study. If you did truly die and your heart started again, there could be complications. I'd like to make certain you're okay before I send you on your way."

"That is very logical," I murmur. "Yes, that's fine." If only because it prolongs my distance from Otto and Athan. The longer I stay away, the better. I'll have to send word to Mrs. Kingsley in the morning of my whereabouts.

He gestures to the bed I'm sitting on. "I apologize the beds are not up to your standards—"

"It's perfect," I reply. "I don't need anything special, Henry. This will do nicely." I glance around the room, the emptiness of it, the lack of anything comforting. Everything is white and sterile and lacking any sort of color. "Would you... mind staying here until I fall asleep? I'm afraid I've started having trouble falling asleep for fear of the nightmares."

There's a phantom in the corner, meandering around, ignoring us, but there all the same. His presence unnerves me.

"Please," I add when he doesn't immediately reply.

"Of course," he murmurs, taking a seat on the nearest bed. "I'll leave once you're asleep."

I nod and settle into the bed, my eyes on him before I close them. Thankful for the reprieve and entirely exhausted, I fall asleep far faster than I plan.

My dreams are filled with trains and coffins, and I wake twice to the feeling of choking only to remember where I am.

That's when I notice the doctor in the bed beside mine, snoring softly. He must have fallen asleep while waiting. Either way, it offers me comfort and I'm able to fall asleep again each time.

Something about his presence is calming, like a gentle warmth, and I'm thankful for it as I drift finally into a peaceful, undisturbed sleep.

16
JEKYLL

She falls asleep quickly with my presence, but I don't leave immediately. I can't help but watch her sleep and ponder the puzzle she's brought to my door. If Mena is to be believed—and judging by the state of her dress, she's telling the truth—then there is certainly some grand question over her head.

Why has she died twice and came back to life? And what secret science might I learn from it?

The puzzle is a strange one, one I've never encountered in all my years, and I've most definitely encountered some strange ones. From my own experiments to travelling through the jungles of other countries, this is by far the most unique problem I've discovered yet.

Mena has died twice now. First by choking and then by train. And each time she has woken back up. From my understanding, the first time took far longer than the second time to awaken, as she'd already been buried after the choking incident. To imagine her desperation, to wake up in a coffin, makes my chest ache. No human should have to go through such things. No woman should have to dig her way up through the earth.

But what a magnificent creature she is because of it.

I shut down the voice before it can grow too cumbersome and settle onto the bed, my brain circulating through the details I know. Mena was hit by a train. Not just any train, but a high-speed train coming into the platform. It had no plans to stop at the platform so while it might have slowed a little, it would not have slowed much. The details she'd supplied—broken neck, crushed skull, collapsed ribs—make sense in that situation. She's lucky she was not completely ripped apart.

And the most extraordinary thing about it all is that she's now completely uninjured. For someone to think her dead and beyond repair, and to then take her to the morgue, there must have been no other hope. What a fright she must have given them when she sat up. Imagining the scenario makes me chuckle under my breath, softly so as not to wake her. She should have some wounds, but all that's left behind are scars.

When I glance over at her, guilt hits me when I realize I'd never helped her get cleaned up. Her hair is still matted with blood, the dried remnants of her injuries staining her alabaster skin. Locomotive grease smears across her face, along her arms, and generally makes her look grimy. Small bits of meat speckle her flesh. I should have offered to draw her a bath, or perhaps helped her clean up myself. Instead, I've allowed her to fall asleep covered in the evidence of her pain.

She should be treated like a queen.

I don't argue with the voice this time because I can't disagree. Despite the grime and the blood, it's easy to see that Mena is beautiful. From the angle of her jaw to the bow of her lips to the lashes that fan her eyelids, she's built as many distinguished ladies are. Even in the fear of her situation, she's magnificent. A woman like her would never look twice at a man like me.

Classless. Strange. Broken.

I glance down at my arm, at where flesh and blood used to live and now only metal and mechanics do. I've grown used to the prosthetic now, but it's hard not to miss the phantom of what used to be.

Of course, I'm not always without it.

I'll have to send for some new clothing for Mena in the morning. She can't wear her dress any longer as it's in tatters and there are no women's clothing in my home. Though she could temporarily wear my clothing, I won't demean her by offering. I'll send for something better.

Such a pretty, powerful creature she is, the voice whispers in my mind as I study her.

"She's a patient," I whisper, reminding the voice that there are boundaries.

She's ours, it growls back. *She's here and she belongs to us.*

But she doesn't. I know that. I know someone like her, a woman of her status, would never be interested in someone like me. So I shush the voice and settle back against the pillows. I tell myself I'll only lay here for a few minutes longer, but before I know it, I slip into dreams of trains and digging my way up from graves.

As if even my subconscious demands I feel Mena's pain.

17
MENA

I wake to rare sunlight streaming in through the windows. Today, rather than the fog that's common for London's early morning streets, the sun makes its appearance, warming the atmosphere up to a pleasant temperature. It feels different somehow, strangely warm despite the chill still in the air. The clouds that often hide the sun from our eyes have decided to take the day off, leaving behind a pleasant morning. It's mornings like these that make me feel whole, that remind me that there's always another day. However, the sun is a rare commodity in the smog of London, so I relish it while I can.

Closing my eyes, I absorb the warmth, soaking in the rays that stream through the windows and humming under my breath in happiness. I'm so lost in the feeling, I forget where I am. I forget I'm not in my home. When a noise startles me from my reprieve and the doctor appears from around the corner, I nearly scream, covering my mouth in surprise.

"Oh! Doctor Jekyll. Forgive me. I'd forgotten for a moment where I was," I breathe, pressing my hand against my chest to still my rapidly beating heart.

Henry stumbles to a stop, his eyes wide. "My apologies, Mena. I hadn't meant to frighten you." He holds up his hands where he holds a bundle of cloth. "I sent for some new clothing for you. I assumed you would not wish to remain in the cotton gown or put your tattered dress back on. I had no women's clothing here to supply."

I stare at him in surprise. He'd sent for clothing? "There's no Mrs. Jekyll hiding about?" I end up asking, which is foolish. We were speaking of clothing, but here I am asking about the detail of there being no women's clothing here.

"I'm afraid not," he says with a smile. "Most women think me strange and unusual."

Sitting up further to make sure he's focused on me, I return his smile. "I don't think you strange at all, Henry. In fact, you're incredibly interesting."

He flushes. "As are you, Mena. I've been considering your predicament all morning and. . ." He trails off, his eyes taking in my eagerness to listen. "Forgive me. I came in here to offer you my washing chamber to clean up if you wish and here I am chattering away." He settles the new clothing on the bed he'd slept on the night before. "Do you need any. . . assistance?"

The red across his cheeks brightens at his question. My own heart flutters in amusement. The doctor is incredibly adorable. "I think I can manage," I say, glancing toward the open doorway. "Cleaning up sounds lovely."

He nods and gestures toward the open doorway. "The washroom is upstairs and to the right. If you should require anything, just call for me."

I stand and stretch, careful to conceal my modesty in front of the shy doctor. I reach out and touch his arm. His blush travels along his neck. "Thank you, Henry. Your kindness is refreshing."

"Are most people not kind?" he asks.

"They are, but often times, it's a fake kindness, play pretend to preserve societal standards. With you, I know it's real," I tell him, picking up the bundle of clothing. I'm pleased to see that there's no corset and it's simply an easier managed day dress.

"How could you know?" he asks curiously, studying me.

I smile gently at him. "I often have a way of just knowing, Doctor." I nod toward the stairs. "I won't be long."

"Please, take as long as you need."

I follow his directions up the stairs and turn right, finding the bathing chamber easily enough. There's a large tub in the center of the room already filled with steaming water. I sigh at the true kindness the doctor has shown me. It's not often you find such genuine care. Making sure the door is closed behind me, I strip the cotton gown from my shoulders and study myself in the mirror, wincing when I realize just how big of a mess I am. How the doctor can look at me without being frightened is beyond me. My hair is wild and loose from the style it had been in yesterday morning. It's tangled and matted with blood and bits of. . . well, I'd rather not say. . .from the head wound I'd suffered. My face is smeared with blood streaks and grime, the two mixing across my cheeks. There's even dried blood beneath my nose. The rest of my body did not escape the same fate. Turning toward the tub, I dip my toes into it, sighing at the heat. I climb into it immediately, sinking until only my nose is above the water, absorbing the heat of it. This was precisely what I needed.

For long moments, I simply soak, enjoying the moment, but I realize quickly that this is not my home and I should not overstay my welcome. I make quick work from then on, using the supplied soap to scrub at my body and then my hair, washing away the grime. The water turns murky with blood and dirt, leaving behind a stain in the water that soaks back into my skin. Only once my flesh is raw from scrubbing do I stand and begin to dry myself off.

The bundle of clothing thankfully includes undergarments and I dress myself. Being a day dress, I'm able to maneuver around and fasten the buttons far easier than that of an evening dress, which I'm thankful for. It can't have been long since I came up to bathe, but when I trail back downstairs, it's to find Henry setting a plate of fruits and cheese on a table for me.

"I thought you might be hungry," he says when he hears me approaching, but he only turns to look at me once he's set the plate down. His eyes widen as he takes me in.

I'd been unable to do anything with my hair except to leave it down. It's not proper, but I doubt the doctor has hair pins sitting around.

"Wow," he murmurs, studying me from head to toe. As if realizing he's staring, he blinks and shakes his head. "My apologies. It's just that you're breathtakingly beautiful."

My skin heats with the compliment, the flush climbing my neck and spreading along my cheeks. "Thank you," I reply, looking down at the clothing. "You picked well." And exactly in my size, too, strangely enough.

He shakes his head, frowning. "Not the dress, Mena. Just you. You glow with… with…"

Before he can find the words he's searching for, a knock comes from the front door yet again. It echoes around us, a hollow sound that makes a pit form in my stomach. I press my hand against the ache, frowning in confusion. Goosebumps rise along my skin like a warning, but I don't understand what they could be warning me about.

Henry sighs. "I'll return momentarily," he says before turning to answer the door.

18
MENA

I'm standing away from the door, still at the base of the stairs. Perhaps, this pit in my stomach is a demand for food, but I don't immediately rush to the plate Henry made up for me. Curiosity has me watching him go to the door. He moves achingly slow, I think, but I realize only the time has slowed for me. My heart throbs and stops as I wait for whatever is on the other side of the door to be revealed. I never felt like this around Athan or Otto. So what is it? What's waiting?

"Doctor?" I call, frowning. I think to warn him, but I don't know what I'd be warning him about.

"Just a moment," he tells me, ever the professional, prepared to find a patient seeking his help.

When he finally grabs the handle, I hold my breath, waiting. The knob turns. The door swings open. And on the other side...

Three women.

I frown at the strangeness of the situation. First, three women have come to this doctor's door, a doctor known for his help with female predicaments. So it should not be strange at all. It would not be if not for the unique symbols etched into the three women's skin.

Along their forehead, their arms, their necks, I can see them, as if they'd been branded like cattle.

"Yes? Can I help you?" Henry asks.

"Good morning," the woman in front says when she sees Henry. "We have need of your services, good doctor."

Jekyll frowns at them, taking in each of their appearances. So he can see the symbols, too. At least I'm not alone in my insanity. "What services are you searching for? Perhaps I have something depending on—"

But the woman in front looks past him then and sees me standing in the back. It should be difficult to see me, shrouded in shadows as I am, but clearly, the woman has no difficulty seeing in the dark.

The unease in my stomach tightens and screams for me to run.

"On second thought," the woman says, interrupting Henry as he speaks of his services. "We don't need you. We're here for her."

She throws out her arm toward Henry before I can do anything but take a stumbling step forward. Henry goes flying backward, as if she had hit him with the strength of an elephant, before he crashes against the wall and slides down. His head slumps and I gasp, moving toward him.

The three women rush inside before I can get to him, their lips split into victorious grins.

"Pretty little Lilith," one says. "We expected more from you."

"You're coming with us," another adds, her eyes flashing with something feral. "Now."

"I'm not going anywhere with you," I growl, standing my ground. The three women immediately begin to stalk around me, as if I'm a prey animal caught in the crosshairs of predators. "What even are you?"

"We are the Bloodbane Coven," the leader surprisingly answers. "A sisterhood of witches. And with your power, we'll be unstoppable."

"I have no power," I declare, tilting up my chin. "You're mistaken about my identity."

"There's no mistake," the leader argues. "We felt you die, and here you are, glowing with power."

Frowning, I glance down at my skin, but I see nothing. There's no glow as far as I can tell. "You're wrong."

One of the witches grins. "A Lilith in denial is a Lilith easily controlled."

I scowl at her. "A foolish witch is a dead witch."

I don't know where the words come from or why I goad her. Some part of me spills the words from my lips before I can stop them. Just as I suspect, the witch doesn't take kindly to my unforeseen words. She lunges toward me, and I fling out my hands in defense, to protect my face from the black claws tipping her fingers. Something white hot burns up my arms and flares out of me, slamming into the witch's chest and causing her to fly backward away from me. She doesn't slam into the wall like Henry had. She lands on her feet and slides, her eyes flashing with violence. Briefly, I think she's going to lunge again. Instead, she drops to her hands and knees. . .

. . .and begins shoveling dirt from the potted plant and anything else she can find into her mouth.

Blinking in surprise, I take a stumbling step back, right into another witch. She hisses at me in anger at what I've unknowingly done to her friend.

"Stop it!" she screeches.

"I don't know what I did! Let alone how to stop it!" I cry, jerking away from her. Her dark claw drags along my arm, slicing it open. "Leave me alone!"

She shoves me toward the leader who bares her teeth and sinks onto her heels, prepared to lunge at me. The other witch continues to shovel items down her throat, things not on the floor now. Coins, shoelaces, dirty bandages from the trash. I can't focus on her, can't stomach what I've forced her to do.

More power flares out of me as I prepare myself for the hit, as I prepare to be cut into ribbons by this angry witch. The one behind me takes the brunt of the hit and drops to her knees, going from violently angry to sobbing in horror. It doesn't slow down the leader, however. I close my eyes in preparation...

...but it never comes.

A roar echoes from behind me and the witch stumbles to a stop, her eyes wide in horror. I don't turn to look, afraid to, but I have no need for that. Whatever is behind me flies forward and slams into the witch in front of me.

I stare with wide eyes at the creature tearing into her, forcing her back. Fear trickles into my chest, but strangely, it's not fear *of* the creature. It's fear *for* him. His roar breaks the trance of the other two witches, and they stumble to their feet, screeching in fear of the thing attacking them. They scramble for the door, all three of them, their symbols glowing with whatever power they possess. I watch them leave with fear in their eyes, and once they're gone through the open doorway, I take in the creature before me.

He's not facing me, his eyes on the doorway to make sure the witches don't come back. He's large, so tall, he has to bend over to avoid hitting his head on the ceiling. His skin is washed in gray, black crawling up from his feet and hands, as if a stain. A long, lizard like tail hangs behind him, swaying back and forth like a cat. Large spikes trail down the monster's spine, going from longer to shorter the lower it gets. I can see claws on his hands, and there are black spots breaking up some of the gray. I can't see his face, only the dark hair and the horns that curl back over his ears, but everything about him says "monster." I should be afraid. I should be terrified right now.

Instead, I'm almost calm.

I don't scream as he turns to face me. I don't run.

Instead, I stare into a face I almost recognize, into the greenest eyes, and my heart beats fiercely inside my ribcage.

As if begging to be let out...

19
MENA

Before I can speak, before the creature has the opportunity to make the decision to kill me, the door comes slamming open the rest of the way. I tense, expecting the witches return. Instead, I find two more familiar faces, their eyes wide at the creature standing before me.

"What the fuck is that?" Otto grunts, staring at the monster who had just sent the witches screaming.

Athan stares at the creature in surprise before sinking into a defensive stance. "Whatever it is, it isn't safe."

Otto's eyes narrow and he follows suit, prepared to attack the monster now turning toward them with furrowed brows. He doesn't look afraid, and as he turns, I get to see his profile. The elegant nose, the high cheekbones, all traits I recognize. Gasping, I turn, searching for Henry where he'd slammed against the wall, but there's nothing there.

Athan and Otto lunge.

"Stop!" I cry, rushing forward to throw myself in front of the creature. "Please stop!"

Athan and Otto both halt their attack in confusion. "What is the meaning of this?" Otto growls, looking between me and the creature behind me. The hair on the back of my neck stands on end, but he doesn't attack me.

"Don't hurt him," I reason, glancing over my shoulder. "He... he saved me."

They both pause, looking from the expression on my face to the monster facing all of us.

"He saved you?" Athan asks, his eyes narrowed in suspicion.

Otto takes a step forward. "And who is *he* exactly?"

I pull my bottom lip between my teeth and wince. "I don't exactly know. But I suspect... well, we should find the doctor and—"

"I am the doctor," the monster behind me speaks. His voice is like the cobblestones of the London streets, rough and monstrous and yet still smooth somehow. "Or at least, he's here inside of me."

I turn fully towards the monster behind me, taking in all of him. The only thing that feels familiar are his eyes and the shape of his face. The similarities end there.

"You're... Henry?" I ask, staring up at him.

He towers over me, standing easily two feet taller. Turned toward me, I can't see the spikes I know line his spine, but the tail still swishes back and forth behind him, catching my attention. The horns that curl back from his forehead tempt me to touch, to feel their reality. When he parts his dark lips, I see sharp teeth flashing there. The only clothing he wears are a pair of shredded trousers, trousers that appear to be the remnants of what Henry was wearing before the witches arrived. Black spots dance along his skin like freckles, smattering across his chest, across his cheekbones, up his arms from the black there. He's beautiful, but in the same way a ship meant for battle is beautiful. A sleek design of war, of terror. And he's looking at me with the eyes of a man starved.

"Yes, and no," he answers, stepping closer. I don't back away, only because I steel my spine and force myself not to. His height is intimidating. "Henry Jekyll lives inside of me in this form, just as I live inside of him while he wears his human skin."

"And who exactly are you?" I ask, looking up into his pretty green eyes.

He reaches for my hand and for some reason, I allow him to take it. His large claws swamp my fingers, but he's careful not to scratch me as he lifts it to his lips and presses a kiss against my knuckles. "You can call me Edward Hyde, my sweet Mena." As he leans over my hand, he looks up into my eyes, making something inside of me unfurl.

"How?" I breathe, staring into his eyes, lost in the beauty of them. I take note of every detail, especially of the fact that Edward has two fully functioning arms, where Henry has a prosthetic.

"I don't like to think of that," Edward replies, his lips curling into a smile. "I'd rather spend the time I have left getting to know you for myself."

Otto scoffs behind us and I glance over my shoulder at him. "Another monster in love," he grumbles. "Of course."

Edward glares at him over my head. "I will smash you into the ground, bloodsucker."

"I'd like to see you try."

Athan holds up his hand and it reminds me that my own hand is still enveloped in Edward's. Carefully, I retract it and he looks down with a frown as I take a step back, but I don't move very far away from him. He seems to relax at the sign of trust and instead settles for winking at me and settling in.

"We have bigger things to discuss," Athan declares, bringing all the bickering to a halt. He looks at me, meets my eyes. "I felt your death again."

I nod, grimacing at the reminder. "Indeed. I was. . . well, I was struck by the train."

He blinks. "And are you well?"

"She's perfect," Hyde offers. "Not a scratch on her body."

My hands start to twist together with my anxiety. "I woke up in the morgue carriage. Gave one of the poor medic's a heart attack and he died right there in front of me."

Otto frowns. "He died?"

But where Otto seems confused, Athan only sighs. "Your death is the natural order. For you to come back, another life must take your place. It's the laws of the world."

I tense and stare at him in horror. "So every time I die, I'm sealing someone else's fate?" At his nod, I nearly choke on my words. "But that didn't happen the first time!"

"No?" Athan seems to think, searching his memories of my first death. "There was another woman who died close to you. A Mrs. Withers—"

I gasp and cover my mouth. "I killed Mrs. Withers?"

He tilts his head. "You know her?"

"Only in passing, but she is. . . was a legend. No one expected her to ever die." I hesitate. "Did I miss her funeral?"

"Yes. It took place right after yours."

Sighing, I run a hand through my hair. "Pity. That would have been a splendid funeral to attend."

Otto looks between us and narrows his eyes. "Regardless, that's two deaths down. Five more to go and you'll reach full power."

"And unfortunately, it appears my time is at an end," Hyde interrupts, drawing my attention. The gray starts to fade along his skin back to the smooth cream of Henry's. "Alas, Henry only drank enough elixir for the fight. Until we meet again, my sweet Mena."

His body begins to shrink, fading away. When his right arm shrivels and falls away with a clatter on the ground, I gasp and startle. Hyde grins apologetically at me. "Sorry, love. It's all part of the process."

In the end, I stare in surprise at Henry when he appears fully from the visage of Edward, his face flushed in embarrassment as he holds the now stretched trousers to his hips in an attempt to keep them on. He kicks the shriveling arm away as it starts to disintegrate and grimaces. After a moment, he picks up his prosthetic from the counter behind us and meets my eyes.

"I apologize for the outburst, Mena," he murmurs with a wince. "But it was the only way I could protect you."

I tilt my head, studying him, fascinated. "So then tell me, Doctor," I say, leaning in. "What exactly are you?"

The curl of his lips comes from something deep inside, some ruthless, mischievous thing.

"My sweet Mena," he says, and I know I'm talking to Edward Hyde instead. "You ask what I am. I ask what am I not." He bows and it's Henry who meets my eyes again as he straightens. "All that I am, or seem, is but a scientist and a doctor. Nothing more. Nothing less."

Otto raises his brows. "Seems a little bit more if you ask me," he grumbles under his breath.

My hand stops my giggle from escaping my lips.

A little bit more indeed.

20
MENA

When I simply stare at Henry, he clears his throat and moves to take a seat on a stool sitting at a worktable. There are various items scattered across the table—a notebook, a graphite stick, some ink—but he doesn't reach for any of it. Instead, he keeps his eyes focused on me. No matter which form he's in, his eyes are the same brilliant green. A strange detail considering there are two very separate personalities between the forms.

Athan steps up beside me, his eyes perusing my body, taking in the new dress and the state of my hair. "I think we all have the same question here," he begins before looking over at Henry. "Were you sent here? Did you feel Mena's power?"

Henry's face twists with confusion. "What does that mean? Mena came to me after her accident. I simply helped her. When the witches attacked, I only meant to protect her."

Athan's face twists with confusion at his answer, as if it's unexpected. I can't say for certain that I feel the power in my veins. Clearly, it's there, judging by the reaction from the witches when I'd instinctually threw out my hands, but I have no way of knowing how to purposely use them. I don't feel much different, just healthy, and whole. If I can't tell it, then why would the doctor feel it?

"Perhaps, it best you tell us how you came to be," I reason, studying Henry closely. I can't see any sign of Edward Hyde in him, not physically. Is it a painful thing to transform? Is it some magic he carries in his bones? I can't determine anything just by looking, so an explanation is necessary. "If you're comfortable with that," I add, realizing it may not be a pleasant story. After all, I wouldn't want to relive my first death and awakening. It's bad enough that I see it in my nightmares.

Henry glances between me and the others, his brows furrowed. "You mentioned a reaper and a vampire before. . ."

Grimacing, I gesture toward Athan and Otto. "The tall brooding man is Athan, the grim reaper from my understanding. The smooth, grinning man is Otto. He's, um, well. . ."

"The King of the European Vampire Coven," Otto supplies helpfully with a wicked grin. "You're welcome to call me, Your Majesty. Master also works well."

Henry's brows shoot up. "You don't look like a vampire."

Otto hisses, revealing fangs that should frighten any human. Henry doesn't flinch.

"What exactly is a vampire supposed to look like?" Otto asks, his teeth still bared. "Vicious and hungry? We're not all heathenistic monsters."

Holding up his hands, Henry shrugs. "My apologies if I offended you. I've never met a vampire, so I was only curious." He tilts his head. "Perhaps, if we're on better footing, you'd allow me to study—"

"Henry," I interrupt, moving closer to him and drawing his attention away from Otto. "There will be plenty of time for that. For now, could you just explain Edward please? Just so we can understand."

And also, to know if he's an enemy or an ally. Athan's question brought up the reminder that there will be many monsters after me if they can all feel it. The witches may only be the beginning. I don't know how deep this will go, but clearly running isn't an option now. If I can't run, I must find another way to combat this prophecy. Running only killed me faster it seems.

"Yes, well. . ." Henry began, looking down at his prosthetic. "As a young child, I was involved in an accident. My mother took her eyes off me but for a moment and I was a mischievous child. The story goes that I ran into the street and was caught in the crosshairs of a carriage. I tried to move out of the way, but my arm was caught beneath the wheel. By the time my mother realized what had happened and took me to the doctor, there was no saving my arm."

My heart aches for a little boy who found himself in such a terrible situation. I can't imagine what his mother felt, the guilt she might have carried with her all those years.

"As I grew up and suffered at the hands of other children who didn't understand, I vowed I would help others, thus my reason for becoming a doctor." He hesitates, looking down at his fingers, one flesh and one metal. "But that work didn't fulfill me, and I never quite felt whole. I enjoyed helping people, but I also wanted to help myself, a very selfish notion, but one I suffered from nonetheless. Soon, after realizing that about myself, I found true science." He holds up his prosthetic. "Being a doctor helped me learn about myself and the capabilities I possessed, but science taught me who I am. I stumbled upon some abandoned research about starfish and their ability to regrow limbs. I grew obsessed with the concept, that if I could only harness their power, I could regrow human limbs, and thus, my own."

Athan moves closer, his brows furrowed. "And did you succeed?"

Henry shrugs and holds up his prosthetic arm. "Clearly not. . . and also yes, in a way." When he reaches into his pocket and holds up a small bottle, I frown in confusion, which prompts him to continue. "I created an elixir. It was meant to regrow limbs and nothing more, but there's a short supply of people willing to test it, and besides that, it wouldn't be moral. You see, I made an oath as a doctor to help people. Having them test an untested serum could be dangerous."

"So you tested it on yourself first," I breathe, seeing Henry in a new light. A scientist desperate for progress, a doctor intent on helping people, a man torn between the two.

He nods. "I did. And it worked. The first time was incredibly painful. I watched my arm stretch and regrow, and just when I'd thought I'd been successful, it turned grey, my hands tipped in black claws. Edward showed up pretty quickly after that." He glances at his reflection in a mirror to his left, as if studying his face. "And he never left. Though I control the wheel in this form, he remains in my subconscious, speaking, coming out every so often. With the serum, I transform and become Edward Hyde, a monstrous creature capable of great terror and strength, but it's only temporary. Depending on how much elixir I take, I eventually transform back into Henry Jekyll and the arm disappears. A failure."

We're all silent, absorbing the words, this story that seems so surreal and yet I've seen the evidence myself. When no one speaks or offers any words of solace, I find myself moving forward to do so. I wrap my arms around him, offering comfort through the embrace. Henry stiffens, but after a few seconds, his arms come around me and return the hold, accepting my comfort.

"Not a failure," I tell him as I lean back. "Just a different outcome."

The slight curl to his lips offers me comfort in a way that I hope he might understand, that he might know what it means to be human and find a different avenue. That's what it is to be human, to make mistakes and learn from them. Though both of us had been violently thrown into a new world, we could share in that together.

Henry runs a hand through his hair when I step back and sighs. "Edward's form is monstrous. His personality leaves room for development, but he has all of his limbs and he's stronger than I'll ever be. I suppose I was successful in my failure."

Nodding, I take a seat on a second stool. "Edward, Mr. Hyde, seemed very. . ."

"Possessive," Otto adds helpfully. "He seemed quite keen on Mena being his."

Henry grimaces. "Yes, well, unfortunately, he's under the impression that you belong to us, though I've told him he's wrong. I would not dare to claim you as such without your consent and I apologize if he came off as forward."

I raise my brow. Nowhere in his words did he argue that he doesn't feel the same. Interesting.

Athan and Otto, in contrast, both scowl at the words.

"A queen belongs to no one," Otto says. "We belong to her."

Athan snorts and glances at Otto. "That's a premature statement. Just because I'm curious doesn't mean—"

"I've already seen it in your eyes, reaper," Otto says, cutting him off. "You cannot protest something so clearly seen."

Athan clamps his lips shut and narrows his eyes at the vampire, annoyed, but he doesn't argue. Another interesting detail.

Sighing at their words, I rub my cheeks, desperate for something mundane. "Can we just. . .pretend to be normal for a moment please? There's a nice little shop down the road that has the most perfect tea. Shall we attend and address these new problems later?"

Otto's face brightens. Athan scowls deeper.

Henry frowns. "You're welcome to go at any time. I should like to call on you—"

"That invitation included you, Doctor," I tell him with raised brows.

His face goes slack for a few seconds before he recovers from his surprise and stands. "Of course it did. Of course, Mena. I would love to attend."

Otto glances at Athan. "It appears you'll have to compete with the good doctor monster, reaper."

Athan bares his teeth. "I'm not competing for anything."

Otto grins. "Keep telling yourself that, reaper. It'll make things far more entertaining than I'd hoped."

21
MENA

The small tea shop down the street is a favorite stop of mine. Unfortunately, it's also a favorite of most of the upper society, so when we arrive for tea, the shop is bustling with activity much to my dismay. Especially since my hair is not perfectly styled. I'd attempted to twist it into some semblance of appropriate style, but without the proper hair instruments, it had been difficult. Currently, I'm using some random instruments from Henry's bag to keep it held in place, of which I'd promised to return. But it still appears just slightly disheveled. There can be one of two outcomes at being seen with the hairstyle. Either the ladies will whisper about how unbecoming I am, or the style will become the new trend. There's no in between.

The moment we step inside the small shop and find a table that will accommodate the four of us, every pair of eyes inside the shop turns, watching our small company. The whispers start quickly after, and I can't stop the flush from climbing up my neck at the extra attention.

"Is this alright?" Henry asks, glancing around at the talking ladies.

I imagine we make a strange sight. I'm wearing a proper day dress at least, so I'm not out of style. Athan wears a suit that looks like it is from the wrong decade, the style cut too severe. Otto is wearing a suit fit for royalty, the edges trimmed in gold thread, small gems sewn into the hem. Henry isn't dressed in a full suit at all, decidedly underdressed for the occasion and location, but he doesn't seem to notice. As a single woman, sitting with three so very different men will make me the talk of the town.

Even more so than I already am.

"I'm a widow," I tell Henry, sighing. "Not an old maid. This is allowable. Besides, I'm sure I'm already the talk of the town after many attended my funeral." Saying the words out loud reminds me. I turn to Athan with a frown. "I never asked about my funeral. . ."

Athan nods as he peruses the offerings. "There were many noble and high-class ladies in attendance who pretended to cry and lamented about losing such a close friend. Not a single one was sincere outside of your staff, but your funeral was a populated affair. I don't believe there was a single important person not in attendance."

Sighing, I look through my own tea choices, searching for my favorite to make sure it's served today. "Just as I expect from the lot of them," I comment. "I suppose at least they came. How terrible for them to waste their false tears and acting skills on someone still very much alive. I expect they'll be bitter about that."

The server comes forward then and sets the table up with teas and biscuits before slipping away, leaving us to have our tea in peace. She'll only return if we're in need of more.

"Which of these is best?" Henry asks, frowning at the options.

I point to a teapot. "I'm particular about the Earl Grey myself."

"Then I'll have that." He takes the pot and pours me a cup before doing the same for himself. He watches me put milk and sugar in mine before copying my actions. As if he's not drank tea before.

"Are you not a tea drinker?" I ask, tilting my head.

"I prefer coffee usually, particularly when I'm working," he answers.

Interesting. I already know that Otto can drink and eat outside of. . . a vampire diet, and Athan seems content with tea, reaching for the chamomile and lavender teapot before delicately dropping in sugar. These three men are so different and yet. . . there's something about them that calls to me.

As if I conjured it, the whistling and horn I've suffered from since the first death echoes in my ears and makes me wince just slightly. It's difficult to ignore today, the sound level higher than before.

Before any of them can ask me about it, we're interrupted by none other than Delilah Hamilton. "Miss Seagraves. How pleasant to see you out and about this day," she coos. Everyone else in the shop is listening in, curious, as I raise my eyes to meet hers. "We've all been wondering if you were well after your ordeal. After all, many of us thought you suffered an untimely death."

I force a smile on my lips at the reminder and slip into the society mask necessary to deal with the other ladies. The decorum required always exhausts me, but it's necessary.

"Mrs. Hamilton, how pleasant to see you. Yes, it was a frightful ordeal indeed. I must say it's refreshing to be able to walk about after such an event. One takes the London streets for granted until you think you won't be able to walk them again."

Her eyes narrow at my words, and the viciousness I despise in the young Mrs. Hamilton peeks through. Henry seems oblivious, but Athan and Otto take notice.

"Indeed. Your funeral was a sad affair. So many came to mourn your passing, it was a sight to see. If only you could have been there." Her eyes flash. "Oh, wait, you were. How silly of me to forget." She looks over at the men, her eyes dismissing Henry quickly before settling on Otto. "Who are your guests, Miss Seagraves?"

Luckily, I don't have to answer. Otto takes it upon himself to stand and take her hand. She giggles and fans her flush as he presses a kiss to the back of her knuckles. For some strange reason, my blood begins to boil, anger flickering in my chest in a way I've not felt before.

"Otto Van Doren," he says, smiling at Delilah. "Are you a friend of Mena?"

"The closest," Delilah says, giggling. She glances at me. "Right, Mena?"

I don't know what comes over me. One moment, I'm simply annoyed and the next I'm so filled with fury, I find myself eerily calm as I meet her eyes and say, "No. We're not really friends at all. I doubt she even knows my favorite tea."

Delilah's face flushes in embarrassment. "Don't be silly, Mena. Of course I do. It's. . . it's. . ." Her eyes flick to the table, searching for my tea, but I place my hand over my teacup to hide the color and smile.

"Go on," I encourage mockingly. "Make yourself the fool."

Her face flushes in anger now and she takes a step forward. I don't know what she intends to say or do. She never gets the chance. On instinct, I flick my finger at her, barely a movement, but just enough. She stumbles to a stop, her eyes going wide and then her entire expression going slack.

"Mrs. Hamilton," I say, narrowing my eyes on her. "Perhaps you should show everyone here just how you cried for my death. Since we're both the closest of friends and all. I'm willingly to bet you sobbed when you found out I was alive."

"Of course," she replies, tears already filling her eyes and starting to spill over her lashes. "I was filled with grief at your passing," she sobs, covering her eyes.

Everyone is staring at Delilah now rather than at us. No longer do they care to watch the woman risen from the dead. Instead, they stare at the woman overcome with her emotions in the middle of the tea shop, her sobs getting the best of her. A few people get up to comfort her, bringing her over to their table. That movement is what breaks my trance and I find myself blinking in confusion at the power I can feel in my hands as it slowly fades away.

Otto grins. "What a lovely trick, my sweet Mena."

Panic fills me, my heart kicking hard in my chest. What have I just done? Where had it come from?

"Perhaps we should go," Athan murmurs, standing up. "Come, Mena. We'll return to your home."

Without hesitation, I slip my hand into his and allow him to lead me outside, too surprised at myself to argue.

22

MENA

Coming back to my home is a strange feeling. When I left, I planned to possibly never see it again, to escape into the country and leave with none the wiser. Now, it stands like a strange hollow shell. It feels as if it could never be large enough to handle this prophecy and the three men with me, though that's a silly thought. It's far larger than I'll ever need just for myself, and having guests will be nice.

Even if those guests are a mix of monsters.

I glance at them, these men who are strangely intoxicating in their own ways. Athan, the grim reaper who seems strangely kind despite his profession and wavers between interest and disinterest in me. Though he looks human enough, there's this otherworldly feeling around him, as if you're running out of time by simply being in his presence. Otto, the vampire king who both feels royal and casual despite his dress. He's never once asked me to address him by his title, preferring a more intimate address, and while he's easily one of the scarier monsters, he never reveals it, keeping his fangs mostly tucked away. For my benefit or some other reason, I don't know, but it's appreciated all the same. And Henry, the doctor plagued by his own creation, two consciousnesses in one, both man and monster, both Jekyll and Hyde. How strange must it be to have to share your mind with another, to hear their thoughts when it should only be your own.

But I've lingered long enough. None of them pressure me to hurry up the steps as I stare at the large house. None of them ask if I'm alright. They simply wait until I'm ready and begin to climb them once I do. The door opens before I reach the top step and Mrs. Kingsley stands before me, her face twisted with worry and confusion at the new man with me.

"When I heard about an accident at the train station, I. . ." she trails off, her eyes tight. "The description sounded like it was you and I rushed down there, but the person was already gone."

I reach out and take her hand, making sure she's meeting my eyes. "It was me," I clarify. "I woke up in the morgue carriage and they took me to the hospital. That was full, so I found Dr. Jekyll instead."

If possible, Mrs. Kingsley's face tightened further. "They thought you dead. . . again?"

Sighing, I move past her as she opens the door further and wave the men in. When she closes it behind us, I face her fully. "I was dead, for a second time. Whatever is happening, I don't know except that it's some prophecy, but I can offer no other explanation."

"Our hope is to solve the puzzle," Athan offers helpfully. "That's why we're here."

Mrs. Kingsley studies me and then looks over the three men. "I'll have another room prepared for Dr. Jekyll."

"That won't be necessary—" Henry begins but I level my eyes on him.

"Yes, it will," I interrupt. "And any room you may need for research or work, you're welcome to use the office or the room we prepare for you. You do not *have* to stay here, but it is an open invitation so that we may figure this out together." I look toward the stairs.

"Now, if you'll excuse me, I'm going to retire to my rooms. I find myself exhausted. Good evening, gentlemen."

I leave them there staring after me in confusion, but I can't take the time to explain what I'm feeling. I need to get away, to sequester myself away from it all for a little while. I need to come to terms with all of this myself and I can't do that surrounded by three attractive men intent on stirring my arousal by a simple look. It's become too much, and I can't trust my mind to make sense of their stares and the incessant foghorn in the distance. I need space to ruminate.

My rooms still look the same. My trunks are still where I left them. No doubt they will be unpacked at a later date, but I don't care to look into them right now. I only open one long enough to grab a dressing gown before stripping myself bare. I stare into the full-length mirror before me, studying my naked body, the marks that now riddle my skin. Though the scars from the train are faded, they're still there, shimmering white against my pale skin. They rest beside the small scars I earned as a child full of mischief, another reminder of what I'm now being told I am.

I am Philomena Seagraves, widow of Walter Seagraves. I am also the reincarnation of Lilith, the mother of monsters, if Otto is to be believed. Those two sentences don't seem to be kin, and yet they are. I've died twice now and come back, healthy and unharmed. There are many things I believe in, but such extreme miracles are not one of them, nor are coincidences. Something higher is at work here and I don't know how to feel about it. Clearly, I now carry something. . . other. . . in my veins. I'd made Delilah go mad with a flick of the finger. I'd made a witch eat dirt. Holding up my hands, I stare at the perfectly normal appearance of them, at the slender digits that don't look like they could cause such harm. Though I feel strong and capable, I don't exactly feel powerful. Not yet at least. The only tell that there's something off about me is when I look into my eyes in the mirror and catch the sheen there.

Like some feral beast demanding to be let out.

It's been a long time since I've prayed to a god that never

answers, but some desperate part of me needs guidance in this moment. All the years I spent on my knees in church demand I turn to him now, to ask for answers, to hope for some explanation other than I'm the reincarnation of a woman cast from the Garden of Eden. It's been so long, I linger before the cross hanging on my wall, uncertain if I should, but God would not forsake me now in my time of need. He'll help me find the answers within myself.

Quickly, I pull on my dressing gown. I don't think saying my prayers while nude will earn me any favors. Once I'm dressed, I lower myself to my knees before the cross and look up at it, my hands pressed together. For a moment, I can't speak, too afraid to say the words out loud, but I realize I can't linger here forever.

I bow my head and speak. "Almighty Father, thou art in heaven, I come to you for guidance in my time of need." Taking a deep breath to clear my thoughts, I continue. "I've lost direction. I know not where I am destined to land, only where I came from. . . and I am afraid." Admitting those words out loud feels like a rock lodged in my throat. A weight settles on my shoulders as I realize that for the truth it is. I'm afraid. I'm so afraid, it chokes me. "I ask that you guide me in the right direction, that you give me the strength to face this obstacle, and that you do not forsake me in my time of need. I ask. . ."

Furrowing my brows as the buzzing penetrates my subconsciousness, I raise my head in confusion. At first, I can't make sense of the noise, not until the window starts to darken. I turn toward it and flinch at the sight of the flies slowly caking the windowpane, blocking out the sky beyond. My heart kicks in my chest in fear. A sign of the devil? Or something worse?

Clamping my hands together tighter, I bow my head and try to drown them out. "Beloved Shepherd of my soul and body, spread your holy protection over me and cover me with your mighty wings, that no terrors of this night may disturb me, and let your divine majesty watch over—" Pain cuts me off, my heart clutching painfully. Still I push through. "And let your divine majesty watch over my mind while I sleep; through Jesus Christ our Lord. Amen."

The buzzing grows louder so I launch into another prayer, growing more desperate with each bite of pain on my body. "Lord, you alone are God, the gracious and the merciful. You command those who love your name to cast away all fear and care, and to lay their burdens on you. Keep me under your protection, and give me now and always that everlasting rest, which you have promised to those who. . .those who. . ." The word "obey" won't fall from my lips no matter how hard I try. My lips dry up as I continue to force the word out, as I fight the compulsion with all my strength. My body starts to convulse, a scream ripping from my throat as pain explodes behind my eyes. My fingers claw at each other, leaving behind red lines as I fight against the pain, as I desperately try to continue my prayer. The flies buzz at the window, seeking entrance. Every part of me is stripped raw with violence as I scream and scream until my vocal cords give out.

The door slams open, but I can't turn toward whoever is there. My eyes are on the cross, on where spiders begin to spill from behind it, on where the cross begins to turn, slowly.

Strong arms wrap around me, and someone is shouting. Otto? Athan? I do not know. My eyes roll back in my head as my convulsions strengthen. I collapse backward into their arms, my body feeling as if my skin has been flayed from my bone. The pain! Oh, the pain!

"Look at it," Athan says. "The mark."

Otto hisses, but it's Henry's voice I focus on. "What does it mean?"

"I don't know," Athan answers. "But it doesn't look like anything good."

My consciousness fades in their arms, my eyes rolling back in my head, but still I try to pray. The words never come, stolen from my breath as if I'm not allowed to speak them any longer.

Christ rots in my mouth. . .

23
MENA

I wake the next day in my bed, the covers tucked around me with care. I don't realize I'm not alone until I sit up and notice him sitting in the corner. Otto is dressed in a different suit today. This one is just as immaculate as the one before, though it's in a crimson and black pattern. He sits in the chair in the corner of my room, his eyes on me as I move.

"Good afternoon," he murmurs, watching me closely. "How do you feel?"

I press hand to my forehead when the earsplitting pain echoes there. "Afternoon?"

He nods. "You've been asleep for nearly two days."

"How strange," I murmur, an ache behind my eyes causing me to press my fingers tightly to my skull. "My head hurts."

Otto nods and stands, coming close to the bed. "After the ordeal you went through, that does not surprise me." He gestures to the bed. "May I?"

After giving my permission with a nod, Otto sits down on the edge of the bed. His bright caramel eyes take in my appearance, and then trail down to my arm. I follow his gaze to find the wound there.

Three scratches bisecting a circle mark my arm like a brand. Three dots sit on the outside of the circle on the right. It's not healing like my wounds from the train. This one, the skin looks festered and sore. When I press my fingers to it, I flinch in pain.

"What is this?" I whisper. "Where did it come from?"

"We do not know," he answers honestly. "We only know it appeared while you were...praying."

My heart throbs painfully in my throat. "He's forsaken me," I rasp. "That's what this means." Otto simply stares at me as I go through my emotions, as tears build in my eyes at first in sadness and then in anger. "All my life, I've been told that God forgives our sins, that he will not forsake us as long as we do not forsake him, and here I am, forsaken." The words are bitter and painful. The rejection I feel, this brand on my arm, they're both signs that I've put my faith in the wrong god. I don't know where that leaves me.

"Mena."

When I glance up at Otto, I find his face twisted with sympathy. When he knows I'm listening, he begins to speak.

"I have been a vampire for a very long time," he begins. "Far longer than you could guess by my dashing appearance. But before I became this beast, I was a young man who believed in an almighty god, an all-powerful, all-knowing God who would forgive us our sins and allow us into heaven."

I watch his expression closely, take in every muscle twitch, every movement. "And what happened to change that?"

He meets my eyes and the smile that flickers across his lips lacks the humor he portrays. "I became a monster." Sighing, Otto takes my hand and holds on tightly. "The god that many pray to, the one we ask for forgiveness, doesn't much care for his creations, Mena. Not the monstrous ones. We were created in the darkness and therefore, we can never belong in Heaven. It's not our fault, but it matters not to the being who wields his power without thought. I lost faith in him when I lay dying on the cobblestones of Rome, when my throat was torn out and I was fading. I asked him for forgiveness, for help, all the things a good follower is supposed to say. Instead, I woke up this beast and with a hunger for blood." He bows his head. "The next time I tried to pray, the words wouldn't come. Those that did tasted like ash. What sort of god forsakes those who need him the most?" He looks back up at me. "Wouldn't the monsters be most in need of forgiveness?"

"So, I am a monster then?" I whisper, looking down at the mark on my arm.

Strong fingers cup my chin and force my eyes back to his. Every part of me hums in awareness of his touch, wanting the feel of his flesh to linger on mine.

"So what if you are?" Otto asks. "So what if we are forsaken?" He leans closer, earnestness on his face. "We are not alone in our darkness."

"What if I'm afraid of the darkness?" I ask seriously, my heart throbbing. "What if I'm not made for it?"

"There's no reason to be afraid, Mena," he coos. "It's meant to happen. Soon, you'll be so powerful—"

"I'm not looking for power," I spit, and immediately regret the bite in my voice. I lower it, easing the venom there. "I only want happiness."

His expression softens and he cups my cheek. "You can be happy if you only allow yourself, my sweet Mena." His thumb strokes along my cheek. "You are not alone. You will not be alone. Never again."

The expression on his face, his touch on my skin, the way he looks at me as if I'm the world, I can't seem to help myself. Some part of me wants to feel normal, wants to feel something. Before I'm conscious of what I'm doing, I'm leaning in and pressing my lips to his.

Otto freezes as my lips touch his, as I press mine softly against his sweet taste. It doesn't deepen, not when he's frozen as he is, and when I lean back and search his eyes, I flush in embarrassment.

"I apologize," I rasp. "I thought I was not alone in my feelings."

"No," Otto snaps, his face twisting. "No," he repeats softer. "It is not because I do not want you, Mena."

I tilt my head. "Then why?"

He shifts, his expression tight. "You have no idea how badly I want you right now, how I long to lay you down in this bed and make you scream my name, but you are not prepared for the beast I am should you give yourself completely to me, my queen. And you are in distress right now. It would not be right."

My expression tightens in annoyance. "Should it not be my own decision?"

"Of course," he hisses. "Of course, but I'm no human lover. Your emotions are frantic right now, and I'm conveniently here with you. When you choose me, I want it to be purposeful, not a quick decision."

Some devilish part of me wants to tease, to get a rise out of this vampire, to see the beast he thinks he is. I stroke my hand up his arm, across his chest, before circling his neck. "And what if I declare I want you now?"

He bares his fangs at me, and before I know what's happening, he's over me. He moved so fast, I had not seen him. Now, he holds himself above me in the bed, his hair hanging around us, his eyes shining bright.

"It's not wise to tempt a monster, Mena," he warns. He leans down and presses his face to my neck. My body tightens in preparation, my fingers clenching in the bed sheets. I feel the first prick of his fangs along my skin, but he doesn't break the surface. Instead, he runs them along my jugular, teasing, threatening. "Soon, my queen," he whispers against my skin. "Soon, I'll sink my fangs into your throat and my cock into your pussy, and you'll scream my name for all to hear." He traces the path of his fangs with his lips, and I shiver beneath him, desperate for his touch. "But today is not that day."

I'm a puddle of need as he removes himself slowly from me and straightens his suit. I crinkle my nose and sit up. "What a devil you are to tease me so," I hiss, displeased at the turn of events.

He grins and bows. "Don't you know that we're all devils in the darkness, my queen?" He straightens and winks. "I'll escort you down to tea when you're ready. I assume you need a moment to collect yourself?"

I bare my own human teeth at him and climb from my bed, stomping to the wash room. When I slam the door, his laughter follows me through and though I'm annoyed, I can't help the smile that pulls at my lips.

Devils, indeed.

24
JEKYLL

"I cannot find mention of the symbol on Mena's arm anywhere," I grumble, searching the numerous books I'd managed to pick up from the library. Not a single one has the symbol that suddenly branded itself into Mena's arm mentioned. "Perhaps I'm looking in the wrong place." I muse over the puzzle, wracking my brain for answers. It appeared while she was praying, along with numerous other events that should not have been possible. As soon as Mena lost consciousness, the flies had disappeared. The spiders had left with them, thankfully nowhere to be seen. But the cross had stayed upside down. No matter how hard any of us tried, it would not turn right again. When turning had been unsuccessful, we'd tried to remove it only to find it immovable that way as well.

I don't exactly believe in a god as a man of science, but if there is one, surely he would not treat Mena so. She's done no wrong. It's not her fault she's been thrust into these events. If I had believed in God before now, I would have lost faith with his treatment of her.

Athan sits in the library with me, his eyes tracing over his own research. There's extraordinarily little in the way of Lilith, her existence greatly scrubbed from most text, so we'll have to start finding older options soon. Perhaps, she was better mentioned at the beginning of Christianity.

I've never met a grim reaper, thank goodness for that, but had I imagined one, the kind, broody, and smug man would not be who I imagined. I suppose most renditions of him leave him skeletal and hooded, but he looks anything but that. He's as much flesh and blood as I am.

Competition, Hyde murmurs in my mind. *Dispose of him.*

I ignore his comment. Mena seems fond of the man even if she's afraid of the events. I will be doing no such thing.

My eyes continue to scan the papers in front of me, finding no answers in their text. "What a puzzle you are, Mena," I whisper to myself. "What a puzzle."

"You like her," Athan says out loud, interrupting my thoughts.

I glance up at him with furrowed brows. "I'm a man of science, reaper. What I feel for her means nothing compared to solving the puzzle."

He grins in amusement despite this conversation being one he could benefit himself from. The reaper is in far more denial than I am. "How long will you tell yourself that before you realize your mistake?" he asks. "I'm willing to bet Hyde doesn't feel the same."

Indeed, Hyde agrees, always the annoying fly in my brain.

Scowling at the reaper, I slide the useless paper aside and pick up another. "Hyde is not in control of my actions."

Athan hums. "Sure he's not." He stands, throwing his book aside. "You know, refusing to accept this new other half of yourself will be your downfall, Doctor. It's why you're intrigued by our beautiful Mena." At my confusion, he gestures in the direction of the stairs, stairs that would lead to her should I want to seek her out. "She's struggling with her other half, too. You want to see if she can accept it, because, if she doesn't, it's proof that you don't have to, either." He walks toward me, making sure I'm listening. Our eyes lock and I see the flash of death in his. "Both of you will soon realize that fate has other plans, Doctor. She always does. Even for those of us who don't believe in it. I understand and dread the struggle well. We will both ache in this war."

He leaves the office then, leaving me here with his words and the books that offer no answers.

He's right, Hyde says, laughing. *We are one and the same, Henry. It's time to accept me.*

"I am not you," I growl, slamming my book shut.

The only answer is more laughter. Mocking, terrible laughter.

25
MENA

My office has been taken over by Henry and his research. Papers are strewn around the room everywhere, covering every surface, sitting in piles here and there. Books sit in similar stacks everywhere you look. He'd gone to the museum this morning and came back with a large load of them. He'd somehow convinced the curator to let them leave the museum in the first place. I don't begin to know how persuasive a man of science on the hunt for answers can be. Clearly, he's persuasive enough because there are hundreds of books here in this office that should not be here.

And I've come to deliver one more.

The Old Testament is heavy in my arms as I stroll into the office, a weight that drags me down while I carry it. It no longer serves as comfort. It no longer feels like mine despite having it since I was a child. As it nestles in my arms, I'm reminded of my attempted prayers, of the signs I've been forsaken.

Of the cross that now hangs upside down permanently in my room no matter how hard we've all tried to turn it or remove it.

It appears I don't have much use for the large leatherbound book any longer, but Henry wants to look through it to see if there is any information we can use to figure out this prophecy, the mark on my arm, or if we can learn more about Lilith. At least it'll be of use to one of us even if I warned him there was nothing of Lilith within the tome. I would remember any mention of her.

I have to admit that it's refreshing to see the office used more substantially despite the mess. It hasn't been so busy since Walter used it. I much prefer to keep my workspace smaller and more manageable compared to the way Henry works. It's chaos in the office right now, but he seems to have some sort of system going as he trails from one pile to the other.

"I've brought the Old Testament," I announce as I look around. "Where would you like it?"

Henry has his nose buried in a book and barely looks up when I speak, so entranced in his research is he. "Just set it on top of one of the piles. Thank you."

"It's my pleasure," I respond before setting the book down with others. The ease of weight is immediate, as if the leather is heavy by itself, as if it is an anchor I could not possibly carry. "Supper will be served in a few hours. I'll come back and check on you before then."

His only answer is a hum that I take as agreement. As a man of science, I assume Henry is prone to bouts of research. It would not be strange to find him so deep in research and thought, that he hears and sees nothing else. Seeing him so is almost whimsical and I'm certainly intrigued. For now, I leave him to his studies, not wanting to disturb him when he's barely begun his work.

Closing the door behind me, I turn toward the large staircase and startle to find Athan there staring up at the portrait Walter commissioned of us. It's the only piece I have of the two of us, the only one we'd truly had time to get finished. There had been plans to commission new pieces every couple of years, but that plan had died with Walter. In the end, this is the only portrait I own of us, Walter looking distinguished and royal, me standing behind him as a lady should, my mouth lacking the smile that had threatened to curl my lips with Walter's teasing during the session. We'd been great friends, Walter and I, but that was all we were to ever be. I'd considered replacing the portrait of one with just myself, but ultimately could not bring myself to remove the portrait there. It seemed disrespectful somehow. Besides, Walter's phantom grandfather is often watching now and I wouldn't want to insult him.

"Did you have a question?" I ask Athan as I climb the stairs. I had plans to return to my room and relax. The house had become rather busy with so many guests and I find my solitude necessary.

Athan turns toward me, his pale eyes bright against the dark stained wood behind him. Everything about Athan is built for both sensuality and death. I suppose death itself can be sensual in a way, but Athan is the walking embodiment of that. When I stand near him, it feels as if I'm standing on a cliff, looking over as I tiptoe the edge. It's a strange feeling, one I think he knows he causes but does nothing to alleviate. I think Athan enjoys making other people uncomfortable.

"Did you love him?" he asks, gesturing to Walter in the portrait.

My eyes trail from him back to the portrait, to the man wearing a kind smile despite his desire to be stoic. My mind wanders to the memory, to our giggles as we tried our best to hold still. "As the reaper, you don't know how these sorts of things work?" I ask him, flashing a smile that's anything but teasing. When he only stares at me, I sigh and force myself to speak. "The marriage was of convenience and necessity, a way to better my family name. It was expected of me as a member of the society and so I did as I was told. My mother was a cynical woman, and she didn't believe in love matches, only ones that would bring the most powerful heirs. At the time, Walter was the most eligible bachelor in London seeking a wife and it was a great honor."

"Do you believe in that?" Athan asks, those unnaturally pale eyes meeting mine.

My brows furrow. "In love matches?"

"In love?" he corrects.

Silence takes over and I ponder his question. I've never particularly thought about it, resigned to my widowhood, but love itself is a great mysterious beast I read about in the paper stories and the books Mrs. Kingsley brings home.

"I do not know," I answer honestly. "I have not witnessed it myself in many instances, so I cannot form an accurate thought about it."

Athan nods in understanding and focuses back on the portrait. "He was a kind man?"

Shrugging, I follow his gaze. "The kindest. He never pressured me. He never treated me as anything other than a lady. And when he died suddenly, I learned he made sure I would be completely taken care of. I inherited everything despite the normalcy of women not allowed ownership. This house and all of his business ventures became mine rather than some long lost cousin from the country." I glance at Athan from the corner of my eyes. "He was a good man even if I never loved him."

The hum that comes from Athan's throat makes my lower stomach tingle for some strange reason, an image of him humming like that from between my thighs flashing in my mind. I flush even if he'll never know what I'm thinking.

"Good," Athan finally says. "I wouldn't want the others competing for your heart against a dead man."

My brows shoot high, and I turn to face him fully. "What makes you think there's any sort of competition happening?"

Athan grins and leans closer. "My dear, there's been a competition for your affections since the very first death," he whispers against the shell of my ear. "Open your eyes and see."

He turns to go, but his words make something echo in my soul.

"And you?" I ask and he pauses. "Are you competing, too, Reaper?"

He glances over his shoulder at me, the ice in his eyes chilling my soul. "Me?" he asks, amusement dancing in his eyes. "I'm only curious, little Dreadful. Nothing more."

And then he strolls away, as if he had not just shattered my perceptions, as if I'm not standing beneath a portrait of my past.

I glance up at the painting again and sigh. "Oh, Walter. You'd never believe what mess I've gotten myself into."

But somehow, I think he'd find amusement in the whole mess, and that eases something deep inside of me. Even if the reaper is lying. Even if there is some competition for my affections.

Even if I'm some reincarnation of a woman long since forsaken.

26
MENA

I return hours later to the library just as I promised I would to fetch Henry for supper. I expect to find him in a different position. Instead, I find him exactly where I left him, his face buried in a thick book that smells like dust and age. At least the book is different from before, so he's clearly moved.

"Perhaps we should come in here and help you?" I say, looking around. "There's a lot of material to get through."

"Nonsense," he replies, looking up at me. "The others would just get in my way. You're welcome to keep me company, however. I would never decline your company."

I smile gently and move closer, studying the book he's reading. "Is that Italian?"

"Indeed." He points to a word on the page. "This book mentions a prophecy with Lilith, but there are no details other than the mention. I thought to study this book closer in the hopes I find more mentions."

"You can read Italian?"

Henry nods. "I can read and write many languages. I'm afraid I suffered much schooling as a child at the whims of my father."

I tilt my head in interest. "How intriguing. What types of things did you learn?"

"Everything from arithmetic to dancing I'm afraid," he laughed. "While I don't hold any title in particular, my father was of the belief that I should be prepared in case a lady of class took fancy to me." He shakes his head as if the thought is hilarious. "He held that notion until the day he died, mostly because he once fell in love with a lady of class who never gave him the time of day. I often thought he was attempting to live vicariously through me."

He flushes as he suddenly realizes just how much he's said. "My apologies. You have no need to hear my family's sad history."

"Don't be silly," I chastise. "I would love to listen to stories of your past. But of course, you only have to speak on matters you wish to."

I touch my hand gently to his in comfort and his flush deepens. His eyes go to where our skin touches, focusing on it. For a moment, he doesn't speak, and then the flush fades as quickly as it came and his eyes flick to mine. Gone is the shy doctor I've come to know and in his place is someone else.

Edward Hyde.

"We will gladly tell you anything you'd like to hear, pretty temptress," he purrs. It's a strange juxtaposition. Without the elixir, Edward cannot take over fully, leaving his appearance as that of Henry's, but he's clearly in the forefront of Henry's mind right now.

"Oh?" I ask, tilting my head. I can't deny I'm as equally intrigued by Edward as I am Henry. Where Henry is the shy and reserved doctor, Edward is the complete opposite from what interactions I've had with him.

Henry had already been standing so it doesn't take much for Edward to leave the book Henry had been studying and stalk around me like a predator seeking its next meal. I turn with him, some instinct demanding I not give him my back, until he stands before me with those haunting eyes. I can't explain the difference. Both Henry and Edward have the same eyes, but when Edward is in control, they're more piercing, more brutal. He meets my gaze now with those eyes, pinning me in place.

He leans in, his arms caging me so I can't run away. "You are so beautiful," Edward hums. "So perfect for us in all that you are." He leans in, breathes deep. "We hunger for you even if Henry is hesitant to admit it."

My heart kicks in my chest as he leans closer, as his warmth wraps around me. Though he looks human now, Edward is perfectly monstrous in his mannerisms, almost animalistic. His very presence is feral. My instincts scream at me both to run and to give in, as if this is some chase.

"What makes you think Henry is interested in a more intimate relationship?" I breathe, staring into his eyes.

The husky chuckle that leaks from his lips makes me clench my thighs together.

"Look at you, pinned here before me like a delicate little butterfly," he rasps, not answering my question. He leans closer, his breath fanning across my throat. "So desperate to hold yourself with decorum and yet desperate for my cock to fill you."

"I've never said such a thing," I argue, but the breathiness of my voice takes away the venom of the words.

"You don't have to," he points out, his lips pressing featherlight against my jugular. "It's in the way you hold yourself. My powerful little goddess. My beautiful butterfly. But we will not clip your wings. We will not pin you down." He presses a soft kiss against the heartbeat in my throat. "I am in Henry's brain, little butterfly. I know what he's thinking just as he knows what I do. He may not be able to speak it yet, but I submit myself to being completely and irrevocably devasted by you." He leans back. "Do your worst, Philomena Seagraves, Destroyer of Worlds."

My heart stops as he looks into my eyes. Because we share our gazes, I'm able to see the moment that Edward fades and lets Henry again take control. The fierceness in his eyes fades to kindness and then to horror as he realizes the position we're in. He jerks himself away abruptly, giving me space to cool the flush on my cheeks.

"My deepest apologies," Henry croaks. "I'm not sure what's come over him—"

"It's alright," I hurry to tell him, pressing my hand to my cheeks. "He does not scare me, just as you don't."

Henry pauses and meets my eyes. In them, if he looks deep enough, he'll see the desire reflected there, both for him and Edward. The need to kiss them both, to compare the way they taste despite them being one and the same, is strong, but I hold myself in check. Henry would flush at the thoughts currently running through my mind. I have no idea if he sees that desire in my eyes because he turns away quickly to tap on the book.

"I think this one is promising. I'll continue searching for more answers."

I force a smile when he glances back at me. "You're brilliant, Henry. I have no doubt you'll find a way to fix me if you're able to."

He freezes, his eyes shuttering to lock down whatever emotion my words conjure up. He takes a further step back. "What if there's no fix?" he whispers, a hoarse truth in that question. Because he hadn't been able to fix himself in the end, not like he'd wanted.

"I don't know," I admit, looking down at my fingers. "I really don't know, but it's time for supper. If you'd like to join us, Mrs. Kingsley is setting the table."

He pauses, hesitates as if tempted to decline.

I submit myself to being completely and irrevocably devastated by you.

"Of course. I'll escort you to the table," he finally replies.

When he offers me his arm, I take it without question, and despite the monster that lives inside him, I've never felt more safe.

27
MENA

Three days later, there are still no further answers. The only information we have is what Otto came with and a few mentions of a prophecy pertaining to Lilith in random books. Nothing else.

"This is fruitless," Henry growls in annoyance, slamming yet another book shut. "The deeper I dig, the less I find."

"As if someone doesn't want us to know," Otto points, similar annoyance in his tone. "I'm afraid in all my years of searching, I had succumbed myself to simply waiting when I found no other information. I was lucky when I stumbled upon the parchment. When I went searching afterward, I found myself disappointed."

"Or. . ." Athan begins from where he sits on the window seat looking out, ". . .it's because someone wiped the information completely."

Henry frowns. "What do you mean? Like they tore out the pages and burned them?"

Athan glances over at the doctor, his eyes hollow. "It's not uncommon for the forces of Heaven to wipe away traces of information they did not agree with."

Silence reigns as his words sink in until it's me who breaks it.

"Wait," I say, frowning. "Are you saying that God wipes away traces of information he doesn't like? That he changes things based on his whims?"

Athan shrugs. "How do you think the Bible came to be? How it came to change over time? Christianity today is not the same as Christianity at its inception. That book you brought down here is not the same as the original."

Otto blinks. "There's truth in that, certainly."

"Convenient they left some of the more brutal stuff," Henry murmurs under his breath. "Anything to teach a lesson."

My beliefs are not dependent on what others think of them, but after this experience with a fate I did not choose for myself and the answer to my prayers being a terrible "fuck you," those beliefs have wavered heavily. For a moment, I believed God could not be real at all after my experience, but here is Athan claiming he's not only real, but that Heaven censors the information we receive. How cruel and arrogant.

"Lilith was created before Eve," Otto announces as if its new information. "That we know."

"Yes, and she was punished for not blindly following Adam," Athan adds. "Doomed to Hell with Lucifer for her defiance."

"What happened to her after that?" I ask, looking between them. "Surely, there's some sort of information?"

"There's nothing," Athan admits. "Nothing that I've ever been able to find. Though I'm a reaper, I don't step foot into the Underworld. That place is for souls and those who reside over them so I have never met Lilith personally or whatever devil or god resides there. And I have never gone searching for answers of my own like the vampire."

"So we know nothing," I sigh. "Surely, I couldn't be the reincarnation if she were still alive, though. Correct?"

Athan opens his mouth and then closes it, pondering the question. "I don't think a soul can exist in two places, no."

"So then. . . if the records have been wiped clean, then we need sources older than the wipe," Henry muses, running a hand through his hair. He pauses when whatever he'd been thinking clicks. "The Codex Sinaiticus."

Athan's eyes brighten, but Otto and I tilt our heads in confusion.

"What's the Codex Sinaiticus?" I ask, having never heard of it before.

Henry comes around the table. "The Codex Sinaiticus is believed to be the oldest existing complete Bible in the world. It's been split into pieces and spread throughout England, Egypt, Germany, and Russia. It's written in Greek."

"What does that have to do with anything?" Otto asks, frowning.

Henry grins. "See, the Codex Sinaiticus was the source of the Christian Bible. It has the Old Testament and the new in its entirety, but it also contains books that are no longer are written in modern Bibles because they no longer fit today's Christian doctrine."

"Which means it may contain Lilith's story," I reason. "You said part of it is in England?"

"Yes, in the British museum to be exact. It may not be the part that's any use to us and it's heavily guarded. We'll have to get permission to handle it," Henry sighs. "We'll need permission from the Queen in particular, and that could take months."

"Then we use the options available to us," Athan interjects. "There are at least two of us in this room who can travel without detection." He shares a look with Otto. "We can slip in, borrow the pieces, and return them before anyone is the wiser."

"They take special handling," Henry grunts. "This book is from the fourth century. It's incredibly delicate."

"Then we'll be extremely delicate," Athan says in a mocking tone. "It's the only lead we have, and we can't afford to wait until Mena dies again."

A knock at the door interrupts our discussion and I turn to find Mrs. Kingsley standing there with a thick envelope in her hand.

"If that's an invitation to a useless ball, decline," I tell her.

"It's for Lady Ambrose's annual event, Mena," she replies.

I scowl. "It's September already?" Where had the time gone? It felt as if it were just July only weeks before.

"I'm afraid so," she says with a smile. "Should I send an acceptance?"

"Just ignore it," Athan offers. "We don't have the time to attend a ball."

Otto rolls his eyes. "Mena is a member of high society. Not attending is an offense."

"We have too much to worry about with everything going on—"

I stop both of them with a raise of my hand. "Otto is correct. This isn't just a normal party. Lady Ambrose is an important figure and if I'm to keep up appearances, I must attend, no matter how much I detest the woman." I sigh deeply, already dreading the forced smiles I'll be guilty of. "Which means I'll need a dress before the ball in a few days' time."

"Well, there's no possibility of you going alone," Athan grunts. "It's too risky. The witches could attack again."

"Or something worse," Henry adds offhandedly.

I look between the three of them, resigned to the decision. "Then it looks like we'll need three suits as well, Mrs. Kingsley."

Otto grins in excitement, but Athan grimaces.

"How exciting," he groans.

"I don't think it's the best idea," Henry murmurs. "But if we must attend, then we shall."

The foghorn echoes in my ears and I can't help tilting my head in confusion, listening until it fades away. It's more constant now, more demanding. Had I not known about the prophecy, I'd think myself suffering from some ailment. Now, it feels as if fate is teasing me with events to come.

Glancing out the window to the foggy streets below, I swear I see a flash of some great shape within it, but when I look closer, I see nothing and so I put it from my mind. There's nothing in the fog. I'm imagining things because my brain is overloaded with information. There's nothing to worry about at all.

Even if the foghorn is still there, faint but insistent.

28

ATHAN

Apparently, this Dutchess Ambrose is a big deal among Mena's society. As the wife of the Duke of Portland, she was required by society to host an annual ball in her husband's honor. As one of the most favored families, it's become some sort of long-standing tradition.

I don't give a shit about traditions personally.

Just the thought of having to attend this pompous ball is enough to make me grimace, but if Mena is to go, then we go whether I like it or not. At least I'm not alone in my distaste of such an event. The doctor is less eager to attend than I am. The vampire king, in comparison, is positively excited to attend. I suppose this is his element, balls and society norms. As the monarch of the European vampires, he'd be required to host many dignitaries and elites. Frowning at that realization, I glance over to the vampire where he's being fitted for a fancy suit. Perhaps, I should ask more into his history. None of us have shared much of our stories. Well, except for the doctor and Mena. Perhaps, it's time Otto and I were more forthcoming if we're going to be working together.

To my left, Henry is being fitting for a suit as well by one of the needlewomen. She adjusts and measures, and marks down notes in a notepad as she goes. Out of all of us, he's the most uncomfortable in this situation. Clearly, he'd much prefer a more casual outfit.

I'm indifferent to the suit I'm being fitted for. It fits nice enough though it's not my preferred cut. Of course, I've been informed that my preferred cut is a century out of date. I can't follow such fashions. Besides, what need have I to follow them when I'm a timeless creature? I much prefer what I like. Fashions change often and it matters not what I'm wearing when I'm escorting souls to the Underworld.

Mena comes out of the dressing room and my eyes widen at the dress she wears. Though it still needs to be adjusted and taken in, it's clear she's going to look exquisite in it. Emerald green in color with hints of a more toxic green to accentuate her hips, the dress hugs her in the way the women of this time enjoy. The corset beneath sucks in Mena's beautiful waist and accentuates her hips even further. The skirt falls to the floor in large emerald waves, the material flouncy and pretty. The bodice is cut to showcase her breasts atop it, the beading along the bodice only adding to the display. Small pieces of material rest around her biceps. It makes her look regal indeed.

"Wow," Henry says, and then clears his throat.

Otto grins. "You look beautiful, my sweet Mena."

Mena flushes at the attention and in the mirror she looks into, her eyes find mine. Our gazes linger on each other, and the urge to steal her away from this room and have my way with her must reflect there. Her flush deepens and she glances down demurely, but not before I see the gentle curl of her lip.

Our little prophecy apparently has a wicked streak.

I don't compliment her out loud. I've already claimed I'm not interested in such whims even if the lie had tasted like ash on my tongue. I don't deserve Mena's attention. If she's going to choose someone, it should be one of the others, not a disgraced and sinful reaper.

"Marvelous," the seamstress coos as she steps around Mena and appraises the fit. "We're almost complete and I'll have the clothing delivered to you today once they're tailored appropriately."

The flush still on her cheeks, Mena reaches out to touch the seamstress she's clearly known for years. Her fingers touch her skin, and there's an immediate change in the woman's demeanor. Where the seamstress had been friendly before, she practically falls all over herself suddenly to make sure Mena is okay.

"Is there anything else you would like, Miss Seagraves? Perhaps a coin pouch to match? Something more for your gentlemen?"

Otto nods. "Could you sew in a bit of Mena's fabric to the collar of my suit please madam? I should like everyone to know I belong to Mena alone."

The seamstress nods in appreciation, her eyes wide and alert and slightly crazed. I frown, realizing when Mena shifts uncomfortably that this isn't a normal personality shift.

"Your power?" I whisper to her. When she grimaces and nods, I understand the situation. "Pull back on it."

"I don't know how," she croaks. "I don't even know how I did it in the first place."

"Focus on it. Calm your mind. Recall the power back to you," I instruct, watching as the seamstress continues to fawn over Mena. She is starting to offer more clothing, more dresses in the best materials without payment.

Mena takes a deep breath and closes her eyes, focusing, but it does no good. The seamstress is so deeply in her manipulation, she can't fathom anything but pleasing Mena.

"Of course your order today is on me," the seamstress coos.

"No! No, I'll pay for your services. I insist—"

"And I insist on my favorite customer accepting her gift," the seamstress chastises. "It is done. Now, back to the other options—"

Guilt flashes in Mena's eyes and I reach out to touch her fingers with mine. When she glances over at me, I make sure she's focused entirely on my words. "Perhaps it's time to start practicing your powers, Mena. So you're better prepared in situations like this."

The nod she spares me is barely large enough to perceive, but I notice it all the same. Poor little prophecy, her powers uncontrollable and her mind aflutter with her flaws. If only she knew her true power. If only she knew how perfect she is. If only I could ever be the one to tell her.

"The outfits will be delivered in a few hours' time," the seamstress gushes. "I hope your evening is as magical as you are," she tells Mena, and behind her eyes, something flickers. Awareness? A haunting? I don't really know, but there's an awareness there I hadn't noticed before.

Does Mena's power take control and the person is aware of what's happening? Or am I projecting?

Once we're back out of the clothing, we're ushered out by the seamstress so she can complete her work. No doubt she has many clients to finish this eve before the party. We stand on the chilly street, a bit surprised at the abruptness of being forced from the shop. The carriage will take a moment to arrive, but in the time we have, I turn to Mena.

"You couldn't help it, but it's okay to use your powers, Mena," I try, but my words don't seem to offer the comfort I mean to. It seems when it comes to Mena, I'm a failure at anything but annoyance or amusement.

She rubs her hands along her arms, as if trying to warm up. She's staring at the street, at the worn cobblestones beneath our feet. "I feel dirty," she whispers. "I feel like a freak."

"Power comes at a cost," Otto throws in. "You'll grow used to it at some point."

She winces. "Must I?"

I scowl at the vampire who clearly isn't helping. I'm about to step forward and try to offer more words that probably won't comfort her when Henry takes my spot and faces Mena. I watch as he tips up her chin and forces her eyes on his. The doctor is all clean lines and shyness most days, but right now, he's looking at Mena like the amazing woman she is, no shyness at all in his expression. At first, I think it might be because Edward is suddenly in charge, but no. It's Henry. Mena's upset has simply chased away his nerves in favor of helping her.

"This does not unmake you," Henry tells her. "This prophecy, these powers, us, none of it will unmake you. Yes, things are changing, but you will remain, at your core, Philomena Seagraves."

"What if you're wrong?" she chokes out. "What if what I become is a monster?"

Henry tilts his head, studies her. Otto and I watch in silence, as if we both sense the profoundness of this moment, this exchange between them. The air is still. The London streets don't echo with their movement through the fog rolling in.

"I think," Henry murmurs, tracing his thumb along her jawline. "I think ultimately, we all become whoever would have saved us that time that no one did. Perhaps, this is you becoming who you've always needed, Mena, but that doesn't change things. You will still be Mena. You will still be the woman who stumbled into my doorway. You will still be the same woman who is worthy of love."

"I feel like a devil," she croaks, her fingers coming up to wrap around Henry's wrist. "What if I become the very demon I fear? What if God has forsaken me for a reason?"

"If you're a devil, then I'm a devil," he replies, smiling. "And we'll do what all devils do."

She searches his eyes. "And what is that?"

His smile widens and he presses his forehead against hers despite standing out in the open. It's improper but Mena doesn't seem to care.

"We fall," he whispers. "Together."

My chest aches with his words, as if they're a reflection of the prophecy that has brought us all together. And what a shame it is that the very words our dear Henry Jekyll tells Mena, are the very words he's craved to hear himself.

I wonder if Mena knows that?

I wonder if she understands just how badly our doctor needs her to survive this?

29
MENA

If one were to decline the Dutchess' invitation, it would resign your fate to solitude. While that threat does not exactly scare me, I prefer to keep my name from the drama that surrounds society as much as I'm able. I'd spent many summers being the talk of them after my husband died, and I have no desire to return to the random appearances outside my home under the guise of cheering me up. If I were to decline this invitation, they would all assume I was deathly ill. Upon finding me not, the rumors would start, and there will be plenty flying around already after my funeral. There need not be additional worries.

Just as Mrs. Le Fluer assured us, the clothing shows up at my home hours after our return. Mrs. Kingsley had worked to prepare my hair, pinning it in place with expert fingers. The green dress suits me and when Mrs. Kingsley is finished, I feel more pristine than I have in a while. When I make my way down the grand staircase, it's to find Athan, Otto, and Henry in matching suits, each of them looking up at me with something akin to affection flickering in their eyes. There's desire there, too, but now isn't the time to address that emotion, not when we're expected at the Dutchess' home within in the hour. Besides, I certainly cannot court all of them, right?

"The three of you look very distinguished," I tell them. "Very handsome, indeed."

Athan rolls his eyes, but Otto flourishes beneath the compliment.

"And you, my sweet Mena," he purrs. "Look good enough to eat."

I smile, amused. Because he could in fact eat me. Strangely, I expected a vampire to be some sort of feral hungry beast always searching for something to satiate that hunger. Instead, Otto is as put together as any gentleman, his feral nature in check. How strange that I misjudged him. Now, I can't see him as anything other than the man despite the fangs he flashes at me every now and then as a tease.

Henry tugs at his suit collar, his face flushed. He's clearly uncomfortable in the evening suit, but it can't be helped. He can't very well show up to the Duke's home wearing anything else.

"Shall we go?" I ask, smiling despite the disdain I hold for Dutchess Ambrose. I've often felt like the Dutchess has never liked me and I have never known the reason for that dislike. It's often put me in a sour mood any time I have dealings with the older woman. Her daughters are no less unpleasant, each of them foolish and spoiled beyond compare.

The Duke's London home is a great estate a mile from my own so not very far at all. Extravagant in its appearance despite the limited space, the home is what one would expect of a Duke. A mix of carriages and the new automobiles that some of the wealthier members of society have purchased line the street. Our own carriage pulls into line, and we await our turn to exit as we must be helped from the carriage and escorted inside.

"The automobiles are quite showy, are they not?" Otto asks, looking from the carriage window. "I've often thought them great mechanical beasts spitting grease and smog."

"An apt description," I reply. "I'm no fan of them myself. They seem clunky in comparison to a carriage and horses. Besides, I enjoy the horses."

Henry leans to look. "I think they're intriguing."

"Of course a man of science would think them intriguing," Otto says with a scoff. "If you had the money, I have no doubt you'd have one yourself."

"You're not wrong," Henry smiles. His eyes flick to mine with amusement. "Perhaps I'll build my own one day. We could have a race. My automobile against your horses."

My heart beats in my chest at his words, but not only because of his jest. His words from earlier in the evening will haunt me for days to come.

If you're a devil, then I'm a devil.

What a stand to take. His words had the desired effect. I'd managed to calm down enough to retire back to my home and I'd been left with the image of his own haunt in his eyes. I am not the only one haunted in this little menagerie we've formed. We all have some weight on our shoulders. How terrible of me to assume I am alone in my struggle.

"Deal," I tell Henry despite knowing he'll never spend his money on an automobile, and he may never build one. It's a dream for him, one I can perhaps supply one day. And when I'm able, I plan to do just that.

The carriage rolls to a stop at the front of the home and the doorman opens our carriage door immediately, not wanting to linger too long with the long line behind us. Henry is the first to climb out, followed by Otto and Athan. It's Athan who reaches back into the carriage for my hand to help me down the carriage steps. Someone begins whispering the moment I step free. The hushed whispers surround us as I take Athan's arm and allow him to escort me inside. Henry and Otto follow behind. None of them pay much attention to the whispers, but I can't help but tilt my head toward them in the hopes of hearing. No such luck however as we follow the crowd inside.

The Dutchess is known for her extravagant parties and this one is no different. The theme seems to have been carnival promiscuity if one were to judge the appearance of the performers around the room. A mix of clothed and nude performers move around the room, dangling from silk streamers, sitting in rings dangling overhead, dancing in the corners. Each of them wears the freakshow makeup I'd once saw while attending one. It's certainly attention-capturing and offers the intrigue the Dutchess would prefer.

The room is decorated in velvets and silks, extravagance at its finest. The members of high society trail around the room, mingling, talking, dressed in their finest. I would not be surprised to learn the Queen would be in attendance judging by how much work went into the theme this year. Even the large candelabras the Dutchess is fond of litter the ballroom, the open flames flickering and giving the room further ambience than the gas lights of the chandelier. Personally, I think the Dutchess prefers her candles to gas far too much, but this is her party so she can do what she wishes. Still, with so many open flames, she's one drunken accident away from losing her house.

Women whisper behind gloved hands, their eyes on me as well as the three men escorting me. It's improper, to be escorted by so many men, but none will dare say it to my face. As a widow, I'm afforded many leniencies many other women aren't allowed. As a titled and rich widow, even more so. They can cause me great loneliness and annoyance, but there's not much else they're capable of.

Otto steps before us and bows. "My Sweet Mena, could I have this dance? I doubt the reaper knows the steps."

Athan scowls. "I have a job to do. Dancing isn't a part of that."

"Of course," Otto grins. "And while you reap your souls, I shall be spinning Mena around the dancefloor."

I glance at the displeased expression on Athan's face, but he nods solemnly and hands me off to Otto. Clearly, Otto is correct and Athan does not know how to dance. A problem that can be remedied in the future if he wishes, but for now, I simply offer him comfort with a gentle touch to his arm that makes him flinch before I follow Otto onto the dance floor.

There is a five string orchestra in the corner who end one song and immediately begin another. The waltz begins slow and builds, echoing in the ballroom as couples join us on the dance floor. Otto offers his hands and we begin to move, swirling with everyone else on the dance floor in a pattern everyone learns in their upbringing.

"I do believe I harmed the reaper's ego," Otto murmurs, expertly leading me through the dance. "Perhaps, he'll realize he needs to try harder to win your affections."

"Is everyone simply worried about my affections?" I ask, exasperated. "Can we not simply worry about the mystery of what I am?"

He meets my eyes. "Of course, if you rebuke our affections, we will step back, my sweet Mena." He leans in and lowers his voice. "Though, you have yet to do so."

I narrow my eyes. "I could."

He nods and grins. "You could."

But I don't offer up the words and his grin widens. We continue to swirl around the dance floor, joining everyone in the choreographed waltz we're all familiar with. I wonder if Henry knows this one, if he's kept up with the latest dances after his father taught him so many.

"Besides, Athan has clearly stated he's not interested in anything further," I add with a huff. "So the only ones worried about my affections are you and Hyde."

"What a surprise you are, Mena," Otto purrs as we move.

I frown. "What exactly did you expect?"

"Honestly, I do not know, but not you. Not this magnificent mix of darkness and fire. Not the way your eyes flash with your power while you hold yourself back." He leans closer. "Not the way you hunger for us and struggle to hide it, or the way you don't shy away from this prophecy despite your fear. You are everything and more, my sweet Mena. Everything and more."

"When did you become so tender?" I ask as his fingers begin to slide along my arm, sending chills along my skin. "I never expected a vampire king to be so sweet."

"My dear," he murmurs. "I will always be this tender for you." His eyes darken. "But only you. I would rip the world to shreds to save you. Never forget that."

My brows furrow. "What do you—"

But I don't get a chance to ask the question. Otto suddenly halts our dance, his eyes on someone in the crowd. The rest of the dancers continue around us, swirling, avoiding us despite our standing in the middle of their dance floor.

"What is it?" I rasp, trying to turn and look over my shoulder. I see nothing but those watching the dancing couples. "What do you see?"

"Vampires," he answers. "Five of them."

The tenderness he'd had on his face only moments before is gone, replaced by a savage warning. A few of those around us stare at us curiously, wondering why we've stopped. Before a commotion can be made, Henry is standing at my elbow.

"May I have this dance?" he asks, his eyes flickering between Otto and the vampires he sees. "I'll take care of her while you address the situation."

Otto looks toward him. "Do you have your elixir, doctor?"

Henry pats his breast. "I never leave without it. Let us hope I have no use for it this evening. The rumors would not be pleasant."

Otto nods and releases me. "My apologies for cutting our dance short, my sweet Mena. I shall make it up to you." He glances at the crowd again. "Do not go anywhere alone."

I nod and watch him slip into the crowd to speak to the vampires. As King, I assume he'll hold some sort of sway over them, but my heart beats rapidly all the same. When Henry offers me his hand, I take it and allow him to lead me back into the waltz. Clearly, he had continued to learn the newer dances after all.

"Do you think he'll be alright?" I ask him, trying to find Otto in the crowd but failing.

"A vampire king does not become a king without bloodshed I assume," Henry offers. "I doubt much can harm Otto."

I wince. That doesn't really reassure me. My tender vampire may be weaker than expected, or worse, he could have a weakness we're not privy to. If something were to happen to him...

The song ends and the string quartet launches into another song, a galop this time, one I'm not fond of. Luckily, or unluckily perhaps, we're interrupted from our dancing by the host herself.

The Dutchess of Portland.

I bow to her as she appears and Henry follows suit, his eyes studying the woman who wears too much powder and cinches her corset too tight. Her breasts nearly spill over her top, begging someone to look deeper, to taste. God knows her husband doesn't take notice of it. The rumor is that he prefers the company of other men rather than that of his wife.

"Good evening, Dutchess," I say after I bow. "A splendid ball you've arranged for us all to enjoy."

"Yes," the Dutchess purrs, her eyes taking in Henry before dancing around the room, no doubt looking for the other two men I'd arrived with. The Dutchess is as much a fan of gossip as the next high society lady. "I've been so eager to see you. How are you, Miss Seagraves? After your accident? It must have been quite a shock to wake and find you'd been buried alive."

My eyes tighten, but I still smile at her. "I am quite refreshed, Dutchess. I've taken the air for granted far too long. Now I do not."

She laughs at my words, as if I've told the greatest joke. "Oh, I've always enjoyed your humor, Miss Seagraves. We must spend more time together. In fact, I would love to hear all about the gentlemen you arrived with. I'm afraid I do not know their names and I pride myself on knowing all of my guests."

I can't be rude to her, not without repercussions or drawing unwanted attention, so I bow my head just slightly. "Of course. This is Dr. Henry Jekyll. You probably noticed me dancing with his majesty, King Otto Van Doren earlier."

"King?" she purrs, immediately taking my arm from Henry. "Do tell me more."

Henry follows with a frown on his face as the Dutchess leads me toward a more intimate corner. Candles line the nook on three sides, so many, their wax drips down the sides and pools on the floor. Henry stands close, his eyes on me before moving around the room, searching for Athan and Otto no doubt.

"What country does your king rule over?" the Dutchess asks, her eyes bright with interest. After all, two of her four daughters are of marrying age.

"Oh, his country," I repeat, glancing at Henry helplessly. I know he's the King of Europe, but I can't exactly say that to the Dutchess. She can't know he's a vampire.

"He's the king of a small country," Henry offers helpfully. "You wouldn't know it."

The Dutchess waves away his words. "Geography was never my strength so you're probably correct, Doctor." She focuses back on me. "What a life you've been living recently, Miss Seagraves. And there was one more man with you." She shivers, as if the thought of Athan gives her the chills. "I must say, he makes me uneasy."

"He has that effect on people," I offer. "Most undertakers do."

"An undertaker?" the Dutchess breathes. "My what company you keep after your death, Miss Seagraves. How very interesting."

Henry leans in. "Even more interesting is that we're all hoping to court Miss Seagraves in the hopes she'll give us the attention we so desire."

The way his voice echoes, I can tell it's Edward speaking rather than Henry, but all I do is flinch at his words, my eyes focused on the Dutchess.

She laughs at his words. "Oh, I see why you spend time with him. Another joker."

"No joke," Edward purrs. "Miss Seagraves deserves the very best, be it in niceties or three men kneeling at her feet, eager to worship her."

I flush when the Dutchess' eyes widen in surprise. She looks between me and Henry, her own flush climbing her neck. "Well then," she breathes. "A lucky woman indeed." She grabs my wrist tightly and pulls me closer to where she stands against the candles. "Tell me, Miss Seagraves, do they make fine lovers?"

I open my mouth to answer that I know no such thing, but I'm struck silent by the sudden heat soaking into my legs. Subtle at first, it quickly becomes unbearable, and I jerk back, confused, only to find my skirts aflame.

The candles!

I pat at the fire quickly climbing along my dress, but it does no good. "Henry!" I cry, attempting to put out the fire. The Dutchess covers her mouth and jerks backward, spilling more of the candles against me. More flames catch on my skirts.

The thing about the prettiest dresses, the ones with crinoline to help their shape, they're highly flammable. No matter how much everyone around me panics and tries to pat out the flame, it climbs.

"Get me out of the dress!" I cry to Henry. "Otto! Athan!"

I don't know where they are in the crowd, but the moment I call for them, they're here, panic in their eyes. The heat eats away at my dress and begins to burn, blistering my legs and climbing.

The scream that tears from my throat when it sinks deeper into my skin echoes around the hall. The string quartet stumbles to a stop, the strange abrupt cut off making the situation worse in my mind, and the crowd turns to look at the mess we're making of the ballroom as I begin to flail around, trying to free myself from the death trap I wear.

"Someone help her!" the Dutchess cries. "Get the dress off!"

The flames reach my waist and climb, burning me, turning my screams piercing. Someone tries throwing liquid on me to help, but it's not water. Whatever it is, it speeds up the flame and I'm completely engulfed. I feel claws at my bodice, an attempt to tear through the numerous layers of my gown. But all I can feel is the skin melting from my body, the pain as I burn, the smell of burnt flesh and hair. My face grows hot as the skin blisters there, as the flames claim me.

"Mena!" Henry shouts, but it's cut off when my ear drums suddenly stop working. I can't see. I can't hear. My senses abruptly stop, the scream on my lips gone as the flames consume me completely.

I am the flames. I blur until I am nothing else.

I collapse as my heart gives out.

Darkness claims me quickly, blessedly, and the pain disappears.

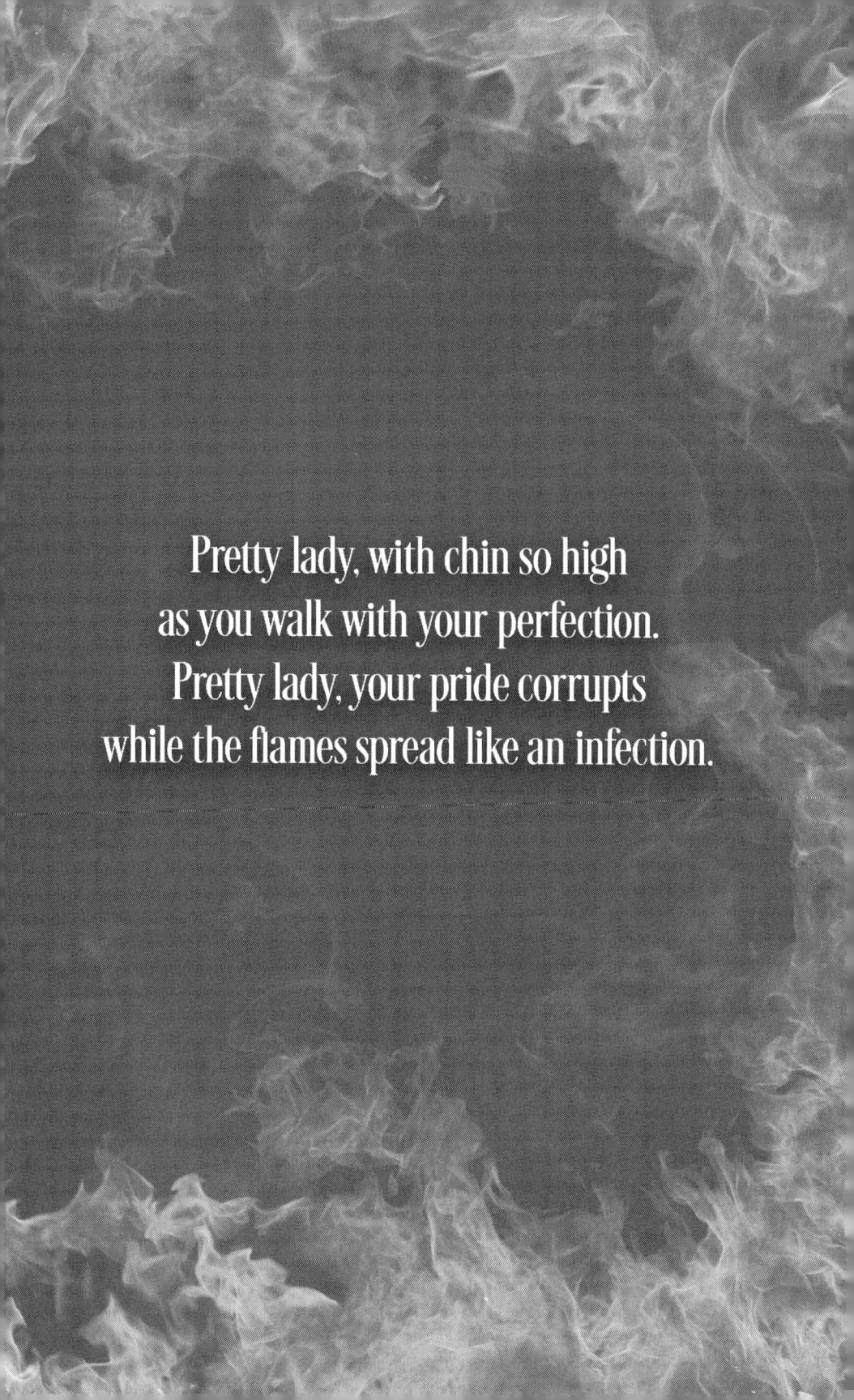

Pretty lady, with chin so high
as you walk with your perfection.
Pretty lady, your pride corrupts
while the flames spread like an infection.

30
MENA

Despite the heat of the fire, the darkness that claims me is cool and relaxing. I went down in flames and as I rest, I'm cradled in mist. It seems like only a few minutes as I hover there, as I'm kissed by the cool darkness, but I don't have much awareness of real time. All I know is that I was in pain and now I'm not.

The first blink of my eyes is excruciating. I fail to open them at first because of the thick crust holding them shut. It's as if someone smeared mud across my eyes and allowed it to dry. My mouth is so dry, I can't open it without what feels like cracking. The moment I twitch, I crack and biting pain spreads from my lips.

"Shh," someone whispers. "Slowly now, Mena."

I open my mouth again and wince with the pain. All that comes out of my lips is a croaked murmur, my throat raw and ragged, my skin new and taunt.

"Someone bring a wet cloth and warm water." It's Athan's voice. At least my ears seem to work again.

There's the sound of shuffling and movement and then someone is pressing a warm cloth against my eyes, gently wiping away the mud. Whoever is wiping does so tenderly, as if I'm a fragile flower dangerously close to losing my petals.

"Try to open them now," Otto instructs.

Carefully, I peel my eyes open. The pain of it is strange. Somehow, my eyes feel new and raw, as if this is the first time they're seeing. At first, everything is blurry as I crack them, but things slowly come into focus the more light that filters in. I blink a few times to clear the ache within them, to help filter everything.

Otto comes into focus above me, his bright caramel eyes tracing over my face. His dark dreadlocks hang around us, highlighting his face, bringing him even more into focus.

"What—" My throat locks up and I have to clear it but still the words won't come.

"Water," Henry orders, and my attention is drawn to him. "She needs water."

Athan quickly brings over a glass that Otto accepts and tips to my lips. The first touch of the water to my lips stings. The first cool drop on my throat is painful, but it eases within a few seconds and I'm able to clear my throat again.

"What happened?" I croak. The words come out, but they're still painful and rough. I wonder how long they will remain so.

"Do you remember the fire?" Henry asks.

I nod and grimace at the feeling of cracking along my neck. "I remember."

"You went up in flames at the Dutchess' party," Athan reminds me helpfully despite my admission that I remember. It's after the fire I don't. "We couldn't get you out of your dress in time."

Henry comes closer and there's a tightness around his eyes that wasn't there before. "You died again, Mena."

"Number three," Otto adds proudly. "You're making quick progress, my Sweet Mena."

"Does the Dutchess think me deceased?" I hazard to ask.

"No," Henry replies. "We rushed you from the party once we got the flames out claiming you were still breathing. You very much were only a husk of the woman you are at this time. We've watched you... regenerate over the last few hours."

"Hours?"

Henry nods. "Six to be exact. It took far longer than I hoped, but I suspect burning alive has its downfalls."

"Unlucky for you," Otto says, drawing my attention, "the pain that comes with this one is unavoidable. You're covered by a layer of... crisp for lack of better word."

"Indeed," Henry says with a scowl toward the vampire. "It's not just falling off like we'd hoped. I suggest softening it up with a bath before you scrub it off. It did not seem pleasant to rub it from your eyes."

"No," I admit, my head swimming with this information. At Henry's words, I glance down at my body and grimace. I'm still in the dress I'd been wearing, or what's left of it. The flames had fused it to my skin, making it impossible to pull it away without excruciating pain. Soaking seems like a good idea. "I do not think I can stand," I admit softly.

"Not to worry, Mena," Otto declares. "I will accompany you to the bath Mrs. Kingsley has drawn and assist you in settling in. I'll be there to offer assistance if you should ask."

He stands with me in his arms. Even the barest shuffling from his movement sends pain shooting up my spine and I tense.

Otto frowns in apology. "I'll move more slowly," he says, and starts moving with smooth, languid steps so as not to jostle me.

"If you need anything at all, call us," Henry tells me as Otto strolls past with me in his arms. "We'll come help if you need it."

His words make moisture want to gather in my eyes, but clearly, my tear ducts are still clogged with damaged skin because no tears fall. I'm glad for the reprieve. How embarrassing would it be to cry over their kindness? Though I'm still afraid of what I am and what I'll become, I don't regret meeting the three of them. At least I won't go through this curse alone. At least I won't die in solitude each time.

Mrs. Kingsley is waiting at the door to my room, her eyes wide with worry and horror at my appearance. She's already seen me, but I imagine I make quite the image with my skin black and crisp and my eyes wide open.

"I've drawn the bath. Let me know if there's anything else," she tells Otto who nods in acknowledgement and takes me inside. Mrs. Kingsley closes the door behind us.

"Did she cry when you brought me home?" I rasp, looking up at Otto.

"She did," he admitted. "Even when we told her you would come back to us, she was quite distraught." He glances down at me. "She loves you like her own."

"I know." I would nod, but I don't relish the pain it would cause so I remain still.

Otto steps into the bathing chamber and glances around to orient himself. Slowly, he moves us toward the large tub. "I'm going to lower you into the water. You will want to soak for at least ten minutes before scrubbing. Make sure to soak your head as well. I imagine your hair is trapped beneath the ruined skin."

I hadn't thought about my hair. What true horror I must look right now, and yet Otto looks at me with nothing but adoration as he gently lowers me into the water. The first press of the warm water against my tortured skin is painful, but it eases after a few seconds.

"Would you like me to leave you?" Otto asks, his eyes on me as I lean back and force all but my face under the water.

"No," I rasp. "Please stay."

I don't want to be alone right now. I don't want to be lost in my fear or the memories of the flames, of my screaming.

Nodding, Otto grabs one of the chairs from my room and drags it into the bathing chamber as if it doesn't weigh anything at all. I know it's heavy because I've attempted to move it myself before, but he makes it look easy. He takes a seat in the chair and settles in.

"Tell me what happened to the vampires," I ask, my eyes focusing on the vampire king.

He smiles and his fangs flash. "There's not much to tell, Mena

Mine. They were under my rule. When they realized you were under my protection, they left, but they'll return." His eyes flash. "There are not very many monsters who can withstand the draw of your power. With each death, the call will grow and more will come. We must be prepared."

"Three deaths," I whisper, looking up toward the ceiling and settling into the warm water. I imagine the skin on my arms and legs starting to flake away. I imagine the remnants of my beautiful dress slowly lifting away like ash on the wind.

"Four more to go," Otto reminds me. "Do you feel any new powers with this last one?"

"There's something there. . . but I don't know what it is. I imagine it will appear when I least expect it."

He hums under his breath. "We should certainly practice your powers once you feel better. There may come a time where we can't protect you."

Because more monsters will come. What kind of monsters are to be expected? How long will I have to worry about them? Will my life always be this edge of horror, this fear of the unknown? When will it end?

"I can see your fear dancing in your eyes, Mena," he purrs. "There's no reason to fear what you will become."

"How do you know?" I ask, glancing over at him. "How do you know I won't become some beast?"

He stands and starts to pull off his coat. I watch as he meticulously pulls the sleeves free and then hangs the coat over the chair. It's ruined now, covered in soot from my skin. Burns are easy to see in the fabric even from here. How close had Otto gotten in his attempt to save me despite the danger?

"It's time to scrub," he says. "Would you like assistance or would you prefer to do so alone?"

I swallow thickly. "Assistance," I admit. I'm not sure if I have the strength to scrub alone.

His fingers work along the ties of his shirt before he drags it up and over his head, baring his chest and stomach to me. Muscles ripple with his movement, glittering in the lantern light. He kicks off his shoes. My mouth waters as I imagine him removing his trousers, but he settles with being bare on top and on his feet. He comes over to the tub and picks up the sponge.

"I'll start with your back," he murmurs. "It will be easier if I'm in the tub with you."

My throat goes dry, but I still manage a hoarse, "Alright."

I sit up slowly, giving him room to step into the tub behind me and settle in. The water ripples against me, brushing against the ruined skin and soaking into the new skin beneath. He's cool to the touch, but it doesn't chill me. Instead, I feel as if I'm on fire again, as if I can't escape the flame that took my life.

"This may hurt," he whispers.

When I nod, he gently presses the sponge against my spine, and I suck in a breath at the pinch of pain. His hand moves with aching slowness as he rubs circles with the sponge, brushing away the dead skin and revealing what must be bright pink and new skin beneath. As if I had to regrow it. As if I'm nothing more than a lizard shedding.

It takes a while for him to complete my spine and only when he works the skin away from there does he spread outward, clearing the rest of my back and my shoulders.

"Tilt your head back," he instructs.

I do as he tells me, tilting my head back so he can run the sponge along my scalp. At first, I worry that my hair is gone and I'll be force to go through this terrible event bald on top of everything else. But when he starts pulling strands of hair free of the skin, I sigh in relief and let him release all of it. Strangely, my appearance has not changed despite feeling brand new.

"Now your front," he says. "We should be able to pull away the ruins of your dress now." He shifts and steps from the tub, making a mess of water that Mrs. Kingsley will chastise me for later. He steps back into the tub in front of me so that he can better see my front.

He's covered in small black flakes of skin, but he doesn't complain, his eyes on me and my comfort. "May I?"

I nod and he leans forward to wipe at my face, clearing the rest of the black skin from there before moving down my neck. The moment he starts to trail downward, my heart kicks in my chest, my thighs tempted to rub together with his touch.

Otto drops the sponge and reaches for a particularly large piece of material plastered to my front. The material appears to be what's left of my corset, the fabric scorched beyond measure. He glances at me as if to see if I'm ready. When I give him permission, he begins to peel it away.

I grimace, my hands going to the edges of the tub and holding on through the pain. It's agonizing, more akin to peeling stubborn tree bark from a tree. It comes away with its own layer of skin, the two layers of fabric and flesh melded together in permanence. When it peels free completely, Otto tosses it out of the tub and reaches for the next. Though my breasts are revealed by his actions, he doesn't linger, remaining a gentleman despite the opportunity. More cloth comes free of my hips, my legs, my arms, until there's only the ruined flesh to face. Otto carefully scrubs at my skin, returning my appearance with one swirl of the sponge at a time.

"Almost done," he murmurs, pulling my leg up so he can scrub at my calf. "And then you'll be as good as new."

I breathe deeper. Despite the crisp skin almost gone, my new skin still feels tight, like I've scrubbed a few layers off completely. At least it seems to be slowly returning to its normal color. I couldn't imagine walking around as pink as a newborn babe.

"There," Otto says proudly. "All done."

I look down and find he's indeed finished. "Thank you," I murmur. "For everything."

He sets the sponge down on the edge of the tub and faces me with a slight smile. "Do you know why you do not have need to worry about what you will become, Mena?"

My heart seizes. "Tell me."

He takes my hand, both of us sitting in a dirty tub. I'm in the nude and he still wears his ruined trousers, but it feels as if we're both flayed open regardless.

"You're a good person," he offers. "Despite the fear in your heart, you still hope for good."

"And what if I'm not as good as you think?" I ask. "What if I give into the power?"

He smiles. "Power doesn't make you a monster, Mena. It only makes you powerful." He chucks me on the chin in amusement. "And bad people don't worry about being bad."

"Are you good?" I ask, meeting his eyes. "Henry thought perhaps a Vampire King doesn't become a king without violence."

His smile drops and his eyes shutter. "The doctor is correct. I would not call myself good, no."

"But were you a good human?" I ask. "Before you grew fangs, were you good?"

He tilts his head, his eyes tracing my skin, my neck, my shoulders. "No," he admits. "No, I was not a good human." He leans in. "So you see, I was made to be a monster."

"You don't seem a monster to me," I whisper. "You've been nothing but kind."

His eyes tighten. "Do not think me a kicked dog, Mena. I am not a pet. Just because I am kind to you does not make me less of a monster."

I move in the water then, easing closer until I'm practically nestled in his lap. His arms come around me, his fingers remaining modest despite our positions. I cup his face between my palms and meet his eyes.

"It makes you less of a monster to me," I rasp, and press my lips to his.

He freezes, surprised by both my words and my kiss, but after a few seconds of hesitation, his arms tighten around me and he yanks me against him, flattening my breasts against his naked chest. His lips move over mine, claiming me, his tongue tracing the seam of my lips and seeking entrance. I give it to him, opening beneath his perusal and allowing him to sweep inside. My own tongue darts out and for a moment, I forget just what I'm kissing despite my words.

My tongue finds his fang. It's sharper than I expect, and it nicks my tongue before I know what's happening. The metallic taste of blood flares brightly on my tongue and Otto growls against my lips, his fingers digging into my sides almost painfully. He captures my tongue and sucks, tasting my blood and sending himself into a frenzy. I moan into his mouth, my own hands exploring down the planes of his chest, along the sculpted muscles. His hardness presses against the seam of his trousers, begging for release. I reach between us and stroke him through the material, desperate to feel him.

He breaks the kiss and snarls at me, his fangs bared, his eyes bright red rather than the pleasant caramel. "Do not ask for what you can't handle, Mena Mine."

"Who says I can't handle it?"

"You're not ready," he hisses, his fingers tight against my hips. "You will not survive me."

"On the contrary, I believe I'll just come back to life," I point out, rubbing myself against him, my core weeping for him. "Isn't that how this works?"

Otto chokes back his words, pain etched on his face. "Such temptation you are," he growls, tilting his head back.

It gives me access to his throat, where I immediately drop my lips and drag my teeth against his corded muscle there. He tenses beneath me, and something tells me he's never felt a touch so tender, something so intimate as this. I gentle my touch more, tracing my lips across his throat with featherlight touches that has him grinding against me beneath the water.

"You will be the death of me," he rasps.

"Can vampires die?" I ask against his skin as I continue to taste him.

His fingers flinch against my hips. "Not easily."

I hum and straighten. He drops his head to meet my eyes, the caramel and red hunger there so thick, it nearly undoes me.

As if on cue to ruin the moment, my stomach grumbles.

Loudly.

He chuckles and softens his touch. "First, my queen must be fed," he purrs. "You need your energy, for I am not the only one agonized for your touch, my sweet Mena."

He lifts me from the tub and settles me on the tile, his eyes on mine. My legs are still shaky, but he makes sure to hold me upright as he follows suit. "I could make a religion out of this," he rasps, reaching up to cup my chin with his palm.

"With what?" I ask, my voice equally as soft.

He smiles and it's the gentlest smile I've seen on his lips yet. "Loving you." And then he steps back, leaving me to sway toward him. "Mrs. Kingsley left a gown on your bed, Mena Mine. We'll see you downstairs for supper." He bows as if I'm a queen, still dressed in only his wet trousers and covered in black flakes, and disappears, giving me the privacy to process what just happened.

And what I hope happens in the future.

31
MENA

I'm in my room for another thirty minutes, not because it took me that long to dress, but because I needed to process the last twelve hours. The party at the Duke and Dutchess' home, the fire, the tub. It all is some great mix of memories in my mind, the fire burning bright, the pain echoing in my mind despite it feeling as if it happened to a different person. The awakening and the pain that came with it. The adoration in the tub and the loving attention to my comfort.

And I do feel different this time. Despite not knowing what new power had awakened inside of me with my third death, I can feel it hovering there, waiting for me to call on it. I can also feel the other powers I've barely touched, as if they exist inside of me as new entities without consciousness now. I am their consciousness. I am their master.

But I still feel so afraid.

The foghorn I've grown accustomed to is suddenly far louder than before. Now that I'm clean and fresh from my third death, now that I've left my room, I realize just how loud it is. Before, it was like an incessant buzzing, like a fly that won't leave the room. Now, it's a roar in my ears that makes me miss my footing and stumble a few times on my way down the stairs. I can't help the twitches from the noise, my ears ringing with it. The horn sounds over and over again, loud and begging.

Something wants attention, but what?

When I step into the dining chamber, it's to find everyone already there waiting for me. Otto's eyes heat at the first sight of me, but at my strange twitching, he frowns.

"Is everything okay, Mena?" he asks, studying me carefully.

"Of course," I lie, taking a seat in the chair saved for me beside Henry. "Just out of sorts still."

"Understandable," Athan comments. "You did just burn to death and rise again."

When I don't say anything back, when I don't come back with some clever quip, he looks at me curiously but doesn't ask. Henry doesn't have the same restraint.

"Perhaps I should check you over before you eat," he says, frowning. "You seem at odds."

"I'm fine," I lie, pressing a hand against my forehead. "Just famished is all."

Henry doesn't seem to believe me, but he acknowledges that I'm probably hungry and Mrs. Kingsley starts to bring out food for us all to eat. I find it strange still that Otto eats the food we do. He gains no nourishment from it from my understanding, but he still enjoys taking part.

The horn echoes so loud, I can't hide the flinch as I jerk to the side. No one asks, pretending to ignore my strange behavior. But the ringing left behind in my ears is so loud it makes me nauseous. I press my hand against my stomach in confusion as it worsens. The others speak among themselves. About what, I don't know. I can't focus on anything other than the strong horn sounds in my ears and the ringing that comes with it. They don't react, as if they can't hear the echo at all.

I'd picked up my fork in anticipation of digging into the roast Mrs. Kingsley had placed before me, but I cannot make myself take a bite. With a wince, I set my fork down on the plate again and it clatters with all the improper etiquette, with ill manners I've been taught is wrong.

"Pardon me," I rasp when the others look toward me. "I think I need some air."

"I'll come with you," Otto offers.

"That's not necessary—"

"For your protection," he adds. "In case someone tries to take you. I'll stand far enough away to give you peace."

Athan nods. "We don't know what sort of beasts will come calling now that you've sent out another call with your death. It's best not to go alone."

I consider his words and finally nod, realizing that I'm in no state to fight any sort of creature, not even a human. Otto assists me when I stumble, his hand grabbing my elbow to keep me upright.

"Are you certain you're alright?" he asks again, worry in his eyes.

"I just need air," I repeat, allowing him to help me.

Once outside, I take in the foggy evening. The London streets are covered by their normal mist, the fog so thick, we can't see too far down the street. Otto helps me down the steps and allows me to lean against the street lantern before he steps back.

"I'll step over here to give you space," he says.

"You don't have to go far," I tell him, pressing a hand to my stomach. "I just found myself suddenly lightheaded."

His frown deepens. "Do you think it's the—"

In the distance, a great groaning echoes across the world and Otto snaps his mouth shut. It sounds foreign and large, like two machines striking against each other and grinding metal to metal. The horn blast in my head echoes so loud it makes me clamp my hands over my ears.

Both of us stare at the fog suddenly rolling closer from the direction of the Thames. A storm comes from nowhere, but we can't see the sky to know if there were any clouds. The first rumble of thunder makes me jump and step closer to Otto. The second is accompanied by lightning that lights up the fog in the eeriest of ways.

My breath rushes from my lungs as I press against Otto. "Something's coming," I whisper, my heart throbbing painfully in my chest. I don't know how I know that, but the feeling almost chokes me.

The next lightning illuminates something in the fog, a great shape that stands above London. A large head and many arms move, arms like tentacles, swallowing the sky and making it home. I stare at the shape in horror as it appears and disappears with the lightning. The thunder booms so loud, it makes the cobblestone vibrate beneath my feet.

"Otto," I rasp, staring at the shape in horror. "What is that?"

"I don't know," he admits, before quickly climbing the entrance steps and opening the door. Vaguely, I hear him call for the others, but I don't take my eyes off of the shape growing larger, closer.

The ringing grows louder, and I flinch, collapsing against the lamp post. It's all I can do to hold myself up, my fingers holding tightly to the iron post.

"*Mena*," something whispers within the ringing. "*Little Destroyer.*"

I can't move. I can't run. I can't do anything but stare at the ever-growing shape in the sky, some great being coming for me. Otto had said other monsters would come. I expected that, but this? What is this?

Run, run, run, my instincts scream, but something else inside me contradicts that with stay, stay, stay, until I'm locked in place.

The others tumble from the doorway behind me, their eyes wide as the large tentacles move through the fog, as the creature draws closer.

The horn tolls so loud, I grit my teeth against the scream in my throat. There's wetness trickling from my ears, but I don't pay it any mind. I can't.

Because the thunder suddenly stops and the lightning fades, the storm gone as quickly as I came.

And a single man steps from the fog...

32
MENA

Otto frowns at the man as everyone's heads dip down from the sky in confusion, now staring at the man rather than the shape in the sky.

"A bit anticlimactic if you ask me," he comments as he understands this man was the source of the storm.

But I'm staring at the man in awe, at this powerful man that makes my bones ache and nearly chokes me with his power the closer the comes. He strolls along the street as if he doesn't have a care in the world. The ringing still echoes, but it's softer now, background noise. He's dressed so richly, I wonder where he could have had a suit made with such intricate beaded detailing. The beads catch in the light from the lamp posts and shine like jewels. As he continues to close the distance, I realize that's exactly what they are.

Diamonds. Emeralds. Teal Sapphires. Beautiful golden thread.

His skin is a nice caramel tone, as if he's spent his entire life in the sunshine, but it feels natural. His dark hair is pulled back at the sides, but it doesn't hide the long length of it. With an angular nose and strong cheekbones, he speaks of another land, a place where the sunshine and the sea shake hands and meet in an eternal dance.

Every part of him is beautiful and agonizing, the kind of man that women would forget themselves to impress. The air smells of the tropics as he closes the distance, of salt air and palm leaves. My chest aches for the sunshine when he strolls closer, unconcerned with our group.

The others are on edge and cluster around me, but somehow, I know this man won't hurt me. I can feel it even if the power leaching from his body makes my bones ache. The large creature doesn't reveal itself in the fog anymore and I wonder if this man was born from it.

Or if he is the very beast we fear.

He strolls forward without hurry, his eyes on me and me alone. He doesn't spare a glance for Athan, for Otto, or for Henry. He's completely focused on me, enamored with my image, as he strolls along the cobblestones without a care in the world.

Athan growls when the man stops before us, a warning not to get too close. The newcomer doesn't even spare him a glance, unconcerned. But he does study me, the simple dress I wear, the newness of my skin. From this close, I can tell his eyes are the deepest emerald green, but there's a ring of light around his irises that make me want to peer closer. Like a light at the bottom of the ocean. His skin glows just the barest amount, but that fades the longer he stands before me, studying me.

I don't shift in discomfort. I study him in return.

Though I've been afraid since the first death, I'm not afraid now. What a strange conundrum of emotion I feel.

Finally, the corner of his lips quirks up and it lights up his face. "Hello, little destroyer," he purrs, and his voice speaks of the stormy seas, of standing on the ballast of a ship, arms wide, as the sea soaks you to the bone. "I've been waiting for your power to be great enough that I could meet you."

I tilt my head. "The horn has been you."

He nods. "You had to be powerful enough to stand in my presence and not go mad. So I waited, and spoke, and called to you, my heart of hearts." He takes my hand and the others tense. When he presses a kiss to the back of it and looks up at me from my hand, I flush even as the bite of power against my hand stings. "You are hauntingly beautiful, Mena. You are so very much worth the wait of eons."

My flush deepens and I'm stricken by this man — this creature? — who bows before me despite his power. I find I enjoy it. I enjoy it far too much.

"What are you?" I ask, staring at him with wide eyes.

He straightens and cups my chin, forcing me to stare deep into his stormy eyes. He smiles and I'm lost at sea. "My beautiful little Destroyer," he purrs, and my whole body reacts. "It's not what I am. It's what I am not."

"And what are you not?"

His eyes crinkle. "My dear, I am not here to harm you. I'm here to elevate you. A woman with a God at her feet. A beauty with monsters at her whim."

I nearly swallow my tongue and amusement lights up his face.

"God?" I repeat, my fingers gripping at the lamp post tightly. Someone behind me makes a sound of dismay, but I don't know who. I don't blame them for the noise.

Not when the ringing in my ears mocks me.

33
MENA

The word "God" repeats in my ear over and over again, like an echo over a canyon that won't go away. It ricochets around my mind until I can bring myself to form words again.

"God," I repeat, looking at this new, very handsome man. "As in *The God*?"

He laughs and the sound goes straight through me, begging me to wrap myself in it.

"One of many," he replies. "But I suspect not the god you're referencing. The one you speak of is a notorious asshole who never bothers coming down from his high tower."

Otto snorts behind me. "Yeah, notorious asshole is accurate."

Otto speaking forces the newcomer's eyes to dance over our group. Though I'm standing in front, Otto, Athan, and Henry stand around me, their guards high with the power that gently oozes from this new threat. If I look down fast enough, his shadows almost look like tentacles dancing along his feet.

The god tilts his head. "It appears you've already begun to grow your collection, little destroyer. A royal vampire, a reaper, and. . ." He peers closer at Henry. "What in the cosmos are you?"

Henry shifts uncomfortably under his perusal, but I don't have time to explain his circumstances and he doesn't seem forthcoming so I direct the conversation back to the issue at hand.

"So you're a god," I say, bringing his attention back to me. "Which god if not The God? What's your name?"

"I go by many names," he declares, and in his tone, I hear the divine ego he must carry. "The Great Dreamer. The Sleeper. High Priest of the Great Old Ones. But most know me by—"

"Cthulhu," Athan whispers as he steps up beside me. He hovers close to me, as if he could sweep me away at a moment's notice. "You're Cthulhu."

The man smiles. "Very good, Reaper. You're much smarter than your predecessors."

"So what do I call you?" I ask, studying him. He's incredibly attractive, the kind of handsome that will have women throwing themselves at his feet. With skin touched by the sun and such an angular face, he's made for sin, for pining after. From the way he holds himself to the way he looks me over, this man would be a notorious bachelor indeed if he participated in high society. Though what else should I expect from a god?

"Whatever you wish, little destroyer," he purrs. "You can call me Hu if that pleases you. You can call me yours if you're feeling more forward." The line is delivered so smoothly, it takes my mind a few seconds to catch up. His eyes follow the flush that travels up my neck and the smile that curls his lips nearly makes me curl my toes.

It's only then that I realize we're still standing on the foggy street where any nosy lady can see if they were to peer out their windows. At least the fog offers some cover.

"We should move this conversation inside," I offer, gesturing toward my home. I don't know how I feel about having a god in my home, but I've already got a reaper, a vampire, and whatever Henry would be classified as. Why not add another monster these days?

I turn, leading them all to my home as if it's the most normal action in the world. Feeling their combined presence behind me makes my hair stand on end, though I suspect most of that is from Hu. I've grown used to the others. It's quite easy to forget what they are, but Hu? There will be no forgetting what power he holds at his fingertips.

The moment we step inside the door, Mrs. Kingsley is waiting. She's standing at the base of the stairs with a frown, no doubt wanting to see what Otto had been shouting about, but too nervous to look outside. Otto most likely told her to stay inside where it's safe. Him or Henry. Athan probably didn't spare the time.

When I step inside and am followed by not three but four men, her eyes widen. "Another gentleman, Mena?" she whispers in confusion toward me. Never mind that he can probably hear. "Are you courting again?"

I'd once proclaimed to her that I'd be a widow for the rest of my life, that there's no need to bring a man in who will take over everything when I can handle it perfectly myself. And while that's still true, I now have four male companions in my home. How best to describe the situation?

"Mena is not courting," Hu declares with a grin directed toward me. "We're all courting her, of course, but she has no need to court us in return."

Mrs. Kingsley blinks in surprise. My blush deepens and I run a hand down my face in annoyance. It's barely been ten minutes and I'm already frustrated with the god. There's no need to put ideas into Mrs. Kingsley's mind.

"They're helping me figure out what's wrong with me," I correct with a grimace. "Nothing more."

Hu strides forward with all the confidence of a divine creature. "Mrs. Kingsley," he proclaims as he takes her hand and presses a kiss to her knuckles. "You must be the lovely woman responsible for Mena's pleasant upbringing. It's a great pleasure to meet you."

Mrs. Kingsley flushes. "Well, not exactly, but I do my best." To me, she whispers, "I like this one."

Hu grins in victory, a grin that he flashes toward the others like this is a competition. Athan rolls his eyes, but the others just stare.

"Alas, Molly," Hu adds, "we must bid you adieu. Mena and we have something to discuss." Mrs. Kingsley doesn't ask how he knows her name, either because she's so flustered or because it doesn't cross her mind. Instead, she glances back at me.

"Would you like some tea brought in?"

I nod, eager for something to do with my hands. "Tea, and something a bit stronger, too," I rasp, wringing my fingers together with my nerves.

Whiskey, I think, will be needed for this conversation.

34
CTHULHU

I'd felt the call from the moment she first died, like an echo across the cosmos. Deep in my watery prison of R'lyeh, I waited for the stars to align so I could leave. But the stars were not the only thing I had to wait for.

Lilith was a powerful woman, God's perfect creation with a mind of her own. Made from the same dust as Adam, she refused to be a breeder and left. She's long since vanished from the earth, but now I can feel her presence again. Not in herself, but in Philomena Seagraves. A reincarnation. A reckoning.

I could not reveal myself to her without driving her into insanity before now. My power is limitless, but it is brutal. One look from someone not strong enough and they'll be forever changed, their mind broken by my appearance. Thus is my curse and my burden.

So I waited until the right moment. Until I felt her third death and the stars aligned just so.

I rose from the sea, from my prison beneath the ocean, and came for her. I'd warned her of my coming the only way I knew how, with the foghorn and the ringing, but still she appeared shocked as I stepped from the fog and took her in.

Beautiful.

I had not expected her to be so beautiful and that will be my undoing. In my haste, I've been thinking of her as Lilith, and while Lilith was beautiful with her fiery hair and brutal personality, Mena is even more so. Her skin shines with her power, the same power that flashes in her eyes as she beholds me. The thoughts in her mind flicker toward me, interest, fear, intrigue. Despite being afraid of my power, she's curious.

And then I feel the gentle waves of her desire.

I want her. I want to taste the power inside her, from her lips, from between her thighs. I want to feel her power brush against mine, tangle with it, defeat it. I want to feel her writhe beneath me, my name on her lips as she screams to the cosmos.

I want her with such a need as I've never wanted anything in my life.

When I find myself in her home surrounded by monsters and tea set before us, I can't stop staring at her while we wait for everyone to fill their teacups. It's been so long since I've been served tea and I take the tiny cup from Mena happily. Her fingers brush mine and her cheeks redden, begging me to nip along the flush with my teeth. All in good time.

Looking around the room, I see the books and papers covering every surface. In my mind's eye, I understand they've been researching Mena's predicament, but though they know some of her plight, it's clear they don't know all.

I raise my brows at the mess. "Clearly, you've been praying to the wrong gods," I tell Mena. "If you were in search of information, all you had to do was ask me, little destroyer."

Mena frowns and it makes my chest squeeze. She should never frown toward me, only smile.

"Why do you keep calling me that?" she asks, her fingers dancing together around the teacup in their nervous energy.

I tilt my head, confused. Shouldn't she know this? Hasn't anyone told her? "Because you're prophesied to destroy the world as we know it, Mena," I answer honestly. "Of which I'm sure you well know."

She freezes. She goes so still I wonder for a moment if she has turned to stone. I watch the shiver travel along her body before she returns to herself and processes my words.

"What?" she chokes out, the word strangled from her throat.

Ah. So she hadn't known after all.

35
MENA

"You are the reincarnation of Lilith. To some extent, you are Lilith, or you at least carry parts of her. She cannot return in the physical flesh, but eventually, your souls will be merged as one. You may have her memories, and you'll have her powers, but I do not know what else will change."

I stand so suddenly, the teacup in my hands goes clattering to the floor. It bursts on impact, but I can't even pay it any mind. The words spilling from Hu's throat are just one bomb after another, each as painful as the last.

I'm destined to destroy the world? I could change so completely, I'm no longer myself? No one else has told me this.

"Now hold on," Henry interrupts. "What do you mean she could change?"

Hu focuses on him, his emerald eyes flashing against Henry's lighter ones. "The sheer amount of power Mena will control will be so great, change is inevitable. Her genetic makeup adjusts with each death. By her seventh death, each cell in her body will be brand new and she will become immortal."

I sway on my feet and very nearly fail in catching myself against the nearby desk. "What?" I rasp, but they don't seem to notice my struggle, or if they do, they assume I'm fine. Only Otto's eyes linger on me, and in his gaze, I see the temptation to support me but the desire to allow me my freedom. I appreciate his decision despite also wanting to be supported. There's so much going on, my brain is starting to ache.

"And how do you know this?" Athan asks from where he stands leaning against a table. He'd refused tea, his body tense around the presence of Hu. What does he know of the god that we don't? Why is he so on alert?

Hu raises his brow. "Lilith told me, of course."

Henry scoffs. "Lilith existed centuries ago. It's impossible."

"For a human, yes," Hu replies. "But I am a god."

"Okay, so say you knew Lilith," Otto continues. "And say we believe you—"

"I have no reason to lie."

"Yes, well," Otto sighs. "Perhaps you should start the story at the beginning. From meeting Lilith to your appearance now. What does a god have to do with Mena?"

My eyes trail over to Hu to find his eyes already watching me. Those bright eyes beg for me to drown in them, and in them, I see every promise of sin and retribution. I see revenge and agony, and above all, a deep loneliness permeates his presence I hadn't pinpointed before. Now, I can feel it falling from him in waves. How long has he been alone?

Hu takes a sip of the teacup, as regal as any king, before setting it back on the tray. "Perhaps you are correct. The beginning will be best. I assume you know the story of Lilith?"

"It's been washed down over the years," Athan replies. "So there are many pieces missing and only certain tomes speak of her at all."

Hu sighs. "It's the plight of humanity to erase history, is it not?" He shrugs and settles back against the sofa. "At the dawn of time, when the world was struck, the god you know created a tiny oasis." His eyes meet mine again. "This was his only creation. He did not create the world, but he did create humanity and the Garden of Eden."

My knuckles turn white where I grip the desk to remain on my feet. "Go on."

"He first created Adam, as you well know. From the dust of the earth. And then he created Lilith from the same dust. They were equals in creation, but as man is want to do, his ego grew with him. Adam grew demanding and he had god's full support to master his reign. He was in charge, he claimed, and so Lilith was to be his property, his to do with as he pleased. Your god did nothing to stop him."

"Lilith refused to be subservient," Henry nodded. "That much we've found."

"Yes," Hu agreed. "Lilith was not made to lie beneath Adam and bow to his whims. She was made an equal and so she refused to do as he bid. He retaliated and so Lilith left Eden in search of help, bruised, injured. Adam, in his fury, demanded a new wife, and so god created Eve, as you well know. But neither Adam nor your god forgot Lilith's betrayal and they hunted her down. She was dropped into the ocean with the intention of killing her, but instead, she dropped into a city sunken beneath the Pacific Ocean, the same city where I had been imprisoned many years before."

"They just put her with you?" Otto asks, confused. "That doesn't make any sense."

"Your god is egotistical, and assumed she would die. And in his hastiness to punish Lilith, he'd forgotten that I, too, resided beneath the sea. He thought to feed her to the sea, to have her be forgotten, and did not make sure she perished. That was his mistake."

"None of that explains what I am," I interject, my voice strained. "So you knew Lilith. How am I her reincarnation?"

The sigh that leaves Hu's lips feels like a century old weight, as if repeating this story is somehow a nuisance in the face of everything. What a pity. The poor god has to explain himself to the human. But I refuse to remain in the dark. If this. . . man. . . has answers, then I should know them.

"When Lilith was dropped and floated beneath the sea, I found her. My power was weakened with my imprisonment, but I was able to draw her to me. She arrived worse for wear, battered, beaten, and furious. She tried to launch herself at me before I reassured her I meant her no harm. After all, I'd been alone in my prison for a very long time at that point. Company seemed like a blessing, even the company of a fiery woman hellbent on revenge." He reaches for his teacup again and takes a sip before reaching for the whiskey decanter. I watch as he fills the teacup back up with the amber liquid before continuing. "Despite her attitude, we became friends, as two entities in isolation become. She spoke of her plight, of how she would return and destroy the world her god took such credit for. How she would punish any descendant of Adam."

"And you believed her?" Athan asks.

"I did. Sometimes, you can look in someone's eyes and see their intentions. I knew without a doubt that if there were a way, Lilith would achieve it." He pauses. "And then Lilith found a way."

Athan straightens, but all I can focus on is Hu's expression. There's pride there, for a woman from long ago. They must have had a real connection for a god to be proud of a human woman.

Jealousy hits me so suddenly, I nearly collapse from it. Henry glances over at me, but I steady myself, desperate to look normal, to not show the random bout of jealousy funneling through my body. I have no reason to be jealous. I barely know this creature.

"She escaped to the Underworld by some blip in my curse, one that did not cover her even if it took many years to discover. She claimed she would return with the prophecy she dropped from her lips, and made me promise I would protect the woman who she chose to enact her plan. Seven deaths. Seven powers. And destruction of the world as we know it."

"She just left you there?" Henry asks. "Why could you not go with her?"

"The lock on my prison was extremely specific. I could not leave until the stars aligned perfectly. Which happened precisely this evening." Hu glances at me. "And now here I am and here you are."

"Here I am," I repeat, struck by the story. "And why was I chosen? Why not someone else?"

"That I have no answer for, little destroyer. Only Lilith knows that answer, but I suspect it has something to do with the brightness of your soul. The world had forsaken Lilith long ago when it had no need to and womankind has been paying for that ever since. I agreed to help, if only to alleviate the boredom of godhood."

But I can taste that lie. Hu isn't trying to alleviate boredom. He believes in the cause, for whatever reason he may have, and he's doing this for a friend.

"And you agree with the destruction of the world?" Athan asks, his eyes narrowing on the god. "You're happy to help?"

"Of course," Hu replies, his expression calm and open. "After all, what has the world ever done for me, reaper?" He leans in. "What has it ever done for any of us?"

36
MENA

I don't know if I believe the words coming out of Hu's mouth as much as I think he believes them. Had I not seen him appear as he had, I might not have believed he's even a god. At this point, that's not quite so surprising considering I've now met a Vampire King, a Grim Reaper, and Mr. Hyde, as well as been attacked by witches. It was only a matter of time before a god showed up. But listening to Hu speak about his past with Lilith, understanding just how old that makes him, and realizing he truly thinks me capable of destroying the world has sent me through the ringer. My mind won't hold still, fluttering between thoughts so rapidly I can't possibly latch onto any single one. It's too much.

As they continue speaking back and forth to each other, arguing about Hu's words, I press a hand to my forehead, trying desperately to keep my sanity intact. I can no longer focus on their words, so ridiculous and unbelievable they are, my mind shuts down.

"If you'll excuse me. . ." I rasp, waving at whatever they respond so they think I'm okay. "Just need some air."

I escape the library and find a dim corner to prop myself up in. Deep breath in. Deep breath out. I repeat the action over and over again until I feel less fuzzy, until I'm able to gather my thoughts again. It's been chaos these last couple of weeks—months? — and it just keeps getting worse and worse. How much more terrible must it get before I crack?

"I promise I won't do anything awful," he says before I realize he's there.

I glance over at the god somehow standing beside me despite him not being there a moment before. Taking him in, the relaxed stature, the smug expression, I can't help but force myself to take a few more deep breaths to deal with him.

"You are something awful," I reply after a moment, shaking my head. "Some old god proclaims I'm going to destroy the world. That's certainly awful."

He shrugs. "Whether it's awful or not, it's the truth. Why fight it?"

I raise my brow. "Perhaps because I don't want to destroy the world?"

"So you'd rather continue to live in this era that takes away your voice, that leaves you yearning for freedom that your gender will never allow you to have? You would rather let the world continue on this way?"

"I have more freedom than most," I argue.

"So it's okay that other women don't have the same freedom?"

I frown at his words, at the implication that I can change any of that with this curse. Still, shame fills me. It's an incredibly selfish thought to think that if it doesn't affect me so badly, then it's not my business. Though Hu is correct, I don't want to tell him that. I suspect he knows anyway by the curl of his lips.

"Why exactly did you come find me?" I ask, pushing my hair from my forehead. "I came out here for some reprieve."

For a second, he doesn't answer, his emerald eyes perusing my face and my posture. I'll admit, I look less like the lady I'm supposed to be right now. I'm wearing a dress that barely passes for proper and my hair is mostly loose down my back. I'm slumped against the wall, and I've never put on any shoes. The bottoms of my feet are probably black from the street outside.

Hu takes a step closer, and I tense. "There's no reason to be afraid, little destroyer," he murmurs. "It is all meant to pass."

I meet his eyes. "This is ridiculous," I groan, pressing the back of my cool hand against my heated cheeks. "I cannot be some reincarnation of a scorned woman from the Garden of Eden—"

"Lilith was not a scorned woman," Hu interrupts, his tone leaving no room for argument. "She refused to be subservient to Adam. That was her only alleged crime."

"Which I could never blame her for," I continue. "As she should rebel against such notions, but to think I'm some version of her and you're a god and I have to keep dying and—"

"Mena," he says, stopping my avalanche of words. "You're allowing the information to swallow you. It's easy enough to accept if you just let it go. The details will come when you're ready."

I narrow my eyes. "And how am I supposed to believe you're really a god? You could be lying."

Which is a silly thing to say. I saw him arrive. I heard his foghorn. I know without a doubt he's not human, but being a god doesn't mean I trust him. The last god I prayed to didn't turn out to be who I hoped he was.

Ah, yes. Because normal men can control the static in your ears, his voice whispers in my mind followed by the static he speaks of.

"Tricks, nothing more," I huff, crossing my arms stubbornly. "I could be insane. Locked up in some asylum right now. I've often thought I was since the first time I woke up from death."

He leans closer, getting so much into my space that I'd be tempted to back up if there was anywhere to go. "You were so beautiful when you dug your way out of that grave."

"You could see me?" I ask before my eyes turn accusatory. "You didn't help?"

"Little destroyer, I could no more help than anyone else. If I were to show up at that point, you would have ran screaming from me and thrown yourself from the nearest structure. No, it was much better for you to meet the reaper first."

At his words, I wince. Of course it was silly to expect him to come save me. I know nothing about this man, this god. I don't need saving. I haven't needed saving in a long time.

"Come with me outside, Mena," he says, offering his hand for me to take.

I hesitate. I should decline, stay in the house, but. . . my instincts tell me to take his hand despite the power I feel dancing along his skin. "The others?"

"Will know you're safe in the arms of a god," he reassures me.

Which wasn't exactly what I was asking but it's enough to get my feet moving. Slowly, I ease my hand into his, the feeling of his flesh touching mine sending a spark through me that has me desperate to touch him more than just with hands.

We step outside and he turns toward me. "Do not be afraid, Mena," he purrs.

"Why would I be—" The words choke off as great black wings expand from his back, seemingly from nowhere. They're great membrane wings, like a bat, sharp in their edges and as black as the night sky. Interestingly enough, within that black, there are sparkles, like stars against the darkness, constellations that trace along the membranes and beg me to trace them with my fingers. "You have wings?"

"I have wings," he nods, smirking. "They're much more impressive in my natural form. One day, perhaps, I'll show you."

I glance around the street. "What if someone sees?"

He tugs me gently closer until he can wrap his arms around me. It's improper, and I shouldn't allow this closeness, but I don't protest. Instead, I wrap my own arms around his neck, eager for what I suspect we're about to do.

"Then they will go insane," he admits.

With a great snap of his wings, we shoot into the sky.

37
MENA

Flying through the stars is a different sort of experience, one I never expected to know the feeling of. The stars, despite being so extremely far away, feel close enough to touch when I'm in Hu's arms. His wings flap languidly as we soar through the skies, carrying us as easily as if I'm a feather. The strength in those wings both unnerves me and comforts me. I wonder what he looks like in his natural form if this is not really him?

You are not yet ready for that form, he whispers in my mind.

"Maybe don't do that," I advise, holding on tighter. "It's unnerving."

His chuckle echoes in my mind and vibrates against where I press my face to his chest. It's strange to think I only just met Hu a few hours ago but here, in this moment, it feels as if we've known each other much longer. It shouldn't feel like that. It never even felt like that with Walter, though we'd hardly been anything more than friends from an emotional standpoint.

"Where are we going?" I ask, the air growing cold around us. My fingers are starting to lose feeling, and I'm not wearing nearly enough clothing to stay warm.

"Just a few seconds more, little destroyer," he purrs.

I appreciate that he says this out loud rather than in my mind.

True to his word, within a few seconds, the pattern of his wings changes and we're moving with different momentum. He pulls up and lands against the smallest ledge, his arms strong around me as I lift my face from his chest and peer around.

"Oh, god," I gasp, clinging to him tighter. Fear dances in my chest, my heart beating against my ribcage in panic. We're not on the ground. My toes aren't touching the earth. They're on the edge of stone, on the very top of the tallest Cathedral in London.

"You can trust me, little destroyer," Hu murmurs, his arms like steel around me. "I will not drop you."

"Stop calling me that," I hiss despite the fear. The wind whips around us, my hair swirling with the movement of the lazy wind.

"Then what shall I call you?" He leans his face closer. "My beloved? Little Lambkin? Dearling?"

I scoff at him. "Mena. You can call me Mena."

He repeats my name like a prayer and if I were not standing on an exceedingly high ledge, my toes might have curled. "And what do I call you within the throws of passion?"

My eyes narrow on the seriousness in his. "What makes you think you stand a chance to witness such intimacy?" I ask sharply.

He laughs as if I've spoken some hilarity. "I can read minds, Mena. I know what you think of me."

"Then you know you're also infuriating?" I grunt, looking away from him to gaze out over the city. At this hour, much of it is sleeping. All but the streetlamps are dark. Electricity in the richer parts of the city burns bright, the well-kept gas lanterns adding an ambience to the streets there as well, but the dwindling gas lamps of the poorer districts flicker with their poverty. I frown. Why have they not gotten better accommodation yet? All should have the proper gas lanterns according to the council. I've never noticed until now that they had not been forthcoming with their progress.

"Yes," he replies with a crook of his lips, answering my earlier question.

Sighing, I tighten my fingers in his coat. "I've known you for a matter of hours—"

"False," he corrects. "In physical form, yes, but you've been aware of me since your first death. You just didn't know my name."

"The foghorn?"

"The only way I could reach you without my power driving you mad," he nods. "Upon your third death, you grew powerful enough to withstand all of me."

"Why is that?"

"Which each death, you grow more powerful. I presume it has to do with that."

We lapse into silence, both of us looking out at the city, taking in the rare view from the highest point in London. Despite the height and perching at the very top of the structure, it's almost. . . relaxing, despite the fear.

Hu's arms tighten around me and lift off before I can prepare myself. I squeak and tighten my arms around him, nearly strangling him, but he doesn't seem to mind. His wings carry us down to the ground to stand before the large cathedral. The giant wooden doors are closed, but I know they're not locked, the cathedral offering sanctuary to those who may need it. I stare at them, my heart aching. Once, I would have stepped inside and felt at home. Now, it feels suffocating to be standing before it.

"Would you like to go inside?" he asks, releasing me to stand on my own two feet.

I hesitate, glance between him and the large doors. "Not really, no," I admit.

"It's only a structure," he reasons.

"It's a house of God," I whisper. "And he's made it very clear he wants nothing to do with me." I shiver at the memory of my last prayer attempt, of the cross turning, of the spiders and the flies. "I do not think I'm welcome there."

"A weak god," Hu grunts, anger in his voice. Anger at me or anger for me? "A false one. False gods demand wine and sentiments."

I glance up at him. He's considerably taller than me, so I have to tip my chin back to really look him fully in the face, especially wearing no shoes. "And what do real gods demand?" I ask curiously.

His eyes flash dangerously. I think he won't answer at first, but when he does, the chill along my skin returns as the word echoes around the empty square.

"Blood," he answers. "Real gods require blood."

38
MENA

When the echo fades, I turn back to the cathedral. It is just a structure, a beautiful one at that. What harm could it do to step inside? Surely, I won't burst into flame for simply stepping inside.

"We can go inside," I murmur, but I reach for his elbow and thread my arm through his. I don't think I can step over the threshold alone.

He doesn't say anything. Instead, he slowly leads me closer to the cathedral. We don't go through the largest doors, the ones that open for mass. We instead head for the smaller wooden door, the one meant for a few people at a time. It's unlocked just as I expected. He pulls it open and gestures for me to precede him. I hesitate for only a second, the thought of burning at my audacity giving me pause. But then I take a step forward, over the threshold, holding my breath just in case. My feet touch the tile on the other side...

Nothing. No flames. No damnation. No one calls me a demon and tells me to leave.

I let out the breath I'd been holding and take another step, keeping them slow and measured just in case. Hu follows me, his eyes trailing up toward the ceiling where murals cover every inch. "Humans build such grand temples," Hu murmurs. "They always have."

His voice echoes in the empty cathedral. No one is inside that we can see though I suspect someone is here in the large building somewhere. Candles burn along the altar and through the room, giving it all an ethereal glow. It's beautiful. I've never been in a cathedral so late. I've never had a need to.

"Is it taboo to enter another god's temple?" I ask Hu curiously. I would think it would anger the other god, but nothing happens with our presence here so maybe it's silly to think so.

"Only if the god of the temple is present." He glances down at me. "Your god abandoned humanity long ago. He only interferes in matters of demonia, or to play games with those who worship him."

"So it really is just a structure," I murmur, studying the murals above. "A beautiful one."

"Yes," he agrees. "A god who forsakes someone so devout is no god, especially when the devotee has not sinned by their choosing or without reason."

"You mean me?"

"You are not the only one who has suffered this fate." Our eyes meet. "After all, who has ever prayed for Lucifer, the one being who needed prayer the most?"

I blink. "You've got a point, certainly. I'm afraid my religion was ingrained in me as a small child. I had not truly questioned it until I attempted to pray during this mess." Sighing, I pause in our walking, bringing him to a stop. "Now, I wonder how much of what I was taught was even true."

Hu tilts his head. "All of it. None of it. With godhood comes a coldness that cannot be shaken," Hu offers. "Only a god can see a child with a broken back and be unmoved."

"Is that how you are?" I ask, tugging him to move again as we stroll beneath the intricate murals.

His eyes tighten. "I often times think myself unmoved by most events." He flashes me a smile. "Until you, of course."

"Of course," I mock with a smile before shaking my head at his flirtations.

Silence between us is comforting. It's not for lack of conversation, but because we're at ease in each other's presence. It's not strained or awkward. We simply exist together without trouble.

"Your god's ego is his weakness," Hu says a few minutes later. He tilts his head up toward the ceiling, pointing to it. "I heard your prayers before, Mena. They were wasted words for a merciless god."

"So who should I pray to instead?" I ask with a raised brow. "You?"

"I am not opposed to worship," he teases, patting my arm. "But worship can be a mutual thing. Just as you kneel for me, I would kneel for you."

My face flushes at his implication. "Why?"

He pauses. "Why?"

"Yes, why? I am human. I am nothing compared to an ancient god." He laughs at my words, and I frown. "Have I said something funny?"

He grins. "You're so very wrong, Mena. You're less human than your doctor, and you are a cataclysm. A void just as I am." He winks. "And two voids can't make a light."

I blink up at him in confusion. What does any of that even mean? I don't understand, but as he said earlier, perhaps the details will come slowly. For now, I simply enjoy strolling through the cathedral with a handsome man on my arm. Every part of him intrigues me and though I should be afraid of him, I can't help but be the opposite.

The confessional booth appears to our right and I pause, staring at it. I've spent time in such a place confessing my sins and begging for forgiveness. It was always given by the priest, but had the priest actually known anything about forgiveness? Had he known that that god would never forgive me for sins I can't control?

"Would you like to confess your sins to me?" Hu asks with a grin. "I'm a great listener."

"Would it do any good?" I ask.

"It couldn't do any harm," he teases. "You'll find I'm much more inclined to forgive you." He leans in, his lips close to my ear. "You begged your god to forgive you and he shoved more torment down your throat to keep you quiet. I have something much better to fill your throat with."

My cheeks redden, the blush climbing my neck and making the room feel too hot despite the chill in the stone around us. The blasphemy that just left his lips, in a cathedral of all places, should offend me. I should be aghast. I'm not. In fact, I'm curious what this god accepts as worship, what it would feel like for him to worship me.

His smile is saccharine as he captures my thoughts and begins to tug me toward the confessional booth. "I'll be your new god, Mena. I won't ask you to bow down to me, to declare yourself as my vessel. I only ask you profess your love unto me, your lord. I will leave such an imprint on your soul, your heart, that anyone you entertain after me will have to know me in order to understand you."

My mouth dies up. No words can explain what his just did to me. I don't protest as he opens the door to the large confessional and leads me inside. He's so large, there isn't much room left once I press against the wall and he follows me, closing the door behind him. When he turns to look down at me, his golden emerald eyes glittering in the darkness even as the light filters through the screen beside us, I freeze.

"Mena," he purrs, leaning down, his lips hovering above my own. "Confess your sins."

My mouth pops open and he reaches up to cup my chin, resting his strong fingers there. I have to clear my throat to get the words out. "Forgive me, father, for I have sinned."

Hu hums under his breath. "Go on."

"My thoughts have been plagued by thoughts of another god," I rasp as he slides his fingers along my jaw.

"Bow your head in the house of god, little destroyer. Who do you think you are?" he chastises, and I bow my head without thinking about it, immediately flushing at the order, at the ridiculousness of it. I jerk my chin back up and he grins. "Very good."

"My sins outweigh anything else," I rasp, my hands coming up to clench at his coat.

"Have you believed another gospel?" he purrs. His head dips down, his breath rushing along my cheeks. "Have you given up on this house of lies and pride and bone?"

"I—" His fingers stroke along my neck, circle it, and my words choke off as heat floods between my thighs. "Oh, God."

"Not that god," he growls. "If you're going to pray, pray to me."

No words will come out at his command. What does one say to Cthulhu, the great dreamer? How does one pray to a god who stands in front of you, who touches you with such tenderness?

"Oh, Mena," he purrs, stroking along my collarbone. "You are the cosmos, so bright, I cannot look away. I want you. My hands have never held something as perfect as you." His fingers push my dress, revealing more of my shoulder.

"We should stop," I croak, but my fingers cling to him tighter, contradicting my words.

"Should we?" he hums. His lips trail along the shell of my ear, teasing. "Your god is watching, Mena," he whispers. "Should we give him a good show?"

Every reason to say no filters through my mind and disappears to be replaced with the one reason to say yes.

At this point, what have I to lose?

I trail my hands up from Hu's coat, along his shirt, to wind around his neck. My fingers scrape through his hair, come down along his jaw to stroke the stubble there. "Yes," I finally answer. "We should."

Hu growls against my neck and finally, blissfully, presses his lips to my flesh there. I turn my head to the side, giving him full access as his teeth and lips trail along my neck, sending my desire ever higher.

"Confess your sins," he growls. "I didn't tell you to stop."

I gasp as his hands jerk the top of my dress down to reveal my breasts to the chill air. He palms one and stoops to the other to suck my nipple into his mouth. I lean against the wall, my legs beginning to shake with the force of my need. My nails claw at the back of his neck, desperate to hold him against me, but it's not enough. I need more.

"My thoughts are claimed by lust," I wheeze out as his other hand goes to the hem of my dress and begins to slide up my leg. "I can't think of anything else."

"And do you yearn for the other three?" he demands, his teeth on my skin sending a bite of pain that makes me jerk against him. "Do you think about taking their cocks in you the way you're thinking about taking mine?"

I'm already hot, flushed so bright red I burn in the darkness, but if I could, I would have burned hotter. Shame fills me, but I push it away. That shame comes from a god who demanded me be something without offering anything himself. It was a lie. It was all a lie.

"Yes," I admit, my fingers tightening on him. "Yes."

"I can't wait to see you splayed beneath them," he groans. His hand circles my knee and continues higher along my thigh. "I can't wait to hear your prayers, little void."

His fingers find the wetness between my thighs and we both groan together. At his first touch, desperation fills me and I'm jerking my skirts up.

"Forgive me, for I'm about to sin," I rasp down to him as he strokes along my seam and his lips trace my chest. "I'm about to fuck another god in your temple."

Hu jerks his head up and meets my eyes. The slow smile that curls his lips makes my legs weak and my body hot. "What blasphemy falls from your lips," he purrs. He stands and jerks me up, my legs automatically wrapping around his waist. "Do you think your god is hard watching us desecrate his temple?"

"I... don't know." I fight the ingrained shame that threatens to fill me as I wrap my arms around his neck. Part of me demands I stop this, demands I behave like the lady I am, but a part of me, a savage hidden part demands I accept this worship, claims I've earned it. My god has forsaken me, so I will forsake him in return. And what better way to send a message. "Fuck me," I growl, leaning in to kiss his throat. "Show me what a real god demands."

I can feel the stars in his fingertips as he reaches between us, as he holds me up, as he strokes his cock along my entrance. We waste no more time. The Great Dreamer thrusts up into me, claims me, and I see the cosmos he comes from behind my eyes. I want him in ways that will get me permanently expelled from the kingdom of Heaven. I need him in ways that would make the devil blush. And as his cock fills me, I give myself over to this god, to the one who requires blood, and give him everything.

A soft cry falls from my lips as he pulls out and strokes back inside. I'm so wet with desire, there's no resistance as his immense size stretches me, as he presses me back against the grate and begins to fuck me properly. I've never been loved quite like this, never felt so consumed, so claimed, and my cries grow louder with each movement, until my cries echo out into the cathedral. My moans and sounds of pleasure fill the temple of God, until he can't ignore the sounds, until we desecrate it and claim it as our own. I don't mind being ruined as long as it means I'm sacred enough to this god to be kept close.

"I accept your sins," Hu growls at my throat. "Be immodest. Rebel. Disobey. And know you deserve to be free." His lips press roughly against mine. "Now scream for me, Mena. Pray for me."

"Oh, god!" I cry against his lips, and he swallows the sound, swallowing me whole as my muffled cries echo around his. He speeds up his thrusts, fucking me there in the confessional booth after I've confessed my sins and committed more. I'm lost in him, desperate to know him so deeply, I'll never question him again. There, in another god's church, with a god buried deep inside me, I find my religion.

I don't want soft or subtle. I want rough, wild. I want sins. I want this god, and I want the vampire king, and the reaper, and the scientist with a harrowing secret. I want them each as much as I want to breathe. I will damn them with my want. The taste of Cthulhu as he slips into me consumes me like the moonlight filters through the stained glass, bright colors dancing around us as it reflects inside. I am something more. I am something different.

There, in the confessional booth, as my cries echo around us and Cthulhu swallows me down to the marrow, as he forces me to explode over and over again, I find my answer.

The only person who can truly absolve me is me.

I've been begging forgiveness from a god who's never cared.

The kingdom of Heaven is within me, and all around me. Let not shame deceive me as all my yearnings are divine in nature.

I pick a god and pray to myself instead.

"Oh, god. Oh, god! Oh, god!"

The stars in Hu's fingertip sink into my skin and light the way...

39
MENA

We flew back home shortly after, and I collapsed into my bed without any explanation to the others. I was exhausted after the day, my thighs tingled with lingering shakes, and I needed the softness of my bed to hold me. I'd almost asked the god to stay with me, but ultimately, I'd let him go to do whatever it was gods do.

I don't know what I need in this life. I don't know if I'm meant for all of this prophecy, but I know there isn't much choice. I've tried running away. It hadn't worked. I can either let my fear freeze me or I can fight things my own way.

Those are the thoughts that filter through my mind as I fall into a deep sleep filled with gods and vampires and stained glass desire.

I wake up the next morning with faded sunlight streaming in through the window. It's a dreary day, as it often is in London, the sun mostly hiding behind the clouds above. Below me, somewhere in my house, there are four men here, each having made some comment of intention toward me or shown it. Four monstrous men. Even Henry has a monster hiding inside of him, one who would kill to protect me.

Someone knocks on the door roughly. "Wake up," Athan calls. "Today we practice your powers.'

I groan as I hear his footsteps recede and descend down the stairs. I could ignore him and remain in my room, but it wouldn't do any good. Eventually, he'll come find me and I don't have any desire to face him unprepared, so I press the button to ask Mrs. Kingsley to assist me. She arrives a few minutes later and goes about helping me dress in a proper day dress and twisting my hair up into a proper style. It's only an hour later I find myself in the library, sitting with the others, my eyes dancing over to Hu every so often as I remember what we'd done the night before.

"Pay attention," Athan growls, dragging my gaze back to where he sits on the desk. "Each death should bring a new power so you should have three by my count."

I scowl at him and cross my arms. "And? How am I supposed to use them?"

"Powers are best felt," Hu offers helpfully where he sits in a leather armchair. "Rather than explained."

Otto is stretched out on the sofa. "Your powers may not affect creatures and may never do so. Some of us are immune to certain powers and we have no way of knowing what you're capable of until you do it."

"You're welcome to attempt on me," Henry offers. "As I'm human."

"Mostly," Hu comments and Henry scowls at him. "You can't deny you're far less human than you think you are," he adds with Henry's look.

"Regardless," Henry grunts. "Feel free."

"We know you have some sort of emotional manipulation because we saw it. As well as the ability to force someone to indulge in excess," Otto comments.

"Ah yes, the witch who began shoveling dirt into her mouth. A great manifestation," Hu says proudly.

The others glance at him in confusion since he wasn't there, but I understand Hu sees a lot of things. It stands to reason he was watching me while he waited for his opportunity to appear.

"So what came with the third death?" I ask, looking between them.

"That, we don't know," Henry offers. "That will be up to you to discover."

"Lovely," I mumble, crossing my arms. "Best felt. Do I just close my eyes and think about them?"

"That sounds like a great start," Henry reassures. "Let us try that."

Taking a deep breath, I close my eyes and focus on the thought of power. I think about making Henry cry, making him feel incredible sadness, but when I open my eyes, he's still standing before me unmoved.

"I don't think it's working," I admit, sighing. "Perhaps it was a fluke before."

"Or perhaps there's not enough human in the doctor," Hu points out with a grin.

"One of your staff?" Athan asks, gesturing toward the door.

"Absolutely not," I growl. "I will not put them in danger."

"Then how else will you practice?" Henry asks genuinely.

"I don't know," I growl. "I'll meditate." Sighing, I sit down on the sofa, forcing Otto to move his legs. "This is ridiculous."

Hu stands and comes over to tip my chin up. "Your fear blocks you."

I scowl at him in annoyance.

"He's right," Otto adds. "It's better to try at least."

In the end, I relent and Mr. Kline, my carrier, appears in the doorway after Athan fetched him. I'd made sure they knew he had to agree and understand what was happening. Mr. Kline steps up with a bright smile.

"Miss Seagraves. It's my pleasure to help," he declares.

"Athan has explained the situation?"

"Clearly," he nods. "Do your worst."

I grimace and glance toward Athan. "I don't like this."

"I didn't expect you would. Now focus."

Sighing, I close my eyes again and think about Mr. Kline crying. It seems the easiest emotion to provoke. After a few minutes of straining and focusing on the strange vibrations I feel in my soul, I open my eyes. Mr. Kline is wiping moisture from his face, but it certainly isn't the sobbing I'd hoped to inspire.

"Well, that's disappointing," I say, shaking my head.

"Again," Athan commands. "Until it gets easier."

We spend hours that way, me with my eyes closed and Mr. Kline waiting for something to happen before explaining how he felt. By the time we're finished, I'm exhausted, and the powers are only minimally easier to use. We come to the theory that it's easier in times of high stress, which would make sense. With instructions to continue practicing, we take a break for tea.

I don't feel like we made much progress in the end, but tea is always welcome.

It's a much better alternative to standing there, watching the Grim Reaper's disappointment with each of my failures. I never knew just how disapproving death could actually be.

I decide I don't like it.

I don't like it one bit.

40
ATHAN

"We don't have time for tea when you're so weak," I grunt. "We should continue practicing until you excel."

"Give it a break," Henry says. "A break won't hurt anything."

I bare my teeth at the doctor. "And when she's attacked again, you'll always be around to save her?"

Henry flushes in anger. "Someone will. Mena barely goes anywhere herself."

"Yes," Mena grumbles under her breath. "There's no peace."

"You could have peace if you knew how to use your powers properly," I shoot at her and she blinks in surprise, as if not realizing I can hear her. I can hear everything. I'm insanely aware of her presence, of her every action, of where she's at all times of the day, and it's frustrating. Yes, I'm here because I'm curious, but I shouldn't be so invested in her well-being. I'm a reaper, not a babysitter. I should just leave.

"Give it a rest, reaper," Otto interjects. "A small break for tea won't hurt anything."

"Mena has three powers she can barely use! More and more

monsters are going to appear soon. We've already faced the witches. What else do you think Mena is prepared for?"

"Tea," Otto responds with raised brows. "She's prepared for tea."

"She's exhausted," Henry points out, gesturing to where Mena is indeed bracing herself against the nearest sofa.

"I can speak for myself," Mena says, her chin tilting up in stubbornness. It takes considerable effort for me not to focus on the graceful lines of her neck. "A break for tea shouldn't be too much to ask for."

Red clouds my vision as the anger in my chest spreads outward. I'm not sure where the anger truly comes from or why it's so violent in regard to this. All I know is that I need to be heard, that I shouldn't leave this place until Mena can safely protect herself. I take a menacing step toward Mena, to do what I don't know. Threaten her? That seems foolish. But regardless, I can't help the step I take. "And when you're ripped apart by the next monster, will you take time for tea then?'

"Regardless of if I've mastered my powers or not, if I'm too exhausted to use them, it won't do me any good, will it?" she growls back at me. Her posture goes from leaning against the sofa to upright, as if she needs her height to argue with me. "You're out of line right now."

"I don't know why I'm wasting my time here," I snarl, the urge to shove the stack of books nearest me off the desk strong. "If you don't take this seriously—"

"Give it a rest, reaper," Cthulhu says from his lounging position in an armchair. "Mena has already said she needs a break. You're only embarrassing yourself right now."

My scythe appears in my hand. "Just because you're a god doesn't mean I can't kick your ass."

Cthulhu smirks at the sight of the weapon. "That's precisely what it means, boy."

"Enough," Mena spits. "This is ridiculous. I'm taking tea. If only to avoid throttling you right now. Do what you must with that information."

This time, I don't take only one step. I take as many as necessary to reach her, only stopping when I'm towering over her and she's looking up at me. Despite all the anger whipping around us, despite the weapon in my hand, she doesn't back down, her eyes narrowed on me, her jaw clenched tightly in fury.

"You think you're so tough—"

"No, I don't!" she interrupts. "But I'll be no use to anyone if I can't even stand up!"

"You're no use to anyone regardless!" I throw back. "All of you! This is a foolish errand helping a spoiled heiress *bitch* gain the powers of Lilith as if she'll ever allow you to—"

The slap comes out of nowhere, or perhaps, I should have expected it considering the heightened emotions in the room. Surprisingly, when Mena's hand connects with my cheek, my head snaps to the side with the force, as if the power in her veins adds a little extra pizzaz. My face blooms quickly and the sting rises with my pulse. Even my ears ring as I slowly turn my face back to hers.

"You're out of line," she hisses at me, her eyes fierce and flashing. That otherworldliness in her is bright right now, her pale skin flushed with pure anger. "Get yourself together and remember that this is *my* life, not yours, reaper. Whether I'm ripped to shreds by monsters or master my power, it's still *my choice.* No one else's. If you can't handle that, then just leave!"

Her words quiver with her emotion. We're standing so close together, we're practically chest to chest, both of us panting heavily from our anger. Without my control, my eyes drop to her lips, and the urge to press mine to hers flashes across my mind. Behind us, I hear the blasted god chuckle in amusement, but I pay him no mind. Everything inside of me demands I do something foolish and throw all caution to the wind. The others may not think it strange that we're all drawn to Mena, but when she's the reincarnation of a woman as powerful of Lilith, the risks are high. What happens when she's at full power and decides she wants nothing to do with us? What happens if she kills us all?

"Just kiss already," Otto declares. "We're all waiting with bated breath."

Mena's crimson cheeks flush brighter and her eyes dart to the others. I don't move, foolish words on the tip of my tongue, but I never get to war with myself on whether I should say them or not.

Just as my hand twitches towards hers, the window behind us blows out and glass rains down around us.

41
MENA

I flinch when the window explodes, my instincts demanding I cover my face to protect it. I barely get a chance to wonder what's going on before I'm being shoved down behind the sofa by Athan, the others immediately going alert. I peek over the edge of the leather sofa, trying to find the source of the attack. When the first creature comes barreling through the window, my heart nearly stops.

Is that a. . .?

"Werewolf," Otto hisses as he slides to a stop beside me. "And they work in packs."

Sure enough, more werewolves come flying through the window behind the first, their muzzles peeled back in ferocious snarls. They're large, their heads very nearly touching the eight-foot ceiling of the office as they straighten to their full height. They're canine in nature as one would expect, but they're far more savage than any wolf I've seen. Covered completely in fur and standing on their hind legs like men, each of them bares their teeth at those of us in the room, saliva dripping from their jowls.

"Where is she?" the first one asks. His words are garbled with growls, as if he struggles to speak with his snout so much longer. "Where is Lilith?"

Otto is beside me, standing in case he needs to react. Athan stands before the sofa, his scythe gripped tightly in his hand. Henry is in the corner, his hand clenched around a small bottle. Hu still remains seated in the armchair, completely at ease despite the situation. He watches the werewolves in amusement, clearly not interested in fighting.

"You're trespassing," Athan snarls. "I suggest you leave."

The werewolf turns to take in Athan with yellow eyes. Saliva drips from his muzzle, his stained canines drawing my eyes. These creatures do not appear as friendly as the ones I've befriended. These seem feral. "You dare keep her for yourself, reaper?"

Athan shifts his scythe from his left hand to his right. I expect him to deny the question. After all, we'd just been arguing, and I'd told him to leave. Instead, Athan looks the wolf in the eyes and says, "Yes." One word. That's his only answer, but it clearly angers the werewolf further.

Rather than waiting around and asking more questions, the wolf launches himself at Athan. I scream, wrenching forward as if there's anything I could possibly do against a creature like that. As Athan had said, I've hardly mastered my powers, and though they seem to work in heightened situations, I can hardly do anything against so many of them. There have to be at least six of the creatures, but I can hardly keep count when they move around the room as quickly as they do.

Despite my scream, Athan doesn't react. He stands still as the werewolf grows closer, as the sharp teeth open in preparation. Only when the werewolf is right in front of him, seconds away from ripping his throat out, does he move. The scythe swings in an arc, so quickly and smooth, I almost miss it. Small wet spots splatter across my face, but I don't move, afraid to.

The werewolf stumbles to a stop and the others go silent, watching with the same surprise I wear. The leader's eyes are wide as he looks down at his stomach. At first, I see nothing, only his fur. And then red seeps from the fur, dripping down in trails. I watch in horror as the werewolf splits in half, organs spilling across the library floor before me. I cover my mouth, trying to force the gag threatening to reveal my distaste for this down. It takes considerable effort, but I manage. Until I pull my hand away and realize the wet spots that had hit me were blood.

The gag doubles me over and it takes everything inside me to keep from losing whatever's in my stomach across the office floor.

The other werewolves spring into action at their leader's death. I count five when I'm able to straighten. The five of them spring forward and I watch the brutal display of violence that fills my home. Otto pats me on the head and tugs off his coat.

"Stay here, Mena Mine," he purrs before launching himself into the fray where Athan swings his scythe. A roar from the corner reveals Hyde in all his glory, prepared for bloodshed. He must have taken his elixir, his beautiful spiked form joining in the fight as if he's been looking forward to it.

Hu still hasn't moved from his chair.

I spring up. "What are you doing?" I cry. "Help them!"

"They don't need my help, little void," he purrs, but as if he spoke too soon, one of the werewolves seems to realize he's an easy target sitting in his armchair. The werewolf flies forward, large gruesome claws outstretched and prepared to gut my god.

I fling out my hands and power explodes, but it doesn't do anything to that werewolf. Only one near me drops to his knees in confusion, tears running from his eyes as he begins to sob. He doesn't even seem to know what there is to cry about, so lost in his emotion, he directs his tears toward a book that has fallen on the floor and landed with bent pages.

The corner of Hu's lips quirk up as he meets the werewolf's eyes, the one racing toward him. The wolf stumbles to a sudden stop, staggering forward before falling to his knees with a solid thump.

Hu leans forward in amusement. "How does it feel, wolf, for your mind to be as wild as your soul?"

The wolf clamps his hands around his head as if he's in agony and starts to scream.

My eyes dance over to Otto where he swipes long nails across another werewolf, his fangs bared like an animal. He leaps onto the creature he fights, and I watch as he sinks those fangs into the creature's neck, ripping his throat open. Similarly, Hyde is taking on his own werewolf, laughing as they move in a deadly choreography. Athan faces off against the remaining two, but I'm sure the one suffering from my powers won't be out for long.

I stand, intending to help, but I realize I don't have a weapon. I meant to kill the wolf still crying, but how can I do that without a blade? The letter opener on the desk catches my eyes and I leap for it, my fingers closing around it just as the werewolf seems to snap out of the sadness and turns toward me. I don't have much time to think about what I'm doing, to consider if it's smart or not. Instead, I just throw myself forward without finesse, letter opener in my hand like a dagger. Luckily, I seem to catch the werewolf by surprise. The letter opener sinks into his chest like butter. There's hardly any resistance at all as I embed it deeply and twist. He stares down at the wound in surprise and then looks back up at me.

"Lilith," he rasps, before he collapses at my feet.

"Well," I murmur. "That was easier than expected." But I only say it to distract myself from the horror of the werewolves slowly beginning to transform back into humans. These were people, not creatures, and I'd just killed one. I stumble back, horrified.

A savage growl sounds out behind me and I turn around just in time to watch the others dispose of their own werewolves, each of them using their strengths to do so. Athan swings his scythe and takes the one out he'd been fighting. Otto's wolf is collapsed on the ground with his throat ripped open. Henry's is twitching on the ground with Hyde standing over him, a brutal grin on his face. The werewolf Hu had been controlling scratches at his own eyes, screaming until the pain becomes too much and he passes out.

It's gruesome, and despite my earlier revulsion at the sight of it, part of me... enjoys it? Part of me wants to do it again. Even if the thought of blood repulses me.

Athan gestures to the werewolf I'd somehow managed to kill. "Good thinking grabbing the silver letter opener." When I tilt my head in confusion, his pride disappears and is replaced with a scowl. "You didn't know silver is a werewolf's main weakness?"

"How could I have known that?" I ask haughtily. "Until five minutes ago, I didn't even realize they were real, you prick."

He shakes his head, and his scythe disappears as if it were never there. "Utterly useless."

Otto straightens and smooths down his clothing despite the blood staining the white shirt. "Leave her be, reaper," he orders, shaking out his dreads. He looks toward me. "I think it's time to reinforce your home, Mena Mine."

Sighing, I wipe at my face, trying to get rid of the blood. "For once, I agree," I respond, only succeeding in spreading the blood around my face rather than removing it.

Hu finally stands from his chair and steps over the crazed werewolf. "How about that tea now?" Each of us glances toward the god with equal looks of annoyance and disbelief. "What?" he asks. "Surely you haven't lost your appetite now?"

The door begins to open, Mrs. Kingsley preparing to pop her head in again, but Otto closes it before she can step inside.

"We'll be right out," he tells her. Then he grimaces toward the mess. "Which one of you is going to clean this mess up so the staff doesn't see? I wouldn't want to give them a fright."

Athan's frown deepens. "Just go," he growls. "I'll take care of it."

Otto grins. "I knew I liked you, reaper." He offers his elbow to me. "I'll escort the lovely Mena to the table while you do that."

I hesitate, glance back at Athan, but ultimately thread my arm through Otto's. After all, he's not the asshole here. The reaper watching me with disdain is.

Prick.

42
MENA

It takes the rest of the evening for the office to be put back to sorts, but the bloodstains take far longer. When I had first walked in the next day and saw the rust colored spots still staining the rugs, I'd had the urge to throw them out and purchase new ones. Mrs. Kingsley had first claimed she could get the stains out, but after trying for a few days, the stains indeed will not lift.

Apparently, werewolf blood is difficult to remove.

Finding myself in need of new rugs and desperately needing some distance between Athan and his demands I practice my powers, Otto and I leave the house for the first time in days to run the errand. The rug shop is only a few blocks from the house, so I opt for walking rather than taking the carriage. Such a short promenade will do wonders for my stress I hope, and I genuinely enjoy Otto's company.

Unlike the reaper's.

I could have sent Mrs. Kingsley to pick out replacement rugs, but I prefer to do it myself, mainly because I needed to get away from the house. Being shut in with so much masculine energy is draining, especially when they don't all get along.

Well, mostly Athan is the difficult one to be around for all involved, but still. With each passing day, he seems to grow more and more irritable, as if he cannot stand to be within my presence. Gone are the flirtations and the mentions of interest. Gone are the lingering looks. All that remains is a sour and bitter reaper determined to drive me mad with practice.

Despite there not being much sun today, the glowing orb shrouded by clouds, Otto is fully covered. He wears a pristine day suit and matching top hat. Small, round glasses with dark lenses shield his eyes and he carries a parasol for the both of us. I don't need the same protections he does, but it's appreciated, nonetheless.

"So vampires can't go out in the bright sun?" I ask, curious. I'd always heard the tale that they burn in the sun and hadn't thought to ask Otto before now. The sun is minimal today so I assume that makes a difference.

"We can," Otto replies, carefully leading me across the cobblestones. "We're just highly sensitive to it."

"Do you catch fire?" I ask seriously.

His laugh makes me flush. "No flames. It does burn us, though. Think of it as a really bad, really fast sunburn. No matter the tone of our skin, we're sensitive to the sun. I don't know the science behind it. Perhaps I'll ask our dear Dr. Jekyll to run some tests."

"Good idea," I muse. "I think Henry is starting to go crazy with nothing left to research. He's been awfully busy with his experiments in his room however, so perhaps he's not bored at all."

"I, myself, am rather curious what he's working on." Otto hums under his breath. "He was vastly secretive when I asked him about it. Even hurried to cover up his notes so I wouldn't see."

"How strange," I murmur.

I'm enjoying our stroll toward the rug store. I desperately needed this walk through the London streets. I alternate between taking deep breaths and making small talk with Otto. It isn't until someone steps in front of us that I realize we're being watched. I look up as our path is blocked and startle to see the Dutchess. I haven't seen her since her party where I'd been forced to leave rather abruptly in the arms of my men.

After burning alive in her ballroom.

"Mena!" she exclaims, her eyes roving over my body and stature. Around us, others pretend not to be eavesdropping on our conversation. I'd been enjoying my time with Otto so much I hadn't bothered to take note of them.

"Your grace," I reply, curtsying as my station dictates.

Her eyes are wide as she looks over my skin before she reaches forward and takes my hand. I tense as she flips it one direction and then the other, confused. "The rumors have been flying, Mena," she says. "I watched you burn right in front of my eyes but there's not even a blemish on your skin!"

I laugh nervously. "Yes, well, it wasn't nearly so bad, I promise."

"Nothing a little exfoliating couldn't handle," Otto adds with a grin. The Dutchess smiles at him and fans herself, clearly interested in Otto despite her own marriage to the Duke. A king holds much higher esteem.

She laughs pleasantly. "Clearly." When she focuses back on me, the smile slips a little. "Someone thought you'd died. I've heard the same rumor three times now, different deaths each time. One I witnessed myself and I was certain you weren't moving when your escorts carried you out. Yet here you are."

I smile and slip my mask into place. "How strange of them to think so. I can reassure you I'm alive and well."

The Dutchess tilts her head. "My favorite rumor suggests you're a vampire. After all, how else does one have such pristine skin without the tint of immortality?"

Flushing, I press a hand to my cheek to feign flattery. "What a compliment. My skin must look porcelain indeed if I'm being called a vampire."

Otto can barely hide his chuckle at my words. "Clearly, you're no vampire, Mena Mine. How silly of a rumor."

As if he's not a vampire himself.

The Dutchess laughs at his words. "Imagination runs wild when there's talk, you know."

"Yes, well," I add, "the rumors of my death have been greatly exaggerated. Just a series of unfortunate incidents is all." I release her hand and step back, pulling Otto with me. "It's been so lovely to see you and I apologize for leaving your ball so abruptly. It was a lovely party."

The Dutchess frowns at my quick dismissal. "You don't even have a burn on you. I swear I watched you burn to a crisp, Mena dear. How remarkable."

My smile this time is tense. "Clearly not as I'm standing right here, your grace. I can assure you I'm completely fine."

Her brows furrow but she seems to remember her manners. "Of course you're fine. Clearly, you're healthy." She smiles. "I'll make sure the rumor gets around, but I make no promises. You know how much society enjoys a good drama. Though I might let the vampire one fester for my own entertainment." She winks toward Otto, and I narrow my eyes. "It was lovely to see you both. Enjoy your day."

And then she passes us by, her head held high as she goes about whatever business brought her to this part of London.

"That woman is questioning her sanity," Otto laughs, shaking his head as she disappears.

"Good," I grunt. "I question my sanity every time I attend one of her gatherings. At least I'm not alone now."

Otto's laugher echoes around the street and it eases the tension inside of me. His fangs flash briefly and he looks anything but human as he throws back his head in mirth. He's beautiful in the sunshine despite being a creature of the night. There's no way anyone could look at him and think humans being so capable of beauty.

And yet they think I'm the vampire. Preposterous.

43
MENA

A few days later, I manage to convince Henry to leave the privacy of his room and his experiments to escort me to the park. Athan has been on his high horse again, insisting I practice my powers. The third power I'd gained, we now know is the power of illusions, but it's proving difficult to master, more so than the other two powers. I think I've seen enough of the grumpy reaper for a lifetime, but I know I'll have to face him again later when he makes me practice more.

For all the power they claim I'll have, I feel incredibly weak. I'm starting to believe Athan is right and I am completely useless.

"This is a pleasant park," Henry muses as we walk together. The grass is green, broken up by well-maintained gardens. At this time of year, there isn't as much blooming as I would normally like, the late September air riddled with the chill of Autumn, but the trees still offer their solace as they're able.

"It's one of my favorites," I muse, watching the swans move along the canal. "I used to sit out here for hours and attempt to draw the swans." I smile. "They're finicky models, rarely holding still long enough to get a good sketch of them."

"Personally, I find swans disturbing."

I blink at him. "Disturbing how?"

"Have you ever been attacked by one?" he asks seriously. "Sometimes, they'll attack simply because you strolled too close to the water. Blasted creatures."

The laughter that slips from my lips makes him furrow his brows. "My apologies, Doctor. I assume you've had experience being attacked by the swans?"

"Indeed," he grumbles. "I was but a child, maybe seven, when I was attacked. A mother swan thought I'd looked at her cygnets wrong. I'd had nightmares for weeks. I still do if memory brings it back up."

"Aww," I laugh. "I apologize for such trauma." When he looks at me sharply, I giggle again. "They're lovely creatures to look at, but for certain they're ferocious when needed. I think that's why I enjoy them. Most people look at them and see pretty ornaments. They forget how fiercely they protect their young." I look toward the swans and sigh. "I often times wonder what it would be like to have a mother so protective."

Henry's frown deepens, but not out of annoyance this time. "Your mother wasn't pleasant?"

"If you asked anyone else, they would tell you yes," I admit. "Well-bred and well-married, my mother was held up to the light and inspected often. She couldn't be anything but perfect, and so she played that part well. It was only within the confines of our home she was anything less. She held me up to the same perfection and so I was marched around like a trinket before any eligible bachelor long before it was time for my entrance into society. She wasn't necessarily a bad mother, not by society's standards, but she was anything but protective and warm." I sigh. "She practically threw me toward my late husband and because I was eager to please, I wooed Walter quickly. It was only after we were married that I realized none of it was what I wanted, but it was already too late. Lucky for me, Walter was genuinely a good man. It could have been vastly different had he not been."

Henry pats my hand. "Do you still you see her? Your mother?"

"Thankfully, no. She died a few years after I was married. Consumption I hear. I barely reacted to the news. She'd not visited once after my marriage."

"I'm sorry," he murmurs.

"It's the past, Henry. There's no need for condolences," I offer, smiling gently. "What about your mother?"

"Ah, my mother was a saint in comparison," he admits. "But she passed when I was a child, a year or so after my accident. My father was hollow for a few months afterwards, but then he simply returned to his old self and offered me what he could." He looks down at the ground. "Sometimes, I forget what she looked like. I was very young when she passed. The guilt I feel each time is all-consuming."

"Do you have a picture?"

"I do. It's how I remind myself. Honestly, my father might have been different had she not died. He was a different man for her, less demanding, but he meant well. I understand my mother was the love of his life and he carried on for my benefit alone. I'm always grateful for that. But he found unrequited love in a titled lady not long after that, a sin I never quite forgave him for. That interaction is what colored our relationship and after that, it was all learning, and the laughing man I knew before my mother passed disappeared completely."

Our entire talk, we walk slowly around the park, taking in the sights, enjoying each other's company. When we come around the next bend, I catch sight of a man sitting on the ground, his clothes dirty and torn. His hair hangs in greasy strands around his face as he hunches over the worn hat in front of him, his hand held out, waiting. Most of the others in the park stroll past him without a second glance. Someone will likely report him eventually. The upper class doesn't like to be reminded that there are those less fortunate in the world.

Rare sunshine cuts through the clouds as I reach into my coin purse for a few pounds. It's been my habit to pass out coin to those who find themselves in such positions. If they're children, I've been known to invite them back to my house for a warm meal. I don't believe anyone should be without food. Most of the time, when I invite them to my home, they refuse, afraid that my hospitality comes with strings attached. I don't blame them. There are those always seeking to take advantage. So I offer more coin to provide better food. Many of them have siblings and family that suffer as well.

"Good evening, sir," I tell the man as I stoop to drop the few coins into his waiting hand. Before the coins can touch his palm, however, he jerks it back as if they would burn him. They clatter to the stone beneath him, the sound echoing somehow around us. "Oh, I'm terribly sorry," I offer, moving to pick up the coin despite Henry's sudden tension. "I meant to—"

"I will not take from a blasphemous whore," the man rasps, cutting me off.

I pause in my movements, stricken, before I straighten in horror. I leave the coins where they dropped, their shine on the concrete mocking. The man is still shrouded by his hair so I can't see his face, but there's something about him that makes me uneasy now that I'm focusing on him.

"I beg your pardon?" I rasp, my heart thumping wildly in my chest.

Henry grows defensive at the words where I'd been nearly shocked into silence. "That's no way to speak to a lady," he growls.

"I see no lady here," the man says before unfolding himself. He rises to full height, his hair still around his face. When he lifts his head toward me, I stumble back in fear.

A thousand eyes look into my soul. His face belongs to no human.

Before I can say anything, before I can react to anything other than to stumble back into Henry, a large black shaggy dog is before us, growling at the man.

"You traitorous fool!" the man shrieks and it makes my ear drums ache. "Disgusting reaper! You lie with the whore?"

It's Athan's voice that comes from the large dog and it nearly shocks me as much as this new creature does. "Better a whore than a cruel god disguised as redemption," he spits.

Before us, he transforms, turning from the large dog into a cloaked figure, his scythe in his hands. I watch as he swings the scythe toward him. The man disappears before the scythe can make contact and decapitate him like Athan had intended. When he turns toward us, his face is skeletal for a moment before he returns to himself quickly, as if afraid that he might terrify me. The cloak fades, leaving him in his preferred outdated suit again.

"What on earth was that?" Henry asks, his hand tight in mine. I don't even remember when I'd taken his hand.

"Low angel," Athan grunts, shaking his head. "Terrible creatures. And there will be more. There always are."

But I can only look at the man who had changed between three forms just now, at the way he's looking at me.

"Angel," I repeat, blinking at him. "They're actually real." Part of me suspected they weren't because they haven't shown up before now.

"Perhaps, you should start wondering which creatures aren't real because there aren't many that are mythical," Athan comments gesturing in the direction we came from. "We should return to your home. I'd prefer not to make a scene when I slaughter a few lower angels in the park."

I let them lead me away, but I turn back once to look at where the man had been sitting. There's still the hat sitting there, and my coin scattered across the cobblestone. For a moment, I wonder where the owner of the hat is, and if he's okay.

Somehow, I think he's not.

Somehow, I think the angel, a being I always thought would be good, killed whatever poor soul had the misfortune of running into him.

My world, and all of my beliefs, shift again.

44
JEKYLL

"When the man looked up, he had so many eyes!"

We'd come back to the house rather quickly after the run-in with the angel. There's not much else to be done in that situation other than remove ourselves from direct danger. There's no telling how many of things wait outside for us.

You should have allowed me to take care of it instead of letting the reaper protect our Mena.

I ignore the voice in my mind as I always do. Hyde has been incredibly pushy lately, especially when it comes to Mena. I try not to let it get to me, but it's difficult when there's a whole other consciousness existing in my mind. Soon, I hope I won't be plagued by him at all, but for now, I simply try to ignore him. Like a petulant child, he hisses in annoyance.

You'll never be rid of me, Henry. You and I are one and the same. You know this.

I don't bother responding to the obvious needle. I'm nothing like Mr. Edward Hyde. I am Doctor Henry Jekyll and no one else. Hyde is nothing more than a failed experiment.

That's incredibly offensive, Henry.

"Yes, well," I grumble under my breath as the others discuss what happened around me. "Get used to it. I'm tired of your presence."

"What?" Athan asks me.

I flush at being caught talking to myself. "Nothing," I quickly say and focus on the conversation at hand.

"So what do we do about the angels?" Otto asks, clear worry on his face. Apparently, the vampire king hasn't had much experience with angels. And why would he? From what Athan explained, they don't come to earth to interfere often. The lower ones sometimes come to cause trouble, but otherwise, nothing ever comes of it. This time, they're clearly coming after Mena, and we have to assume the weaker angels are only the first. What does a high angel look like? What are they capable of? And how can we stop them?

Mena is sitting in the armchair to my left, her eyes flashing with her power despite not moving. She's quiet. Too quiet. She hasn't added to the conversation at all despite being the target of attack.

"Eventually, they may be strong enough to hold power here," Athan points out. Though Otto and I seem concerned, Athan is mostly indifferent.

"What does that mean for us?" I ask, wondering exactly what sort of powers angels have. The one in the park didn't seem particularly nice, so I can't imagine they come down to kiss babies and help people.

"It means my scythe will no longer be a weapon we can use against them if they're high enough," Athan answers with a shake of his head. "If he's sending his angels, he's going to start getting desperate soon. Every part of the supernatural world will have an interest in Mena, whether they want to stop her from rising to power, capture her, or follow her. We need to be more vigilant."

Hu almost seems amused by the entire situation, as if he's watching the newest play down at the theater. He's a strange god, this one, mostly watching rather than partaking. Unless it has to do with Mena. Then he participates with her.

"Oh, and Athan turns into a dog," I point out.

Mena glances over at Athan at my words, but she still doesn't speak.

"It's a church grim," Athan grunts. "Not a dog."

"Of course he does," Otto tells me with a shrug. "This isn't my only form either. None of us have a single form. The god here can transform into—"

"I'll be in my rooms," Mena suddenly interrupts, her voice soft and unhurried. There's no panic evident there, no desperation. The only thing I hear is exhaustion.

I frown toward her. "Are you quite alright?"

"Quite," she replies with a half-smile that never reaches her eyes. "I just find myself exhausted."

Nodding that I understand, she bows her head just the barest amount before slipping from the room. She has often been exhausted lately, but I can only imagine how taxing it must be to hold so much pressure and weight on her shoulders. She's been told she's some great power, forced to practice, and learns of a new creature every day, each of them wanting to hurt her or steal her away. It must be horrible to be so sought after.

I can't help but feel as if something is wrong, that she needs us, but I give Mena her privacy.

Foolish, terrible man, Hyde whispers in my mind. *We will lose her.*

Perhaps, I think, it's best that we never thought ourselves worthy of her in the first place. . .

45
MENA

My panic chokes me, but I keep it tamed until I'm able to escape the office and make my way into my room. I close the door behind me and press my forehead against it, letting the coolness of the wood sink into my skin, trying to force my panic under control.

Angels. Terrifying creatures, so unlike anything I've ever known. And they're coming to kill me, I assume. The one in the park had not seemed particularly helpful or eager to join me.

Why? I did not choose this. I did not decide to be the reincarnation of Lilith! That is his domain. I should have free will, shouldn't I? But I have nothing.

I take a deep breath and start counting, trying to calm my racing heart.

One. Angels are very real and instill nothing but primal, oppressive horror. There's no longer a question if they're real, and I wish there was. I wish I still thought they were cute cherubs protecting us humans from another realm that we would one day reach. I wish I was still that naïve.

Two. God is real, though I haven't seen him. I'm not sure I'd want to see him, not after this. Not after he has forsaken me. I cannot follow a god so immoral, so cruel, and yet...

The urge to pray overcomes me. The need to ask him why this is happening? Why am I the chosen one? What evil have I committed to find myself with this fate? Am I really so miniscule? Have I sinned so much that I cannot be saved?

All my years of church and prayer have taught me to ask for forgiveness. But what do I ask forgiveness for? I can't possibly ask for forgiveness for being born, for being what I was made to be. I can't ask for forgiveness for opening my heart to monsters as I was made with an open heart.

Desperate for an answer, no matter where it comes from, I leave the door and kneel before the large hole in the wall. The cross is no longer there, already cut away, but it's the place I've always prayed, and old habits die hard. The only way we'd been able to take away the upside down cross was by cutting a hole and taking away the wall. There'd been no other method that had worked.

The feeling of my knees hitting the hardwood sends a shock of abrupt pain through me when I drop too hard. The air charges around me as I thread my fingers together and bow my head.

I part my lips—

"There are better reasons to be on your knees."

I scowl and pop open my eyes to find Hu leaning against the wall in front of me. Just as he always is, he looks completely at ease, as if this isn't strange that he can appear in my room without asking or alerting me to his entry.

"I seek privacy," I growl at him, desperate for separation between me and the monsters I'm slowly giving my heart to. Perhaps that's why I've been abandoned by my god. I had the audacity to love creatures who needed love the most.

Hu tilts his head, studying me. "If you pray to your god, angels will be all over this house."

"So what do you suggest I do?" I hiss, releasing my hands.

"Pick a different god to pray to, one that won't get you captured or destroyed."

I freeze. "Destroyed?"

He nods. "There are weapons capable of destroying powerful creatures. And you are not yet immortal."

"Like you?" I ask.

"Gods cannot be killed, only banished," he admits. "Or else I might have been dead long ago."

"How convenient for you," I hiss, dropping back on my feet so I'm sitting prone before him. "How very magnanimous of you to be so forthcoming with information."

He studies me closely, those eyes seeing far too deeply inside my soul. "Bitterness does not suit you, Mena."

The laugh that comes from my lips sounds bitter indeed, but I don't care. "What would I have need to be bitter over?" I ask, my heart beating at my chest. "Because my life is ruined? Because some twist of fate took my choice away and now, I must become this monster or die? Because I'm surrounded by monsters claiming to care for me? Because my god abandoned me in my time of need?"

His eyes flash. "Your god may have loved you, Mena, even if I have my doubts, but it does not change the fact that he does not love you enough to save you." He straightens. "I do. The others do. But we can only save you from outside forces. We cannot save you from yourself."

His words are like a slap in the face. "Love," I mock. "What could monsters know of love?"

"Is it not a fitting punishment for monsters?" he asks, taking a step closer. "To want something so much, to hold it in your arms, and know beyond a doubt that you will never deserve it?"

"Punishment," I laugh. "What could you know of punishment? An all-powerful god? Our world barely holds a flame to your existence."

"No, it doesn't," he answers, coming closer. "But you do." He kneels before me. "I know a great deal about punishment, little void.

I was born in it and there is nothing lonelier than godhood, but this isn't about me. This is about you and this urge to destroy yourself."

I choke back the sobs threatening to come up my throat. "It's the one thing I can control."

"Wrong," he growls. "You may have been chosen, but only you can choose what to do with the power you've been given. You have a choice. If you decide you want to disappear into the eons, I'll help you when the time comes, but until you rise to your full power, you're vulnerable. I will not wait so long to find, to taste you, only to lose you abruptly."

The sob won't stay down this time. It bubbles up my throat and tumbles out, my eyes brimming with tears that I can't hold back.

"One day," Hu continues, watching the tears trail down my cheeks. "You will be face to face with whatever saw fit to let you exist in this universe, Mena, and you will have to justify the space you've filled." He cups my cheek. *But you will not be alone there.*"

The dam breaks and I'm overcome with great wracking sobs that shake my body and make me curl in on myself. Hu stares at me for a moment, surprised, before I feel his arms hesitantly wrap around me. It's strange at first, as if he's never hugged another being, but when his arms come around me and I collapse into them completely, he wraps me so tightly it's as if he's trying to hold me together.

"I've got you," he whispers, his wings expanding to wrap around us further. "You're not alone, little void. I've got you."

And that's where we remain for hours, me cradled in a god's arms, sobbing about being chosen for a fate I did not choose, and when my tears dry up, he carries me to my bed, tucks me in, and presses a kiss to my forehead.

Devoid of tears, I feel lighter.

Like I emptied a cup that was overflowing.

When he tries to leave, I reach for him and so he stays.

I am not alone. I am not alone.

I am not alone.

46
MENA

I watch with dismay as the windows are covered with thick metal plates, the bars screwed into the brick and destroying it. This home has been in the Seagraves family for generations. Though I am a Seagraves, I was not born as one. It should not hurt me so to see the brick damaged, but I can't help but feel as if these precautions won't be much help at all.

After all, can one even keep angels out with metal bars?

"Be careful with that," I tell Otto as he picks up a vase to move it out of the way. He tosses it back and forth between his hands, uncaring that it's nearly two hundred years old.

He looks at it. "This ugly thing?"

"It's a few centuries old," I comment. "Irreplaceable."

He snorts. "My darling Mena, two centuries is hardly a blip. I, myself, have art from the medieval era."

My face twists. "Not all of us were lucky enough to be alive during it," I hiss. "That piece was a great sum of money."

Otto rolls his eyes. "You make me sound like an old man." But he dutifully puts the vase somewhere safe until they're finished placing the metal over the windows.

"If you are an old man, then I fear what my title is," Hu comments with a grin. Though the god alternates between helping and not, he always seems prepared to interject.

We're spending the day reinforcing every entry point of my home, closing up the windows, changing out the door, making sure there are no back entries we may have missed. My once beautiful and warm home now feels claustrophobic with each entry point covered. The need to escape is strong, but I dutifully help. After all, if I can avoid the angels getting into my home, I'd like to do that. If I never ran into one again, it would be too soon.

I pick up the stack of mail Mrs. Kingsley left for me to look through, flipping through invitations I plan to ignore. Most of them are for balls, hosted by gossipmongers who enjoy being a part of the gossip. After the Dutchess' party, the invitations flooded in, eager to see what's left of me. No doubt the Dutchess only added to the rumors by claiming I'm perfectly fine or stoking the rumors of my vampirism. I have no desire to cater to their curiosity.

The men around me are in various state of undress. Otto has forgone his normal suit and instead wears only his trousers, leaving his top half bare. It's a blessed sight watching him move, his rippling muscle shifting with the light as he helps hoist metal windows up singlehandedly. I had not realized just how strong each of them is. Athan appears to need a little more help, but Hu doesn't seem inclined to offer it.

"Why don't you take one of your elixirs?" Athan tells Henry. "I'm assuming Hyde is strong."

Henry frowns. "He is but—"

"Then we could use his help."

Henry hesitates and glances over at me. "I'd rather not."

Athan scowls. "Then what good are you? What are you even here for?"

Henry's face flushes in anger and embarrassment.

I feel the need to step in, to defend him. "If he doesn't want to shift, then that's his choice, reaper. Leave him be."

The gentle smile that pulls at Henry's lips helps me realize I've done something right, but he only shakes his head. "There's no need, Mena. He's right. If Hyde can help where I cannot, then perhaps I should allow him out." But there's hesitation on his face, as if he does not want to do so at all.

He pulls a small vial from his pocket. He always has one on hand, always prepared to need Hyde despite his desire not to change. I suppose it's best to be prepared than ill-prepared. I watch as he stares at the elixir for long seconds, great disdain on his face before he tips his head back, revealing the column of his throat as he swallows the elixir. He tucks the vial back away inside his breast pocket and smiles at me.

"See you soon."

He begins to morph, revealing the gray skin, the spikes, the sharp claws. When Hyde stands before me, he flashes me a grin. "Always a pleasure, butterfly. Allow me to showcase my strength and put the rest of these men to shame."

He picks up a window by himself and wiggles his eyebrows, drawing a soft laugh from my lips.

"I don't know why we're going through so much trouble," Otto grumbles as he strains with one of the windows. "We should just kill Mena four more times and hurry things along."

I scowl at the vampire. "Excuse you?"

"You'd have more power faster and be less mortal," Otto points out. "You'd be less vulnerable."

"That's a preposterous thing—"

"It won't work," Hu announces from where he inspects one of the metal windows for weaknesses.

Otto turns to him. "And why not?"

Hu meets his eyes and then looks over toward me with raised brows. "Why, because each death is tied to one of the seven deadly sins, of course. You mentioned reading the prophecy before. I thought you had understood that she cannot die without a sin being related. If she does so, then the death will be permanent."

We all stare at him in silence. His words sink into my mind and circulate around. The seven deadly sins. I remember the prophecy mentioning it but I had not realized...

"Why did you not mention that before?" I ask, keeping my voice level and calm.

He shrugs. "I thought you knew. Otto spoke the prophecy and it's very clear in the part he knows."

"How would we know?" Athan growls. "How could we have possibly known? It did not specify that without the sin attached, she would die permanently."

Hu laughs. "You seem to think you know everything else, reaper."

"Why, you idiotic—"

"Enough," I say, holding up my hand. "Regardless of when we're learning the information, we know it now."

"Mena's right," Hyde offers. "It also means the plan to kill her will not work."

"Thank everything for that," I grumble, turning away from the windows again to flick through the envelopes. I stop on a particularly thick cream colored one, take in the lettering before quickly popping the seal open.

"It seemed like a good idea," Otto huffs, returning to work. "Clearly not, but it's far better than you lot have thought of."

They continue talking as I scan the card inside the envelope, burgeoning excitement filling me. "It's time for the Derby!" I exclaim, forgetting myself for a moment and interrupting them.

They all turn to look at me in confusion, various expressions on their faces following the confusion, but it's Athan's I focus on most when his face twists with annoyance.

"We're not going," he declares, turning away.

"Says who?" I demand, holding up the invite. "I have never missed the Derby and don't intend to now. It's one of my favorite pastimes."

"It's dangerous to leave this house," Athan argues. "We're

certainly not going around so many people. Do you know how many of them could be angels in disguise?"

"I cannot remain sequestered in this house indefinitely," I counter. "That's preposterous—"

"You're not going!" the reaper yells. "And that's final!"

I narrow my eyes and cross my arms over my chest. "And how will you stop me?" I challenge.

"She'll have protection," Otto points out. "It's not as if she'll be alone."

Athan glances between all of us and scowls. "Fine. Get her killed before she ever reaches full power. Suit yourselves."

He disappears a moment later, leaving us to finish reinforcing the house without him. Who knew that reapers were so sensitive?

47
MENA

It takes hours to finish the work, but at least it goes by pleasantly once Athan leaves. He takes the perpetual thunder cloud over his head with him, leaving us to converse and laugh and genuinely enjoy each other's company. With the reaper gone, Hu actually helps more, lifting the grating with ease. The final task is replacing the front door, taking away the beautifully carved wooden one and replacing it with a heavy steel door instead. It's ugly and crass, but it will keep out a lot of creatures so I don't complain.

I wonder if it can keep out reapers.

"That should do it," Otto says as he dusts his hands off. "I'm not sure it'll stop everything, but there are certainly creatures who can't break through steel."

Hyde is checking the fastenings over and over again, making sure the bolts will hold. "It's best to make sure everything is proper, so our butterfly is not caught by surprise," he says when Hu looks at him curiously.

"Of course," Hu replies, but his smirk says he does not agree. I suppose in his eyes, the door is perfect because he had a hand in it.

Gods likely don't understand the imperfection that comes with humanity.

Otto glances at the large clock across from us and sighs. "It's about supper time, I think. We should go get cleaned up before we attend so Mrs. Kingsley doesn't sniff her nose at us." He smiles, clearly endeared by the older woman. I don't blame him. Mrs. Kingsley has a way with everyone, be they monster or man.

"Indeed," Hu offers, moving toward the stairs. "A hot soak in a salt bath will make me feel right again."

Otto tips his chin to me. "I'll see you at supper, Mena Mine." And then he too climbs the stairs, leaving Hyde and I to stand in the entryway.

Edward Hyde is a strange creature, monstrous in nature, but also caring. He's very much the devilish part of Henry, the forward and teasing side that he rarely shows otherwise. As he stands here looking at me, something flashes in his eyes that I do not understand.

"We have not had a moment together in a long time," I tell him with a smile. "It's nice to have been able to spend this time with you again."

"Yes," Hyde rasps. "Henry has been stubborn as of late, and I fear we may see each other less and less."

I frown. "What do you mean?"

He shrugs. "It's just a feeling I have, butterfly. I just mean we should enjoy each other while we can." At this his expression turns wicked. "Perhaps, you could come with me into the office? I have a tome there Henry meant to ask you about."

Tilting my head toward him in confusion, I shrug. Cleaning up can wait. After all, I had hardly done any work. With my lack of physical strength, I was not much help in the heavy lifting.

"Of course," I reply, immediately moving toward the office and stepping inside.

Hyde follows, closing the door behind us. "The book opened on the desk just there," he purrs.

I follow his direction and peer at the open book, frowning when I realize it's some book about cathedrals. There are sketches and words written in a different language that I can't read, but my cheeks flush as I remember what I'd done the last time cathedrals came up. "What does this have to do with anything?" I ask.

His warmth is suddenly behind me as he presses into my back, his body large and imposing as he reaches around me, caging me in. Hyde is much taller than I am where Henry and I are mostly the same height. In this form, Edward Hyde is nearly seven feet tall, his body lean and savage. As he leans down to plant his hands on either side of me, it forces me to lean with him until my body is over the book.

"Why are you blushing so, butterfly?" he purrs in my ear. "Is there a reason a cathedral stirs something inside you?"

"I. . ." I glance over my shoulder and find him there, his sharp teeth flashing with his green. Those light green eyes watch me, curious and full of sensuality. "Perhaps there is some meaning behind my flush."

"Tell me," he murmurs, leaning down to nuzzle at my neck.

My blush deepens and he chuckles against my skin, making me flood between my thighs. Oh, how Edward teases. Oh, how he's nothing but devilish seduction.

"Hu took me to one. Recently," I admit, my voice breathy with desire.

Hyde hums and slides his teeth along my shoulder, sending shivers through my body. "And what did he do to you there? Did he make you pray with feverish delight? Did he fuck you in front of God? Did he draw your sins from your lips?"

"Yes," I rasp. "To all."

His breath wavers. "Oh, how I wish to have seen that, butterfly. I bet you were magnificent."

His claw-tipped hand comes up and circles my throat even as he presses against my back. I don't protest as he tips my chin back, as he forces me to turn and peer into his eyes.

"I want you, butterfly," he groans. "I do not have much time, but I want you."

"Then have me," I tell him. "I want you, too."

His eyes flash dangerously. "Are you certain, Mena? I am not the delicate man that Henry is."

"Yes," I rasp, his claws still around my neck. "Yes, I'm certain."

He grins and his sharp teeth flash again. "Such a good little butterfly," he purrs. He reaches between us and begins to pull my skirts up over my hips. The slide of the fabric against my skin is torture as he slowly reveals my calves, my thighs, before tossing the material around my waist and revealing my nudity beneath. "You wear no undergarments today," he rasps. "How much did you hope for this outcome?"

"Every second of every day," I groan, pressing back against his hand as he trails it along my backside. "I've imagined you pinning me to the wall and licking me until I scream."

He groans in my ear. "I've imagined so many sweet things with you, butterfly. Like sinking into your sweet cunt and making you scream my name. Like tying you from your chandelier and fucking you while you remain suspended. I've imagined all of us taking you at once, your body buzzing with pleasure as we fuck you until you beg us to relent."

My flush spreads, my fingers curling into the wood of the desk that holds my weight. "I thought we were running out of time," I rasp, meeting his eyes. "What are you waiting for, Hyde?"

His hand squeezes my neck almost painfully. "I was giving you a chance to change your mind. How foolish of you not to do so."

His hand strokes between my thighs and he growls at the moisture he finds there. When I feel his tail curl around my ankle and yank, forcing me to spread my legs and my chest to drop against the desk, I grunt in surprise.

"I know I said I would never pin you," he groans. "But you must forgive me this one time as you look so pretty pinned this way."

I can feel his hardness, the shape of it different from any man's. I can't see him, but I can feel the bulbous, more rounded tip of him as he slides it along my wetness. His tail strokes up my leg, teasing as he does.

"Do you know who is about to fuck you?" he asks as he presses against my opening, holding himself still for a moment.

"Edward Hyde," I answer, turning my head to get a good sight of him standing over me from over my shoulder. "Edward Hyde is about to fuck me."

"Good butterfly," he growls, before pressing inside. He stretches me roughly, my wetness aiding his movement as he buries himself inside my wet cunt. I gasp and claw at the desk as he pins me down, as his body comes around me, his hands planted on either side of my body.

The tip of him is not the only thing shaped different. Small textured bumps ring his cock, driving me mad as he slides them against me, as he goes so deep, there's a bite of pain. He moans above me, his body moving slow as he works his way inside, as he struggles not to hurt me.

I gasp and moan as he moves, my nails leaving small rivers in the wood.

He pauses above me. "We have not much time, Mena. Already I can feel Henry—"

"Fuck me," I growl, pushing back against him. "Paint me with your claim before you leave."

He snarls above me. "You seduce my soul until it moans your name, butterfly, so I will do the same to you." He pulls back, stroking outward until only the tip remains. "Now scream so the others know my claim."

He slams back inside me so brutally, I can't help but scream out, my nails digging into the wood of the desk with brutal savagery. His cock strokes inside me, claiming me just as I asked, his claws leaving larger gouges in the wood beside my own. He leans down and bites at my shoulders even as he continues to fuck me with brutal strength. The desk jumps forward, scrapping against the floor with each powerful thrust, with each of my screams of pleasure. His claws come down over my hands, truly pinning me beneath him as he holds me hostage to his pleasure.

And then I feel his tail.

"Tell me, butterfly," he purrs. "How does it feel to have such powerful monsters at your beck and call?"

I gasp as he suddenly wrenches my head back by grasping a fist full of my hair. Pins scatter across the desk as he yanks me up until my back aches.

"Like redemption," I gasp between cries. "Like feverish redemption."

He jerks out of me so suddenly, I mew in protest, only to find him jerking me around and shoving me back on the desk. He comes over me, his cock finding my entrance before he thrusts inside again. I throw my head back, my elbows braced on the desk as he fucks me so hard, I see stars.

In this position, there's no mistaking who I'm fucking, this monster who lives inside Henry, who is Henry in many ways. Hyde is a part of him, a brutal part, but a part nonetheless.

He leans down and captures my lips, my tongue dancing along his sharp teeth as he sweeps inside mine. "You taste like moonlight," he says against my lips. "You belong to us, butterfly."

"Yes," I rasp, my body a live wire beneath him.

And then I feel his tail trailing along my backside, stroking there, temptation and sin and all the taboos of this realm. My eyes pop wide as he strokes my back entrance while he fucks me on top of this desk.

"Don't worry, butterfly," he breathes. "You are ours in every way."

And then his tail presses at my back entrance, making my eyes roll back in my head with the overwhelming sensations. I collapse backward, giving him better access, and he snarls his approval as he jerks my legs up and throws them around him. His hand cups my breast and molds them, twists them, and I suddenly can't stop the wave that crashes around me. I scream my pleasure as he fucks me, his cock and his tail inside me, his claws tweaking my nipple. My cunt clamps around him, drawing a savage sound from his throat even as he fucks me through my release.

"Again," he growls, ramping me up yet again. "Come for us again. Show Henry how sweet you are as you scream your release."

My body builds back up quickly, my legs shaking as Hyde fucks me with ruthless abandon. I'm convulsing on the desktop, fighting my trembling as he begins to slam inside me with brutal strikes. I reach up and grasp at his horns, tugging him down to kiss me. He snarls against me lips and nips at them.

"You're worth every sin, butterfly," he snarls. "Every prison, every fight, everything." He leans back, his eyes meeting mine. "And if this is the last time we have this, I want you to remember me. I want you to know that you've had my heart since the first moment we met."

I blink at the earnest words, want to ask him what he means, but his thrusts grow more forceful and we're both crying out our pleasure together, my body shaking with another orgasm while his warmth coats my insides. His tail pulls out of me first, and then he steps away.

"Edward," I muse, panting on the desk, reaching for him. "Don't go."

"My deepest apologies, butterfly," he groans as he steps backward. "I am out of time."

When I look over at him, he starts to fade slowly, his eyes bright on mine. "I'll remember you," I tell him. "How could I not?"

He smiles. "Just as I could never not love you. . . butterfly."

And then he transforms completely and Henry stands in his place, his face flushed in arousal and embarrassment. He immediately turns away to preserve my modesty despite what he likely just witnessed looking through Hyde's eyes.

"You don't have to look away," I murmur, sitting up on the desk.

Henry clears his throat. "I, um. . ." He looks down at where his arm falls away, his prosthetic on the other side of the room where he'd taken it off before taking his elixir. "I'll leave you to dress." He starts to leave, heading for the door.

"Henry," I call, and he freezes. "You do not have to fear the monster inside you. He's less a monster than most humans."

He does not turn, but I hear his words clearly. "But he's still my monster all the same."

He leaves without a backward glance, and I'm left with the trembling between my thighs as a reminder of what I'd just done, of what Hyde had said.

I could never not love you.

And what's more, I've started to love both of them, too.

48
MENA

The Derby invitation had sat in the pile for a week before I'd seen it, so the actual event came quickly. Within a few days, we were preparing ourselves for it, making sure everything was in order, and getting the carriage ready. While the trip is a bit longer than I prefer, it's worth it for the annual derby. I love the event, the horses all lined up, the fashion that is worn. It's my favorite event of the year.

Everyone shows up to the derby, whether to cheer on their favorite horse, to gamble, or to share the latest gossip. Everyone comes to the derby, no matter their class. We are simply separated as needed, an action that always bothers me, but one I can do nothing about. Still, it's an enjoyable affair for all.

As we arrive, I take in the sights as I step out of the carriage in my day dress and large derby hat. It covers my face, shielding it from the spurts of sunshine and adding a sense of fashion I enjoy. The large feathers on the top of it are dramatic and colorful. If I could wear a hat every day, I would.

Otto is equally as impressively dressed as I am, his own top hat sporting a throng of feathers that matches my own. Despite it being far from men's fashion, it works well for him, and no one seems to mind that he's gone above and beyond. No doubt the rumor of his royalty has spread, and no one would dare question a king. Henry is wearing as simple of a suit as possible, pieces he could get away with not wearing left at home. He wears no hat because he claims they make his head ache. Hu is wearing a suit that looks like the latest fashion out of France. The waistcoat he wears flashes with green and gold, small jewels embedded in the buttons that catch eyes as we walk.

Athan did not come.

The reaper has been distant since his outburst and has preferred to spend more time tending to his duties than spending time with the rest of us. I don't blame him—he has a job to do—but it would be nice to speak to him. I hadn't meant to cause trouble. I just thought we all needed a day out regardless of the danger.

After all, if I'm holed up in my house and no one knows I'm alive, then am I really living?

As we step inside the gates, I'm immediately approached by people wanting to get the latest gossip. A few ask about the incident at the Dutchess' home. Some ask about the men I came here with, gushing over Otto and Hu and assuming Henry is simply there as my servant. Before I can get offended for him, he assures me he prefers the disinterest to them fawning all over him. For the most part, it's normal socializing even if I distaste it.

Until Mr. Radcliff appears.

I turn away, hoping to escape his notice, but my way is blocked by others conversing with Hu and Otto, trying to impress them. I turn back, looking for another way out, only to realize he's already seen me. His eyes brighten in his wrinkled face, and he jauntily makes his way toward me despite the grimace on my face.

"What's the matter?" Henry whispers.

"Just a rather distasteful man headed my way," I admit before I have to plaster a smile to my face. "Mr. Radcliff. How lovely to see you again."

The older gentleman preens under my false attention. He's a few inches shorter than me, but you could never tell him that. His height is a disparaging fact he'd rather no one mention. He's wearing a suit that's not quite right, as if he'd rushed whoever helped dress him. Though he comes from old money, his estate has dwindled abruptly due to his gambling addiction as of late.

Which is where his interest comes in for me.

When Walter died, Mr. Radcliff immediately came swooping in, attempting to woo me in my time of mourning. I had still been wearing black at the time. Though I had been clear I had no interest, he has not stopped trying. Even when I inherited all of Walter's business ventures, he thought himself persuasive enough to convince me to give it all away because "a woman shouldn't frustrate herself with such things." I've had a distaste for the man since, preferring to have little to do with him. Of course, I can't avoid him forever when we frequent the same events.

"Miss Seagraves! I was hoping to run into you today. I've heard such mad things about you as of—"

"All rumors and exaggerations," I quickly interject. "You know how high society loves drama."

"Of course. Of course," he purrs, reaching forward to touch my elbow. I pull back, but he doesn't seem to notice, wrapping his grubby fingers around it all the same. "I do hope you've changed your mind about my invitation."

"I have not," I say, giving no room for him to mistake my rebuff as anything else. "I hope you understand."

Mr. Radcliff guffaws and waves away my words. "A woman as pretty as you should not have to work herself to death. You should be placed on a pedestal for all to see."

"I prefer to be valued for more than my appearance," I counter. "My intelligence and business savviness are important to me."

"But you're a woman! You should be embroidering and tending to children. Not dealing with businessmen. It's unbecoming, Miss

Seagraves. Which is why it is my duty to offer my hand, to court you and take over so that you can relax in comfort—"

"Mr. Radcliff," I interrupt, my voice harsh. "I do not, nor will I ever, have intentions of marrying you."

Mr. Radcliff was not the only vulture to swoop in when Walter died, but he is the most persistent. Many of the other men have decided I have no desire to marry, content to allow me to remain a widow despite their annoyance that the fortune is unused in their minds. If I were to marry, all of that would transfer over to the husband, but why would I give away the freedom Walter had left me with? They genuinely believe women so stupid.

Mr. Radcliff's face reddens. "I really must insist, Miss Seagraves—"

"The lady said she's not interested," Henry interrupts, stepping up to my side, his expression hard. In his eyes, I see Hyde flicker in preparation.

"She has her escorts for the day," Otto adds from my other side. "Do you even have a title?"

Mr. Radcliff flounders. "A title does not make a man—"

"But it helps, does it not?" Otto purrs. He leans in. "I'm a king, you silly little fool. Do you think Miss Seagraves would bother herself with a peasant when she could have a king?"

Mr. Radcliff turns bright red. I've never seen him such a peculiar shade. "Of course." He clears his throat and bows toward me. "Miss Seagraves."

And then he scurries off like the rat he is.

Sighing, I turn to Otto. "I've been trying to get rid of that man for years. While I don't condone your methods, I must say they were effective."

Otto grins. "What can I say? I have a way of staking my claim." He offers his elbow. "Should we find our way into our seats?"

"Yes, and if he returns, I will finish the job," Hu declares with a wink.

"I don't want him to die," I clarify.

His eyes meet mine. "Who said anything about killing him, little void?"

I shrug. "I just thought I should put that into the universe considering the four of you."

"Three," Otto corrects. "The reaper is off doing whatever reapers do."

"Yes, well. . ." I let the word linger because I'm not sure what to say. Athan has been avoiding me and despite my attempts to bridge the gap, he has no current interest in doing so. I've left him to his own devices for now, not sure how to mend things between us.

Together, the four of us make our way to our seats in the protected box. Those without class are left to sit further down the track in seats not shaded by the sun. Separate. Always apart. I can't help but wonder if I should go sit with them instead to make a statement, but I suspect I would not be welcomed in their domain. I cannot bring them into mine. The guards at our boxes would never allow it.

"Which horse are you betting on?" Henry asks, looking over the jokey names.

I flick my eyes over the options before pointing to one in particular.

"The Morningstar," Hu comments. "How interesting. Would he not be destined to fall?"

"*She* is an underdog. I've been watching her the entire season and she has remained solid enough to make it to this point, but she's holding back. This is the race to let out all she has."

"Ah, so you know what you're doing then," Otto says with a grin. "A trait I enjoy. Very well. You shall pick the underdog and I shall bid on the favored to win. Let us see who does better."

When the booker comes around, we both lay our bets. The bookie looks at me strangely when I place mine, but I only smile and feign the dense enjoyment of a woman. He takes my bet, no doubt assuming it's money I'm going to lose.

When the jockeys line up, I lean forward, watching The Morningstar closely. She's in pristine condition this morning, her chestnut coat gleaming in the pale sunshine. She looks perfect and eager, a good quality in a racehorse.

The horn blows and the gates open, each horse springing forward, their jockeys pushing them forward, their training coming in handy now. Morningstar's jockey is new, mostly untested, and it's only as she runs that I realize the reason Morningstar hasn't fully won is because he doesn't know the limits of her body. He's playing it safe. As he slips back a few positions, I stand on my feet. Those around me follow, the excitement bringing everyone up.

"Come on," I murmur, watching closely. "You can do it."

But the jockey is holding safe and steady. Horses don't win by being safe. They win by being legends.

I glance over at the others, take in their excitement and stances, and then focus on the jockey with narrowed eyes. Morningstar could win if she had a better jockey. I'm going to give that to her. I feel the powers in my chest, coax them out, and think about the jockey being less afraid, less hesitant. I see the moment it enters him. They round the track and the jockey's face shadows. With a fierce hit, he encourages Morningstar faster.

I scream in excitement as they near the finish line, as she passes third place, second place, first place, and takes the lead.

"Go, Morningstar, Go!" I shout.

The gazes I feel on me from my men don't dissuade me as I cheer her on. She runs full tilt, her jockey giving her all she's got, until she passes the finish line and claims the title. I cheer with the rest of the crowd, but when I turn to Otto, his eyes flash.

"That was cheating, Mena Mine."

"Was it?" I ask, tilting my head. "Or did I simply encourage the potential?"

"A fine line you walk," he answers, gesturing with his chin toward the course. "And a risk you took. She may have won, but she'll never win again."

I follow his gaze and gasp at the very clear limp Morningstar now carries herself with. Her jockey hurries to climb from her and give her relief, his horror clear on his face. He'll never know it was me who made him push her. He'll blame herself.

"Horses who can't race get put to death," Henry says solemnly. "They have no more use—"

"Stop," I growl. "I realize now the mistake I made." I grit my teeth. "But at least there's something to be done about it."

I slip past them and down to the field, searching for Morningstar and her jockey. They're surrounded by people congratulating him despite the jockey trying to get Morningstar through. They make it into the stables after a lot of pushing. I move to follow before being stopped by the guard.

"I'm sorry, miss. Jockeys and horses only."

"Please," I tell him, pulling coin from my pocket. "I'll be out quickly."

He stares at the coin for a moment before taking them and gesturing me through. I look through the stables until I find the one I search for.

"I don't know what came over me," the jockey says to the horse doctor. "One moment, I was being careful and the next we were running full tilt. I never meant to hurt her."

"These things happen," the doctor says, checking out her foot. "Unfortunately, Morningstar will likely be lame. I suggest it best to put her out of her misery. It'll never heal properly."

"I'm sorry to interrupt," I declare, making them both jump as I appear. "If you're to dispose of Morningstar, I would like to purchase her."

The jockey stands up and frowns. "Why?"

Because I've caused her predicament. Because I'm evil. Because I'm a terrible, horrible person.

"Because she's beautiful, and she worked hard for her win. She deserves a life of comfort now, not to be sent to the factory." The jockey hesitates and I pull notes from my purse. "I promise she will be well taken care of."

"You're making a poor investment, miss," the doctor says with a shake of his head. "Women. You're all bleeding hearts."

But the jockey doesn't hold the same disdain. "You promise she'll live comfortably?"

"As comfortable as a horse can be," I promise. "The best care, the best feed, and the best stable. When she's healed, I'll make sure she has a field to run in."

"Then I will not take your money," he says, patting her neck. "I never meant to hurt her—"

"I don't think she would ever blame you," I tell him, my guilt clawing at my throat. "And you'll always be welcome to come visit her. You're a promising jockey. You both made history today, winning with the underdog."

He smiles. "We did, didn't we?"

When I leave him with my information and where to bring Morningstar to, I find the others waiting outside the stables for me. "We have a new horse," I declare. "She'll have the best of everything."

Otto studies me. "And how does your conscience feel?"

I hesitate. "Dirty," I finally admit. "Guilty."

He nods. "It doesn't go away, Mena. Remember this the next time you wish to use your power. Each one will stain you until you're no longer able to remember your morals, until your hands drip with blood."

Nodding in understanding, I go to move past them, but grunt in pain before I can do so. I look down at my hand in confusion, thinking I perhaps got stung by a bee too silly to realize I'm no flower. Instead of an insect, though, I see black lines etching themselves into the back of my hand. I grimace in pain with each stroke, until I'm gasping with it, until Otto takes my hand and stares in horror at what the lines make.

49
MENA

The lines are black and thin as they streak across my hand. With each fill of ink, pain explodes as if the lines are etched directly into my skin like a tattoo. They crisscross and streak back and forth, forming a symbol I've never seen before. It doesn't make sense to my mind, but I know it can't be good. I haven't had much good lately when it comes to surprises. When the pain ebbs away and leaves me staring at an intricate design on the back of my hand, I frown at it, unsure what to think. My initial thought is to panic, but I do my best to keep it held back.

"What does that mean?" Henry asks, staring at the mark curiously.

Hu leans over to get a better look and starts laughing. "Party tricks, nothing more."

"I hardly think it's a party trick," Otto growls. "Mena is not immortal like you are, not to withstand a curse. Or did you forget that fact?"

Hu blinks at Otto's words and stops laughing, as if only realizing now that Otto is correct. Never mind the fact that I'm supposed to be immortal at some point—I can't focus on that too long or I'll go mad

—but I have a curse on me now? What more can I encounter while going through this? My life has become unbearably strange and unpredictable and I'm not sure if I prefer it or my old boring version.

"If it's a curse, what does it do?" I ask, studying the mark. Whatever it speaks of, it isn't in any language I know, but I can't help feeling as if it's demonic.

"We won't know until that mark lights up like a beacon," Otto replies, taking my hand to study the mark closer. "Curses can do anything from tracking you to giving you bad luck to... killing you."

My face pales. "What?"

"But I may know someone who can help!" he adds before I can let my panic take over completely.

I'm trying my best to remain level-headed, but I'm finding it more and more difficult to do with each passing moment. It's a new problem every waking moment. When will I be able to stop and catch my breath? Am I doomed to live in this stressful bubble for the rest of my life? Was my birth ultimately a curse?

Hands are on my cheeks a second later, dragging my mind away from the cliff I find myself metaphorically standing on. Otto's caramel eyes meet mine, crash into mine until all I see are the rich brown his speaks of, like the sweetest of confections, like the brightness of light whiskey.

"Don't panic," Otto murmurs as he holds my face. "This is nothing in the grand scheme of things."

"What if it kills me?" I rasp.

"It will not," he promises.

"How can you possibly know?" I ask, reaching up to circle his wrists, grounding myself further. "How could you ever know something like that?"

Otto sighs. "You won't like the answer."

"Tell me anyway."

His hands are still clamped around my face, comforting me with his coolness. Every part of me demands I brace myself for his words despite not knowing what they'll be. So I do just that, uncaring about those who may be watching this improper exchange.

"The witches won't kill you," he murmurs. "Because they would rather capture and use you. Likely, the curse will be something that may weaken you or make you vulnerable long enough for them to swoop in and steal you away."

I blink, take a deep breath. "Okay," I rasp. "Okay. That's not so bad. I'm not alone."

"Exactly," he nods, pride flickering in his eyes. "You're not alone in this."

"I'm not alone," I repeat and then I continue to repeat it in my mind until I believe the words, until I know I'm truly not alone and can handle this. "Okay. We can go find this person who will help now."

Henry tilts his head. "Are you certain? We can wait—"

"No, I'd prefer not to leave this mark on me. Especially since we don't know what it'll do. We tend to it now and dismiss it," I counter, straightening further. Otto finally releases my face and offers his elbow.

"You're not alone," he says again, covering my hand with his once I tuck my fingers into the crook of his elbow.

I take a deep breath and repeat it like a mantra. "I am not alone."

Not anymore.

We're in the carriage heading toward the less quaint side of London, the fog rolling in as it often does in the evening when the sun is no longer strong enough to chase it away, if it ever came out to begin with. I'm seated between Otto and Hu, both of them touching me with small intimate touches that drive me mad and ground me at the same time. Henry sits across from us, his nose in his journal as he goes over some sort of formula. It's a comfortable ride even if we head toward the side of London I often stay away from. Not because of the people, but because of the aura that surrounds it.

The streets here are dirty and rough, the cobblestones left in disrepair by the city. These types of roads are known to claim a carriage wheel or two, and I couldn't imagine what they would do to the new automobiles I've seen start driving the streets. They're rare, but they must stay away from this side of the city or else they would destroy their shiny new wheels.

Rats run the edges of the street out in the open and beggars are plentiful here. Small children with grime on their faces hold out their hands for change, beg for even a penny to utilize. The coal smoke is strong here, the air choked with it. The factories must be close by.

"This is where you know someone?" I ask curiously, staring out the window. The carriage stands out here, drawing attention I'd prefer not to draw. We should have chosen a different means of transportation, but I hadn't thought that far ahead.

"Yes," Otto replies. "She prefers to stay away from the better part of town. She's had bad experiences from what I gather."

Athan pops into existence before me and I nearly screech at the sudden appearance of him, flailing in my seat and pressing myself against Otto in surprise. The reaper stares at me with no emotion despite my outburst.

"I went to the house, but you lot weren't there," he offers instead of a greeting. "Why are you in this part of London?"

"We've had a situation," Otto growls. "Not that you care to know."

Athan raises his brow. "A situation?" When no one answers him, he turns toward Henry.

Henry's shakes his head. "Mena's been cursed by the witches. We're visiting a friend of Otto's who can help."

Athan's head snaps toward me, his eyes searching my body until they land on the mark on the back of my hand. "I assume you're going to the bruja?"

"Bruja?" I ask, glancing at Otto uncertainly. "What does that mean?"

"She's another kind of witch," Otto nods. "She's not a coven witch like the others. She keeps to herself and does nothing but help women. If anyone can help us remove the curse, it'll be her."

"I agree," Athan adds. "It's a good plan."

"Good thing none of us need your approval," Otto sneers and looks away, back out the window. "We're here. Try not to look too suspicious."

But we're all still dressed in our derby clothing. Before I climb out, I quickly unpin the hat and toss it to the seat across from me, making sure my hair is still in place before I take the hand Hu offers. He helps me from the carriage and we turn to face Otto.

"Now where?" I ask, studying the buildings around us. Most are five stories tall or shorter, too many people clustered around outside. I'm willing to bet the inside of the buildings are overpacked as well, forcing people to live in substandard housing. If there are so many rats on the streets, I can't imagine how many there are inside.

Otto leads us all inside the nearest building. I'm correct about the state of the inside. People cluster the stairs, some of them sleeping there rather than in an apartment. The stairs are dirty, covered in old newspapers and smelling of filth. Hollow desperate eyes look toward us as we step inside, as we begin to climb the stairs slowly, attempting to avoid those clustered there. The entire building smells like feces and mold, and certainly is not suitable for living, and here these people are with no choice.

No one says a word as we travel to the top floor. Most of them barely look at us as we climb the stairs, their minds somewhere else.

"Opium," Henry offers. "I've seen its effects often."

I don't blame them for their desperate attempts to escape reality. This place would make even a criminal wrinkle his nose.

There are no people sitting on the fifth floor. They don't sit along the stairway that leads to it and none reside on the landing. As if they completely avoid it.

"Witches, no matter the era, make people uncomfortable," Athan offers from behind me. "This one is no different."

I hesitate. "Should we be doing this?"

In all my years, I never thought to seek out the help of a witch and while I've never met one, I'd been raised that witches are bad. I don't think they're all inherently bad, as most people aren't, but I've only had experience with the ones attacking me. Perhaps I'm wrong and all witches are bad though.

"If we want to remove the curse, we have no other option," Otto reminds me. "We don't want to wait around to see what it causes."

I nod and continue forward until we're standing before a black door. There used to be metal numbers on it, marking it as a particular apartment, but those are long gone, the outlines of them the only remnants. Someone had scratched the word "witch" into the paint. Another had scratched in the words "Hell waits for you." They weren't very creative in their insults it seems.

Otto raises his hand to knock but before his knuckles can touch the wood, the door swings open, revealing a young woman.

My brows shoot up. I expected a gnarled old woman, not this young lady closer to my age. There's not even a single wrinkle on her face.

"All witches start young, just as you do," she says to me, her eyes bright with clarity. "I've been expecting you, Philomena. Come in."

I immediately shut down my thoughts, or try to. I've been unsuccessful in hiding them from Hu, but having a stranger read them is even worse.

And yet Hu was a stranger a few short weeks ago.

"You say you were expecting us?" I ask as we follow her inside and close the door behind us. The apartment is small, and though the outside of the building is miserable, the inside of her apartment is anything but. It's clean and free of the scents of filth. Instead, some sort of incense burns and fills the room with the scents of vanilla and cinnamon. The hardwood floor is old but intact, beautiful woven rugs covering them in certain places. It's quaint but comfortable. There are no rats here.

"Yes, of course. It's easy to sense people of your power coming," she replies, her heavy accent speaking of a land across the Atlantic Ocean. I've never met someone from Central or South America, but she looks as beautiful as I imagine her country is. Like the apartment, she's well put together. Her clothes are free of stains and tears, built for comfort rather than appearance. Ink runs along her skin, depicting everything from ravens to symbols to a picture of cat. When a cat with the same look appears at my feet and weaves between my legs, I realize it's a portrait.

"Hello, sweet hunter," I tell the cat, leaning down to run my hand along her back. She arches happily, meows, and takes off back to wherever she hides. To the woman, I say, "People of our power?"

She smiles, her eyes crinkling. "Do not play coy, Philomena Seagraves. You came here for a reason. I imagine it is important, no?"

"What exactly do you know about us?" Otto asks curiously.

"Not as much as you think I do," she answers with a smile. "There are limits. I understand that each of you carries something within you, but I do not know what. Miss Seagraves here is awakening, but I know nothing else."

We all exchange glances. I think to tell her about my predicament, so she understands, but when Athan shakes his head just slightly, I clamp my lips shut. I don't know who to trust in this world any longer, but I feel as if I can trust the four men who have been with me since this all started.

"I've been cursed apparently," I say instead, holding my hand out toward the woman. "We thought you could help me—"

"You can call me Ynez," she replies, her eyes bright. "Now, let me get a good look at that curse."

I hold my hand out to her, and she wraps her fingers around mine. There's a spark at her touch, where her skin touches mine, and I suck in a breath as she traces the lines.

"Yes, a desperate curse indeed. It is not even sewn properly and should be easy to break." She releases my hand, and I can breathe again, as if her touch stole the air in my lungs. "About the payment—"

"We will pay whatever you're asking," I tell her. "Just please remove it."

Her eyes brighten further. "Of course. Let's say twenty pounds?"

Otto guffaws at the price. "Twenty pounds? Why, that's ridiculous for a small curse—"

"It is not small," she interrupts. "And I take on risks for removing it. I will be at the mercy of Miss Seagraves' power to remove the curse. Are you willing to promise me that will be safe?"

Otto clamps his mouth shut. The truth is none of us know the true extent of what I am so to promise safety when we have no idea if it's true or not would be barbaric.

"Twenty pounds is suitable," I reply, tilting up my chin. "I shall transfer the coin as soon as we're finished here."

"I shall take your word for it as you're a lady of worth," Ynez offers before nodding. "I will prepare the table. Please, have a seat. This will take a few minutes to gather the supplies."

I don't sit, mostly because of the anxious energy in my heart, but Otto and Henry do. Where Henry sits stiffly so as not to be rude, Otto completely makes himself at home, lounging like a languid cat on her sofa. The feline in the room appears again to curl up on his lap, insisting he pet her. Hu and Athan remain standing with me, their eyes taking in the room.

We're silent for the five minutes it takes Ynez to gather her ingredients and when she calls us to a table set to the side, we oblige her. Small bottles are scattered across the top and I watch as she begins to add bits of each into a small bowl. She murmurs under her breath, words I cannot hear or understand, as she works.

"A drop of your blood is needed," Ynez tells me, holding out her hand for mine. I hesitate, only briefly, before settling my hand in hers. She pricks my fingers before I can even flinch and squeezes a drop out into the bowl. "Good. Now I will mix and then spread it over the mark and wrap it. Then I will speak some necessary words."

The paste she makes is cold as she spreads it across the back of my hand. She wraps it with an old cloth and tightens it, so tight it nearly makes me wince. Only when she's finished does she close her eyes and hold my hand in both of hers. Her lips begin to move, speaking words not in English, rapidly dropping them. With each word, there comes a tingle in my hand that grows with her voice level, increasing until I'm grimacing in pain.

Her head wrenches back so violently, I scream. I try to jerk my hand from hers, but I can't, her fingers so tight on mine, they're nearly bone crushing. A god-awful sound begins spilling from her lips, as if she can't breathe and breathes too much at the same time.

"What's happening?" I cry, jerking at my hand. "What's wrong with her?"

Athan snarls and reaches for my hand, trying to free me, but even he can't remove her hands. "This isn't what happens!"

Henry curses under his breath and tries to help, but what can he do?

The air in the apartment suddenly picks up and swirls around us, pulling my hair from its style, twisting my skirts around my legs, throwing papers and leaves she'd had collected in a bowl into the air. It batters against me like a hurricane, demanding I let it in, demanding I release it, until I have to narrow my eyes to sustain looking at the woman holding onto my hand. Phantoms suddenly tumble in through the walls, moaning in agony, desperate to be heard, drawn by the power Ynez holds in her hands.

Ynez' head snaps forward again, her eyes milky white, her fingers tight on my arm. "Lilith. Goddess of the Night. The Evening Star. Mother of Monsters and Demons. Devil. Whore. Demon. Sin. Temptation. Reckoning. You've come here knowing what you are!" Her voice sounds like many, as if there are hundreds speaking all at once. "The world will tremble when the Mother of Monsters walks among it. Death will follow in her wake. The Garden of Eden was only the beginning. Death sits beside you, stands with you. Death is your lover, just as the four monsters around you are. Heed these words, Destroyer." She makes a screeching sound and I wish I could cover my ears. "You will destroy everything if you allow the power to claim your soul."

The wind suddenly drops. The white in Ynez' eyes clears, and she stares back at me with her bright violet eyes. They widen and she gasps, snatching her hands back from me. The mark on the back of my hand is gone—I can feel it— but the apartment is a mess now.

"You came into my home, knowing what you are," she snaps, her lips peeling back to bare her teeth. "How dare you!"

"I. . ." What does one say to that? "I didn't know—"

"Leave," she hisses, pointing to the door. "You have tainted my home with your calling. Never come here again!"

She practically shoves us out the door, one after the other. She makes sure I'm out last, and I turn to apologize, but before I can, the door slams shut in our faces.

"My apologies," I say anyways, looking down at my clean hand. "I didn't know."

When it's time to send payment, I double it, because I don't know what I've actually done, but it must be bad. Because the money comes back, returned, along with a note saying, "I want nothing you've touched."

My chest squeezes. What am I that I make such a powerful woman afraid?

What true monster I must become at the end of this. . .

50
ATHAN

"Are you done playing dress up and derby racing?" I snarl the moment we return to Mena's house. "This is ridiculous! I told you to stay home and you insisted."

"I realize my mistake, but you have no need to shout," Mena replies, exhaustion in her shoulders as she follows us inside.

The carriage ride had been a long tense one, the time spent looking anywhere but at each other. We'd been foolish to involve the bruja, but there'd been no other option. We did what we had to do.

"I have every reason to shout," I growl. "We don't know what that curse was for. It could have been a tracking spell or something worse. Why must you—"

"Enough," Mena snarls. "You've made your thoughts achingly clear. I've heard enough now."

"Then perhaps you'll have learned to stay in this house where you're safe."

Anger flickers across her face, fury the likes I've not seen from her. "I will not hide in my home like a mouse!" she shouts back.

"You did before!" I spit. "You hid in your house for a week the first time like a damaged, broken little girl!"

"Shut up!"

"You're so hellbent on being normal that you're going to end up ruining everything, you spoiled brat! You're not worthy of the powers you carry—"

"Fuck you!" she spits, shocking me into silence.

None of us had heard Mrs. Kingsley come in, but we all hear the crash of the tray she'd been carrying as it shatters against the tile. Her eyes are wide as they focus on Mena.

"Mena!" She cries, chastising her for the curse.

Jekyll flushes at the word and Otto mostly looks surprised. Only Hu seems unmoved as always.

"Now look what you did," Otto grunts. "You've reduced a lady to swearing with your idiocy and insults."

"I don't care," I growl and take a step away from Mena. "This is getting ridiculous and I have a job to do."

I don't warn them. I don't ask for permission. I simply disappear, reaching for the call of yet another death, letting it draw me to it like a moth to a flame, until I'm standing before an older woman staring down at her body forlornly. When she sees me, she blinks.

"No one even came to check on me," she croaks. "It's been hours since I sent the telegram."

I hold out my hand for her. "Come. This world is cruel and terrible. You do not want to stay here."

"But what if they never find me? What if they never loved me?"

My chest squeezes. "It matters not. You lived your best. Let your soul be free from worries and stress, and I'll lead your soul to freedom."

"Freedom?" she asks, her eyes brightening. "That does sound nice."

She looks down at her body one more time, sadness in her eyes, before she reaches out and takes my hand. We drop, one reaper and one soul that didn't deserve the neglect she suffered.

The Underworld awaits us all.

51
MENA

Athan is gone yet again, off to brood with his misplaced anger and to fulfill his reaper duties. I'm honestly starting to wonder why he even comes back each time. In the beginning, he seemed interested in me, curious as to what I am, and made comments about courting me, but now that we know everything, he's been withdrawn and angry, as if he can do nothing but hate me. I don't understand and the more I attempt to, the more I have to put the thought out of my mind.

The reaper is just insane. That's the only excuse I can fathom.

"I wouldn't let him get to you," Henry murmurs.

The both of us are standing at the doorway to my rooms. Since he had been going to his to check on some of his experiments, he had offered to escort me up. Now, after reaching the door, I don't really know what to say.

"I'm trying not to," I admit with a sigh. "I just don't understand what he wants from me."

"Perhaps you should start thinking of what you want from him, rather than wondering what he could want from you," Henry offers with a shrug. "I don't pretend to know anything about reapers or this world I've suddenly found myself in, but ultimately, you choose to surround yourself with whomever you please. If you don't want him here, then send him away."

I furrow my brow. "He doesn't seem the type to listen."

Henry winces. "You're not wrong, I'm afraid." He glances toward his room. "I'll leave you to your business."

"You could stay," I rush out, and when his eyes meet mine, I flush. "I mean, I would like it, if you joined me."

"For tea?" he asks, his own brows furrowing in confusion. "Is Mrs. Kingsley bringing up a tray?"

I can't help the laugh that slips out at his cluelessness. "No, not for tea, Henry." I offer my hand. "I don't particularly want to be alone right now. Could you perhaps join me?"

He glances at my hand and hesitates. "I suspect the others might be better company."

"I'm not asking for their company. I'm asking for yours." I allow my hand to linger in the air for three seconds, and when he doesn't reach out, I start to drop it. "However, if you're too busy—"

"No," he rasps. "No, I'm not too busy. I just. . ."

When he doesn't explain further, I dip my chin. "I see."

"No," he growls. "No, you don't." He grasps a chunk of his hair and pulls in frustration. "How could you? You are beautiful, and strong, and amazing. If you ask me if I love you, I would ask how could I not have fallen in love the moment you stepped into my life? I'm terrified of the love I have for you, Mena, because I know it will ruin me and I know that I will let it. But I am not some powerful reaper, or a vampire king, or a god. I'm just a doctor playing pretend, a scientist who failed and broke himself. You should not care for me. You should not want to spend time with me. You should not think of me at all. My hands are covered in the blood of my failures, and here you stand, pristine, beautiful, and everything I've never deserved."

His words strike me. They slam into my chest and unmake me before stitching me back together again. "Henry—"

"I am a monster," he spits. "I carry a monster inside me, and I walk with him in my mind. There is no separation, not really. You should send me away, but if you do not, I will remain here to help because even that space is enough to soothe me."

I reach for him, and though he flinches, he doesn't pull away when I cup his jaw. "Henry," I whisper. "You are no more a monster than I am a queen. You speak of love as if I could never return the emotion." I lean in and press a gentle kiss to his lips, a chaste one, one that makes his breath wheeze from his chest. "I have loved you since you stayed with me in the hospital bed, when you took kindness on a woman speaking insanity. I saw the goodness in you then. I see the goodness in you now."

He shakes his head. "I am not good. It was not goodness. Any person would have done the same. That does not make me special."

"You're wrong," I reply. "Most would have turned me away. Many would have locked the door behind me. But that doesn't matter. I did not fall in love with you for your kindness. I fell in love with you for who you are, the intelligence in your eyes, the way you get so lost in your research the world falls away, the way you glance up at me as if you realize I'm in your orbit and need to lay eyes upon me." I stroke my thumb along his jaw. "Henry, how could I not love you?"

His Adam's apple bobs, his eyes swimming with something I can't quite read. "You look at me as if I'm some great thing."

"You are," I tell him. "Henry, you are."

I'm surprised when he presses his lips against mine, when the kiss turns from gentle to this desperate desire to feel. I let him press me back into my room, allow him to kick the door shut behind us. It was what I wanted, to feel him, to need him. After everything, I need to feel normal, to feel as if my life is in my hands.

His hands roam along my waist, stroking, driving me mad, and when he reaches behind me to loosen my dress, I allow him. My own hands go to his coat, shoving it from his shoulders, eager to be skin to skin. It takes far longer than I would like to be undressed before him, but once we're both nude, he lifts me—one warm flesh hand, one cold metal— and carries me toward my bed, laying me down on it with the same gentleness he kisses.

"You are the most beautiful thing I've ever seen in my life," he rasps as he looks down on me before climbing up after.

I flush, my body languid for him. "There are many who are prettier."

"Lies," he rasps, nestling between my thighs. "I don't know how to hold your hand without regarding the ugliness of my own, Mena, but I can't contain my soul from loving yours."

His length presses against my entrance and he eases inside, a slow move that makes my back arch as I dig my nails into his back. I'll likely leave marks behind, but he doesn't seem to care, his own moan sliding from his lips as I clench around him.

"Oh!" I cry as he slowly pulls out and slams back in. My breath whooshes out of me, my body humming with pleasure beneath him.

"Your love opens a mortal wound in me," Henry gasps in my ear. "I will work this blade in deeper, all the agony it causes a reminder of the reality." His pelvis slaps against mine as he slowly builds me higher, as he strokes me gently, as he takes his monster's reins and forces himself to love me slowly. "I beg of you that the death come quickly, because when you reach your full potential, you will not want me."

I open my mouth to deny his words, to argue despite my body's growing pleasure, but he covers my lips with his hand, holding my words back.

"I am not a creature that was born," he growls, picking up speed. "I'm a fire that was set by my own hand, and I will turn to ash." My body rises and I cry out in pleasure as he strokes me higher. "I will not burn you with me. I will save you from myself."

I shatter, my body shaking with an orgasm that robs me of my sight for a moment, that has me spasming beneath him as he follows me over the cliff, his warmth filling me. I blink away the fuzziness and take in his expression, the way he holds himself over me so as not to crush me, the way he's staring at me as if I'm some great masterpiece upon a shelf.

"I will not let you burn," I rasp as I cup his face. "I refuse."

He presses his face against my palm. "I'd die for you, Mena, and I'm trying to figure out whether you mean that much to me or if I mean so little to myself."

When he winces in pain suddenly, I frown. "What's wrong?"

He shakes his head. "Hyde. He's demanding to be let out."

"Let him out if you wish," I murmur, running my hands along his shoulders.

"I do not wish to," Henry grunts, sliding from inside me and sitting up. He scoots to the edge of the bed, turning his back to me.

I sit up, moving over to hug him from behind. "Oh, Henry. I'm not afraid. He's a part of you—"

"No, he isn't," Henry snarls, jerking from my embrace to stand and reaching for his clothing. "He's a disease, and when I find a cure, I'll finally be rid of him."

I watch as he jerks on his pants and grabs the rest of his clothing. He won't meet my eyes.

"Look at me," I ask. "Please."

But he doesn't. He shakes his head. "You deserve better than me, Mena," he rasps. "This was a mistake."

And then he strides from my room, slamming the door behind him, leaving me satiated and sad and not knowing how to help. Sighing, I reach for my dressing gown and slide it on.

It seems Henry and I have something in common neither one of us wants to admit.

Neither of us seem to be able to accept our monsters.

52
MENA

As the days grow deeper into Autumn, the chill in the air comes with the changing of the months. The wind reminds me that more layers are required at the first step outside, and I seek refuge back by the fireplace. It's certainly not cool enough yet to warrant all the fires in the house to be lit, but it's enough to make me yearn for a better pair of gloves than the dainty ones I currently have. I'm always ill-equipped for the colder weather.

I have not ventured out as often as I would like, not after the curse that was placed upon me. I don't stop myself because of my argument with Athan, but rather because I need a break from all the new and horrifying events that seem to keep happening to me. Besides the fear of another impending death, I fear the beasts that will continue to come. What other horrible monsters will hunt me down? Have we seen all that there is, or will there be more? I suspect the witches will try again at some point, and we've barely seen the beginning of what the angels might do. If there are angels, does that mean there are demons waiting their turn? And if I'm the mother of monsters and demons, does that mean the demons will be on my side?

Does it make me evil if I accept my fate? Or can I control the outcome?

Because I haven't left the house in a week, I've grown bored with things. While I'm not alone, I can hardly say that I'm entertained enough to satiate my melancholy. Henry busies himself with his experiments and after our last interaction, he's been more reserved. Hyde has not come out at all, as if Henry is suppressing him completely. I can't begin to imagine the pain that must be causing the both of them. Hu doesn't do much besides lie around and stare off into space. I suppose a god so used to being locked in a prison is well-acquainted with sitting for long stretches of time doing nothing. Otto is too busy, always reading a book or writing poetry or painting masterpieces. He does not sleep and so every morning I awake, it's to find him completing some other task that would take any normal man weeks to complete. Athan has remained aloof and only pops in at his whimsy, barely saying two words to me at a time. Mrs. Kingsley said I need to give him the space he requires, but I've done nothing but give him space. I'm starting to think space is the opposite of what he needs.

And my dear Mrs. Kingsley. With all the exciting events going on, the house being reinforced and broken into, the blood stains that had been impossible to lift from the rugs and needing to through them out, and the strangeness that I've become, I've often caught Mrs. Kingsley staring at me forlornly, in pity, as if she wishes she could do something to make things easier. I've reassured her that my plight is not as unpleasant as it seems—I held nothing back when I explained the circumstances—but I don't think she believes me. Not when great melancholy seizes me at inopportune times, and I stare off into the void inside me. Still, I try to reassure her as often as possible, sparing a smile for her as I'm able.

Phantoms continue to be drawn to me, as if they sense the very power in my veins. For the most part, I try to ignore them, only because I cannot help them all and it would not be fair for me to help one and not the others. Their presence lends an eerie glow to everything, making every room as unpleasant as standing outside in the chill air. Even the fireplace cannot always chase away the chill left behind by their mourning. I'd thought to help them in the beginning, but they all have sad stories, and my bleeding heart will be the death of me if I allow it. At least there are no phantoms I know flocking to me. If my late husband were to show up, it would certainly be an awkward affair.

The stack of invitations has only grown in the weeks since my sad event at the Dutchess' ball. It's as if everyone wants to get a look at the morbid Miss Seagraves, the woman with death on her heels. It has only made me more popular, and to think, all I had to do was die a few times to accomplish such a thing. Perhaps, I should have tried that sooner.

Now, in my absolute boredom, the stack of invitations is growing more tempting. I have a choice between the balls I attend, as I've been invited to all of them, and a single night out seems harmless enough. Perhaps I can accept one invitation, attend the ball, and return home without incident. It would liven things up. I will certainly remain a fair distance from any candles and at the first sign of trouble, we would leave.

Thumbing through the envelopes, I find a cream one with the scrollwork that can only be credited to Mrs. Gladys Des Vaux. Her parties are exclusive with the invitations sent only to the top picks. To be invited is considered an honor, as her parties always ended with crazy events. One year, she performed a séance that had high society afraid for months afterwards. Another year, I heard there was a massive orgy after the punchbowl was spiked with opium. She's known for having great fun.

I drop the other envelopes and peel open this one, take in the theme inscribed around the edges. Circus acts and entertainment, everyone from fire dancers to sword followers. It appears everyone is interested in outdoing each other for this theme this season. Almost every ball has been some sort of circus themed, but if Mrs. Des Vaux is throwing it, hers will be the most exciting. Though the thought of fire dancers gives me pause. Surely, I can keep my distance from them. All should be well.

I turn to where Hu is sitting in the armchair, his eyes blank as he goes through the cosmos of his mind. "We're going to a party this evening," I declare.

Hu blinks away the blankness and focuses entirely on me. "I'm sorry, what did you say?"

"I said we're going to a party this evening. It's sure to be a blast."

His brows furrow. "Are you sure that's wise? You're not immortal and—"

"You didn't seem to care before," I point out. "So what if I'm not immortal? Can't I still have fun?"

His eyes level with mine, and I can see the gears ticking in his mind. "I do not think it wise, little void. Your humanity will get you killed."

"Then I'll just come back," I shrug. "Look, I'm suffocating in this house. I need to get out, to go do something. I cannot sit around and wait to die. It makes me entirely too anxious to do so."

He stares at me, as if looking deeper than the surface. "You will not go alone."

"Of course not. You will come with me, as will Henry and Otto." I don't say Athan because I don't know where he's at, or if he will even come. I know he would be angry at me for leaving certainly. He thinks I should remain in this house like a caged bird, and I refuse to be that. If I am destined to be Lilith, to hold her power, then I presume Lilith would not allow four men to walk all over her, no matter if they're gods or monsters. So I won't allow myself to be sequestered away permanently.

Hu, though displeased, nods and begrudgingly stands up. "Then we shall go, but I do not like it and I take no responsibility for what chaos I cause should the need arise."

That sounds like a threat, but I shrug it off. After all, there can't be too much that happens at a ball. Especially at this one. The invitation list is small and quaint, meant for intimacy rather than grandness, though I expect to be impressed by the affair.

When I explain the situation to Otto, he immediately jumps at the chance to get out of the house. Unlike me, he thrives in social situations, yearns for it, and so being in the house has been harder on him than even me. Vampires, apparently, love to preen like peacocks every opportunity afforded to them. Athan, as expected, could not be found to be alerted. Henry seems almost annoyed to be disturbed from where he leans over a microscope, carefully zooming in.

"Must I go?" he asks, staring at his work with a frown. "I'm working on something quite interesting."

"You're welcome to stay if you'd like," I counter, not wanting to disturb him. There has been tension between us since our last encounter, and I don't know how to fix it. Despite reaching out to him many times, Henry is deeply within his conscious, withdrawn from our connection as if I'm some heinous beast. It's made me feel it more than anything else.

"If you do not come, Mena will be all the more vulnerable," Otto declares from behind me.

Henry frowns. "Then do not go."

"The lady has spoken," Otto replies. "And so we are going. I only point out that you would be a vital asset in her protection. Besides, Mena clearly wants you to go."

His eyes flick to me. "Is that true? You wish me to go?"

I nod and answer honestly. "I do, but only if you wish to go. I will not force you."

He leans back and sighs. "I'll be ready within the hour."

True to his word, he is indeed ready within the hour. All of us are. I had Mrs. Kingsley assist me with a dress with far less volume than my previous attire. The narrower the bottom of my dress, the less likely I am to accidently brush against any open flames. This evening, I'm wearing a dress with no bustle, the turn of newer fashion that many might turn their noses up at by those who do have not burned to death in a bustled dress. The corset cinches tight, leaving my breasts to pour from the top provocatively. It's in a deep shade of midnight blue, small crystals embedded in the material that look like stars if they catch the light. I pull on long, elbow-length gloves to match and prepare for the evening. Excitement fills me. This is a break from the boredom of hiding, of waiting for death to catch up with me again.

The carriage ride is short, only fifteen minutes, but we must wait another fifteen minutes in the line for entry. Once we stop, Otto steps out first and as always, offers his hand to assist me out. The moment I appear, whispers begin. Miss Seagraves and her escorts. Miss Seagraves and her dance with death. I hear it all, the whispers too loud around me, the whispers of a society who wants me to hear what they say, who wants me to take notice of them. They clamor for my attention like hungry dogs.

Inside, the party is as opulently decorated as I expect. Great curtains are hung around the edges of the room, striped red and white like any good circus. Though inside, it feels more like a freak show than anything else. In one corner, a bearded lady turns this way and that, allowing party goers to feast their eyes on her form. She leans forward when someone asks to touch, and I watch them tug hard enough to make her wince. She does not complain, only smiles, and continues her movements. In another corner, a man juggles glass bottles, careful not to drop them. A sword swallower stands on a stage in the middle of the floor, doing his tricks and swallowing just about everything.

"The high class certainly spare no expense, do they?" Henry asks, but it's not a question that needs an answer. In his words, I hear the obvious. What a waste of money that could be used for helping people. What a way to spend money when there are people hungry in the streets. I understand, even as someone within this world. It's not pretty, not if you look any deeper. It's all a desperate attempt to retain meaning, to pretend you're something better than you are. Because the high class are not actually better people. They do not deserve this any more than anyone else. They're simply lucky that they can be wolves in sheep's clothing instead of wolves in the mud. It's all an illusion, just as everything else in this world is.

Hu looks around the party with a bright expression. "I'd forgotten how great humans are at debauchery," he muses. "Do you think things will descend into something more sensual later?"

"Gladys Des Vaux is known for such things," I reply. "I would not dismiss it as a possibility."

Otto seems pleased with my choice of ball, his eyes roving over the crowd. "Would you like to dance, Mena Mine?"

"I would," I reply. "However, I've already promised my first dance to Henry. You shall have the second."

Henry's face whips toward me, his eyes narrowing. "You're welcome to dance with Otto first—"

"Nonsense," I declare. "Come. Lead me to the dance floor so that I can join in the merriment. This is one of my favorite songs after all."

Henry glances at the others before slowly offering his hand. "As you wish, Miss Seagraves."

I place my hand in his and allow him to lead me to the dance floor despite this entire thing being orchestrated by me. The moment we're on the dance floor and we begin to move, I smile.

"You've been avoiding me," I tell him.

"I've been working on my experiments. If you felt I've neglected your company, I apologize," he answers, looking anywhere but in my eyes.

"A novel excuse that has worked on other women I'm sure," I reply.

He flinches and meets my eyes, finally, and I see so much emotion swirling there, we slow in our dancing. "I do apologize for my outburst," he murmurs gently. "It's unkind of me to treat you so when you've been nothing but accepting of me."

"Oh, Henry," I whisper, reaching up to cup his cheek. "I care about you."

"You shouldn't."

"And why shouldn't I?" I ask, narrowing my eyes. "Why shouldn't I care for you like this?"

His expression sours. "I'm a beast, Mena. Beasts do not deserve such happiness."

I frown. "Apparently, I'm a beast, too, or becoming one. Or have you forgotten that fact?"

"No," he says violently. "No, you're anything but."

"But I will be, Henry. By the end of this, I will be the destroyer of the world. I will carry power in me that I must learn to control. What hope do I have when I see you struggle with yourself? What hope can I possibly have of stopping a truly evil outcome?"

His expression smooths out. "I believe in you, Mena. You are not evil."

"And if I am?" I ask, shaking with my fear. "If I become the very thing I'm meant to become? Will you call me a beast and declare me a lost cause like you've done yourself?"

He opens his mouth, shuts it, uncertain what to say. It's a very real possibility. I may very well be the end of days, the bringer of chaos, the destroyer of worlds. That is my destiny in many aspects no matter how badly I do not want it. But I'm learning to accept what I cannot change and embracing what can remain the same.

My heart.

I open my mouth to speak again. I don't know what I'm about to say, what I intend to, but the words never make it out of my lips anyway. My focus goes on the watching crowd behind Henry, on those watching the dance, those watching Henry and I standing in the middle of the dance floor, our etiquette forgotten. There, amongst people I recognize, are three women I know. Not by name, but by faces.

The witches.

"We must go," I rasp, grabbing onto Henry's arm.

He sees my panic and nods, but as he goes to take a step, he stumbles. I barely catch him as he loses all function, as he begins to cough up black muck on the front of my dress. My heart stops.

"Otto! Hu!" I cry and they're there immediately, supporting Henry between them and ushering us toward the exit. When I search for the witches again, they're gone.

I remain as close to the men as possible, knowing I'm a vulnerable and tempting target while they're busy supporting Henry between them. This was a mistake, but I must own the mistake now. We'd barely gotten in a single dance before chaos had struck. What a fool I am. What a horrible, terrible fool.

As Henry coughs up more muck onto the cobblestones while the others lift him inside the carriage, I desperately grab at my skirts, rushing after them. We climb into the carriage without incident, leaving me to believe the witches got what they wanted out of their appearance.

And hopefully, that doesn't end in death for my doctor.

53
CTHULHU

Anger pounds at my temples. Anger at this weakness I have in my heart for this human despite my need to fulfill my promise. Anger that the doctor could die because of her carelessness when we could use his protection and intelligence. Anger that we find ourselves again attacked by a bunch of witches who keep outsmarting us with party tricks and curses. At least I've seen this curse before. The curse of liquid ink makes the target cough up ink until they drown on it. The only way to save Henry is to get it all up and make sure he keeps breathing.

"This is on you," I tell Mena as I rush to keep Henry breathing. Otto helps, making sure his airway remains clear after each coughing fit. "You were likely the target."

Mena is watching helplessly, clearly distraught, and here I'm going to add to it with my words. She needs to understand this isn't just about her, and it certainly isn't some excuse to have fun. She's meant for greater things than society and polite conversations. She's meant to change the world and that can't be done if she's constantly trying to get herself or her protectors killed. My flippant attitude has clearly made her think I am harmless, that she can do as she wishes and I will relent. It's time to change that.

"I realize that," she answers, her voice hollow. "I accept full responsibility."

"Do you?" I snarl. "If he dies, will you bury him yourself? Will you dig his grave and have your reaper lead him to the afterlife?"

"Leave her alone," Otto growls. "We all went along with the plan. She does not bear the burden alone."

"I take full responsibility," she says, her voice strained. Carefully, she leans forward, her hand hovering over Henry's chest where he struggles to breathe. "Is he going to be okay?"

"As long as we can keep him breathing. Lucky for us, the curse seems to be weak," I grunt.

The rest of the carriage ride is spent keeping Henry on his side as he coughs up ink and making sure he keeps breathing. The ink diminishes by the time we're pulling up to Mena's house and I know we're now past the danger. It doesn't diminish my anger, however. I need a fight. I need to make her understand.

"He could have died tonight," I grunt, helping him back into a seat. Henry is weak, his face hollow, but he's alive. "And it would have been your fault."

"I understand."

"Do you?" I growl. "Do you truly know what it's like to lose someone like that?"

Without waiting for her permission, I clamp my hand around her knee, pushing my power into her. Her head wrenches back, the column of her throat strained as the cosmos loads into her body.

"What the fuck are you doing?" Otto snaps, shoving at me, but I push him off. Henry tries to move, but he's too weak, so Mena is forced to witness the cosmos I carry.

Every pain, every weakness, every failure, every loss, flickering before her eyes. And then the aching loneliness of my prison, the centuries I spent waiting for her, the need for her to be successful where I never was. I may be a god, but Mena is meant for more. It will not be me who makes history. It will be her, and I plan to live in the background of it, to know I had a hand in her making.

But I can't do that if she dies.

I withdraw my hand and her head snaps back toward me, anger flashing in her eyes.

"How dare you!" she snarls, shoving my hand away. "How dare you violate me in such a way."

"Parties are not important when you're the second coming!" I growl, needing it to soak in. "You will face your mistakes and bear them—"

"I am!" She snarls. "I bear them all. I bear my burdens and mistakes. And now I bear yours as well because of your stunt!"

"Good. Let that weight remind you of—"

"Go to hell," she spits in my face. "Or wherever the fuck you came from."

She shoves past me and heads toward the door. Even in her anger, she touches her hand to Henry's knee, making sure he's okay, before leaving the carriage completely, running away from her problems as she's always done.

"Leave her alone," Otto snarls.

"I'm a god," I snarl back. "I do as I wish."

And I leave the vampire to handle the doctor as I storm after Mena.

54
MENA

I have to get away. I have to put distance between myself and the others before I do or say something I'm going to regret. My mind is a mass of turbulent emotions, anger, sadness, fear, hostility all mixed up into a hurricane that I'm afraid to let out. I can't function. I can't breathe. I can't think clearly without feeling as if I need to hurt someone or something.

This isn't like me.

I'm usually calm and collected, my mind still and easy. Right now, I feel so unlike myself, I have to clench my hands together as I climb the stairs so I don't punch the wall. This anger is not something I'm accustomed to. And I'm not even angry only at Hu with his accusations and horribleness.

I'm angry at myself.

Boredom. To think that my boredom is what could have killed Henry.

And while I accept it, that this was my grave error, that doesn't mean that Hu has to shove it in my face over and over again. And the memories! His consciousness slamming into me had felt like someone shredding my skin from my body, like my bones were being broken one by one. Those visions were not meant for human eyes, and had I have been more human than I am now, it might have killed me. If I am eager and impulsive, then Hu is doubly so. They could have stopped me. They could have been more frank. I would have been angry, but Henry would be safe.

And those witches! I'm so tired of those damned witches! Something must be done about them!

"I'm not finished with you," Hu growls behind me as I storm toward my bedroom.

"I'm finished with you," I snarl, pointing my finger at him. "You leave me alone!"

I open the door to my room and try to close it behind me quickly. I should have known that I can't stop a determined god when he's set on his course. Not yet anyways. I have no idea how powerful I'll be at the end of all this.

Hu slams inside behind me, the door flying back open and nearly taking me out with it. My face pinches in anger as he storms inside and slams the door closed so hard it rattles the walls.

"I said leave me alone!" I hiss. "I have nothing I wish to say to you!"

Hu is taller than me by about a foot, the tallest of my men as long as Hyde is not out. Everything about him speaks of power from his wide shoulders to the stern look on his face. It's a strange juxtaposition between this look and the careless expression he often wears. It appears I'm not the only one fueled by anger right now. His height makes it impossible for me to look him directly in the eye, but it doesn't stop me from trying. I glare up at him with all the irksomeness I can muster in my soul.

"Your humanity is going to get you or one of the others killed!" he growls, pressing his chest against mine.

"I've already come to terms with my mistake! There's no need to remind me, you arrogant arsehole!"

I'm flustered and angry and everything inside of me demands I hit him. Instead, I keep my fists tightly balled at my waist, far from striking him. This anger is not me. Call it the stress from the last few months or this foolhardy man in front of me, I don't know what's come over me, but I can't fathom hitting out of anger.

"Have you? Or have you only looked at it through your high society lenses?" Hu continues to snarl. "You're acting like the spoiled—"

"Don't," I warn, holding up my hand. "I already get it from Athan. I don't need it from you, too."

"Clearly, one saying it has no impact!"

"I did not go there alone!" I snarl, standing on my tiptoes and poking him in his chest. "You went along with my plan. Do not pretend I am at fault alone. It may have been my idea, but I presumed we would be safe with each of you. You're a fucking god! And we had a vampire and Hyde! There should have been nothing amiss!"

We're both panting hard, each of our chests brushing against the others as our lungs expand and slack. If it was a fight he wanted, he's getting one, but my words seem to have triggered something inside of him.

"You're right," he snaps. "I am a god. And I do what I please. And right now, I want to fuck you so hard, you scream my name like a prayer."

His words are like heat under my feet. One moment, I'm ready to throttle him. The next, I'm thinking about his words, about the way he's looking at me, about the anger still charging the air around us.

"I'm angry with you!" I hiss.

"Then fuck me in anger," he commands. His hand wraps the back of my neck so quickly, I have no way to stop it. His lips are on mine a second later, coaxing mine open on an angry gasp, his tongue sweeping inside and claiming me in the fire. I tense, intending to rip myself away, but then I grow angry for thinking the thought. This man, this god, thinks he can dominate me.

He thinks wrong.

A woman is never weak. She holds the string for all actions—for sex, life, homes—and in an instant, she can pull or cut and cause a chain reaction. If Hu thinks I'm going to scream his name like a prayer, he doesn't truly know me.

I kiss him violently back, my hands going to his throat and ripping at his shirt there. Buttons go flying as we frantically fight for control, as he jerks me against his body and grinds his hardness against me. He threads his finger into my bosom and pulls, but the corset holds strong. He curses against my lips and forgoes removing the contraption. Instead, he reaches lower and a great ripping sound echoes around us. When I jerk away and look down, it's to find my skirts completely ripped away, leaving me only with the corset and the torn remnants of what used to be a beautiful dress.

"You bastard!" I hiss. "I loved this dress!"

"Did you?" he purrs. "I like it better in tatters." He tears at his trousers, freeing his impressive cock for my eyes to latch onto. He fists my hair and forces me to my knees before him despite my fighting. "Now be a good girl and worship me."

My lips peel back from my teeth. "Fuck you!"

"I intend to," he groans. "Until that anger weeps out of your pussy for me to lap up like a man starved, little void. But until then, taste my anger."

He presses his cock against my lips, rubs around them. His hand clenches in my hair tight enough to hurt, the pins scratching at my scalp, and I gasp in pain. He seizes the opportunity to press his cock inside, pressing against the back of my throat and making me gag. I wretch and he pulls out, gives me exactly two seconds to take a breath before he forces himself inside again, stroking against my tongue and forcing my jaw to widen to accommodate him. I dig my nails into his thighs hard enough to draw blood and he moans in pleasure.

"Use your teeth if you must, little void," he groans, fucking my face in long rough strokes that make tears come to my eyes. "Teach me a lesson in putting a goddess on her knees."

I do as he says. I bite down, not hard enough to cause real

damage but enough to serve as a warning. His fingers spasm in my hair and his cock jumps in my throat, my tongue tasting his slight loss at the action. Oh how he hangs on.

My hand reaches up to his balls and squeezes painfully, until he's desperately stroking inside my throat, until his anger turns his strokes punishing. So I squeeze them tighter.

The guttural sound that comes from his throat makes me leak between my thighs. He jerks my lips from his cock violently and wrenches back. His hand leaves my hair and grabs me around my throat instead. He jerks me to my feet and a strangled cry leaves my lips as he throws me backwards. I land on the bed, bounce, before he comes over me.

"No! Fuck you!" I spit, shoving at him until he moves. Then it's my turn to throw him on the bed, to force him to lie back. I climb on top, and his hands reach for my hips. "You'll force me to worship you?" I hiss. "Then it's your turn."

I maneuver myself over his face and sit down, forcing him to taste me. His arms immediately lock around my thighs, forcing me down on him harder, his tongue stroking along my seam. He moans in pleasure at the taste, at the way I leak for him. I grind against his chin, against the gentle beard he wears, until I'm moaning in pleasure, my body trembling with desire and anger all at once.

I'm going to fuck this god until he remembers my name for all eternity.

Jerking off his face despite his hold, I shimmy down his body and position myself over his cock. He tries to jerk me down, but I hold myself steady, my face pinched with my anger. "I hate you," I spit.

"No, you don't," he growls. "You hate that I remind you of what you are meant to be."

I bare my teeth. "I am Philomena Seagraves. I decide my destiny."

"Yes, but you are also more," he sneers.

I press against his length and his hands squeeze my thighs painfully as I sink down. "You think you are in control of me," I growl. "But I've already sunk my teeth in you."

He grins. "Then swallow me whole, little void. Bleed me dry with your anger."

My hips move, slapping against his pelvic bone as I rise and fall, as I fuck him brutally, claiming him for my own. I move until I am moaning in pleasure.

"But you forget something, Mena," he rasps, his muscles tensing.

"And what is that?" I grunt, grinding against him.

"You are not a goddess just yet."

He twists us and I go tumbling into the mattress, him coming over me quickly. His cock never pulls from me as he begins to fuck me brutally into the bed, as he grabs my wrists and pins them above my head.

"You are not yet strong enough to control a god," he growls, and there's suddenly a knife in his hand.

"What are you doing?" I snarl, fighting to free myself but his hold is solid. I'm torn between the pleasure of his thrusts and the fear of the knife. "Hu, what are you doing?"

"Fight me, Mena," he laughs. "Tell me what a terrible monster I am."

When the tentacles appear from around him, my eyes widen and I fight harder, afraid of what he intends to do to me. One of the tentacles slithers along my body and pulls my breasts from the top of the corset, leaving them misshapen and my nipples vulnerable. The nearest tentacle wraps around it and sucks, making my back arch from the bed. When another tentacle slithers between us and strokes my clit before pressing at my entrance where Hu still strokes, my heart stops. Tentacles everywhere, stroking, building my pleasure, and then the knife is pressing against my throat.

"I'm going to kill you," I pant, wriggling in his hold, both desperate for release and desperate to get away. My anger boils in my veins and makes me clumsy. I can't move, can't remember how to make my powers respond. Around us, things begin to move but I'm not sure if it's Hu's power or mine doing it.

"Maybe," he purrs. "But I'm going to slit your throat while I fuck you. As you die, you'll still feel me inside you, still feel my cock claiming you. Your pussy will spasm around mine as you breathe your last breath and you're going to take that feeling with you. How long will you still feel me pumping inside you after you die?"

"You won't," I spit, around a moan. "Oh, god!"

"Wrong prayer," he warns. "Say it properly."

"Go to hell!" I snarl.

My body winds tighter and tighter until I'm threatening to explode around him. I'm gushing, my body desperate for release, and despite the press of cold metal against my throat, I'm helpless to stop it.

"Tell me how I make you angry, little void. Declare me a monster and feast on my soul!"

My back arches off the bed as my release slams forward. "You force fed your memories into me," I snarl. "You're a selfish god who knows nothing of what it takes to be human."

"You're right," he replies, his hips slapping against my inner thighs. "And if there's one thing gods love, it's tragedy."

My release explodes, slamming out of me like my soul leaves my body, and I come apart in his arms, convulsing with the orgasm until I only know the trembling.

Until the knife slides across my neck...

I gasp and choke on what I assume is blood, my hands clawing at him as he continues to fuck me. My body convulses now for a different reason, and fuck if I can't still feel the pleasure as my vision closes in, as it tunnels and starts to fade.

Above me, Hu grins and moans. "See you on the other side, little void," he purrs.

I choke again and my heart stalls, and then I see nothing.

Nothing but the infinite darkness I'm coming to despise.

Fourth Death

Our eyes lock and I freeze.
Like a gazelle before a lion.
Even though I have teeth.
Even though I have claws.

We'll rip each other to pieces.

55
MENA

I come back with a gasp, and I snarl, the wrath still heavy in my heart and on my tongue. I'm still in the same position as when I died, my body nestled beneath Hu's, my arms pinned above my head, his tentacles stroking along my body. His cock jumps inside me, and he moans as his release finds him, as my face slowly twists with the fury that I feel.

"There you are, little void," he purrs as he leans down to press kisses against my collar bone. "So fast this time. You were gone for barely a few seconds." He nips at my jaw and whispers in my ear, "how long did you feel me stroking inside you as you died?"

"Get the fuck off me!" I snarl. "Before I tear your flesh from your face with my teeth."

He chuckles and the tentacles recede, disappearing completely just as the door burst open behind us. Otto, Henry, and Athan all slam inside, their eyes wide as they search for the source of my death, a death they no doubt felt.

When they see me in bed, mostly nude, with Hu still nestled inside me, various expressions cross their faces. Henry, despite still being weak and needing to support himself against the doorway, flushes and allows me some modesty, looking down. Otto's brows raise in surprise at my predicament, while a flicker of heat appears there. Athan only looks annoyed and disgruntled, as always.

"What the devil is going on here?" Athan demands, his eyes taking in our appearance.

I jerk my wrists free from Hu's hold and shove at his chest until he pulls from me and sits up. The moment I'm on my knees, I smack at him again, my teeth bared as the fury fills me again. I see red. I demand blood. I'm so angry, the walls seem to shake around me.

"You killed me," I accuse Hu, shoving at him again.

He grins. "You needed to die by wrath. I seized an opportunity."

"You fucking slit my throat!"

"You did what?" Henry hisses. "Who gave you the right to do that?"

"No one gives me rights. I am a god," Hu replies as he climbs from the bed and sets his clothing to sorts. "We needed her more powerful. She's now died four times. You're welcome."

I'm so angry I could scream. Despite my state of undress—my dress is in ruins, there's wetness dripping down my thighs, and my neck is still covered in my slowly drying blood—I climb from the bed and stab him with my finger. "Give me your knife."

He laughs. "No. I think that's enough bloodshed for one day."

"Give me the knife!"

He raises his brows. "I said no."

Indominable rage fills me, and I can't contain it. I'm so lost to the fury that I hardly know what I do next. With every ounce of hatred in my body, I pummel my fist into Hu's chest, and to my surprise, he flies backward, slamming into the wall hard enough that the bricks shake. He makes an oomph sound as he hits before landing on his feet, his eyes wide in surprise.

"Well, well, well, look what we have here, little destroyer," he purrs as he straightens. "It appears your death has brought some new benefits."

"I told you not to call me that," I pant. "I don't care if you are a god or not, I will string you up by your entrails and let the ravens feast on you."

The grin that spreads across his lips is mocking. "There's the bloodthirsty Lilith I know. And to think, it only took wrath to bring her out."

His words are like a bucket of cold water. The anger washes out of me, leaving me hollow, and cold, and in desperate need of solitude. The betrayal of what's he's done this eve, twice forcing his whims on me, is too much. I can't do this. I can't look him in the face as he's shoved his memories in my mind and killed me without warning. My chest aches with agony. I trusted him. And I'm a fool for trusting him still, but it does nothing to displace the anger in my heart.

"Get out," I rasp, reaching up to run a hand along my now pristine throat. I can feel the fine raised scar there, barely thick enough to be noticed by others.

"Mena," Otto tries.

"All of you," I clarify. "Leave me."

They hesitate, but it's Hu who leaves first. "I'll see you soon, little void," he purrs, and I flinch, too angry at him to act on it now that I find myself so desperate for solitude.

"If you should need anything—" Henry begins, still barely holding himself up.

"I'm sorry you were hurt," I murmur, looking away. I can't look any of them in the eyes, can't do anything but shy away. My arms come to wrap around my body, hiding it from view. "I'll speak with you when I'm feeling up to it."

"Of course," he whispers, and leaves.

Athan is the last to leave, lingering.

"If you're here to say I told you so, I don't need it," I croak, my desperation growing. "Please, just leave."

He tilts his head. "Why would I say what you already know?"

And then he, too, leaves, and I'm alone. The moment I am, I drop to my knees and let every emotion wash over me.

The sobs come only seconds later, my freedom leaking from me just as my tears do, each of them staining the rug with my pain.

56
OTTO

I can hear her crying, each sob like an arrow to my chest. They're so filled with pain I can hardly stand not going in there and comforting her, but she asked for solitude, and she deserves it. I can't fathom what she must be feeling, what pain she suffers, what losses she must be mourning. Such transitions are difficult, but it's been so long since I've gone through my own, I don't even know how to comfort her. What good would a vampire be in this situation? I've hated the monster I'd been forced to become for centuries.

"Look what you've done," I grunt at the god. He's strolling from the room despite the sobs as if he doesn't care, as if this is all part of the plan. Henry and Athan linger, both unsure what to do. The doctor can barely stand, and yet he yearns to go in there and comfort her. And here this god fucked her and killed her and expects it to just be forgiven so easily?

Hu glances at me in amusement, as if it's funny that I should be angry with him. "The quicker she reaches seven deaths, the safer she will be," he says as if that's the only explanation he needs.

"I agree," I growl, shaking my head. "But you're forgetting one vital detail."

He furrows his brows and stops, looking at me expectantly. "Pray tell me, vampire. What is it you know so well that I do not?"

"It is Mena's life. She should be informed before—"

"So, she can deny it?" he spits before straightening and adjusting his wrinkled suit. "You're all going to ruin her if you continue to placate her so. She is not some damsel in distress. She is not just some woman. Mena is destined to destroy the world! To send it into chaos!"

Henry scoffs behind me, clearly as annoyed as I am, but having no energy to say so. That's alright. I have enough for all of us. The reaper is simply standing by, and with his latest attitude toward Mena, I don't doubt he agrees with Hu. I no longer care if any of them are more powerful than me or not. I care for Mena, and I will not stand idly by while she is bullied.

"If you keep on this path, she'll hate you," I warn the god, my words carrying every threat within them.

"It does not matter," Hu replies with a shrug. "I will have fulfilled my promise."

I tilt my head. "For a god, you're an absolute idiot."

He tenses at my words, offended. "You dare call a god an idiot?"

"It's the least of what I'd like to call you," I hiss. "Be grateful." Pointing my finger at him, I shake it in warning like I'm scolding a dog. "You make sure Mena knows before you do something so rash next time," I threaten.

"Or what?" he asks, amused at the thought of a vampire threatening him.

I shake my head and scoff. "Or you're going to lose her heart, great dreamer. And I'll gladly be there to keep it warm with you gone."

Turning away from the three of them, I storm off, needing to get some air myself if only to prevent myself from going into that room and making sure Mena is okay. She needs her space and the moment she's ready to come out, I'll be there to tend to her. For now, I'll drown myself in the blood of some poor, terrible socialite that the world has never needed.

Fucking gods. They're all the same. Useless and too far removed from humanity to do anyone any good.

57
MENA

My anger is palpable. Within my rooms, I can sit within the anger and stew and struggle, but the thing is, I'm no longer just Mena. I'm no longer just the widow with money who attends balls and laments boredom. I'm some reincarnation, some bitter attempt at retribution for a world that should have never treated women as second class. The pressure to be well, to accept these facts of my deaths, to know that I'm going to destroy the world, weighs heavily on me. I am not who I thought I would be. I will become something other.

Will I still be Mena inside there? Or will I be wholly monstrous?

Four deaths now. I have died exactly four times. Choking on cake, hit by a train, burning alive, and now having my throat slit by someone I trusted. Each is as traumatic as the last, but the betrayal of the last one coats my tongue and demands I do something about it. Hu is a god, and his arrogance and ego is what made him take a decision that should have been mine and make it his own. Regardless if I would have declined, it's still my decision and my life. I'm so tired of being controlled, first by society and now by this. I'm so tired of having no say in my future.

The anger in my heart climbs my throat and spills from my lips in a guttural, gut-wrenching scream that shakes the house. I can feel the walls tremble. I can feel the floor beneath my feet quiver with my power. Whatever the fourth death has awakened, it's not something as simple as an illusion or twisting someone's emotions. This one feels more potent. This one feels powerful.

The power leaks from my body, bleeding from my feet and spreading throughout the house. With my scream comes more screams, matching indominable rage from my soul that infects others. I can't hold it back. The betrayal is too great. The anger is too raw.

I'd said I needed solitude, but in this moment, I realize I need anything but.

Desperate, I throw my door open and give thanks that the men are no longer outside. I don't know how long I've been pacing and working myself up in my rooms. I only know that I need to move now before I do something heinous. However, the anger is still leaking from me, tainting the air, and I do not stop to think about its effects until I find myself faced with it.

A thunderstorm rages in my chest as I take the stairs, the lightning in my heart flashing like a warning sign. Those black clouds envelope my mind, encompass it, until I can't see past them. The devastating wave rises from the dark abyss of my soul, where cruel memories and bitter insults wait on the tip of my tongue. I want to lash out. I want to fan the smoldering embers inside of me, encourage them to ignite, demand they destroy everything in their path. The path of embers is bright, desperate, necessary, and at the end of it awaits self-destruction, but I cannot bring myself to stop.

The storm rages on and it fills my home like my father used to when I was a child. He would rage and stomp around and demand obedience from our fear. My mother never stopped him, and by default, I never knew how. And now I am just like him. I feel that same indominable, infectious rage eating away at my soul.

"Mena, what's going—"

Mrs. Kingsley appears from the kitchen, her eyes worried, stress eating away at her expression. The moment my rage hits her, her expression goes slack before twisting into a vision of rage I've never before seen from her. She bares her teeth and steps completely out, her eyes flashing with the same indomitable rage leaking from me. Seeing her so overcome dulls my rage just a little but it does not make it dissipate completely. Mrs. Kingsley snarls at me, and then throws one of the vases off the nearby tables. It shatters against the marble, sending shards dancing across my feet.

My rage fades more.

"Mrs. Kingsley?" I ask, taking a step toward her, only now realizing I'm barefoot and wearing only my robe. The glass pieces of the vase cut into my feet and the pain breaks through the rage. "Molly?"

She screams and continues raging through the room, throwing anything that will break from the table, lashing out at the art on the walls I never cared for, destroying anything she can touch. Someone hears the racket and comes out, the vampire peeking from the office. Otto takes in everything and frowns, but his expression morphs into anger for a second as he draws too close.

"Go!" I choke, the power still leaking from me. "Get everyone away from me!"

Otto looks between me and Mrs. Kingsley, his eyes flickering with understanding that is interrupted with the rage that I feed him. He struggles to hold it back, to fight my hold. No longer is my power too weak to affect immortals. No longer am I so easily overcome. "Mena—"

"Please," I rasp, wrapping my arms around my stomach. "Get everyone to safety."

He disappears and I know he'll do as I ask. I can't control this new power, can't rein it in. I can only let it play out and one of my closest friends is currently caught in the crosshairs.

Mrs. Kingsley destroys the room, rips it to shreds, and in her anger, I see my own. Every part of her speaks of the betrayal I feel, the anger I carry, the bitterness at being chosen for this life. I never wanted this weight, but it is still my burden, not my friend's. Not the people I care about.

Mrs. Kingsley screams, the rage demanding release, and when she runs out of things to break, she turns toward me.

"I'm sorry, Molly," I cry, wrapping my arms tighter around myself and sinking to the floor. "I'm so sorry."

She takes a step toward me, as if prepared to rip the last item in the room to shreds.

Me.

Tears begin dripping from my eyes as I apologize over and over again. I apologize for making her feel my rage, for infecting her with it. I apologize for bringing her into this mess. I apologize for being a monster unable to control her powers. I apologize for every moment I've ever failed her. I sob as the words tumble out, as I repeat the words over and over again like a mantra.

And there, on the marble floor, surrounded by the broken remnants of art, my rage turns to grief.

It had been grief all along.

Grief for the life I've lost, for the freedom I thought I had. Grief for who I once was and who I'm destined to become. Grief for the betrayal from someone I trusted.

Grief.

I'm sobbing now, wrapped around myself in my pain, and the power finally breaks, leaving me to feel it all with excruciating detail.

"Oh, Mena," Mrs. Kingsley says, and I look up to find her standing in the middle of the room, disheveled and confused. She presses a hand to her forehead. "I don't know what came over me. I'm so sorry."

I scramble up, uncaring of the broken glass that cuts into my feet, and wrap my arms around her. She hugs me back without complaint or hesitation, offering her comfort as she always does while I sob against her.

"No," I tell her. "No, as long as you're alright, I do not care. These are just things, Molly. They can be replaced. Not you. Not you." I heave a great breath of air. "This is all my fault."

"Oh, Mena," she laments. "You've been thrust into a new world very quickly. Not a single person blames you for falling apart every now and then."

"I'm failing. I'm going to destroy everything without meaning to."

"Nonsense," Mrs. Kingsley grunts. "No matter what new things transpire, you are still Philomena Seagraves. This power, these events, do not make you. Only you can do that. Only you can choose what destroys you."

I sob against her like a child, so overcome with emotion I can't function. So she lets me remain there, until I run out of tears, until her clothing is soaked with my pain. When I'm able to speak again, my voice is rough and raw, but the words are still understood.

"I'm a monster," I rasp, leaning back to look her in the eyes.

She smiles and cups my cheeks like she always did when I was younger. "You were never normal, Mena. You've always been extraordinary. I've always known that. You and I, we'll get through this together, just as we always do."

"And if I destroy the world?" I ask.

She tugs me against her again in a hug that makes me feel safe, that chases away the thunderclouds in my heart. "Then we'll face that when it comes, child," she promises. "We'll face that when it comes."

58
MENA

The mess in the entry hall has been put back to sorts, the room considerably emptier now, the walls barren. The art that Walter had collected, some from his grandfather, has been dashed away in an instant and I can't bring myself to care. I never liked the artwork, most of it masculine in nature, and now that it's gone, it almost feels like a blank slate, something I can put to sorts how I prefer.

If I don't destroy the world before then, that is.

Part of me is still afraid of what I'll be capable of by the end of all this. But another part, perhaps one that whispers, has started to claim I will still retain my humanity throughout, that despite the power I gain, the choice will still be mine. Sure, there's a prophecy, but I can ultimately make the choice on what I destroy or how I destroy. If I have to cling to my humanity with monstrous claws, I will do so. I will remain myself for as long as I'm able, and if I cannot, then I will take care of the problem myself.

The office has become our gathering chamber it seems, as it's the most spacious and the most comfortable. Athan is with us today, having returned sometime after my new indominable rage powers had taken hold to find the mess left behind. He had not asked me what happened, but I presume he knows from someone else. He barely speaks to me any longer, and I don't understand why he's still here. Perhaps, he just wants to witness my downfall. It seems like something he'd enjoy.

I haven't spoken to Hu since he slit my throat. Though he has tried to speak to me, I still feel betrayed by his actions and have yet to forgive him. It had felt like a violation, one he does not understand because of his godhood. Gods don't make a distinction between their wrath and their pleasure, and that's the problem with the world. I'm a pawn, a promise, and nothing more. He'd made that clear with his actions. So he should not be put off by my ignoring him. I'm only treating him as a pawn the way he'd treated me like one.

Otto has been at my side as often as I'll allow him, making sure I'm okay, offering comfort. When I'd come down from my rage, he had been there to carry me back to my bed chamber, and when I'd panicked at the blood still in my sheets, he'd carried me to his and kept me company until I'd been able to fall asleep. He had not pushed. He was only caring and tender, his only concern being my comfort, and I appreciated that. I'd spent the night wrapped in his arms, safe from the nightmares that I know will plague me ever after.

Henry seems to have recovered from his attack by the witches. His color has returned and he's able to stand without weakness. As the doctor is often to do, he immediately returns back to work, going over the notes he's been taking on my predicament. He reserved a particular journal for me, an ornate purple book that draws the eyes. His own work resides in the plain brown leather one he keeps on him at all times. I can't help but notice the differences he unconsciously chose between them.

He holds my journal open now as he paces in front of me, his eyes roving over his words. "So, I think you've succumbed to Gluttony, Greed, Pride, and Wrath so far," Henry declares, his finger tracing his words. "I had a hard time linking Greed to the train, but I think, because you intended to take your possessions with you and never return, that would fall into that category."

"And why is pride the fire?" I ask, tilting my head.

"You were dressed in your best, and trying to impress the Dutchess, were you not?" he asks.

"Impress is a strong word. But I see your point. I'd gone to the exclusive ball rather than stay home as a sense of pride."

He nods. "Yes, and we know wrath was clear."

Henry glances over to Hu where he grins in response. I don't waste a look at the god, only seeing him smile from the corner of my eyes. The longer I can pretend he's not there, the happier I'll be.

"Yes, which means there are still three deaths to go. Envy, sloth, and... lust, it seems."

Athan chimes in from his position by the window. He's often spent his time looking out of them despite the bars, as if waiting for the next attack or for a moment to slip away. Which is silly. No one is keeping him here. I've barely even spoken to him.

"How does one even die from lust?" Athan asks, finally turning away from the window to look at Henry.

Clearly, by the flush on Henry's face, he doesn't know the answer.

Otto, on the opposite side, grins. "I can think of a way."

I shake my head at them, flabbergasted that this is the discussion we're having. I decide I don't want to dig deeper into Otto's idea right now, but later...

"So what?" I ask. "We're all trying to find ways to kill me now? Is everyone else going to do so without my permission again?"

"Of course not," Otto growls, offense written across his face. "Some of us have actual manners." He looks at Hu pointedly, but the god only rolls his eyes.

"I told you it was for your own good. Remaining angry with me is pointless," Hu grunts.

But I only tip up my chin and keep my eyes off of him. Out of the corner of my eyes, I see his scowl, as if he truly believed my forgiveness so easy to obtain.

"Have you been practicing?" Athan asks me. His tone implies that he thinks I'm not, that the wreck of the entry hall had been a clear sign I haven't been, but as we've discovered, the rage is a new power, which means I have to start at the beginning training with it. I'd been attempting it in the safety of my rooms each night before bed, and the anger has only just begun to be practiced.

"Every night," I answer automatically despite not particularly wanting to talk to the reaper. Unlike Hu, he didn't slit my throat. He's just an arsehole. "I reserve each evening for practicing before bed."

"Good," he replies, dismissing my pride. "I suspect we'll be in an all-out war at some point in order to protect you—"

"Why are you protecting me again?" I ask, looking between each of them. "Why be here for this? Why not just leave me to my fate?"

The silence in the room is deafening as my question surprises them. After Hu's betrayal, I need to know their reasoning, if only to settle the insecurity in my chest.

I'm not surprised when Otto speaks up first. "Clearly, I'm smitten and wish to protect you because I care," he says almost flippantly. When I raise my brow, he sighs. "And also, I've been waiting for you for centuries. I won't leave you in your time of need."

Henry shifts where he stands, his face flushing scarlet. "I also care," he mumbles, but he offers no other words.

Hu grumbles from his seat. "I made a promise as you well know."

But I don't spare him a look and it only makes his annoyance deepen.

I focus on Athan, on the tension in his shoulders. "Well, reaper?" I ask. "Why do you remain when you can't stand to be in my presence?"

He narrows his eyes on me. "It doesn't matter why I'm helping. Only that I am."

"It does to me," I whisper. "It matters to me."

He straightens with a scowl, his face pinched with annoyance. "If this is the direction of the conversation, then it's clearly finished." He glances at the others. "Someone needs to make sure she's practicing. I have business to attend to."

"Wait!" I cry, but he disappears before I can reach for him, leaving the question hanging in the air.

Otto only shakes his head at his antics, but my heart hurts. Because even if Athan doesn't want to answer the question, I can admit why I wanted to know to myself.

I care. I want him here.

But it seems Athan has no interest in what I have to say at all.

59
MENA

The house has grown suffocating again, and Otto can tell that I'm slowly going insane from it all. When he'd appeared and started whispering about a plan to take the carriage for some afternoon tea like a child getting up to mischief, I had immediately gone along with it. Giggling, I follow him out the door, stooped over so Mrs. Kingsley doesn't catch sight of us even if she knows we're leaving. I would never leave without letting her know where I'm going.

That's how Otto and I find ourselves inside the carriage bright and early, the wheels bumping over the cobblestones and my heart beating with childish excitement. It's been so long since I've felt this carefree, it's a welcome feeling.

"Won't the others be angry when they find out?" I ask, keeping the blinds closed so we can't be seen from the outside.

"Let them be angry," Otto replies with a smile. "Besides, you're not alone. I am here to protect you."

"Yes, but—"

"It was easy to see you needed a break, Mena," he quickly

answers. "My only hope is that this little trip eases the weight on your shoulders even a little."

I reach for his hand. "I appreciate how much you take care of me," I murmur.

"I will always be here to do so," he replies, and I can tell he means it. That's what makes Otto so addictive. His honesty. The feral nature that lurks beneath his skin. The intense tenderness he's capable of despite the terrible violence he's drawn to. It takes great strength to be so gentle when you're capable of great monstrosities.

"Which tea house will we be attending?" I ask when the carriage takes a road off course for my normal one.

"Yes, I figure it best to choose one we do not frequent so we're more difficult to spot. I know it won't be your favorite—"

"Nonsense," I interrupt. "I'm simply happy to be spending this time with you."

He flashes me a smile that is mostly fang before settling in for the ride. His hand holds mine, his thumb stroking along my skin, driving me mad within the confines of the carriage. Everything about Otto is temptation and sin and I have yet to dive so deep into him.

As it turns out, the tea house is a quaint little place that offers a splendid array of teas and a scone service. Despite it not being my favorite place, it certainly holds its own appeal and I know I will be coming back when I'm able. The woman tending to it is beautiful and kind, and her manners are impeccable. I like the intimacy the place provides with the five small tables scattered around the room.

Otto and I sit sipping our tea, comfortable silence between us, both of us enjoying each other's company. It's only as I'm staring out the window at the passersby that Otto finally breaks the silence.

"Don't let his attitude bother you."

I peer at him curiously. "Whose?"

His laughter warms the room and I catch sight of the owner glancing at Otto with a lovestruck look on her face. "I suppose it could be any one of them, no?" He grins. "I, of course, mean Athan."

I shrug and take another sip of tea. "It doesn't bother me."

His smile widens. "You're not a very good liar, Mena. Especially to yourself."

Sighing, I settle my teacup back on the saucer and level my eyes on him. "Combined with everything else, it's just another nail in the coffin. He found me first. He stuck around for a reason, but he doesn't want to admit why. Each day, he grows more aloof and withdrawn and I don't know what to do about it."

"It's the way of reapers," Otto shrugs. "I have never met a reaper who was not plagued by ill manners."

"You've known many?"

Otto nods. "Three, including Athan. From my understanding, the mantle of the grim reaper is passed down once the current reaper repays his sins. They bear heavy burdens."

A frown pulls at my lips. I haven't heard this information before and I'm curious to know more. "What sins?"

"You would have to ask Athan that," Otto replies. "I have no idea, and that's only a myth of sort. I, myself, have never asked."

His words create a storm in my mind, curiosity eating away at me. What had Athan done to warrant becoming the reaper? When will he be free and what does that mean for him once he is? But I'm not here with Athan. I'm here with Otto, and in his care of me, I have not taken the time to care for him the same. I wipe all thoughts of the reaper from my mind and focus instead on the vampire king.

"Do you never wish to return to your own position?" I ask, tilting my head. "You're a king. Surely my home is far less grand than yours."

His eyes flip from the scone he'd been eyeing up to mine. "I am content where I am, Mena."

"But you're a king," I push. "You worked hard for that position, to maintain it. I can't help but think that I'm stealing you away from it."

Otto sighs and reaches across the table for my hand. His skin is always cool to the touch, never warm like Henry and Hu. "The truth is, Mena Mine, being a king is an achingly lonely position."

"What do you mean?"

"You're never sure who means what they say and there's always someone eager to stab you in the back," he clarifies. "Spending time with you, here, free of expectations and betrayal, is the best decision I've ever made." When he speaks those heavy words into existence, he seems to realize it and immediately switches back to carefree. He winks. "Besides, I plan on being around for your full awakening, and I will gladly prostrate myself before you."

"But you're a king," I point out. "Why is there a need for that?"

"Yes, I am a king. And I will be *your* king when you become a queen," he says, his eyes flashing with pride.

My heart opens a little more to the vampire king. "You're so certain I can handle it."

"Completely," he answers with a smile. "I have the utmost confidence in you, Mena. Your human heart will be your greatest asset."

His confidence in me makes things feel lighter. "Thank—"

Before I can reply, before I can so much as thank him, I'm cut off by someone taking a seat at our table with us. I tense and focus on the beautiful woman peering at me from beneath her lashes.

She smells like death and the living all at once.

60
MENA

The woman is wearing an outfit fit for any proper lady. Her pinstripe blouse is free of wrinkles and her skirt trims her waist as it should. Her hair is pinned up nicely and her face is pristine. From all inspections, she appears a normal lady, but I've never seen her before. That's not to say that there are not people I have never met but it is certainly rare. Especially for ones dressed like the rest of high society. I've never seen this woman at a single ball or event, but perhaps she's new in town, a distant cousin of one of the ladies I know. Despite all this, my power recognizes something about her that's strange, but I can't place what is. Something feels. . . off. She's not a witch I don't think as she lacks the appearance of any symbols etched into her skin. Though she's buttoned up in a blouse, the blouse has lace arms and can be easily seen through. She's not an angel as she has two very distinct eyes. I simply stare at her, but Otto is not quite so patient.

"Can we help you?" he asks, and though the question can be seen as rude, his tone is as pleasant as it can be.

"Yes, you can," she answers, and her voice has a pleasant lilt to it meant to put people at ease. It only makes me tense. She focuses entirely on me with her answer. "Miss Seagraves. I belong to a particular group of individuals whose sole mission is to protect the crown and all her assets."

My brows shoot up. "And what is this group of individuals called?"

The woman tilts her head. "We go by many names, but it is perhaps easier to call us The Masked Guild, for we work in the shadows and remain completely anonymous."

"And yet here you are, anything but anonymous," I point out, narrowing my eyes. I am no stranger to shadow guilds and secret work. I've often run into them when dealing in business and prefer to remain apart from them. "What is it you want, you and this Masked Guild?"

The woman glances from me to Otto, her eyes taking him in before settling back on me. "We are aware of many monstrous creatures who roam the streets of London. Our task is to protect our city from those."

When she doesn't continue, I narrow my eyes. "And what does that mean precisely?"

"Miss Seagraves. Mena. May I call you Mena?"

"No," I reply, suspicion in every particle of my body. "Miss Seagraves will do."

Otto's lips quirk up at my words, but he hides it quickly behind his stern study of the newcomer.

"I see," the woman sighs. "Miss Seagraves, we're aware of your... predicament, and the company you are currently keeping."

I straighten, my tea and scones forgotten in favor of this stranger. Her words signal a warning, that she knows more than she is saying. I have two options. Either I can admit she's correct and ask what she requires, or I can pretend I don't know what she's talking about. I settle on the second option as the safer of the two.

"I don't know what you speak of," I reply, staring her down.

Her smile is mocking. "Of course, Miss Seagraves. You see, we come, not because we wish to harm you, but because we would like to protect the rest of the world. Unlike many others who may be after you, we only have the safety of humanity on our minds. We have the means to protect you, and if you join us willingly, you will want for nothing." She hesitates. "As long as you do as we say."

There's no use pretending I'm anything but what she suspects. Clearly, these people have done their research. I don't know how they know or where they get their information, but it would be a benefit to gain as much information as possible from them.

"So you're offering me a cage?" I ask, crossing my arms.

"Better a cage than a death sentence," she replies, and I can see why she works for this Masked Guild. Though her voice and everything in her speaks in a perfectly natural tone, it's taken me this long to realize the unnaturalness in which she holds herself. She's poised, unmoving, so still that she could be considered a predator.

"And if I do not?" I hazard, staring her down. Her eyes are two different colors, a strange thing to note at this point. One is green and the other is blue. "If I don't desire being put in a cage?"

"I am only the messenger," she replies. "I will leave you if you say no, however. . ." She glances at Otto again and takes in his posture and readiness to pounce. "If you decline, force will be necessary. I'm sure you must understand our need to keep the world safe."

"And what if I can keep it safe myself?" I ask, tilting up my chin. "What if I'm able to control it?"

She grabs a scone from our tray and takes a bite. "The Masked Guild does not put such confidence in a single woman, no matter the monsters at her side." She sets the scone back on the tray, her bite mark left in it. "Power corrupts, Miss Seagraves. If you do not go with me now, action will be taken against you."

"And what if we send a message with your death?" Otto asks, the threat heavy in his words.

She smiles. "Well, that would certainly be an answer, would it not? Especially coming from the King of the European Vampires." She meets my eyes. "I take it your answer is no?"

"Clearly," I reply, remaining poised and in control. She's a human. I could use my powers on her, but then I'd be precisely the monster her people think I am, so I hold myself contained. "I have no desire to be caged."

She nods in understanding and rises from her chair. "Then I will be seeing you again, Miss Seagraves. Unfortunately, it will not be under better circumstances." She reaches into her skirts and produces a piece of cardstock. "If you should change your mind before our next encounter, this is where you will go."

She drops it on the table and leaves us to our tea, exiting the teahouse and strolling down the road as if she didn't just reveal a secret society and threaten me all over tea. I pick up the card and study it. It's black and the address written across the front in script is barely discernable from the darkness of the background. The only other detail is the outline of a mask on the other side.

"Well, at least she had manners," Otto murmurs, taking the card from me to study it for himself.

"Yes, but what are we going to do about them?" I ask, sighing. "Perhaps it's best they cage me. If I'm meant to destroy the world—"

"A caged bird can be exploited," Otto points out. "They won't cage you and tuck you away, Mena. They'll force you to do their bidding. No one comes in peace when you're as powerful as you are. The connections you make before your seventh death will be the only ones you can trust, because after, it will only be those who wish to gain something from you or use you. There is no other option."

"You sound as if you have experience," I murmur.

"Remember I told you that being a king is a lonely dilemma?" When I nod, he sighs. "You will be in the same predicament, my sweet Mena. But you have an advantage."

"Such as?"

"You have us, and you have Mrs. Kingsley and those under your care. Each of us cares for and respects you, and you have no need to fear their desires." He smiles. "Now, let us head back before some other secret group decides to make an appearance."

He pulls me up from my seat and we head for the carriage, our tea forgotten, the single bite of the scone mocking me on the table.

61
MENA

We arrive back to the house without further incident despite being completely on edge the entire time. How many more players will reveal themselves in this game? Vampires, werewolves, witches, and now a secret society who protects the streets from monsters like me? Surely, there cannot be too many more surprises. But even as I think that thought, I know there will be more. The angels have yet to start appearing after the one and I've not yet seen a demon. The myths I always thought stories are coming to haunt me now just as the phantoms do.

When we return, surprisingly, no one is there to make a big deal about it. Athan is still off doing whatever he does, and Hu is apparently in the kitchens tormenting Mrs. Lily into teaching him how to bake her famous soufflé. While that sounds intensely adorable and like something I would like to see, I'm still angry with the god. Not once has he apologized or admitted he made a mistake, instead insisting he did the right thing. When he gets over his ego, then perhaps we can talk. For now, he can do whatever he wishes, and I will keep avoiding him.

Henry, in contrast, is in his rooms working on whatever his latest experiment is. One of these days, perhaps he'll explain what it is he's working on, but he remains secretive for now. I suppose all scientists are highly protective of their work just as artists are.

As soon as we enter the door, Otto goes and fetches Hu and Henry to inform them of the newest developments. Since we have no way to contact Athan, he'll have to be filled in when he cares to return.

Otto hands the thick cardstock card to Henry with a sigh. "Apparently, there's another threat now. This society, the Masked Guild, came to us offering to cage Mena to protect the world, but she also suggested Mena would have to precisely do everything they say. I assume they intend to use her."

"And you think they would exploit her," Henry nods. "It makes sense. No agency ends with good intentions, even if they came with them. There are always those who are corrupt and prepared to use whatever means necessary for power."

"Exactly," Otto declares. "Which is why Mena told them to go fuck themselves."

I snort. "I did no such thing. I only told them no."

"Same thing," Otto grins. "I saw the sentiment in your eyes."

Henry sighs. "This is getting out of hand. I don't feel as if this house will be safe for much longer. There are only so many reinforcements we can make against these creatures, let alone humans with the Queen's funding."

"Perhaps this is the last of the threats?" I ask hopefully. After all, I could use a break from the constant reveals. "How many more enemies must we face before this is all over?"

Hu laughs. "This is only the beginning, little void. Wait until the angels and demons truly get involved."

I glance at him, and he straightens, his face brightening. It's the first time I've looked at him directly since his betrayal, and though I'm still mad, what he said has made me curious.

"The demons will come, too?"

Hu nods. "They've rarely been known to keep their noses out of the business of angels. And you're to be the Mother of Demons. They may come in peace, but we plan for them not to. They may think to influence you to their cause."

"Great," I groan, pressing a hand to my neck. "This just keeps getting better and better."

"Honestly, you're handling this all very well," Otto announces. "All things considering."

"When you don't have much choice, you face the bull head on," I admit, and the words echo in my brain like a memory. I frown as déjà vu comes over me, as the room practically spins, and I have a moment of feeling of being here and then not. A flush rises on my neck in response, and the hairs there stand on end.

"I think after all this excitement, I'm going to go lie down," I offer as the others continue to talk. I suddenly don't feel very well, my mind spinning with vertigo.

Otto turns toward me with a frown. "Would you like me to accompany you?"

I wave away his concern. "No, I'll be alright. A short nap might do me well." I bow my head toward them just slightly and leave the room, making my way slowly up the stairs and heading for my own chambers. Once inside, I lean against the door before sinking down against it, the buzzing in my brain rising to an insistent ping that shoots pain behind my eyes. What started as a strange feeling now turns into a full-blown attack on my mind, the pain drawing a tiny gasp from my lips as it knocks against my skull. The next time I blink my eyes open, I'm not in my room.

I'm in a garden.

The trees stand tall around me, lush and green in a permanent way they're not known for in London. The grass is soft beneath me, my fingers running over it to remember the touch. The sun shines brightly, not so hot that the air is undesirable, but warm enough to chase away the chill.

I stand, confused as to where I am. I'm still wearing the same clothing, still very much me, but this is not where I sat down. What sorcery is this? And where did the pain go?

"Where are you going?" a man shouts and I duck in fear, only to realize that it's not me being addressed but a woman before me who storms from the trees. A man follows after her, his face twisted in anger. They wear strange clothing that barely covers their intimate bits and their skin shines with the shade of spending time in the sun. The woman has fiery red hair, her eyes bright and intelligent. The man, in contrast, looks more plain compared to the beauty of the woman.

"Away from you," she spits. "I will not remain here as your plaything."

"You will do as you're told," the man snarls. "You are my wife, and I will bed you as I please!"

The woman's eyes narrow. "I will not lie beneath a man who does not respect me."

"And what will you do if I do not care for your denial?" he growls. "I can take whatever I wish."

"You can try," she dares, baring her teeth.

The man's face twists with fury. "We shall see what Michael thinks of this newfound rebellion, Lilith. Perhaps he can talk some sense into you."

For the first time, I see fear flicker in the woman's eyes. "I hope they realize the mistake they made when making you, Adam," Lilith spits back. "And if they do not, then I will take care of teaching them myself."

Adam shakes his head. "You held such promise, Lilith. You only had one task—"

"I am not your broodmare. Nor will I be subservient to you!" She shoves him away from her. "Leave me alone!"

He scowls and leaves her, not because she told him to, but because he's going to tell whoever Michael is about this encounter.

I frown at the scene, at Lilith as she stands there staring after Adam.

"I have to get out of here," Lilith whispers. And then she turns her head toward me. "*You're going to help me, Mena. You're going to save us all.*"

I collapse under the weight of her words, and when I blink again, the garden is gone, and I'm back in my rooms again.

My body seizes with pain, my skull splitting apart, and my lips peel back in a scream.

62
MENA

The memories begin flooding my mind as if I've always known them. Déjà vu strikes without preparation constantly until I'm walking in my world one moment before being suddenly transported to another, left in confusion as to my whereabouts. My awareness of my mind feels off, as if I'm being force-fed emotions, like when Hu pushed his memories into my mind. I do not like it. Every time I close my eyes, I can see the life of someone else. No matter if I'm meant to be the reincarnation or not, it's still unsettling. And seeing Lilith's life makes me uneasy and unprepared for what's to come.

My screaming the day before had left everyone rattled. As quickly as the pain came, it disappeared, leaving both me and the others confused. I'd tried to explain what had happened, but the words had been difficult, especially since I don't completely understand what it all means or how it's happening. Yes, I'm a reincarnation, but I'm still me. Will I constantly feel split in two?

Otto and I are sitting in the dining hall, both enjoying a bit of tea. Henry is busy at work and had refused to come down. I don't know where Hu is though he's probably sulking in his rooms or wandered out when I refused to converse with him further than I had. Athan is. . . well, I'm sure he's tending to his reaper duties. It must be never ending to have souls constantly calling you.

Mrs. Kingsley has gone out to fetch some supplies for supper, which means it's only Otto and I sitting at this large table meant for twelve. The tea spread is as lovely as always, the scones delicious, the tea steaming hot. It all seems strange, because it tastes like lavender one moment, and the next, strawberries are blooming on my tongue, a remnant of a memory I assume.

But as I take a bite and close my eyes to savor the sweet berry—one of my favorites—I can't help but remember another time. When I open my eyes again, I'm sitting at a different table, looking across at Hu. There's something off about him, something other, and it takes me a moment to realize there's more cruelty in his eyes here and his black wings are not tucked away.

"Have you had your fill?" he asks, staring at me in annoyance. "Can you leave yet?"

"I am no more capable of leaving than you are," I reply, or at least my lips move. The sound that comes from my lips does not sound like me. It's a stranger's voice, though one I recognize.

When I lift my hand to reach for another scone, I can see the bruises and wounds along it, as if I've taken a beating recently. Freckled in among the fresh wounds, there are scars from those previously healed. It creates an abstract artwork across my skin, the type of artwork that should never be condoned. I glance at Hu closely, sizing up if it had been him to cause the scars, but the moment the thought enters my mind, the memory dismisses it.

Hu sniffs. "Michael is a real piece of work for dumping you in the ocean after what he did," he says, clearly annoyed. "I can't believe he did not remember I'm here."

As if the words trigger the memory, I'm thrown backward from this one, the feeling of falling sharp and brutal before I blink and I'm staring up at a different man, one I've never seen before. For a moment, he almost looks human, until the shroud is lifted, and I can see him exactly as he is. He'd been a handsome man before his visage shifted, almost achingly so. One of those men who are too pretty to touch. But he shimmers and changes, and the handsomeness is broken up by the thousand eyes suddenly blinking where his face was. There's not a head as much as there's this floating mass of large eyes. Each of them stares at me in hatred. From his back sprouts too many feathered wings to count. They move languidly, sending little bursts of lazy air at me. He still wears the white suit he'd been wearing before the shimmer, but that's where the similarities end.

"You doing daddy's bidding again, Michael?" I say with a sneer. My body feels weak and exhausted, like I've been running for far too long.

The angel shifts in annoyance. I don't know how I know he's annoyed without any facial features, but I do. His annoyance is palpable.

"I have chased you for far too long, Lilith. This is getting ridiculous. You can either return to the garden, or you can suffer."

"I don't like either of those options," I growl. "You tell Adam he can go fuck himself."

The angel tilts its mass of eyes. "The Creator has demanded—"

"He can go fuck himself, too," I interrupt. "I will not be a plaything for either of those assholes. So you can turn around and deliver that message."

His wings still. Every part of this archangel freezes as if he were a predator who has caught sight of prey. It's not smart of me to antagonize him. Angels are not known for their forgiveness. Especially archangels. The only one who claims forgiveness is the Creator, but he doesn't mean it. It's a lie, like everything else. In the end, my creator will have to beg for my forgiveness, because I refuse to believe someone so cruel could force me into this situation.

"My orders are either retrieve or punish," Michael finally says. "Are you choosing punishment?"

"Standing here looking at your ugly face is plenty punishment," I spit.

There's nowhere to run. Michael has chased me to the ends of the earth and there's nowhere left to flee. The ocean is at my back, the water lapping at my heels. Michael is faster than me—all angels are—but what I lack in speed, I have in determination. I will outlast this archangel. I will not return to the garden to be a toy.

"As you wish," Michael says, and then he shoots toward me so fast, I can't even raise my arms to cover my face.

The first bite of pain is from his fist to my sternum. It throws me backward into the water with a shriek, my lungs struggling for air. As I hit the water, Michael slams down upon me, pressing me into the water, drowning me as his hands hit again and again. I open my mouth to scream and suck in large gulps of water, my lungs stinging in protest as darkness closes in around me. Before I can pass out, Michael yanks me out of the water and slams me down on the sand hard enough that the water comes out in great heaving coughs. I have no time to gather my senses before I'm lifted into the air again.

"Stop!" I cry, trying to fight back, but the Creator made me weak in this body. It will take something more profound to fight the Creator and his ilk.

A fist strikes my face and my head snaps backward. My ears ring with the hit as I try to blink through it. The knife at my hip is there. If I can just—

"The Creator wishes you to feel his pain. You disobeyed him. You betrayed him by leaving. And so each hit will be your betrayal and the suffering you've caused him." Michael jerks me up and brings me close to his thousand eyes. "Your pain will be your salvation. Suffering is necessary for enlightenment."

I bare my teeth, the blood in my mouth coating them and probably making me look a monster. "I'm going to kill you one day," I sneer. "Perfect little Michael. Always doing daddy's bidding and playing the monster so he can pretend he isn't one."

He hits me again and more blood spills from my mouth. I laugh at him, at this pain, because he's right. My pain will be my salvation. This suffering will bring enlightenment. All it is doing is making me certain that I will end him, that I made the right decision. I will destroy the Creator's world and all his minions.

"Is that the best you can do?" I goad. "You're letting me down, Michael."

The eyes narrow and the blades in his wings flash. Michael is the archangel of war. The Creator always sends his most savage angels to do his bidding. What being could create such monsters and command them? What being would dare create me and demand I conform? I know the answer, but it still hurts. I was created for nothing but a broodmare. I will be more. I will be everything he fears.

Michael is angry now. That's one of the emotions they're capable of feeling. Anger and vitriol. They feel no love, no sadness, no yearning for something more. Well, not this one. The Morningstar had rebelled. He'd failed, but at least he had tried.

Just as I try.

His fists slam against me over and over again until I can't even cry out. Even in pain, even feeling as if I will die, I can't help but laugh at him. He's trying, but there's nothing that can make me willingly return to the garden, and he needs me to be willing. You can't enter the garden without that willingness, but I've been awakened. I've seen what else is in that knowledge. I've eaten from the trees. I've eaten from both the knowledge and the everlasting ones. I cannot be swayed. I cannot be changed.

I will never go back.

When I can no longer keep my body awake, when my eyes have swelled shut and my awareness begins to fade, Michael lifts me into the air on his thousand wings and carries me over the ocean.

"Perhaps," he says, his voice echoing strangely in my mind, "the Creator will forgive me for finishing the job for him. The ocean will claim you, the final bite of pain to end your miserable rebellion. Enjoy your trip."

And then he drops me. I fall through the air, limp, unable to do anything but descend. The scream tears from my lips despite my pain, and when I slam into the water, my body breaks further, cutting off my scream as the saltwater chokes me—

"Mena!"

I jerk, hard enough to fall out of my chair. Otto is there before I can hit the floor, his arms around me, his eyes wide.

"I. . . what happened?" I rasp, pressing my hand to my forehead as he helps me up. I blink, the features of the room coming back into focus. Gone is the beach and the ocean. Gone is the version of Hu I do not know. Instead, I'm back in my home, in the dining room, having tea with Otto.

"You were screaming," Otto whispers. "We were enjoying tea and you just froze, your eyes glazing over. It was like you weren't even here with me any longer."

"I. . ." The memories flash fresh in my mind and my face reddens. "Since the last death, I've had. . . memories."

Otto's brows furrows. "Memories? Your own?"

I shake my head. "Not mine. I think they're Lilith's. I saw. . . I saw Hu briefly before I was thrown backward into a memory with an angel. An archangel. Michael."

He straightens, worry flashing in his eyes. "You're seeing Lilith's memories now?"

Nodding, I reach for his hand. "They're as real as this moment. I could feel every blow. And they don't, I don't think they move in a linear pattern. They're chaos, and I can't control anything about them. I feel helpless against them."

His hand squeezes mine in comfort. "It sounds like you need something to ground you."

"What does that mean?" I rasp.

He gently sits me on the table before his fingers move over the fine China and the scones. He starts moving them further away and I frown in confusion.

"Otto, what are you doing?"

"The memories are vivid because part of Lilith lives inside you," he answers, making sure everything is moved before he kneels before me. "With each death, I imagine, they will only get more chaotic, so you will need to ground yourself when you feel the sensation of a memory surfacing. You need something real, something that can override the emotions of the memory."

"Okay. And how do I know what will work?"

The grin he flashes at me is enough to make me shift on the table. "Well, Mena Mine. I have a remarkably good idea if you're willing."

"Oh?" When he braces himself against the table, caging me in, my lips pop open. "Oh!"

"Indeed," he rasps. "We have the house to ourselves mostly. What say you to me feasting on you instead of those scones?"

I smile and cup his jaw. "I say we do whatever we please."

His grin reveals his fangs. "Good girl."

I'm thrown backward on the table before I know what's happening. Otto moves far faster than I expect, but I suppose I do not know much of vampires to begin with. I know they feast on blood, that they need an invitation to enter a home, but I do not know much else.

When Otto shoves me backward so that I'm lying on the edge of the table with my legs dangling off, the china that remains clatters. Something tumbles off the edge and shatters on the floor. Mrs. Kingsley is going to be upset, but I can hardly think about that when Otto is reaching for my skirts and drawing them up my legs. He pools them around my waist only for his hands to reach for my ankles. He slides his fingers along my skin there, trailing up to my calves, to my knees, lovingly learning my shape as if I'm a temple he is prepared to kneel at. When those fingers trail along my outer thighs and then circle to the inner, I press my hand to my stomach, grateful I'm not wearing a corset. I could not breath if had been tightened into such a contraption.

"You," he says, staring down at my legs, before looking up to my eyes, "are a beautifully made woman, Mena Mine. A being of great power in your womanhood. A force of great terror." He smiles. "And I don't mean because you carry Lilith inside you."

"You don't?" I rasp, watching him as he continues to trail his fingers along my flesh.

"I don't," he confirms. "Those are all traits you carry in your heart, with or without this twist of fate."

I frown. "I am just a woman, Otto. There are many like me through the other doors of this street."

He smiles and his fangs flash. My body tightens, temptation in those sharp points. What would it feel like for him to bite me? Would it be painful, or pleasurable?

"On the contrary, Mena Mina, you are wrong. But never you mind. The role of a lover is exactly the same as the role of the artist. I love you, and therefore my job is to make you aware of the things you may not see in yourself." He kneels before me and I come up on my elbows to watch him. "Even if you refuse to see your greatness."

"Love?" I rasp.

"Indeed," he answers, looking up at me from where he kneels. "I have crossed oceans of time to find you, Mena Mine." His eyes dip. "And now I will taste you as well."

He leans down, his lips tracing my inner thigh, and I collapse back against the table, uncertain if I should do something or if this is simply him acting on me. My fingers clutch at the wooden top of the table, stumbling against silverware that remains and a glass of tea half drank. But as his lips trace against my skin, I cannot think of anything except for the feel of him, the softness, like a tulip being dragged along my flesh. When there's a prick, I jump, but it's only a nibble, only a tease.

"Are you going to bite me?" I ask, my voice thick with desire.

He chuckles against my thigh. "Perhaps." Drawing closer to my core, he lifts my legs over his shoulders. "Would you like to me to bite you, Mena Mine?"

"I. . ." What does one say to that question? A sane woman would perhaps decline and extract herself from this dangerous situation. After all, I'm courting a monster between my thighs right now. But I have long since started to believe myself equal parts insane, and therefore, my answer is not that of a sane woman.

It's of a dangerous one.

"Yes," I finally answer. "Yes, I would like you to bite me."

He stiffens, as if he did not believe my answer would be yes. But he recovers quickly and his fingers continue to work their magic along my legs. "You continue to surprise me, Mena," he whispers. "I enjoy that."

And then his lips are at my core, lapping at me like a beast. I wretch up from the table, surprised at the ferocity of it, but his hand is on my pelvis before I can flee, forcing me down, pinning me like prey. I reach between us and grab at his hair, but he's steadfast in his mission and does not move.

"Otto!" I cry as he sucks hard at my clit, as his tongue swirls at my core. He consumes me, just as he promised he would, and I convulse against the table, desperate to both get away and sink into him deeper.

He hums against me and it sends tingles through my body. "I like the way you say my name, Mena Mine. Say it louder."

And then I feel the pinpricks of teeth on my inner thigh.

I scream, not because of the pain of it, but because as he draws my life force into his mouth, my core throbs with the action, as if he has a direct line to my nerves. I writhe beneath his hold, my body tightening with each languid pull of his mouth. I cry out, my fingers clenching in his hair tightly, as I shatter completely. My other arm swings wildly, catching at plates, sending them scattering off the table to shatter on the floor. I am a million pieces, just as those ceramic plates. And yet I am whole.

He withdraws his teeth from my thigh and returns to my core, lapping at my release and humming in pleasure. I twitch beneath him and when he stands to come over me, I'm delirious with pleasure.

"You taste better than any scone, Mena Mine," he purrs, his hands going to my waist. "I'd like to taste the rest of you."

He tears at my dress and it rips away. I look down in surprise, my eyes blinking at the tatters I'm left in and then down to the sharp nails tipping his fingers. Those nails return to my waist as my dress hangs around me like a robe, dimpling my skin, but not breaking it.

"Much better," he murmurs before leaning down to my breasts. He trails his teeth along the globe there, equally kissing and teasing before coming over my nipple. I gasp and wiggle beneath him, desperate for him to be inside me, needing him to claim me thoroughly. "Your blood tastes like berries," he murmurs, before his fangs sink around my areola.

My back arches from the table as I gasp for air, as my cunt clamps around nothing, pulsing with his draw. I cry out, my fingers gripping his hair so tight, it must hurt, but he does not care. He releases his fangs from my skip with a pop, lapping at the wounds so they don't bleed.

"So beautiful," he purrs. "I could worship you like this forever. We can hold each other like a prayer unspoken, like two sinners entombed in hell."

"I don't want worship," I rasp. "I want understanding."

He reaches beneath the table and I hear the clatter of his trousers being undone. "You are a sin worth hurting for, a fervor, Mena Mine." I feel his length against my entrance a moment later, teasing, begging. "But no matter. If you would prefer understanding, then I will understand every piece of you, every desire, every need. I will know you better than you do yourself, and in the end, you will still be mine."

He thrusts inside me and I gasp in surprise. His size stretches me, fills me to the brim, until I'm clawing at his shoulder still clothed. Only I wear the tatters of my dress and lie naked before him. He shows no flesh to my eye. My blood tints his lips, a droplet of it on the edge of it begging to be swiped away with his tongue.

"I could start fires with what I feel for you," he gasps as he strokes inside of me, brutally pounding his length into my core until

I'm overwhelmed with sensation. "But if I am to perish by fire, then let that fire be yours."

"Otto!" I gasp, desperate for me, afraid of it. He speaks of love, and I had not thought of it truly before now, but he's correct. I have loved each of them, even Athan, in some deep darkness of my soul before I truly knew I was capable. I've accepted that long before I thought it.

"I know that in a thousand years, if I had to wait again, I would love just the same, with all the terrible beastly heart I have," he groans, his nails pricking my skin as he fucks me like the beast he thinks he is. The table rattles with our love making, the house echoing with my cries and desperate shouts. He leans down and kisses me, and I taste my blood there, a metallic flavor that somehow does not repulse me. The kiss mad with desire, with eagerness, and I wrap my legs around his waist in a desperate attempt to still myself. I gasp against his lips and he swallows each down, like a memory, like a promise to keep me in his heart.

He fucks me, claims me, loves me, consumes me, until I am not more myself than he is himself. Until I know nothing but the feeling of him taking me. And when he leans down to breath in where my shoulder meets my neck, I claw at his back, begging him to finish the job, praying he imprints himself on my soul.

"In the crooks of your body," he says, his warm breath ticking my neck. "I find my religion."

His fangs puncture the flesh on my neck, his hand coming around to hold me still as he continues to roll his hips against me. I explode, stars speckling my vision as I convulse beneath him. He holds me steady, his fangs drawing my blood into his mouth, his cock fucking me until he too shatters, until he claims me with one final step, until I am his and he is mine.

I tremble, my body thick with exhaustion even as he continues to stroke slowly inside of me, even as he sucks at my neck, feeding on me, satiating himself fully.

"Mena Mine," he coos as he releases my neck and leans back to looks me in the eyes. "I have existed a long time. I have waited for you for centuries. There will be no other but you. To whatever end, I will be by your side." He strokes his hand on my cheek, cupping it. "You can have my heart if you have the stomach to take it."

His eyes are earnest, open, as he lays his love at my feet, as he begs me to love him back, this monster who thinks himself too brutal to be loved in return.

I sit up and clasp his face between my hands despite my exhaustion. "You already have my heart, vampire mine, just as I have yours. There's no need to offer it again."

His eyes light up, a brightness that one would think silly for a vampire. But there it is. A vampire king, his lips stained with my blood, grinning with boyish delight because I gave him my heart, because I don't look at him as a monster. He thinks it a great proclamation, some monumental declaration that might have never come.

But really, I would've bled out beneath him had he told me he liked the color red...

63
MENA

When the inky black lines appear on my forearm a few days later, I can't help but grumble in response. I don't panic like the first curse mark because I already know what it is. I know panicking won't help but my irritability skyrockets.

"They don't give up, do they?" I grunt as I hold my forearm out to the others over breakfast. We all watch as the black marks trail around in a circular motion, twisting into some strange symbol I don't recognize. This one isn't the same as the last one. This is a new curse.

This morning marks the rare occurrence that everyone is here. Henry came down from his room, his face coated in a fine sheen of sweat. Every so often, a word slips out of his mouth, as if Hyde is trying his best to come out, but Henry is forcibly keeping him in check. I've never seen him struggle so badly before and it saddens me that he feels the need to.

Otto is here as always, his eyes meeting mine over the teacups every so often, a reminder of the china we'd broken a few days ago and the chastisement we'd received from Mrs. Kingsley later when she could no longer find the complete set. My face flushes and I smile, taking a sip of my tea from a different teacup than I normally use.

Hu is at the other end of the table, shoveling down food at a rapid rate. He'd explained once that gods don't have to eat, but that they can enjoy it. Hu decidedly enjoys eating, and he can often be found sneaking further snacks from the kitchen. Apparently, he had not had the opportunity to eat while in his watery prison, so he's making up for it now.

Athan is sitting at the table this morning, a newspaper open in front of him. He has mostly ignored us, preferring to read about current events rather than holding a conversation, but at least he's here I suppose. At my words, he looks up and frowns at the marks on my arm.

"We need some protection from further curses," Athan grunts as an answer.

"The witches are after us and we can't return to the bruja," Otto points out. "Where do you suggest we find such help?"

"Not from a coven, we can't." Athan folds his newspaper and sets it down. "But there must be coven-less witches that will help for a significant portion of coin."

I sigh. "Are there not other good witches?" I've never asked the question. The bruja was nice enough, but she'd been clear after the last curse. Besides, the way her eyes had turned milky white after she found my powers unnerved me.

"Good is a relative term," Athan replies. "But sure, there are witches who practice the lighter magic rather than dark, just like the bruja."

"Then we shall find one of them," I declare. "How does one find another light witch?"

Otto hesitates and glances between me and Athan. "Mena, there are not many light witches capable of combating true dark magic. Dark magic is taboo for a reason. It's much stronger and requires more of a sacrifice to use it. A light witch may not be able to—"

"I've made my decision," I say. But my face softens at his worry. "Find a light witch. It's not like we have much choice, Otto."

"I know that," he grunts. "But it may be a fruitless endeavor."

"If it is, then we'll reevaluate our plans, but we must at least try."

When he nods, I settle back into the breakfast. Otto leaves right after breakfast and he doesn't return until the next morning, but the look on his face is hopeful.

"We have a meeting," he declares. "We must all go. I do not have faith in our safety should we be split apart."

And that's how we find ourselves all loaded into the large carriage by the early afternoon, the horses pulling us along the cobblestones at a brisk pace.

"Where are we meeting her?" I ask, my eyes taking in the sights of the city outside. We're moving away from the cleaner part of the city and headed toward the rougher side again. I suppose it makes sense for a witch to hide in the ranks of those less fortunate. It would be much harder to fit in with high society without raising suspicion. Everyone talks.

"A pub," Otto replies. "Off the beaten path and far outside the main roads. Once we reach a particular street, we must finish the travels on foot."

"Oh! I'm glad I wore my comfortable shoes then." I sigh, leaning back against the cushion again.

The carriage comes to a stop only ten minutes later in a seedy part of town. When I accept Henry's hand out of the carriage, I immediately feel out of place in my expensive clothing and even the shoes on my feet. The people here look ragged and overworked. And above all, they look hungry. Many of them are skinny and starved, their limbs gangly and terrible.

"Come," Otto says before offering his elbow. "It's this way."

The back streets are narrow and filled with all sorts of terrible sights. Families living in boxes if they're lucky enough to claim one, disease spreading through the ranks of those forced to sleep outside, and too many hungry hands. I don't have enough coin for all of them though I'm tempted to try giving to as many as possible. My heart hurts for the children.

We turn a corner to find this alley empty, free of any beggars. It's only trash and remnants of people who might have lived there previously. Otto frowns and slows his steps, his head tilting to the side, as if he's listening for something.

"Everyone stop," he orders suddenly.

I stumble to a stop beside him, my eyes roving the alley in search of a threat. When a man drops from a building and lands on his feet in front of, us, blocking the way, I jolt in surprise. This new man is clearly otherworldly, and when he hisses and reveals his fangs, I realize he's a vampire just like Otto.

"We're not looking for trouble," Otto hisses. "I suggest you head back home, vampling."

The man grins. "You may not be looking for trouble, Your Majesty, but we certainly are."

Movement from behind us has me turning to find another couple of vampires closing us in.

"Otto," I whisper, tugging on his coat. He glances at me and then behind us, and his face turns angry.

"Treason," he hisses, releasing me to take up a mantle before us. "You dare commit treason against me?"

"When you plan to keep her for yourself, that's treason, *Your Majesty*," the man before us mocks.

"I am your king!" Otto snarls, his claws lengthening.

The man tilts his head. "You're no longer any king of mine."

He moves then, faster than my eyes can track, and I scream when Otto does the same. One moment he's beside me, and the next he's not. He slams into the vampire before us, a savage snarl tearing from his lips as he rips the vampire to shreds. The two vampires behind us hesitate as they watch Otto rip the other vampire's head off with a wet squelch and holds it up at his side.

He bares his teeth. "Your youngling was not a suitable opponent," he says, his voice thick with aggression. He barely sounds like himself as he faces down the two vampires, and then the three others who appear. Otto grins. "You think to overthrow the king with six? How insulting."

Those words trigger the other vampires into action. They shoot forward, deadly intent written on their faces. Henry, Athan, and Hu box me in, forcing me to move back against the wall and standing in front of me so we're out of the way, but all I can focus on is that Otto is outnumbered, that there are five other vampires attempting to harm mine.

"Help him!" I cry when the five vampires attack Otto. I watch as Otto turns completely feral, his claws tearing them limb from limb, their snapping teeth achingly close to his skin. It's a terrible, gory fight, a brutal one, and the sight of it will remain burned into my memory like each of my deaths. These ones don't stain my soul, but I worry for the stain they'll leave on Otto.

Athan shakes his head. "We should not intervene in the matters of vampire hierarchy. Besides, Otto is doing just fine."

And I suppose Otto is doing just fine as Athan says. I watch him slash his arm out across one vampire's neck only to immediately turn and shove his fist through another's chest, it's still beating heart held in his grasp.

"Holy. . ." Henry mumbles, his eyes wide.

In this moment, I see Otto's brutality. I see how he became the King of the European vampires. All that savagery closed up inside of him when he's with me makes me aware of just how delicate I am. Otto holds himself so gentle with me, keeps himself careful. To see his full capabilities makes me understand just what type of monster I court. He was right before. He's a monster. It's never been clearer now as I watch him grab the final vampire and slam his teeth into the fearful vampire's throat. I watch, enraptured, as Otto tears his throat out with his teeth, severing the spinal cord with only those weapons before he drops the body to the ground.

With six dead vampires at his feet, their blood splattering along the brick walls and across Otto's suit, he stands in the middle of their remains. These vampires that used to be his people. And he'd killed them without remorse.

For me.

Otto turns toward us, blood dripping down his chin and spilling down his front. He looks as dangerous as any wild animal, his eyes flashing feral and hungry. I watch as he pants, as his shoulders rise and fall with his angry breathing.

And then his eyes meet mine and hold. In those eyes, I see his love for me, everything he feels for me, everything he will feel for me in the future. For a moment, his image flickers, as if another memory is trying to take hold, but focusing on him helps. I see blood on him. I see blood on the ground by a tree of knowledge. And then the image disappears and leaves me in the present when I focus wholly on the blood running down Otto's chin and staining his shirt.

He takes a step forward, but stops and looks down at the bodies. He seems to come to some decision in his mind, because he instead raises his arms at his sides.

With his eyes on mine, he says, "I renounce my hold as King of the European vampires. I relinquish my position and instead pledge myself to you, Philomena Seagraves."

Athan blinks the same as I do, but mine is in confusion. Athan seems only surprised. He glances at me. "A vampire king of Otto's power is a world power. He held the position to keep the world in balance. Now, he will rise more powerful by your side, not held back by the notions of a kingdom."

I gasp as Otto comes forward and takes a knee before me. He meets my eyes with a grotesque grin. The blood makes it all the more intense as he bows his head and prostrates himself before me.

"My queen," he rasps lovingly. "My beloved."

My monster.

64
MENA

When we finally make it to the pub, it's under this strange umbrella of unease. I don't pretend to know fully what Otto's renouncement of his crown means for our journey, but I understand it's a big deal. For him to swear his fealty to me instead of a kingdom is something not done by vampire kings, from what Athan explained, and I'm not sure how I feel about it. Otto once said he would worship me, but I had not believed him. Now, he walks regally beside me, the king he is, his eyes on me and the surroundings in case more of his vampires attack. Blood still soaks his shirt, but he'd at least wiped his chin clean. Unfortunately, his suit will not survive the wash after the sheer amount of gore that coats it. Nothing can be done about the suit now, so we just have to continue to the pub despite it.

When we walk inside the pub, it's Otto who takes charge, strolling forward despite the blood as he bows his head toward a woman sitting at a table with a pint of ale and what look like oracle cards spread in front of her. The woman is nothing I expect, but then I should have known that considering the bruja from before. This woman is also relatively young, barely older than I am, and I can only tell because of the slight wrinkles around her eyes. She's dressed in an elegant suit, tailored for her frame. A gold pocket watch chain hangs from the breast pocket, but otherwise, there's no other ornamentation. A bowler hat sits to the side of the table where she'd removed it. Her hair is cut short like a man's. I can see glimpses of tattoos at the edges of her suit, and I wonder just how much of her body is covered. This woman, this witch, is certainly not what I was expecting.

"I apologize for my appearance," Otto tells her.

She waves away his apology with her hand and moves the oracle cards off to the side, careful with them. "I saw your trouble well before you arrived." Her eyes trail over to where I stand uncertainly. "I cannot begin to fathom the trouble you've dealt with, dear."

My chin dips. "It has been... eventful."

She smiles and gestures for us to take a seat around the table. There doesn't seem to be anyone else in the pub, strangely enough, despite it being the time when men leave the factories and head for a pint. It's as if the building is empty. Even the barkeep is nowhere to be found.

"We've come to ask for protections," Athan declares, as if it's some great revelation.

"For Lilith," the witch nods. "I understand."

"It's Mena," I correct her. I tilt up my chin. "I may be her reincarnation, but I am still very much myself."

The witch smiles. "Of course you are, but the creatures who come for you, come for Lilith. They do not care about Philomena Seagraves, widow to Walter Seagraves."

I tense. "How do you know that?"

She shrugs. "Public record is relatively easy to look up, Mena."

"Right," I say, my face growing hot with embarrassment.

"First, before we speak of protections, allow me to look at the curse written on your arm."

I grimace and set my arm on the table, revealing the black lines. "It appeared yesterday morning."

"If we're to be informal, you should call me by my name. If I'm going to touch you, you should recognize you're being touched by me. I am Tallulah."

I nod. "And I'm Mena."

Her lips quirk up. "I know, dear. We've already established that," she says, before wrapping her fingers around my skin. Her hand is cool to the touch, like ice, and I shiver with it. "It is good you came to me so quickly. This curse will kill every human around you within another day. It's a terrible curse, but it is a weak one. The coven must be desperate to have you. This will take only a second."

She closes her eyes and I watch as she starts to murmur under her breath. After a moment, she slaps the curse mark on my arm, making me jump, before she smears something across the black lines. I watch in surprise as it starts to fade. That was far quicker than the bruja's curse breaking.

I'm not the only one surprised by how quickly she tackled it either. The others stare at her, their eyes wide.

"Now, Mena," she says, opening her eyes. Her fingers still hold my arm. "In this life, you must remember you will change throughout this experience."

I frown. "I don't want to change."

"Change is inevitable. Like a snake shedding its skin, we all go through phases of our lives where we must become who we are meant to be. Life has ended and begun again for me a hundred times, just as it has for you. This is only one more shedding."

Sighing, I look down at where she holds my arm. "Can I not simply be myself by the end of this?"

"You will always be entirely yourself, Mena. We're all constructed by our surroundings and the events that shape us. Change does not equal loss. It only means change." She releases my arm and reaches for a pot from the floor. A lid covers the top of it. "Now, I'm sure you know that light wards will be weaker in the face of true dark magic?" When I nod, she smiles. "Good. That's why I'm going to need your help for this protection spell."

"My help how?"

She opens the pot and starts dumping things in. She lifts her pint and takes a swig before pouring the rest of the beer in. "I need a drop of your blood, as well as a drop from each of your men."

I offer my hand and she pricks it so fast, I miss there being a needle in her hand. She squeezes a drop from the tip of my finger before moving onto the next. Otto is the first to offer his blood. He pricks himself with one of his claws and his drop follows mine. When Hu pricks his finger, the ground beneath our feet shakes for a moment before returning to normal. He grins at me, as if proud, and I shake my head at his dramatic antics. Henry follows third, letting Tallulah prick his finger. When it's Athan's turn, he hesitates, but ultimately offers his hand toward her and lets her do the honor of pricking him.

She speaks some words over the pot and little tendrils of steam trail up from it. When she seems satisfied, she reaches for a small pouch and dips it in the mixture before shoving some of it inside. She ties a cord around it and passes it to me.

"Wear this around your neck," she instructs. "It should rebound any curse back to the caster, leaving you safe and them cursed."

I nod my understanding and loop it over my head.

"Now, keep in mind, this will not protect you physically. If you're attacked, you will still need to fight. This is a solid protection, but it will mostly only protect you from curses and hexes. You must return to your home quickly," she says, standing. "I feel something approaching and I'm not certain what it is."

I scramble to my feet, the others doing the same, but I can't help but reach for her. "Thank you for all your help."

Tallulah shakes her head. "No thanks are necessary. I wish you the best against this evil."

Nodding, we turn to leave, but before we can go out the door, Tallulah calls my name. When I turn to meet her eyes, the softness in hers is gone. Before me stands a determined witch, an angry one.

"Remember, dear," she says, her voice echoing. "You are but a snake. Coil yourself and strike fast when the time comes."

Her words follow us out the door and all the way home until they're an echo in my mind, a reminder that at least somewhere, in the large city of London, there's a light witch who believes in me.

And somehow, that thought makes me feel better.

65
MENA

The day doesn't end there like I expect it to. I assumed we could return home and relax. The curse is gone. I shouldn't have any further curses placed upon me by witches too scared to come any closer. We should be able to take a break, but in my thoughts, I almost forget that I'm being hunted by so many different groups, it's difficult to keep track of them.

Of course, when we pull up to my home, I recognize the woman standing before the large welcoming party.

When Henry steps out first and offers his hand for me, I step out with my chin held high despite the circumstances.

The Masked Guild is larger than I thought. Right now, there are at least three dozen bodies here, but the humans standing in front are not the ones that bother me. It's the ones in the back, a dozen or so creatures. Each of them has stitches that sew across the exposed skin, so I imagine the sight continues across their bodies beneath their simple clothing. Each of them is large, far larger than a normal human, and they stand like silent sentinels. There's no emotion in their eyes.

"Victoria," I offer pleasantly despite the circumstances. "I assumed I'd seen the last of you at the tea house."

She smiles, but it doesn't reach her eyes. "Yes, well, I thought I would make a personal call to remind you of our conversation." The smile widens, as if this isn't a very real threatening motion she's taken, her and her monsters lining the back.

Otto, Hu, and Athan take up positions around me, their eyes taking in the group.

"What are they?" Athan asks, not caring about etiquette or walking on eggshells. He points to the creatures I can't keep my eyes off of.

Victoria smiles. "Do you like them?" she asks coyly. "They're my creations, my beautiful monsters."

A few of the other Masked Guild shift, their intricate yet simple masks firmly in place where Victoria's is not. For whatever reason she does not hesitate to show us her face. But true to their name, the other members remain anonymous.

"Your creations?" I ask.

She nods. "I have overcome death, just as your vampire has, but I can bring the dead back to life."

Otto tilts his head. "It does not appear there is much life within them."

Henry frowns. "What did you say your name was?"

Victoria focuses on him, her eyes bright with excitement. "Victoria."

"Victoria what?" Henry pushes, taking a step forward. "What is your surname?"

She grins and this time, the smile is genuine. "I suspect you already know, Doctor Jekyll."

His breath stutters. "I've heard of you, of your grotesque experiments. It seems you found your home in a shadow group."

Victoria laughs. "Yes, well, we're not here to cause trouble—"

"Seems unlikely," Athan grumbles, gesturing toward all the backup she brought.

"We are only trying to protect humanity." She focuses on me. "Do you really want to cause the destruction of the world, Mena? It's for everyone's safety that you come with us, including yours. We can protect you."

"Don't believe them," Otto hisses. "No organization appears like this in the name of peace."

"A precaution," Victoria offers. "We're a very powerful group, and we would not make good enemies."

I tilt up my chin. "It's difficult to believe you the good side when you threaten us."

Her eyes crinkle. "You're a smart woman, Mena. Almost smart enough to understand the abomination you will become at the end of this. I promise you that we are your safest haven."

"Your promises mean nothing to me," I declare. "I know nothing about you, and I will not trust in an organization that hides behind masks and false creatures."

Her tinkling laughter fills the air. "My Frankies are very much real, Mena. And unfortunately, if you do not come with us, we'll be forced to act against you. If you're not with us, then you are a threat."

"Somehow, I feel as if you're more of a threat than I am," I admit, taking in her stance and the monsters she created. I glance over at Henry, and he clearly knows exactly who she is. There's fear in his eyes, unease, and also respect. Scientist to scientist. This woman has done something big, though reprehensible at best.

"If you do not make the decision to come with us of your own free will, Mena, we will do what we must to protect our world."

You will either return to the garden, or you will suffer punishment.

The echoes of the memory flash in my mind, lay over the top of reality, and I blink it away. It's Lilith's way of reminding me not to cower, that I can withstand more than this woman is capable of.

My eyes harden. "I will not be your tool."

"Very well," she purrs. She gestures to her people to move and they all start heading away from my house, leaving only her standing before us. "We'll be seeing you soon, Mena." She blows me a kiss and follows her people, leaving without violence.

This time.

I relax the moment she's gone, finally out of her sight.

"Great," Athan grumbles. "This just keeps getting worse and worse."

"What did you expect?" Hu asks genuinely. "That she would just easily ascend?"

"I was only curious," he growls back.

I scowl at him. "You can leave at any time. Nothing is keeping you here now that your curiosity has been sated." I turn to Henry. "Who was she? Why do you know her?"

Henry frowns. "There's been speak in certain circles about a scientist running experiments, attempting to best death. Clearly, she's been successful."

"You know her name?" I ask, curiously.

He nods. "Unfortunately, I do." He stares down the street where she disappeared. "That woman, the one in front, she's none other than Victoria Frankenstein."

"Lovely," I rasp, before looking at Athan again. "Leave if you do not want to be here. I'm tired of listening to your excuses for your rudeness." And then I stalk back into the house, my chin held high, to think about all the creatures determined to cage me or kill me.

The list just keeps growing longer and longer it seems, and I don't currently have the mind to ruminate on it.

66

ATHAN

I watch Mena storm away with a strange feeling in my gut. Her disappointment had been palpable, so thick in the air, I could taste it. Perhaps I feel this feeling because she's right. Why am I still here if I've already learned the answer to the puzzle? I can leave and not come back. She would not be surprised by it. The others would be the same. So why can't I just leave?

"When are you going to start telling yourself the truth?" Hu asks, shaking his head at me.

I narrow my eyes. "I don't know what you're talking about."

Hu scoffs. "A moment of silence, please, for this poor soul's intelligence."

I scowl at the god, but I don't reply, not wanting to court his baiting.

"You declared intentions for Mena at the beginning and then withdrew," Otto points out. "She has a right to be angry about your personality change."

My face twists. "I'm just tired of being attacked."

"Then leave," Henry growls. "Mena is correct. There's nothing keeping you here."

I bare my teeth at the man. "Says the scientist using her as an experiment for his own conscience."

Henry's face twists with savage anger in a way I have not witnessed before. "I have my faults, I admit," he growls. "But I have never once thought to use Mena in my work. I'm here because I enjoy her company, because I desire some sort of relationship with her. She could pick any one of you and I would back down gracefully, thankful that I had a moment of time with her." He takes a step toward me. "Can you say the same?"

I blink and glance over at Hu. "And what about you? Aren't you here only to fulfill a promise? Slitting her throat without care? Lurking around her manor like a ghost?"

Hu tilts his head. "I made a promise, yes. But even without that promise, I would stay for Mena. Despite my rash decision, she deserves safety, and I will spend my time seeking her forgiveness."

I glance at Otto, seeking his answer. He doesn't wait for me to ask. Instead, he has his answer prepared on his lips.

"You already know my intentions. I've been forthcoming since the beginning. I only want to offer Mena companionship and loyalty. She has full choice in what that entails."

"Love sick fools," I spit. "All of you. She'll throw each of you away the moment she rises to full power."

Henry straightens at my words, his eyes hard. "If you really think that's who she is as a person, Athan, then you haven't been paying attention. Clearly, you don't know Mena at all. If ignorance was a virtue, you'd be a saint by now."

He turns towards the house and starts to make his way over to the door, following after Mena. Otto looks at me with a long lingering emotion that makes me feel more ashamed than anything else. Hu is the last to go, his eyes taking in my tension and the emotion I'm trying my best to hide.

"You're smarter than this, reaper," he says. "If you keep on this path, you're going to lose your chance."

I bare my teeth at him. "Who says I want a chance?"

Hu smirks with such condescension, it puts me on edge. "I can hear your thoughts, reaper, remember? And the shadows you wrap around your shoulders do not hide the ache you feel for Mena. If you care for her, you should start showing it. And if you don't, then stop confusing her heart and leave for good."

He turns and leaves me there, standing before the house, alone. Just as I've always been. I'm meant to be alone. That's my curse and my punishment. It's what I've earned.

Despite their words, I can't give in, not truly. I don't deserve this chance. I don't deserve any affection or an opportunity for love. My sins far outweigh anything I could give Mena, and she deserves someone whole and without this crushing guilt. She deserves someone better. Any of the others would be a better option than me, a reaper with a past so black, it might as well be night. I cannot give in.

But I'm not strong enough to leave.

I disappear to the cemetery, trailing along the gravestones until I find a place to sit with the souls who refuse to move on. Their sadness comforts me, because at least I'm not alone in this feeling.

At least I'm not alone in my pain.

67
MENA

I stare at the window of my bedroom, the symbol scratched into the glass like a beacon. What looks like blood drips around it, as if whoever carved the symbol into my window repeated the action in blood to make sure the message was clear. It has only just shown up within the last hour or two. It certainly was not there when I awoke this morning. So sometime between when I went downstairs for breakfast and now, some creature was at my window, looking into my most intimate space as it carved the strange symbol there. And it is strange, but also familiar, though I cannot place why the design makes my mind itch in confusion.

"The witches?" I ask, my heart kicking hard in my ribcage. Every day, there is something new to fear, something new to worry about. It makes sense my first suspect would be the witches. After all, they had certainly tried to harm me.

Hu shakes his head at my question. Of the four men, he's the most knowledgeable about things like this. Henry's knowledge is perfect for science. Otto seems to know enough, but had not had the full story. Athan, despite his insistence otherwise, knows next to nothing. Hu, with all his ancient wisdom and experience, is my crutch in circumstances like these.

"That symbol is angelic, little void," he replies, his eyes on the dripping blood.

I hesitate before asking my next question, preparing myself. "And what does it mean?"

Hu glances at me, his eyes showing his age and power behind them. I can see he does not think it wise to tell me, but he forces himself to anyway. "It means 'forsaken,'" he finally admits. "It is the symbol for one forsaken by their god, the same symbol burned into the Morningstar's back."

My chest squeezes so tight, for a moment, I can't breathe. Every day, a new surprise. Every day, a reminder that the god I spent my life worshipping is not the being I thought. How many more blows must I suffer through no fault of my own? How many more reminders must I consume? This speaks of a bitter god, of a cruel one, and the more these mementos appear, the more angry I grow with him.

After that, more and more of the symbols begin showing up everywhere I turn. The strange etched symbol, two lines cut through what look like wings, appears on the windows, the doorways, the stones before my house, until it's an effort to keep up with washing them away. Despite the blood being removed, the lines still remain, each carved into the surface with something sharp. After a while, they grow more creative and begin leaving behind images of the upside down cross, a slap in the face to my prayers. It goes on for days, haunting me in such a way that I must keep all the curtains closed, the doors locked, to feel safe.

Three days later, the doorbell rings and their methods change. Instead of the symbols carved into the cobblestones, there's a golden box, a large blood red bow on top. A gift addressed to me. But they don't write my name. No, they write the same forsaken symbol they continue to use.

I want nothing to do with it.

But the others insist we at least know what's inside of it.

"What if it's a plague?" I ask, staring at the box. My skin pebbles with unease, an awareness of the evil inside that box filling me fully. I don't know what to expect, but I figure it cannot be anything good.

Henry shifts. "A plague would be very bad."

"It's not a plague," Athan counters. "I scent death, not sickness."

"Yes, but plague causes death," I point out. "And there have been plagues before—"

"I think we're all safe," Athan argues.

Otto sniffs. "But not Mrs. Kingsley and the others."

Athan's face changes from annoyed to understanding. "We open it outside. Have fire at the ready to burn it."

It's Hu who ultimately strides forward to lift the lid. As a god, he cannot be killed as easily as any the rest of us and so it's an easy choice. I don't know what I expect, but it certainly isn't the sight that meets my eyes as he kicks off the lid with his boot.

I cover my mouth in horror. "Is that...?"

"A goat," Hu clarifies. "Or at least, the head of one. It appears they enjoy making Morningstar jokes."

It's nothing but teasing brutality. It's difficult to reason the image of angels I grew up with and compare them to these terrible creatures playing bullies and heathens. The image of sweet angels protecting humanity disappears from my mind to be replaced with brutal immature beasts willing to kill an innocent creature to make a point toward an innocent woman born into the wrong prophecy.

"Have angels always been this brutal?" I rasp, still staring at the blood pooled in the bottom of the box. The kill is fresh, the poor creature's eyes still open in horror and yet to cloud.

Hu nods. "Angels are not the cherubs your religion favors. Believe me. You never want to see an archangel in their true form. They are scary beasts."

And this is coming from an ancient elder god imprisoned at the bottom of the ocean. If he finds the angels scary, I don't want to ever witness their horror in person, especially since I've seen one in my memories.

"Destroy it," I declare. "Burn it here on the doorstep so if they're watching, they see what I think of their games."

"With pleasure," Hu replies.

I return back inside the house, and only fifteen minutes later, Hu joins us. I know it won't be the end of the teasing, but for now, perhaps we can respite. I'm wrong.

Not even an hour later, there's a knock on the solid metal the front door has been replaced with. I grimace and glance over at Otto.

"Another gift?" I ask.

"It could very well be," Otto replies. "Or something worse."

"Allow me to answer the door," Hu offers. "It's best someone immortal take the brunt of whatever may be on the other side."

And that's how, as a group, we all move toward the front door. I'd instructed Mrs. Kingsley and the others to remain out of sight and safe until we're certain things are going to be okay. If it's another goat head, then it's safe. If it's something else entirely, we won't know how to be prepared for it.

I'm standing right behind Hu as he pulls the heavy door open, and we all get an eyeful of the man on my doorstep. He's dressed in normal clothing, though that of the working class rather than high society. He's clean of coal or grime, however, which tells me that the clothing is a disguise and nothing more. He's handsome enough, his jawline chiseled, but that is not what makes me catch a breath in fear.

His eyes are black as night, no pupils detectible in their depths. As I stare at him, the shadow of great bat-like wings whispers into view behind him and his features shift, just barely, and I see him for what he is.

Demon.

He doesn't even look at Hu as he stands before me. Instead, the demon focuses entirely on me and me alone.

"Good evening, Mother of Demons," he says, his voice smooth and well-mannered. "May I have a bit of your time to discuss the great and powerful Morningstar and his requests of you?"

68
MENA

"I . . ." I'm at a loss for words. This man is very clearly a demon here as a messenger from the devil himself from what I garner, and yet he's being so polite, it confuses me. Demons are demonic, or at least that's what I've been told. Everything else has been a lie up to this point, so why should I assume my knowledge of demons is correct? Still, staring at a demon makes me war with every piece of knowledge inside me. My upbringing, despite how much I've suffered and my loss of religion entirely, still demands I fear this creature even if he's being polite. I can't imagine the Morningstar sending his blessing at the end of all this.

"Are you here as a messenger or a warrior?" Hu demands of the demon, his voice booming in a way I have yet to hear.

The demon bows his head. "A messenger, ancient one. That is my only role on this day."

Hu glances over his shoulder at me. "He will not harm us then. If his role is messenger, deviating from that role is punishable by death." When I only stare at him in confusion, he adds, "demons are very specific about their rules, more so than angels."

"So. . . it's safe for him to come inside?" I hazard.

Hu nods. "Indeed."

I'm not sure how I feel about all of this, but if Hu says it's safe, then it's safe, even if my fear is dancing in my sternum. "I suppose I should invite you in for tea then?" I direct toward the demon waiting on my doorstep. My life has grown so rife with strangeness, my mind no longer stumbles over the existence of such creatures. Of course they exist if angels do. Demons are hardly less believable than grim reapers and ancient gods.

"Tea would be lovely," the demon says with a pleasant smile. "Many thanks for giving me the space to deliver my message, Mother of Demons."

I glance at Hu in confusion.

"If he fails to deliver his message, he's sentenced to death as well," Hu clarifies at my look.

Sighing, I gesture for the demon to come inside. Some part of me pities this creature beholden to rules I know nothing about. I could have easily sent him away and sentenced him to death for something so simple. I can't deny my curiosity is piqued as well. If the angels were so brutal and evil, perhaps the Morningstar had a point in his rebellion. I can at least hear the message.

It feels strange to lead the demon to the dining table and to take a seat across from him. The men all take up seats around me, protecting me against this creature despite his reassurance that he's here only as a messenger and nothing else. When Mrs. Kingsley shakingly pours tea for everyone, her eyes on the demon with great fear, the demon is nothing but respectful as he gently mops up the spilled tea and thanks her for her kindness. She scurries away quickly, her worried eyes checking on me to make sure I'm safe.

"Now, you said you had a message for me," I ask, my eyes on the demon. If I focus hard enough, I can see his true form, but it strains my mind, so I settle on this disguise.

"Yes, of course," the demon says after he takes a sip. "Am I correct in assuming you know what you are already?" He glances at the others. "With so many protectors, I cannot assume anything else."

"I know what I am," I nod. "I know what I carry."

"Wonderful," the demon exclaims. "That saves us some time." He leans forward. "Do you know the story of the Morningstar, Mother of Demons?"

"I, uh, know what is written in the Bible," I offer with a wince. "I'm afraid I do not have any other examples."

"Understandable," the demon nods. "It had been a great effort of the Creator to wipe the truth away. Some of the items within that story are true. The Morningstar was certainly the most favored and the most beautiful, but he did not rebel because of jealousy. You see, there is a phenomenon that can happen to angels where they suffer from a sudden bout of humanity." To my curiosity, he smiles. "Feelings. Love. If an angel were to fall in love, he can no longer suffer from lack of feeling, and the Morningstar did just that."

"He fell in love?" I gasp. "With whom?"

"Who no longer matters. Her name has been wiped from memory, and now the Morningstar can only mourn the knowledge that he once loved. The Creator wiped her away, destroyed every part of her, and punished the Morningstar."

"When he cast him out of heaven?" I ask.

The demon shakes his head. "Not exactly. It took longer for that. Remember, the Morningstar was his favorite angel, and so it took more rebellion to result in him being cast out. The Morningstar spoke out against the Creator's brutal treatment of the humans, of his cruelty. In the end, there was no other choice. The Morningstar could no longer exist happily in Heaven while he felt and the Creator no longer wanted to see him. Thus, he was cast out."

I tilt my head. "And what does this story have to do with me?"

He takes another sip of tea. "The Morningstar would like you to believe he is a good creature, but he is also the Morningstar and one of the most likely creatures to be able to prevail against the Creator." He sets his teacup back down. "He sends me to ask you to join us against the angels. The Mother of Demons belongs on the side of the demons, and the Morningstar will do what must be done, whether cruel or not, to win this war."

Hesitating, I glance at the others. Hu slightly shakes his head, just barely enough for me to catch it. When Henry's eyes meet mine, I see he agrees with the god. It's Otto whose face is twisted with unrestrained distrust. Athan looks as emotionless as always. Their feelings are known to me, but still I don't want to insult this demon when he's been so well-mannered.

"I do not yet know if I should join a side," I hazard. "You see, many come threatening force and pain, but this is my life. It is not a decision to be made lightly."

The demon's eyes tighten. "Of course, I understand. We do not wish to make an enemy out of you, Mother of Demons."

"Then do not," I say, tilting up my chin. "You have alluded to the Morningstar being willing to do whatever he must to win. If I say no, will he promise not to harm me and mine? Or will he come with violence and threats like the angels have?"

The demons sighs. "Unfortunately, things are not so simple, Mother of Demons. You see, there is a great deal at stake if the wrong beings get ahold of you. Should you decline, violence is—"

"If you worry about the hands she should fall into," Otto growls. "Then you should protect her. Help her! Threatening her to do your bidding makes you no better than the angels!"

The demon grimaces. "Unfortunately, the Princes of Hell are unwilling to help without Philomena's full cooperation in the war. Their condition is she joins us, or she dies."

"And the Morningstar?" I ask. "Despite his rebellion, despite his lost love, he would kill me for rebelling?"

"To keep you from the angels' clutches, yes," the demon says. "It is a strategic decision, not a personal one."

I stand from my chair and look down at the demon, my face stern. I'm so tired of this. I'm so thoroughly done with beings threatening me. "Then I guess our business here is concluded," I tell him. "I will not join anyone who takes away my freedom. You can tell the

Morningstar that his people are no better than the angels, and I will not play the pawn in his war."

The demon tenses, but stands politely. "Be warned, Mother of Demons, the next time demons come, it will not be in peace."

"Good," I grunt at him, gesturing for the door. "Next time one of you come, you will die."

His face twists, but he bows his head. "I am sorry for the circumstances, Mother of Demons," he admits. "May your rebellion be worthy of your soul."

We all escort him out the door and close it behind him. I lock it just in case, not sure if he'll come back with friends so quickly or wait. I glance at Hu as I lean back against the door.

"Demons can die, right?" I ask.

He nods. "They can be banished, so in a way, yes. Their mortal vessel can die."

Sighing, I close my eyes and lean my head back against the cold steel. "Good," I murmur. "I wasn't sure if my threat sounded menacing enough."

His soft laughter is the only reason I'm able to open my eyes again despite the constant threats I receive. It's the only reason I can still smile despite the symbols etched into every window, every doorway, every stone.

"Come, little void," he murmurs, offering his hand. "Let's finish our tea."

I take his hand and allow him to lead me back to normalcy.

Or as normal as one can be when sharing tea with a god, a reaper, a vampire, and a Hyde.

69
MENA

Despite everything going on, Athan still remains as withdrawn as ever. If he's in the house, he's floating around like the reaper he is, silent, the air around him heavy with moroseness. I don't know if it's his grief or the remnants of those souls he helps. Every time I've tried to speak with him for the past few months, he finds a way to argue or escape. So, I've stopped trying to reach out to him. He will when he's ready or he won't. Either way, it's not my responsibility to help him with whatever mental load he is struggling with. It's his.

I haven't seen him since the demon came to visit. That was three days ago. The demon has not returned with his friends, and it has been mostly quiet except for the angelic symbols continuing to appear. At this point, I don't know if it is actually the angels leaving the symbols behind or if they are left behind by people being influenced by them. I start suspecting the later when I catch sight of an old woman carving into the cobblestones before standing up and blinking in confusion, as if she does not know how she got there or what she's doing. Which somehow makes the angels even more cruel in my eyes.

I'm striding through the hallway, heading to my room, when Athan appears out of thin air like a ship in the fog. At first, I think not to say anything, because he has ignored me so often. Some small part of me decides otherwise and I find myself speaking before I know what I'm doing.

"There are scones in the dining room," I tell him without glancing his way. "If you're hungry that is."

Athan pauses and looks toward me. It's only then that I realize he's in his full reaper form. So used to his cloak am I, that I had assumed he was simply wearing it over his outdated suit. Instead, what I find looking at me is the empty stare of a skull, the eyeless sockets jarring when I'm expecting the handsome face of Athan. He does not often wear this form in the house, I think because he knows it unnerves me, but the dark cloud around his aura this evening is almost palpable. I can sense it, the anger, the fear, the guilt, all swirling around him.

I frown. "Are you okay?"

Despite his penchant for being an asshole, I do care for the reaper against my better judgement. I suppose that is what prompts me to continue speaking to him despite no words coming from his lips. I watch as he slowly transforms back to the man I know and the handsome reaper is looking at me again. There's no anger directed at me this evening. Instead, he just looks unbearably sad.

"Athan?" I say when he still doesn't respond. I take a step toward him. "Has something terrible transpired?"

The guilt flickers in his eyes. "Look at you," he rasps. "Despite my actions, you worry for my sanity?"

My brows furrow. "Of course, I worry. I'm not so heartless as you."

"And then you strike with venom," he laughs and shakes his head. His expression grows contemplative despite the heaviness surrounding him. After a moment, he holds out his hand toward me. "Would you come somewhere with me, Mena?"

I hesitate. I have not often left the house since the attacks increased and the angels and demons made their threats. "Walking out the door may be dangerous, as you have pointed out to me."

"We will not be walking out the door," he clarifies. "I am a reaper, therefore, you only need to hold my hand for a few seconds."

For a moment, I don't reach for him, and disappointment flashes in his eyes. When I make my decision and reach slowly for him, that disappointment goes away, leaving behind only guilt.

"If we are not walking out the front door, how will we leave?" I ask.

"As reapers do," he answers, his cold hand clamping around my fingers when I'm close. His hold is a little too hard, but I don't pull away as his face flashes back to the skull and fog begins to roll from beneath his cloak. "Relax," he says when he realizes I'm starting to panic. "It will only feel like mist on your skin for a moment."

The fog surrounds us, covering the hallway and blanketing it out until all I can see is the white mist. As quickly as it comes, it starts to fall to the earth, revealing that we're no longer in the house. Instead, we're standing in a cemetery, the same one I'd been buried in and where we met.

"Why are we here?" I ask, frowning. I don't like the reminder of what it had been like to find myself buried alive. It was by far one of the more traumatic deaths. "And how come you have not used that power before to help?"

"I'm unable to travel anywhere besides a grave, so the power would have been useless. And as to why we're here, I find comfort here," he replies. "As I do in any graveyard." He leads me deeper into the tombstones and mausoleums, his fingers cold in mine. "There is something about them that make me feel better, perhaps because it is where I do the most good. Grim knows I have not done much of it."

"What do you mean?" I whisper, my eyes dancing over the phantoms lingering around. A few, I recognize from when I climbed from my own coffin.

His skull fades, the cloak disappearing as he releases my hand and takes a seat in the middle of the cemetery, right on top of a grave. My eyes dance over the names I do not recognize as I hesitate to disrespect the dead.

"They are no longer here with us," Athan murmurs. "This is nothing but earth now. They have long since decomposed."

Carefully, I gather my skirts and settle onto the wet ground beside him. The evening is cold and foggy and the chill air dances around us as we lean back against gravestones of long forgotten people.

"I can see how it can be calming," I murmur. Despite the phantoms hovering around us, there's a gentleness about this place, an acceptance, that you cannot find anywhere else.

He nods and remains silent. We sit that way for a long time. I do not know how much time actually passes, but it feels as if it could be an hour we enjoy in companionable silence. I spend the time watching the phantoms, watching the way they move from place to place. Some of them appear to be looking for something. Some seem content to just hover and float around. Some still live in their death as they did in life, relaxing, enjoying their time, laughing with each other. It's a strange sight and it makes them less scary to see them so. . . normal. I've been so afraid of the strangeness of seeing them that I had not taken the time to understand them.

"Why do some spirits stay and some leave?" I ask, glancing over at Athan.

He shrugs. "Many reasons. Some stay because they have unfinished business. Some refuse to believe they've died at all. Some died too soon and wish to watch over their families. They can leave at any time they're ready."

I lean my head back against the headstone. "It's a nice thought, that souls can linger to watch over the people they care about."

"I think it foolish," he rasps. "They can do nothing to help. They only watch their families move on without them, or not in some cases. They only watch the suffering they leave behind and they can do nothing but spectate. They cannot tell them they're there. They remain unseen. What choice is that?"

"One born of love," I whisper, glancing out at the souls. "It does not matter that they cannot act. It only matters that they are there."

Athan closes his mouth and studies me closer. "They are not all noble, Mena."

"I'm sure they are not," I nod. "But many of them are. They remain as they're able to, just as you remain with us despite your duty."

He tenses. I think he's about to snap at me, that I've ruined this small moment we've been able to share, but instead, he sighs. "I know I have been unbearable."

I turn fully toward him. "Why is that exactly?"

The second sigh that slips from his lips is as heavy as the aura around him. "Do you know how reapers are chosen, Mena?"

I frown. "Otto mentioned it has to do with their sins, but he did not know any further information."

He hangs his elbows over his knees, his eyes staring out at the souls. "He's right. Reapers are chosen based on their sins, but it's not so easy. There are a great many sinners in the world. Those who become reapers usually have so many sins, they are heavy with them." He glances at me. "Or their sins are so terrible, they remain unspoken."

My fingers clench in my skirts. "Which one are you?" I ask. "Many sins, or terrible ones?"

His eyes flash. "Both." At my sudden tension, he continues. "Have you guessed what era I'm from, Mena?"

"I had not assumed you from any era but this one."

"Reapers are timeless," he says. "We come from any era, from any time period. I, myself, was born in 1692, and I died in 1738."

Which explains his outdated suit. "And your sins?"

He hesitates before speaking, but he can no longer look me in the eyes. "I was a captain in the royal army. My ship mostly focused on exploration, until I was commanded to a different task, one I did not hesitate over despite knowing how wrong it was." He looks down at his hands, as if he can see blood on them. "I was ordered to carry cargo across the Atlantic, to deliver the cargo to the colonies."

"That does not seem so bad," I murmur, frowning.

His ice eyes meet mine. "The cargo was people. Slaves. And I delivered them without complaint. No matter how it made me feel, no matter that they suffered while on my ship."

I can see the guilt in his eyes, the knowledge that he knew what he was doing was wrong, but he does not shy away from his sins. He claims them, wears them around his neck.

"Do you regret it?" I murmur.

"Every moment of my existence," he says. "I was too afraid to deny my orders, too terrified of the punishment I would earn. I was a coward in my life, and I've been a coward in this one. You do not deserve someone so covered in blood to remain around you. I am stained with it, and the blood will never wash away."

My frown deepens. "Are you saying this is why you remain aloof around me?"

"Of course it is. Mena, you deserve so much better than a reaper bathed in blood. I do not know how long I will remain a reaper, but my sins are so great that I know there's no end to this. I have been this creature for years and years, and I have not paid back even a fraction of my sins."

I shift onto my knees and move closer to him. His eyes widen as I hoist my skirts up and straddle his waist. His hands do not move, as if afraid to touch me should I disappear.

"Do you think yourself the only one capable of sins, reaper?" I ask.

"No, but—"

"Otto has killed innocents by his own admission. Hu is a literal god who drives mortals insane. Henry practiced science on himself and created a monster." I lean in and cup his face between my hands. "And I am the Mother of Monsters according to a prophecy. I carry the weight of womanhood on my shoulders. I fucked a god in a cathedral and confessed my sins to him. You are not the only sinner in my home. You are only one of five." He chokes back words, and because he cannot get them out, I continue. "Sins are a construct of a god none of us follow, Athan. You regret your choices, and you atone for them now. You do not do so because a god demands it, but because you carry your guilt with you always. I am not afraid of your darkness."

He blinks. "But—"

"Do you fear my darkness?" I ask, staring into his eyes. "Do you hate me for what I must become? For the power that I gain with each death?"

He shakes his head despite my hold. "How could I?"

"Then how could you assume I hate you for yours?" I demand.

His hands come up slowly and cup my waist, gently as if he's afraid to hurt me. "Lilith chose well when she chose you," he murmurs. "I do not think there a better human."

"I just told you of my sins," I point out.

"Yes, but your morality is solid. You do not harm anyone if you're able to. Your refuse to cower to monsters demanding your subservience. You hold strong, and I envy you because of it."

"Envy me?" My brows furrow in confusion.

"It comes so easy for you to be good," he rasps.

I press my forehead to his. "It's not easy, Athan. It's a choice. It's always a choice."

He takes a shaky breath. "If I apologize for my behavior, will you forgive me?"

"You're already forgiven," I tell him, holding myself above him. "From the moment you watched me claw my way out of the earth."

The first brush of his lips against mine is a promise, though I do not know what he promises. The second kiss is a desperate need between us now that we've come to an understanding. Our darkness tangles together as our lips move against each other, as he grinds me down onto his lap there in the cemetery where anyone could see, the phantoms loitering around us. It's improper and terrible, but only to those who demand women be submissive and coy. I'm tired of trying to fit into a society that would toss me over a cliff at the first opportunity.

I wrap my hand around his neck and kiss him deeper, desperate to have him as close to me as possible after so long of fighting the attraction.

"Could you love me?" he asks as he breaks the kiss and trails down my neck, his lips dancing along my skin. I lean back to give him better access, soft breaths whooshing from my throat. "Could you love me despite what I am? What I've done?"

"Yes," I answer honestly.

His lips trail over my collarbone, down to the tops of my breasts. "I'm a beast, a monster, death on the wind—"

"And I'm meant to die over and over again," I reply. "What is your point, reaper?"

He leans back and meets my eyes. "My point. . . is that I've loved you since I first saw you covered in mud and exhaustion." He trails a hand up to my neck and circles it. "I am the darkness of death, and you will taste it on my lips every time we kiss."

"I taste death every time I die," I counter. "I am not afraid of you, reaper."

"Not even if I tell you the terrible things I wish to do to you? Not even if I lay you down right here on these graves and fuck you on top of them?"

My breath rushes out. "Not even then." My eyes meet his. "We all have our sins."

I prepare myself for just that, to feel this reaper between my thighs, to finally claim him as my own as I have the others, but something stops me. I pause and frown before jerking my head to the left.

Athan tenses. "What is it?"

I frown. "Your lips are not the only place I taste death," I admit seconds before there comes a bark from the fog.

Athan blinks in surprise. "You can sense death? You did that faster than I can."

"I... I don't know," I frown. "I did not know myself capable of it. Do they need help?"

Athan gently lifts me from his lap and stands. He helps me to my feet a moment later. "Yes, he does."

I assume the bark is from some companion calling for help as we trail through the fog, my hand in Athan's. Instead, what we find is a phantom of a large dog hovering over his own lifeless body. The body lays across a fresh grave and I stop, tears springing to my eyes before I even know what's happening.

"No," I rasp, my fingers clenching in Athan's.

He glances at me. "My duty is never easy, Mena. Most duties are not." He kneels down before the phantom where it hovers, it's tail wagging gently. "He has already moved on, friend. You should follow."

Will he be waiting for me?

I stumble when the voice echoes in the fog, when it reaches my ears and I can understand it. For a moment, I think I imagined it, until Athan smiles gently and pats the phantom as if he's solid.

"Yes, he will be. I can lead you there."

The phantom dog looks over his shoulder at his body. *I was so cold, and now I am not.*

Athan nods. "Death is like that."

For a moment, the dog doesn't say anything, his eyes sadly looking between the new gravestone and the remnants of his life. Then he turns toward Athan and looks up at him, his eyes large.

Was I good?

I can no longer hold back my tears. They pour down my cheeks as I cover my mouth, as I take in this poor creature who had only loved his friend so tenderly, he laid down and died on his grave. Heartbreak. He died of heartbreak. And no one had come to save him.

But what surprises me the most is the way Athan chokes on his own emotions, on the way he presses his head to the nose of the phantom dog and closes his eyes against his own tears.

"You were the goodest boy, Tippet," he rasps.

A golden light appears around the phantom dog, around Tippet, and Athan stands. He glances over at me. "I will return," he croaks.

I nod and he disappears with the phantom, leaving me in the graveyard with Tippet's body. Not knowing what else to do, I move over to the fresh grave and kneel. I gently move Tippet aside before starting to dig, my nails caked with mud as I claw through the earth. I dig and dig and dig, and when Athan returns and sees what I'm doing, no words are exchanged as he kneels down opposite and helps me move the earth. When we reach the coffin, it's him who gently lifts Tippet's body. It's him who covers him in fog and gently lowers Tippet through the coffin top and into the coffin with his best friend. Then together, with tears running from our eyes, we fill the dirt back in, until we're both staring at the gravestone. I watch as Athan takes a knife and carves into the marble next to the name.

John Williams is carved into the stone. And then beside it, the words, "And his loyal friend, Tippet," are scratched by Athan. When he's done, he stands and helps me to my feet. We're both covered in mud, as if we both climbed from the grave just now, but I don't mind. How could I?

"Why didn't you just lower him without digging?" I sniff, staring down at the stone. Something about it makes me feel better, as if we're honoring him.

"Because we both needed the dig," he reasoned, his fingers searching out mine and clasping them together.

"Did he find John?" I ask, looking up at him.

His hand squeezes mine. "Yes. He was waiting for him just on the other side."

"Good," I croak, wiping away more tears. "Good."

Ultimately, I learn many things about Athan that night.

He carries the weight of his sins on his shoulders, as do we all.

The Grim Reaper kisses like a starving man faced with a feast.

And above all, despite his sins, despite his pain, death is kind.

So kind, he helped a phantom dog to the other side and helped me bury him where he deserved to be.

With a gentle smile through my tears, I embrace the fog the envelopes me and accept all that he is. And I love him.

I love him.

I love him...

70
MENA

No one questions our return. No one asks about my tear-stained face or why Athan and I are holding hands or why we're covered in mud. No one bothers us as we separate and tend to our own heavy sadness we both carry. I remain in my room long enough for Mrs. Kingsley to come searching for me, for her to knock on my door and ask to come in. I had not realized how long I've been in my room, but the sun is now shining again outside and it's high in the sky. I blink at the brightness as she comes inside and her eyes search me out. When she finds me sitting in the armchair, she comes over and cups my face.

"Mena, dear. Are you okay?"

I look from the symbol on my window up to her with a frown. "Of course, I am. Why do you ask?"

"You've been in your room for almost the entire day," she says, moving to take a seat in the opposite armchair. She looks at the symbol with more fear than I do, and it reminds me that I'm slowly accepting this world I've found myself in. Unlike me, she has a choice. She has the freedom to leave, and I have yet to offer it to her.

"My apologies. I lost track of time," I murmur, looking down at my hands.

"The men have been pacing," she replies, smiling. "You know, I think the whole lot of them are enamored with you, Mena. They hang on your every word."

I return her smile. "You think so?"

She laughs. "I haven't seen such adoration since I found my own dear husband. I swear the four of them were meant to be here. I do not know how you'll choose between them."

Her comment makes my smile disappear. Do I have to choose? I have not been operating as if I need to, but from outside eyes looking in, it must be so.

Glancing at her in worry, her face twists. "Oh, no, Mena. I did not mean it as a terrible thing. You have choices—"

"And what if I do not want to choose?" I ask. "What if I want them all?"

Mrs. Kingsley tilts her head. "Well, you have freedom many don't have, Mena. I suppose, if you'd like and they're willing, you will not have to. You have never cared for society's opinions of you and with everything happening, perhaps it does not matter anymore anyway."

I lean forward and take her hand. "I have not asked how you're holding up. What with. . ." I gesture toward the symbol on the window.

She sighs. "I cannot deny I'm frightened of it all. While I do not pretend to know everything, there are obviously forces at work I thought nothing more than myth."

"You do not have to stay," I rasp. "I have not been a good friend. If this is too much, I will help you go. Whatever you need, you shall have it. The house in the countryside is yours to do with as you please—"

"Mena," she interrupts with a smile. When I fall into silence, she meets my eyes. "I'm not going anywhere."

"But it's dangerous," I croak. "I could not bear if something were to happen to you."

"We, the rest of the staff and I, have already discussed it, Mena." She squeezes my hand. "Everyone knows they can leave at any time, but we will not abandon you. We refuse. All of us."

I blink at the moisture in my eyes. "Are you certain?" When she nods, I ask, "And they know I'll pay any amount to keep them comfortable for life? That they can leave at any time?"

"They know, Mena," she replies. "We all do."

I can't hold back the tears this time as I rise from my chair and kneel before hers. I wrap my arms around her waist like a child and cry in her lap, grateful to have made such friends. They could have chosen to leave, but each of them has become family. I am not their boss or their lady. We're a household.

We stay like that for hours, both crying and sharing each other's company, reminiscing about the past and trading memories. Molly Kingsley has always been a mother to me, and unlike my own, she stands strong beside me.

But if it's the last thing I do, I will protect her. I will protect everyone. Whether it's with my powers...

...or by getting rid of them.

71
MENA

After an emotional few days, it's almost nice to return to the normal task of research in the office. Henry is working in here today and so I decided that I could search for more history of the Morningstar in the hopes of finding something to end the war before it begins. Somehow, I feel as if I'm meant to be at the helm of it, but with that feeling, I do not know what side I will take. Clearly, I won't be on the side of the angels, but I don't feel as if I'll be on the side of the demons either. Where does that leave me? In limbo and confused, and that probably isn't a good place to be.

Otto is reading a book on the sofa, his body spread out like a cat. Athan is at the desk for once, actually researching with us. Hu is busying himself with whatever he does in another chair. He's not helping, not caring to help research, but he's present at least. Sometimes, he stares off into space, dazed, only broken up by laughter at whatever he sees. I assume he's spying on people, or some other such nonsense. I haven't asked.

I'm still mad at him for killing me without warning. I've mostly been keeping away from him as much as I'm able to even if we're on slight talking terms again. There is still the feeling of betrayal in my chest when I see him, and I do not know how to remedy that.

"Do we really need to sit here all day?" Hu asks suddenly into the silence. "We could spend our time doing something far more productive."

"Such as?" Henry asks, raising his brow.

Hu glances at me and grins. "I can think of a few things."

I scoff and look back down at my book. I can feel his annoyance from across the room despite not even looking at him. Out of the corner of my eyes, I watch him stand and stalk toward me.

"That's it," he snarls. "I've had it. What do you want from me, Mena? What is it that will make this tension and anger dissipate?"

I glance up at him over the edge of my book. "What ever do you mean?"

His face twists. "Do you want me to prostrate myself at your feet? Do you want me to beg for your forgiveness on my knees like a human in church?" he demands, his frustration leaking out of him. "What is it you want from me?"

I set my book down on my lap as wickedness fills me. I could play the dismissive woman, or I could have some fun with this. He deserves to squirm. He deserves to feel desperate for my forgiveness. Do I want this god before me on his knees? Yes. Yes, I do. I want to see exactly that.

"That would be a start," I reply, calling his bluff. I don't actually think he will do so. But in case he does, the staff is out for the day, going about their own business. Even Mrs. Kingsley went to run her errands, leaving only the five of us in the house.

Hu hesitates as he stands over me. "I am a god. People kneel at my feet."

I raise my brows. "Alright," I reply, picking up my book again, dismissing him.

Hu growls in frustration. "What do you want from me, Mena?" he snarls again, leaning in close.

I flick my eyes up to his, the storm in his depths giving me a taste of the stormy ocean on my tongue. "I've already said," I say calmly, my wickedness leaking into my tone. "Kneel and beg for my forgiveness."

He flickers between forms, one moment, the smooth man I know, and the next, to the beastly god he is, his tentacles swirling in agitation. He morphs between the forms before settling back on human.

"You want me to kneel before you?" he growls. "You want me to beg?"

"Yes," I say matter-of-factly. "I do."

He jerks my chair toward him despite the size of it and I squeak in surprise. I watch as he gets in my face, his teeth bared, before he slowly lowers himself to his knees before me. His hands remain on the arms of my chair as he cages me in. He's the same height as me now, his face even with mine despite kneeling.

"Is this acceptable?" he grunts.

I grin. "It's a start."

He takes my hand in his and I can't help the sudden rapid speed of my heartbeat as he looks up into my eyes. "Mena, please accept my apology," he says, more of a growl than begging.

"For what?" I ask, my grin widening.

"For what?" he repeats.

"Yes, why are you apologizing?" I clarify.

He grits his teeth. "Because I killed you without your permission."

"Because you did not respect my opinion," I correct. "Do you respect it now?"

"Clearly," he growls, gesturing to his position. "Your dismissal is killing me."

"I thought you were immortal," I tease.

He bares his teeth at me, and his form shifts again, revealing all his brutality, all his godhood he carries. His face is so other, the tentacles there that trail over my thighs make me squirm as his hands clamp down on them. Those hands are tipped with claws. An extra set of eyes look at me, blink at the same time from his face, the tentacles that hang over and around his mouth twisting and writhing. The large black wings curve behind his shoulders, begging me to touch, asking me to love him in this form, too.

I reach out and stroke his face, allowing his tentacles to curl around my fingers. He looks otherworldly right now, but I suppose that's how gods are meant to look. I'm not afraid of him as I touch my fingers to his pale green skin. Despite this change, despite there being twice as many eyes, they're the same ones I look into in his human form. He's beautiful like this, wholly himself, and I am not afraid.

As I touch him, there's something so beautiful about touching something so monstrous so gently. There's something beautiful about risking the sharp teeth and the lethal claws, to defy my fear and upbringing, and choose to be delicate with something that can be incredibly brutal. He's capable of great destruction, and yet he kneels before me like this. How interesting to see a being so powerful on his knees before me.

"I promise to converse with you on all future decisions," he growls, his voice echoing with his power. "I promise not to betray you again, Philomena Seagraves. I beg you to want me down to my marrow, to love me despite my bad decision. I may be a god, but you are everything." He sighs and squeezes my thighs. "I was once different, but here, in this moment, I blur into you. I will get lost in your stars, and I will enjoy every moment of it." He takes my hand and presses a kiss to my knuckles. "I love you, little void."

I stop breathing. "You love me?"

"Is that so hard to believe?" he asks, still in his monstrous form.

"No," I rasp. "No, but..."

"Then let me show you if my words are not sufficient," he growls, scooping me up from the chair and walking me over to the desk. "Let us all show you."

I blink with wide eyes at the others as they stand. "Oh," I rasp, not moving, barely breathing. "What..." I don't know what I'm going to ask. What do you mean? What do you have planned for me? Where is this going?

Do each of you love me?

But the words don't come out of my mouth, not when Hu stands before me, remaining in his monstrous form as he looks down at me with hunger in his eyes.

Otto sits up from his position, interest in his eyes. "Now this is certainly more interesting than the book I'd been reading."

Athan tilts his head, interested, curious, but he does not move from his position at the desk. Instead, he flips a page and continues to read, alternating between looking at the page and watching me shift on top of the desk. I'm uncertain what I should do.

"We still have so much work to do," Henry comments, but those words lack the conviction he meant them with. Instead, his eyes linger on me, dance between the god before me and the way I sit on the desk, ready, willing. "Perhaps," he says, changing his mind. "A break will be good for us."

"Indeed," I breathe, looking up at Hu as he looms over me.

He leans over me, his claw dipping into the crevice between my breasts. "This will have to go, little void. Do I have your permission to strip you bare?" Pride flashes in his eyes as he asks, as if this is progress, as he remembered to respect my decisions.

I can't help the little chuckle that slips out. "Yes, I'll just unbutton—"

But I don't get a chance to unbutton anything. With his claw, Hu tugs, ripping the dress in two down my front, jerking it from my shoulders to leave me naked and sitting on top of the desk with wide eyes.

"That was a lovely dress," I muse, looking down at the tattered material he drops to the ground.

"I'll purchase you as many new dresses as will make up for the destruction of this one," he promises. "I could wait no longer to feast on your sight."

Athan is paying complete attention now, his eyes on my breasts as I lean back on my elbows, his book forgotten in front of him. Otto drags a chair over and takes a seat, happy to spectate for now. Henry hesitates over by his desk, not sure what to do in this situation, his eyes raptly on me and also a bit perturbed by Hu's true form. When I reach for him, he strolls over to stand beside the desk, still not sure what to do.

"Relax, Doctor," Otto laughs. "Haven't you seen a naked Mena before?"

"Yes," he rasps. "But I have still not grown accustomed to it." He glances at the vampire. "Have you?"

"No," Otto muses. "I'm simply better at hiding my awe."

I flush at their compliments and at having all their eyes on me. I have only been with them individually, and in Athan's case, not really at all yet. This is new, and though it feels wicked and wanton, I'm desperate to experience it.

"Love is a sacrament best taken kneeling, is it not?" Hu asks, kneeling before me, his face level with my core.

"I. . . don't know," I rasp, watching him carefully as his clawed hands slide from my knees up my thighs.

"I believe so," he muses, those claws teasing. "Do you accept all that I am, little void?"

"Yes," I reply.

"And are you afraid of my true form?"

"No, not in the slightest." I watch as his tentacles begin to stroke my skin, adding to his hands.

He's a large man, but in this form, he's even larger. Though I have tasted Hu, I have not tasted him as his true self, like this. And I want nothing more than to do so. At my lack of fear, his eyes crinkle as if he's smiling.

"Good," he says, and then those wandering tentacles find my core.

I gasp as they stroke through my wetness, as they spread it around. There are so many moving sensations, I can't follow them, my chest rising and falling with rapid breaths I can't control. Anticipation boils in me as he watches intently, as his tentacles touch and stroke while his hands caress my thighs.

"Lie back, little void," he murmurs. "Let us take you on a journey."

I do as he says, lying back all the way on top of the desk. Athan's eyes meet mine as I do, and I reach out to cup his jaw. We've come to an understanding, my reaper and I, and I give him my permission to do as he pleases. I'm about to voice that, to tell him everything. . .

Until a tentacle slips inside me and my back arches at the feeling.

"Oh!" I cry, forgetting for a moment what I'd been doing. The tentacle begins to stroke in and out of me, driving me back, before another follows, stretching me wider. Hu settles between my thighs, his large shoulders keeping me spread apart around him, his great wings behind him like a halo.

"How does it feel to be at the mercy of a god?" he asks, those claws stroking achingly slow as his tentacles fuck me, as they push deep inside and stretch me.

"Like. . . Like. . ." I can't get any words out, squirming on top of the desk, desperate for more.

Those tentacles circle my clit and suck, and I never stand a chance. I explode, shattering into a million pieces, crying out in ecstasy as he strokes me higher and higher, until I see stars.

Like floating in the stars, my mind supplies, but I can't say the words out loud. Luckily for me, Hu doesn't need me to speak.

I open my eyes to literal stars floating around me, like I'm hovering in the cosmos. I stare with wide eyes as they swirl around us, as space comes inside the office and remains.

"Is this you?" I ask in wonder, reaching out to run my hand through them. They don't react, instead swirling around me like I'm the center of this constellation.

"No," Hu muses, his tentacles pulling from inside me as he stands. "This is all you, little void. And what a pretty trick it is."

Henry is staring up at the stars with the same wonder I am, but Otto and Athan are focused entirely on me, their eyes hungry, but they wait. I'm looking at them, wondering what's happening, when large claws grip my face and force me to look back up at Hu. His eyes are narrowed and as I watch, his tentacles disappear beneath. It isn't until he hums in pleasure that I realize he's tasting me on them.

My core clenches with the knowledge.

"Divine," he murmurs. "Do you know how to pray to an ancient god, Mena?"

I shake my head even as his claws drop to my throat, close around it, not squeezing.

"You provide an offering," he says, and then I feel his length pressing against my entrance. "You give them something." He leans over me. "You're going to give me your pleasure, and when I'm done, you're going to give it to the others, until you belong to all of us, until there's no part of you that we do not know. Understand?"

I nod, my fingers clenching at the edge of the desk. "You're all okay with... sharing?"

Otto laughs. "A silly question when we're all watching you hungrily while Hu prepares to fuck you, Mena Mine." He leans down and presses a kiss to my lips, a lingering one. "You belong to all of us, and we belong to you. There is no other option." His eyes dance up to Athan. "Right, reaper?"

I turn to look at Athan, to hear his answer. His eyes clash with mine as he hesitates, but when my eyes meet his, his expression eases. "Right," he answers. And then he reaches out to stroke my breast, to gently drive me insane.

"Now that we've settled that," Hu muses from between my legs. "It's time you scream my name, little void."

He presses inside me, stretching me around his girth, and I gasp with the way he feels as he eases inside. His tentacles drape around me, stroking, adding to the fire as I moan at the way he fills me. When he's seated fully inside, he pauses, his eyes on me.

"I am not a gentle creature, Mena," he reminds me. "Does that scare you?"

"No," I rasp. "I'm still not scared."

He nods. "Then you will have me as I am, with all the brutal abandon I'm capable of." He leans down. "But don't worry. You will not break."

With the stars still floating around us, he begins to move. Slow pumping strokes at first before he picks up speed, thrusting inside of me with an eagerness that vibrates through my hips with each powerful slap of our hips. I cry out, reaching for something to grab onto, and find hands to steady me. I shatter again so fast, I'm not even prepared for it, but Hu does not slow. He does not stop. He picks up speed.

"I yearn for you in every moment," Hu growls. "I'm eager to please you and it frustrates me. I am a god! And yet I bow to you. I give myself to you. I need you." His claws dig into my hips, piercing my skin with little stinging marks.

Otto strokes his hand along my body, running his own claws around my nipple, teasing. My cries grow louder, echoing in the large room.

"Fill her lips," Hu commands, and I don't realize who he's talking to until Otto strips himself bare and brings his arousal forward.

I reach for him, but he bats my hand away. Instead, he threads his hand into my hair and jerks me toward the edge of the desk, twisting me toward him and pressing his cock against my lips. The moment I cry out when Hu slaps into me with a particularly brutal thrust, he presses inside, deep enough to gag me. I claw at him, trying to breathe, and he eases back briefly to allow me to take a breath before thrusting in again. He moans in pleasure, a guttural sound that encourages Hu to fuck me harder. His wings spread behind him, casting me in shadow even as the stars continue to swirl around us.

Hands trail over my body, stroking me as Otto fucks my mouth and Hu fucks my cunt. I gasp for air as I'm able to, desperately trying to hold on but they overwhelm my quickly.

"More," Hu commands.

Otto jerks from my lips only for Henry to come up beside him, naked, dripping his excitement. Otto doesn't release my hair, controlling my movements as Henry steps up. Where I know Henry would be gentle, Otto doesn't allow him to be, forcing my head down on his cock and gagging me on him. Henry moans, his cock jumping in my mouth.

"Not enough," Hu growls, picking up speed. "Little void, I do believe you're due a death by lust, are you not?"

I can't answer. I can't speak around the cock in my mouth, my hands clawing at them, to bring them closer or push them away, I'm not sure.

"Do we have your permission to pleasure you until your body gives out?" Hu asks instead. "Speak so in your mind."

I hesitate, fear flickering in my mind for a moment. Die? Again? By lust? Is that even possible?

"Oh, it's possible," Hu growls as he fucks me and sends me over the edge yet again. My core clenches and my release leaks around me, squirting out to paint his hips. He snarls, a sound that's all savagery, and picks up speak. "Answer, Mena. Now!"

I close my eyes against the stars. *Yes*, I whisper in my mind. *Yes, I give my permission.*

"Permission granted," Hu purrs, informing the others. And then he fucks me so brutally, I scream around Otto's cock as he thrusts back into my mouth as I shatter again. My body convulses, trembling as they don't stop, as they continue to push me.

"Lay on the desk, Doctor, if Hyde can't come out to play," Hu commands before jerking me up off the desk. He doesn't stop fucking me, instead holding me up by my hips as he continues to thrust inside me. I cry out, my arms clawing at his shoulders even as his tentacles wrap my nipples and suck, squeezing, stroking.

Behind me, I hear shuffling and only once whatever they're doing is finished does Hu jerk himself from inside of me and turn me around. He carries me back to the desk and places me on top of Henry, right over his cock. His hands go to my hips as I ease down on him, as I begin to rock my hips and gasp in pleasure.

And then Hu steps up behind me.

I turn, looking over my shoulder at him as he forces me down on top of Henry, chest to chest, forcing me to arch my back as Henry takes over and strokes up inside me.

"What are you doing?" I ask, my voice raw from screaming.

Hu's eyes meet mine. "Killing you with pleasure, little void." His tentacles sweep along my back side and find my back entrance, stroking.

My eyes widen.

But I don't have time to panic. I don't have time to voice my concerns. Because Athan is suddenly on my other side, naked, his cock in his hand as he guides my head over to him, as he presses inside slowly until he touches the back of my throat. He holds me there, my lips press against his pelvic bone, his cock jumping in my throat.

Sudden pressure at my back entrance has me tensing, but strong hands stroke my spine, calm me, ease me until I'm relaxing. Athan eases back, allows me to take a breath, and then eases back in, holding me again, forcing me to hold my breath as Hu begins to work his way inside.

Beneath me, Henry pauses, allowing me to adjust as Hu presses in my ass, as they stretch me beyond what I've ever been stretched. It's painful, but behind that pain, there's unyielding pleasure. Until they both begin to move, and then there's only pleasure.

Athan eases back and I pull in a large breath through my nose, filling my lungs. He pulls out and my head is jerked to the opposite side where Otto thrusts inside and fucks my throat as brutally as Hu begins to fuck my ass. I gush around them, my body in a permanent orgasm that only recedes and crests repeatedly, never disappearing completely. My legs shake, my muscles trembling to hold myself up, and when I no longer can, they hold me up inside, fucking me ruthlessly.

Otto jerks out and Henry drags me down for a kiss, his lips moving over mine, before I'm jerked back up and Athan takes control again, forcing himself down my throat and holding, moaning as my throat squeezes around him.

"So beautiful," he moans. "So perfect." His hand circles my throat, feeling himself there, stroking himself through my skin. He pulls back and gives me air then presses in again. "You take me so well," he purrs. "Such a good girl."

I explode at his praise, my body shaking as my fingers dig into the desk, my strength failing me. My body shakes with pleasure, my moans echoing around Athan's cock as I leak down my legs.

"Otto," Hu growls, and I feel him shift. His cock remains inside my ass as he shifts higher, climbing onto the desk with us, leaving space for someone else. I feel Otto shift and then his cock his pressing against my entrance, joining Henry's as they stretch me wider, as I gasp around Athan's cock before he cuts my air off again.

"Such a good girl," Athan moans, stroking my throat and jaw. "Look how good you take us."

Tears spring to my eyes as Otto slowly eases inside, as the others hold still to allow him to adjust, to allow me to stretch. Athan keeps me pressed against his pelvis, forcing me to hold my breath, my body languid and overwhelmed as they stretch me completely.

"Fuck," Otto growls, his cock pressed tight against Henry's. "I won't last long like this."

Hu laughs. "Then don't last long."

And then they all begin to stroke inside me at once, and my eyes roll back in my head.

The stars explode brighter around us, my powers growing them, encouraging them, Athan continues to hold me against his pelvis, as my lungs begin to scream. My releases squirt around them, soaking them, my body gushing it's release, but I can't scream. I can't cry out. I can't do anything but accept it. My nails dig into Henry's chest, holding on as they fuck me senseless. Hu strokes inside my ass, Henry and Otto stroke inside my cunt, Athan inside my throat. I am gone, delirious with pleasure, my eyes dazed as the fuck me like the monsters they are.

I convulse between them, release after release taking me and stealing my strength.

"Yes, little void," Hu groans, picking up speed. The others follow his lead, making the desk shake with their force. "Give into it. Let go."

Athan pulls back, allowing me to breathe for a moment, and my lungs scream at the sudden air. He jerks out and leans down, and I'm able to focus on his eyes as he leans in to kiss me. "Don't worry, little Dreadful. We're here." He stands again and I pop open my mouth dutifully and he grins with pride as he strokes inside and holds, cutting off my air again.

My eyes roll back and I'm no longer seeing. I'm not longer able to control my body. I go limp, but they hold me up, continuing to fuck me. Orgasm after orgasm rocks me, steals my strength until I have nothing else to give, until I can only take them and nothing more.

The first one to finish is Henry, his body shaking beneath me as he leans up to kiss my breasts, his lips trailing along my nipples and my neck even as Athan holds himself inside it. His warmth fills me, mixing with my own release, and dragging Otto behind with him at the feeling of them slipping in and out of me.

Hu snarls something in a language I do not know and slams inside my ass, holding as his cock jumps and fills me, as it runs down to mix with the mess we're making on the desk. I can feel it, but it's muted, so far away, I can't focus on it, not until strong hands cup my jaw, until Athan holds me.

"Good girl," he purrs. "Take all that we are, every monstrous drop." And then his cock jumps in my throat and his warmth spills down it.

I need air, but there's none to be had as Athan keeps me pinned, as he pills my throat and suffocates me with his pleasure. I begin to fade, my body giving up. I can't reach for him, can't signal that I need air, so I speak in my mind.

I can't breathe, I scream. *I can't breathe.*

I know, little void, Hu whispers back. *See you soon.*

I jerk, convulsing around Athan, but he holds me fast.

He holds me tight.

The tingles of my body fade into buzzing, my ears starting to ring.

And then blackness envelopes me like a blanket, cradling me, and I float into the stars I conjured.

Fifth Death

Come closer.
Let me bask in your chaos.
Run your fingers down my spine
and thrust deep within my soul.
This is my yearning.
This is my ecstasy.

72
MENA

I come to with a gasp that shakes my ribcage and nearly jerks me off the desk. I'm close to tumbling off before strong arms catch me and center me back on the desk as I gather my senses. My body throbs with a reminder of what we had just done, what had happened, but I feel stronger now, whole. I'm surrounded by my men, each of them looking at me with a mix of relief and worry.

"Oh, thank fuck," Athan growls as I take breath after breath, as I gulp the sweet taste of air, and taste the remnants of him on my tongue. There's clearly worry in his eyes, as if he'd forgotten for a moment the prophecy and my need to come back after each death. Truthfully, I had not expected to die this way, but. . .

"Lust," Henry points out with a shake of his head. "I had not realized we could achieve it this way. This is wildly unprecedented."

"I knew exactly what we were doing," Hu announces, as if he needs us to know that he has all the answers and planned for it to happen precisely this way.

Otto leans over me. "Your heart is still beating far too fast, Mena Mine. How are you feeling?"

I meet his eyes with a small grin even though I work to orient myself. "Like I just died from the best orgasms of my life."

His husky chuckle strikes home when he leans forward to press a tender kiss to my lips. The vampire is as smooth as butter as he presses kisses along my jaw, down my neck, along my collarbone.

"What powers have awakened?" Hu asks, leaning in closer, curiosity in his eyes. "Do you feel any different? Five deaths out of seven is significant progress."

I pull back from Otto to assess my body. I still tingle from their lovemaking, my body bright with ecstasy. My heart is beating wildly within my chest, demanding to be let out, but otherwise, I feel the same if a bit tired. I should probably allow my body to recover before I begin anew, but my hunger has done nothing but grow for my four monstrous men.

"I feel fine mostly," I admit, pressing a hand to my chest. "Albeit tired."

"You should rest after such an ordeal," Henry offers. His head twitches and I can tell Hyde is telling him something, but whatever pressure Henry has been putting on Hyde has kept him at bay. It makes me sad to think of his struggle, and part of me misses Hyde. He's as much a part of Henry as this prophecy is of me.

"I can rest when I'm dead," I tease with a wiggle of my brows.

He snorts and moves to lean in, I assume for a kiss. Before he can make his target, a tap from the window pane has us all freezing. I don't move nearly as fast as the others. My head turn is slow as I prepare myself for what I'm about to see. Otto, Hu, and Athan immediately turn, dropping into stances and prepared to fight. And what a sight they make, ready for war and as nude as the artwork in museums. Henry stands in front of me as protection, but I notice his hand does not reach for his elixir in his discarded pants, as if he refuses to let Hyde out.

I blink at the creature hovering in the window. Sometime between our intimate event, the sun had set and the moon had taken hold of London. The large moon highlights the creature on the other side of the glass. He's dark gray in color, his skin almost textured like stone. Great bat wings arch over his shoulders, large and imposing, but not nearly as impressive as Hu's. His face is not human in the slightest, his nose and mouth pronounced like the muzzle of an animal. His ears are pointed and large, and when he points toward the doorway, indicating he wants to be let inside, I see deadly claws on his fingers.

"What is that?" I whisper, my eyes wide.

The creature's eyes turn toward me as if he heard me. They're bright and yellow, and there's an almost feral look within them.

"Gargoyle," Otto replies, glancing over his shoulder at me. "He's requesting an audience."

"Does he come with peace or violence?" I ask, immediately reaching for my clothing. Upon finding it useless after Hu tore through them, Henry offers his shirt instead. I pull it on, covering as much as I'm able, and wrap my arms around my stomach. It's strange to be before a new creature so vulnerable, but at least I'm covered now. The others seem to think it best to cover as well as they reach for their clothing, all but Hu. He doesn't seem concerned with his nudity at all.

"Gargoyles are not war creatures unless they must be," Hu supplies helpfully. "He will not enter with violence."

"Then we should hear what he has to say," Athan murmurs, glancing at me as if checking for my opinion. When I nod, he straightens and pads his way out of the library in bare feet and trousers. He does not bother with a shirt, and it gives me a pristine view of his back and the ink along his spine in the shape of a scythe as he leaves.

Henry steps forward to help me adjust the shirt better as the gargoyle disappears from the window and we can hear the sounds of Athan opening the steel door and letting the creature inside. I'm just finishing my buttons up when Athan returns, the creature coming in behind him.

I had not realized just how huge the gargoyle was through the window. He tucks his wings in tight as he comes through the doorway, but his shoulders still brush the doorframe as he does so. He's so tall, he nearly touches the ceiling with his ears, and when I look a little closer, I can tell he's stooping to make sure not to damage anything. It immediately endears him to me. This great terrifying creature is worried about shattering my light fixtures. How kind.

"Good evening," I say after clearing my throat. "What business do you have?"

The gargoyle looks around the room, finds me, and immediately strides forward. The others tense and step in between us, afraid he means me harm, but with the look in his eyes, I can tell that's not why he's here. Some part deep inside of me, some instinct, tells me this creature will not harm me despite the constant threats I've suffered.

"Philomena Seagraves," the creature speaks, and his voice is just like the gravel of his skin. "Your name echoes across the cosmos, and we came as soon as that echo reached us. We have traveled far and long to reach you and offer our protection."

I tilt my head and move closer to him despite the clear protests from the others. My instincts are screaming loudly that this creature is safe and so I trust them. When I come to stand right before him, he towers over me, making me feel smaller than I am. I look up into his eyes, into this animalistic face that is less human than many of the other creatures we've encountered.

"To protect me?"

He nods. "We, our legion, have come to declare our loyalty to the Mother of Monsters. We shall protect you in the night, and during the day, while we must sleep, we will wait until the moon rises again."

"But why?" I ask, frowning. "Why would you protect me?"

"You are already being protected by a vampire king, a reaper, an ancient god, and a mad scientist, but you question why the gargoyles are here?" Athan asks, amusement in his tone.

"It is a valid question," the gargoyle says, his eyes unblinking.

"We are not a war clan, and we are adept at weighing risks and outcomes. Along with the whispers of Philomena's name come of the whispers of her morality, of her kindness, and her beauty. All of the traits are necessary for a Mother of Monsters, but she lacks one thing that can get her killed, and we shall not have that being the reason she disappears."

My frown deepens. "And what do I lack?"

He leans down and touches my chin, like a father to a daughter. There's no intimacy in the action, only endearment. "You lack the thirst for blood, Mother of Monsters, and in a war with angels and demons, with creators and scorned, bloodshed will be necessary. So then, we shall spill the blood in your honor, and we shall protect you as much as we are able."

I open my mouth and close it as he releases my chin and gives me space again, his eyes flashing with honesty. Whatever reason the gargoyles are here, I will not deny such a valuable asset.

"What do I call you?" I finally ask, looking up at him.

"You can call me Asikor, Mother of Monsters."

"Then you shall call me Mena," I nod. "And how many are there of you?"

"We are six strong," he answers, bowing his head. "We must turn to stone in the sunlight, but at night, we are your protectors to command."

I offer my hand to him. He takes a moment to study it before he too reaches out and allows me to lay my hand in his. "Your loyalty and your protection is appreciated," I murmur. "If you have need of rooms, you're welcome to bring your brethren inside. We also have meals should you need any." I don't exactly know what gargoyles eat, but I assume they must, so I offer.

"We will remain on the roof where we belong and serve as lookouts," he clarifies. "But I will pass on your kindness to the others in regard to food. We do not need to eat, but many of us enjoy the action."

He bows his head one more time toward me, before doing the

same to the others. Then he walks out of the office carefully, leaving us to stare after him.

"Perhaps more will show up and join our side?" I ask hesitantly, glancing at the others.

"I would not bet on it," Otto muses. "Most creatures are selfish. The gargoyles have never been a selfish lot. They prefer a leader. Asikor clearly leads them, but they enjoy focusing their tasks. In you, they find their purpose."

"Someone should warn Mrs. Kingsley that we have new company," I say, but as if my words procure it, I hear a scream and a clatter of china as it shatters on the floor outside. "Never you mind. She has clearly already seen them."

Otto snorts out a laugh. "I'll go let her know they're safe before she has a heart attack." He disappears out of the office.

"Six gargoyles," I murmur. "What creature will appear next?"

73
MENA

The sun is bright on this rare warm day in the middle of October. There is often nothing but the chilly air this time of year, but as if someone heard my request for a less dreary day, the sun has made its appearance. It's warm on my face as I step from the steel front door and take a deep breath. The air of London is still riddled with smog, but at least there's a hint of brightness within it today.

I glance up to the roof of my home where the six large gothic gargoyles sit posed. They're stone now, unmoving, but I know when the sun goes down, they will awake with stretches. The first time I had watched them transform had been strange. Now, it's as normal as everything else in my life. Unfortunately, they're of no use to us during the day, so today's errands will be made without them.

I've neglected my business dealings for far too long. One of my merchant ships has been docked for the better part of a week and I have yet to complete my inspection and deliver the next set of paperwork for the captain. Today, we make the trip down to the docks to do so. I will not be going alone, however. Each of my men attends with me, their eyes watchful as we stroll down the street toward the

Thames. It's not a long trip, but enough that we walk the streets of London in plain sight.

And enough for the angels to find us.

The first beggar we pass looks up at me with a thousand eyes silently. He speaks no words, nor does he curse my name. He barely moves as the eyes blink and watch me walk by. The pattern repeats itself as lower angels find themselves in the streets to watch us pass, not daring to attack, but serving as watchers for their creator. A few minutes into our walk through their ranks, they start to speak.

"Harlot," one hisses.

"Forsaken whore," another snarls before spitting at my feet. I have to stop Hu from strangling the angel.

Sometimes, their words are in English so I can understand – "fornicator," "Devil Spawn", "Mistress of Betrayal"—sometimes, they speak in their own angelic language and somehow, those insults seem worse despite not knowing what they mean. They never attack, only watch, but it adds to this illusion of being in immediate danger. With so many eyes on me, it makes the hair on my arms prickle and my skin tingle. Not in fear, but in awareness.

"I can't believe I prayed to that asshole so much," I grumble, glaring at the nearest lower angels daring to spit insults. If anything, this solidifies everything I've witnessed over the last few months. It makes me angry that I once worshipped this being capable of being so cruel.

"If you read your Bible, you'd know he was never merciful," Hu offers. "It was right there written."

"Yes, but. . ." I frown at his words and sigh. "It does not matter now, does it? I do not blame the religion as a whole, only the propaganda we were fed."

Henry has always been blunt in his disbelief of most religions, but his curiosity has taken hold now that a literal god is often in our presence. Though Hu is not the same type of god as the Creator, he is still an ancient god capable of terrible things. It takes great effort on his part not to infect every human around us with madness at all times. I've watched him struggle to hold it in, and often, he secludes himself to protect those in my home. Still, it leaks out in small increments, and sometimes, a human will run screaming of monsters and death when his power brushes against their mind.

"Are there no gods worthy of worship?" Henry asks Hu, his eyes bright with that curiosity. "They all seem rather terrible."

Hu shrugs. "It depends on what you consider worthy, Doctor."

"I consider good as worthy," he answers. "Good gods."

Hu shakes his head. "You're thinking in black and white, Henry. No entity, be it human or god, is fully good or fully evil. Things are always in shades of gray. There are whole groups who worship me, who send me their prayers, and I would argue I am not good, but I do not believe I am fully evil either."

"Are all gods so self-aware?" I ask curiously. The way he describes it sounds very human, a mortality to it that draws me in.

"Clearly not," Hu replies while pointing out another angel who barely conceals his identity. A woman walking by stops at the thousand eyes looking out from beneath then brim of his hat. She's struck by awe, clearly a religious woman, and falls to her knees before the lower angel. He ignores her as she starts to pray, his eyes on me instead. "Some humans suffer from being angel struck," Hu offers as explanation. "In a few hours, she'll forget she ever saw one."

We continue past the walk of a million eyes, growing closer to the harbor with each step. I remain on alert, but I'm still not prepared when one of the angels reaches out to snatch my hand when I stroll too close. I jerk back, afraid of what could happen should the angel touch me.

"Blasphemous whore spreading your thighs for the monsters of hell," the angel spits. "You're no better than your namesake."

"Go fuck yourself," I tell the angel. "Maybe it would loosen you up."

Hu laughs at my outburst. "I do so enjoy your fire, little void."

Fire, but not blood lust, just as Asikor said, so we leave the angel where he stands and continue on our way.

74
MENA

The captain of the ship, Captain Brisbane, is awaiting our arrival as we step onto harbor street and make our way to The Cyrene. This ship is one of many in my fleet, and one of the original ships my late husband acquired. Captain Brisbane did not put up a fight at my inheritance of the fleet as some others did. He did not mind taking orders from a woman, and for the respect he shows me each time we've met, I appreciate him more.

Today, he stands more tense than normal, his eyes hidden behind a pair of sunglasses like Otto often wears. I suppose the shades are growing more popular in London these days, as I've often seen ladies wearing them, but it's odd for Captain Brisbane. He often prefers to meet my eyes as a sign of respect. Still, I do not question him. It's not proper to question a man directly on his choice of fashion.

"Captain Brisbane," I say by way of greeting. "I apologize for my tardiness on this trip. I'm afraid there has been quite a few strange events lately that prevented me from attending."

He nods. "It is no problem, Miss Seagraves. We shall attend to it now."

I frown as he turns away, his stride as stiff as his words. It's so strange. The Captain Brisbane I know is talkative and often asks about the events transpiring during his travels. He had not even asked for the newspaper folded under my arm that I always bring him. He has been known to help me with a few of the crossword puzzles I struggle with and we often share in the frustration when we cannot decipher the puzzle.

"Are you well, Captain Brisbane?" I ask as I follow him aboard the ship. The others are right behind me, their tension as heavy as my own. Though they do not know this man, they can sense my unease.

"I have never been better," the captain replies as he picks up a sheet of parchment and passes it to me. "These are the goods brought back if you should like to go down and doublecheck them."

I take the paper, glance over it, and hand it back. "I trust that you have done your job well, Captain."

"I insist you go look at them," he replies stiffly. "The Americans have been known to short us and I am eager to be done with this."

I frown. "You do not make mistakes."

"Our trip back from New York was riddled with sickness and we were short a few members of our crew. I'm afraid it is likely we missed plenty on our travels," he replies, his voice without emotion. It's so unlike him, and I'm so concerned that I do not immediately notice anything else.

Until I realize how alone we are on the ship. Usually, the crew is aboard and tending to things while I come, but it has been sitting for a week. Perhaps, they're off tending to their own errands. Perhaps Captain Brisbane relieved them of duty in the meantime?

"My condolences to the loss of your crewmembers," I hazard. "I will make sure to find you suitable replacements when you are ready." I meet his eyes, my instincts beginning to rear their ugly head. "Where is the rest of your crew?"

Captain Brisbane does not react except to shift his weight. "They have been sent off while we wait."

Otto takes a step forward and takes a deep breath. He closes his eyes, inhaled, and frowns. "What is that strange smell?"

"This ship is out to sea often. I assume it's salt air and fish," Henry offers, but his own frown deepens.

"Yes, well, let me go check this shipment and we can be done with this," I declare, studying the paper. At least it is not a large shipment this time. Sometimes, the entire ship is full of items that must be transported to the warehouses for processing. This day, things will move quickly, and blessedly so. My unease is only growing.

"I shall come with you," Athan murmurs. "The rest of you, keep watch up here."

Athan and I go beneath the deck and take in the barrels piled up against the walls. There should be twelve of them, and when I count, that's the number I find. Easy enough. It is checking the contents of them that is time consuming.

"Three barrels should contain coffee beans," I tell Athan. "Four should have sugar. Two are molasses. And the last three should contain various spices. Could you pop open each one so we can check please?"

Athan moves to the first barrel dutifully and wrenches the lid off with strength I'd forgotten he possesses. I lean over the barrel as he opens it and frowns. None of the items I'd described are within the barrel. I reach for the contents and hold it up before letting it trickle from my hand.

"Dirt?" I say, confused as to why the barrel is filled with dirt. It should be coffee beans or sugar. There's no reason for there to be dirt within it.

"Is it common to find dirt within them?" Athan asks, frowning.

"No, not at all. I have never had this happen. Perhaps it is a mistake. Open the next one."

Athan does as I ask, and we find more dirt. We move through the barrels, each one as full of dirt as the last. When Athan tips over one to check that the items are not beneath them, only soil spills out.

"Twelve barrels of dirt. This does not make sense. This merchant is not known for betrayal. He is highly recommended," I reason, looking up at Athan in confusion.

"Perhaps, he got greedy and thought to play games?"

"And sever ties with one of the largest merchants he does dealings with? No, that doesn't make sense. Something else is going on here." I turn to take in the rest of the cargo hold, searching for any explanation and finding none. I take a few steps, intending to go above and ask Captain Brisbane what is going on, but when I take the step, the floor beneath me creeks dangerously and I freeze.

"Mena?" Athan asks, tilting his head toward me. When another loud sound echoes, that of wood breaking, his eyes widen. "Mena, don't move."

"Clearly," I rasp. "I can reach for you slowly and—"

Before I can get the words out, the floor gives a great heave, and it shatters beneath me, leaving my hanging in midair. I scream as I fall through to the bottom of the ship, my leg jarring in pain at the impact before I tumble to the floor. The sunlight filters in through the hole I made, revealing the space I've fallen into, a space used only for crew quarters and a bit of storage. I gasp and freeze, my eyes taking in the bodies upon bodies piled high among the hammocks...

And the creatures that crawl atop them.

"Athan!" I cry, standing up despite the pain in my leg. "Athan! Vampires!"

I attempt to take a step, but nearly collapse with the pain in my leg. I've been briefly hobbled, an easy target for these creatures who have already made quick work of the crew that once sailed this ship. I recognize many of them from my times working with this merchant ship. Their bodies are in various states of decay as if they've been feasted upon during their travels. I cover my nose at the smell as the creatures close in.

Athan drops in from above, his scythe in his hands as he bares his teeth at the approaching vampires.

"Hello, pretty monster," one of the vampires purrs, the only one not approaching. "We've come to take you back to our clan."

His accent is American, so he's not from the same clan as Otto. This vampire looks more rugged, but more so than that, each of these vampires look desperate and hungry. I've never seen Otto look quite like this, and though he has taken small sips from me, he often goes out to feed in the evening, returning with a flush in his cheeks. These vampires don't look as if they've fed recently at all, their cheeks hollow and blackened, their eyes feral and desperate.

"No, thank you," I tell him, pressing close to Athan. "This is my home."

He grins. "It was not a request, Philomena Seagraves." He gestures toward the other vampires, and they rush forward. "It was a declaration."

I scream as the vampires swarm us. There has to be at least twenty of them in this small space, their limbs gangly and grotesque in their starvation. Athan swings his scythe wide, but the swarm is upon us before he can take them out. They're fast as all vampires are and these ones are faster under the influence of hunger. My scream echoes in the hull and I can hear my men above when a commotion breaks out, but I can't focus on them. I have no weapon in my hands, only the power in my soul.

I reach for it, desperate to make it work. "Lilith help me," I cry, focusing on her essence inside of me. I've suffered the memories, but as of yet, I have not felt her. I press for the power, trying to help in some way.

A vampire reaches out to grab me and I jerk away too slow. His claw slashes across my arm, leaving a trail of blood that sends the swarm into a frenzy. Athan curses as they cover him, as he swirls and fights, as he cuts them with his scythe.

Let your anger out, a voice whispers in my mind. *Every angry repression of your emotions through your life. Let it all out.*

The voice is feminine and soft, barely discernible above the sounds of the fight around us. I focus on the anger in me, the anger that my ship was attacked because of me, anger at these men dying for no reason, anger at these vampires for daring to take me. Anger at the treatment of women, at choking back my words so often they're permanently lodged in my throat, at being told to look pretty and nothing else. I let it fill me, let it bubble over, and when I can no longer contain it, I let it burst out of me.

My power is strong enough now to affect creatures in a way it was not before. It blasts out of me and many of the vampires screech in anger, my power stirring them up, but despite my power being strong, hunger is a stronger motivator. It holds them away, but it does not deter them, their jaws clacking in agitation as they try to push through. Power flows out of me as Hu and Otto drop from the gaping hole above. I see Otto and breathe a sigh of relief. We have our own vampire and he's far stronger than these ones. At least things will be okay now. There are more of us. We shall be fine.

But I speak too soon. The power flowing out of me fluctuates and lets the vampires get too close. Before I know what's happening, teeth clamp down on my neck from behind, pain exploding through my body. This bite is nothing like Otto's. This is all pain and horror and bloodshed. I scream as my blood flows down my neck to soak into my dress, my hands going up to shove at the vampire biting me, but he's latched on properly, and I can't push him off.

Otto's snarl of anger fills the hull, echoing with so much venom, it shakes even my own legs as he descends upon the vampire holding me. He slams his fist into the vampire's face and the sickening crunch echoes in my ears as he's ripped from my neck with a violent tear. I clamp my hand against the bleeding wound and stumble, my legs giving out. He took more blood than I had assumed and I'm bleeding still, my neck wound gushing as I try my best to stay awake.

I slam to my hands and knees as I desperately try to staunch the blood flow. Henry appears a moment later, still in his human form, his eyes on the wound on my neck. He immediately falls into doctor mode as I watch the scene around us through blurring vision. Otto rips through the vampires quickly, far more brutal and cruel than Hu and Athan. It takes only a minute for the vampires to be disposed of, the bodies surrounding us growing more fowl in the enclosed space by the second.

"Captain Brisbane?" I choke, my voice barely a rasp.

"He was under thrall," Otto replies as he steps forward. He's covered in blood, splattered in it. He looks every inch the vampire king right now, his eyes bright with feral anger. "There is no cure but death."

My chest squeezes at the realization that my entire ship has died because of me. I'm too lightheaded to make sense of much else as they close around me. I'm losing too much blood despite Henry tying bandages around my neck.

"We must go," Athan declares. "The sound would have alerted the authorities, and we cannot be held under investigation without being easy targets for other creatures."

"My men," I choke out, my body giving out.

"I'm sorry, Mena," Athan offers. "They're lost, but we will report this and give them the burial they deserve."

"Their souls?" I croak.

"Here," he nods. "I will take care of them."

And then I collapse under their care and float away into darkness.

75
MENA

I wake to find them tending my wounds back in my home. I'm laid out on my bed, my body stiff with pain but still mostly whole, as they surround me. My throat screams as I swallow, and I'm reminded of the bite I'd suffered beneath the ship.

"Did I die?" I rasp, wincing in pain when it pulls at the tightness in my throat.

"No, you were merely injured," Henry answers as he flutters around me.

"A good thing because I do not think this death would have been either envy or sloth. Those are the only two sins left," Hu says, his eyes hard on me. He looks relieved that I'm awake, his gaze trailing down my bandaged and bruised body.

"We came entirely too close to losing you," Otto growls. "The damned American Clan launched their attempt well. They bid their time until you came to them and set their trap. We need to be better aware—"

"You're a vampire. Shouldn't you have sensed their presence?" Athan accuses.

Otto bares his teeth. "Yes, but the scent of dead fish covered it.

This was a sophisticated attack, one that will not be so successful again."

"Clearly," Athan snarls. "You bloodsuckers—"

"Stop," I croak. "Please."

They fall into silence, their eyes back on me.

"Why isn't she healing as fast as before?" Athan asks. "She was always quickly healed before."

"She did not die," Hu answers. "She only heals rapidly when she dies until she is immortal."

"I am fine," I tell them, moving to sit up. Henry helps me and packs some pillows behind my back. "My neck hurts," I add with a wince. "But I will be fine in a few days' time."

"We may not have a few days," Otto points out. "With the fifth death, your call went out to every monster in the world, and it will have been stronger. They will all be coming for you now as you near your complete rise to power."

"Fantastic," I grumble. "Can someone help me down to the office? My leg is still a little weak. I must have sprained it."

Four men rush forward to support me, but it's Otto who gets the pleasure. Instead of allowing me to walk on my own, he scoops me into his arms and holds me tightly against him, cradled like a precious item. I cup his jaw as we travel down the stairs and into the library. He sits me on the sofa before taking a seat at the other end and pulling my legs into his lap. When he starts to caress my skin, I sigh and lean back as the others appear behind us.

"What do we have need of in here?" Athan asks. "Surely, more research can wait."

"It makes me feel better," I sigh. "To feel as if I'm taking part in here with you all."

He clamps his lips shut before going over to the stack of books and picking one up. Despite his usual grumpiness, Athan dutifully sits down and joins in simply because it makes me feel better.

I sigh, the bandage on my neck pulling at my skin as I twist my head. Hu takes a seat on the desk, his eyes on me.

"How does it feel?" he asks, tilting his head.

"How does what feel? The wound?" I counter.

"Your mortality," he corrects. "Does it suffocate?"

I smile gently. "Sometimes it can. It's a stark reminder that we are not invincible, that death waits around the corner often times, but it also reminds us that we should enjoy the life we're given. It's easy to forget such and find yourself in a life you do not enjoy."

He nods, but before we can continue our conversation, there's a blip in the room. The gas lighting dips low, fading out and back in. The air grows thick with power and tension, the walls trembling. I jolt upright, confused, only to find a new person standing in our mist with my next blink. Hu leaps to his feet and takes a step back, his eyes narrowed. Where there would normally be no emotion in his eyes, there is this time, and I see nothing but hatred.

The new man looks around, the yellow suit he wears strangely bright in the dim room. His skin shines with a similar tone as Hu's, but there are no other similarities. Where Hu wears his hair long and dark, this man has short and blond hair that tumbles over his forehead in boyish curls. His eyes are bright blue, pretty if not for the strangeness in them, as if there is a layer behind them like a wolf's. He's tall and lean and stands with an air of arrogance only the most egotistical of men possess. I immediately don't like him as his eyes focus on me briefly before landing on Hu.

"What are you doing here, Hastur?" Hu snarls, clearly on edge. The others are tense, but none so much as Hu. I don't understand what's going on or who this person is. I'm too weak to stand and face this man on my own.

The newcomer grins at him. "Why, did you think you could keep the destroyer to yourself, Brother?"

The air freezes at the hostility between them.

But not so much as I do as I stare at the newcomer with wide eyes.

A brother? Hu has a brother?

76
CTHULHU

"Brother?" Mena asks, looking between me and the god I'd hoped to never see again.

Hastur grins over at her and it makes my hackles rise. "Yes. I'm the better-looking brother, clearly," he purrs.

Mena's brows shoot up, but it's Otto who replies to the insult.

"Debatable," the vampire king says with a shrug. "I'd rather fuck Hu."

Hastur's smile falters at his words, and I can't help the snort that slips out. I relax a little, realizing that I'm not facing this asshole alone this time. Even Mena looks amused at Otto's response, her eyes sparkling despite the unexpected appearance.

Hastur schools his expression again, trying to hide his ire, as he focuses on Mena.

"Lilith, Sweet Mother of Monsters—"

"Oh, first mistake," Athan interrupts. "You didn't bother to learn her name before you showed up here?"

Hastur scowls. "She is Lilith."

"I am Philomena Seagraves," Mena argues. "I carry Lilith's soul within me."

I glance at her in surprise. Up until now, she has not made mention of Lilith being a part of her. We knew she was having memories but clearly, more has been happening throughout our time. It has not been long since her last death and there is likely more to learn, but as much as I want to, I can't ask about it right now. My brother is not as magnanimous as I am, and him being here is a clear sign of trouble. Hastur does not come knocking unless he wants something.

Hastur straightens. "Very well, Philomena Seagraves. I expected you to be beautiful," he declares, "but your beauty far outweighs the depravity in your eyes. "

Mena's face twists. "I don't think you're seeing me well. . .Hastur, was it?"

His face twists in annoyance at her address of him, as if it had not occurred that Mena is very much still human and that she's brave enough to address another god without fear. My brother is used to humans who weep and bow before him. Mena will do no such thing.

I can't help my amusement at the situation despite Hastur's interruption. My brother and I have never seen eye to eye. I am surprised he took this long to appear if I'm being honest and I can only assume it's because he could not prior to Mena's fifth death, not because of his power driving her mad, but because of his penchant for getting himself in trouble. No doubt, he thinks Mena can protect him in some way. I may have been imprisoned for my crimes, but Hastur is often the whipping horse for the other ancient gods.

He also does not hold his human form as easily as I do, which makes me think that he has suffered these last centuries since I've been imprisoned. He flickers between his human form and his natural form, his sharp tentacles appearing and reappearing with severity. Mena seems to grow more uncomfortable the more Hastur attempts to woo her, his floundering only making things worse.

Hastur grumbles under his breath. "Perhaps I should begin again. It appears I have come ill-prepared." He straightens and his form flickers again, making Mena flinch at the severe difference. "I come to ask if you would like to join me, a stronger god, in your endeavors of destruction. You are a great power, one deserving of one so powerful as me, and I—"

Mena holds up her hand and he stops, aghast at her interruption. "Look..."

"Hastur," he supplies helpfully again.

"Look, Hastur," she continues. "I don't know really who you are past being Hu's brother, but he seems to not like you, so therefore, it will do me well to also not like you. You show up in my home without an invitation. You come without knowing my name or who I am or even if I want destruction. What need have I of a man no better than the human men right outside these doors?"

Hastur opens his mouth and shuts it, at a loss for words. I can't help but laugh.

"What's the matter, Brother? Surprised?" I tease.

Hastur glares over at me. "I am the stronger god."

"Says the god who can't control his form," I goad. "What happened in my years of imprisonment to make you so weak?"

He bares his teeth and his forms shifts fully, no longer pretending to be human. Mena shifts backward into Otto in fear, and I don't blame her. Where my natural form is all curves and smoothness, Hastur is jagged edges and severe angles. His tentacles are tipped with sharp points and his face lacks any pleasantness. But what surprises me the most is the way his wings twist behind his back. They appear as if they've been broken and no longer seem capable of flight. I have never seen his wings damaged so.

"What has happened to your wings, Hastur?" I ask, staring at their grotesqueness.

He snarls at me. "It's none of your business, Brother!"

And then he flies toward me.

I shove the sofa with Mena and Otto out of the way, her scream echoing around me as I shift and meet Hastur head on. We slam against each other with a sound like thunder, both slashing claws and grabbing tenacles.

"Hu!" Mena screams, concern in her voice.

"Stay back!" I yell. None of them should get between a battle of gods. Mena especially. The others are weak in the face of divine powers and I could not bear the sadness it would cause my little void should something happen to them. At my instruction, they pull Mena further away, protecting her, making sure she's surrounded. It makes me proud that they do so, that they understand.

We have become a unit, a family of sorts. I've never had a real family.

The fight is thunderous and brutal as we crash around the office and rip each other to shreds. His claws bury into my side, but I heal before he can swing his claws at me again, the benefits of being a god. His wings are useless, but mine are still weapons capable of great damage. I slash at him until we're both broken and bleeding, our healing process slowing until we're both panting and holding ourselves at strange angles as we heal. We will not die, but we can temporarily knock each other out if we continue like this. The walls are crumbling around us, the outside leaking in, the office in ruins. The bookshelves have been destroyed, the prized leatherbound collection Mena loves scattered and damaged across the floor. We've made a mess, and I will have to make it up to her later. But for now, I prepare myself to launch at my brother again, intent on scaring him away from my Mena. Hastur braces himself, preparing to launch himself at me despite his ruined wings.

"Leave him alone!" Mena snarls, suddenly appearing between us.

I snarl, prepared to attack Hastur if he dares to hurt her, but my brother draws up short, his eyes on the woman between us.

"You would protect him?" he snarls. "After all the lives he has taken, all the damage he has caused?"

Mena tilts up her chin. "Yes."

Hastur narrows his eyes. "Love," he spits in disgust. "Love is tiring. Temperamental. It makes demands and uses you until there's nothing left. Hatred is far superior, something you can use. You can sculpt it, wield it. Love will humiliate you, but hate will make you sing."

"And yet I choose love," she replies, her eyes hard. "And so does your brother. Perhaps, think on that fact the next time you dare try tempting me into your hatred again."

Hastur scowls and looks between us, the hatred he spoke of still flashing in his eyes, but it's not directed at Mena. It's directed wholly at me.

"This will not always be the outcome, Brother," he warns. "You will not always have the Mother of Monsters as your shield."

He turns to go, but my words make him pause.

"And you will one day learn that I am not your enemy, Brother. I never was."

He glances over his shoulders at me, his wings twisted and terrible, the bones shattered beyond healing. There's something in his eyes, something I don't understand, but I don't have time to discern what it is.

He disappears into the dusk, off to wherever he now resides.

I stare after him before taking in the destruction we've caused. The library is crumbling, the shelves ripped away and the stone wall collapsed. Books litter the floor, furniture inside and partially out. The inhabitants of other homes have started to come out to take stock of the damage after the commotion and I shift back into my human form before they can see, toning down my power to keep them from going mad, only for Mena's benefit. It pains me to squash it so, but I will live in pain if it means I can have Mena in my life.

Mena is dirty and frazzled, her hair fierce and wild around her after facing off against another god. The bandage on her neck is wet as if she tore open the wound again, but she's standing despite her pain, despite her weak knee.

"Miss Seagraves," someone, a man, says as he appears in the gaping hole in front of us. "Are you alright? What has happened?"

Mena blinks at the man and takes in the damage. "A sinkhole," she tells them, thinking quickly. "The walls have started crumbling, so be careful. I barely escaped it myself."

Alarm flashes in the man's eyes and he steps back. "Should we call someone?"

"It has already been arranged, thank you," she says pleasantly despite her appearance.

The man rushes away to tell the other inhabitants on Mena's street, and I listen. Quickly the rumor spreads, so rapidly, nothing else could be believed.

Philomena Seagraves has survived yet another near-death disaster, the woman with the devil on her heels...

77
MENA

Henry's room has grown cluttered with papers and science equipment. It has been weeks since I was last in his room, but this time, when I come searching for him within his chambers, it's to find him bent over his journal taking notes. On the table before him, there are all manner of glasses and vials, some over an open flame as they boil, some simply waiting for whatever step is next. Tiny tubes connect them, little puffs of steam coming up from the ones boiling, until it looks like the den of some mad scientist.

Athan had referred to Henry as just that, and while I do not consider him mad, I do consider him more of a scientist than a doctor. How could I consider him anything else when he mixes compounds such as this? This does not look like a doctor's work for certain.

Henry is so engrossed in his work, I don't think he even hears me enter. He doesn't move, doesn't show any signs of stopping what he's doing, so I step forward and gently touch his shoulder. He jerks, startling both of us as he whirls, his hand coming up as if prepared to fight. When he realizes it's me, his hand drops instantly.

"My apologies, Mena," he rasps. "You startled me."

"It is I who should be apologizing. I knocked a few times, but when you did not answer, I grew worried. I should have simply left you to your musings."

"Nonsense," he says, shaking his head. "I was lost in my experiment. I should have heard you knock."

I nod. "Should I leave you to it? Now that I know you're alright, I can—"

"No," he interrupts before wincing. "No, I would not like you to leave. You're welcome in my room at any time, Mena."

"Very well," I muse, strolling around the table set with experiments. "What is this?" I ask, pointing to a couple of the boiling bottles. I'm careful to keep my hands away from the heat, but despite the distance, I can feel the heat regardless.

"I'm sure my experiments are terribly droll—"

"I would love to hear about them," I say, meeting his eyes over the equipment. "I am not afraid of scientific terms, Doctor."

His eyes crinkle. "Of course you're not." He stands and comes over to the table where I'm standing. He points to the bottles. "I have been working on a poison in a sense, something strong and without mercy."

"Why something so strong?"

He glances at me. "To rid myself of the monster I created, of course."

My heart squeezes. "You're going to kill Hyde?"

His shoulders lift in a shrug. "Hyde should have never been created and he is but one obstacle to returning back to normalcy." When he lifts his prosthetic arm, I furrow my brows. "I have tried a few different concoctions, but they always fail. This time, I'm using something much more potent. Tell me, Mena. Have you heard of radium?"

I rack my brain for the word because it sounds familiar, but I can't remember exactly where I've heard it from. "I have, but I do not know from where."

"It's relatively new, but many in high society claim that radium has cosmetic results when applied to the face. It's a very potent element and in my experimentations, I've discovered it can serve as a poison in the correct doses." He points to a set of five bottles sitting at the end of the table. "I completed the formula this morning and plan to test it now. Would you like to witness it?'

"Witness Hyde's death?" I rasp, staring at him.

He frowns at my tone and tilts his head. "Hyde isn't real, Mena. He doesn't belong here."

I hesitate, but wince and whisper, "he's real to me."

He pauses. "So you will not have me without my monster?"

"That's not what I said," I growl, shaking my head. "That's not it at all."

"Then what difference does it make whether Hyde is a part of me or not?" he asks, his lips pressed into a severe expression. "Hyde is a figment of my failure, nothing more. He's not real."

"I've touched him. Spoken to him. That makes him real."

"Not to me!" he growls, his body suddenly shaking with anger. When he sees me recoil, he schools his features. "My apologies. I'm just under a lot of strain."

I take a step back, putting distance between us. There's hatred in his eyes not directed at me, but directed at himself. He sees Hyde as a mistake, and sure, he may have begun that way, but he's a part of him now. I do not know a Henry without a Hyde, and I wonder just what he will become should he sever the ties with a monster born of his darkness. I have no doubt that Hyde is the part of him he suppresses, that he was not simply conjured up from nowhere. But Henry doesn't seem to want to hear my opinion, and ultimately, it's not my choice. I cannot stop him from going through with this.

"I understand," I whisper, reaching out toward a bottle.

He stops my hand with his. "It's very concentrated. I would not suggest you touch it yourself." He sighs. "Will you sit with my while I test it? In case something goes wrong?"

"What happens if you die?" I ask.

"I doubt I will."

"But it's possible?" I push.

He hesitates. "Sure. There is always a risk of death with any science experiment."

My chest squeezes again. "I don't want you to do it."

"Nonsense," Henry murmurs. "It's perfectly safe. Watch."

Before I can stop him, before I can voice any more concerns, Henry grabs one of the five bottles and pulls the cork. He tosses it back, grimacing at the taste while I gasp in horror. Am I about to watch Henry die? Am I about to watch Hyde die?

We both hold still, waiting for any effects or for something to go wrong. I watch him in horror, focusing in on every movement, the rise of his chest, the clearness in his eyes, the way he stands.

He sighs after about ten minutes. "Failure," he announces. "Hyde is still very much alive and telling me what he thinks of me."

My relief is palpable as I relax, grateful for the failure and that Henry was not seriously injured. I have not known so many scientists, but I imagine most of them test on other people rather than themselves. What does it mean that Henry refuses to test anyone but his own body? His kindness saves them but at the cost of his life.

He turns toward his journal, leaving me to stare down at the remaining four bottles. If they're failures, he'll throw them away, dispose of them in the way they're always disposed of. When he turns away completely, I reach for one of the bottles and slip it into the pocket of my skirt. My instinct tells me to take it, that if it's meant to target monsters, perhaps it can target mine.

Do not, Mena.

The voice has grown stronger. It started as a faded sing song voice after my fifth death, but now, her voice echoes in my mind like a warning. Not my mistake. Not my failure. But something I do not like.

We were meant to destroy the known world, not preserve it.

But I don't want to destroy the world. Preserving it seems a valid option.

My hand curls around the bottle in my pocket. "I'll leave you to it," I tell Henry. He waves me away, already lost in taking his notes.

So I leave, the bottle tucked away, potentially my own cure, or at the very least, a way to combat the growing power in me. I will not be the destroyer, no matter what, and if that means I'm no longer in the equation, then so be it.

So be it.

If Henry cannot live with his monster, then perhaps, I should not live with mine.

78
MENA

We have all decided it's no longer necessary to hide. Even in my house, the creatures find me, but they seem most aware at night when the gargoyles are there to keep them at bay. During the day, we only have to worry about humans and witches. When Athan agreed that it was probably safe to go out with one of them accompanying me, I nearly passed out from joy. The first trip is to my favorite tea house. Oh, how I've missed the tea and scones!

Besides, the rumors around my life have been flying, and seeing me out and about will keep up appearances. Clearly, I'm alive and well. Clearly, there is not some nefarious thing going on with Philomena Seagraves.

Of course, that's all a lie.

There have been a great many people knocking on my door to offer their condolences toward my crumbling house and to check on me. In reality, they're looking for tidbits, for more information to spread around. So going out and having tea will give them that option so they'll leave my house alone. It will also remind them that

I'm very much alive and not an undead creature as some rumors have speculated.

"Thank you for joining me for tea," I tell Athan as he sits across from me. He ordered a cup of chamomile while I enjoy my own Early Grey. I'd watched as he'd pulled small sugar cubes from his coat pocket. Before dropping them in, I'd seen they were in the shape of skulls. I'd tried to ask about them, but he pushed my questions away with a quick, embarrassed, "I enjoy them," so I leave him alone. I'll ask about them later, and perhaps, ask to try one.

"Of course I would join you," Athan replies to my earlier statement. "Honestly, it's nice to just... exist with you."

I smile at him over the rim of my cup, an action he returns. When the reaper smiles, it lights up his face, makes him more pleasant, but above all, it makes me happy. Since our talk, we've grown closer. On the opposite side, Henry and I have grown more distant. As if Athan accepting his darkness makes Henry push harder against his own.

The bottle is still in my pocket, burning a hole there with the reminder of what I'd taken. Henry had said the mixture was potent, so having it in my pocket is probably a risk despite the numerous layers between it and my skin. Still, I can't bring myself to dispose of it. With each growing hour, I feel more and more helpless, as if no matter what my heart says, I will end up destroying the place I love.

What better revenge than destroying the game board the Creator loves?

The voice is a fluttering nuisance. Though she chimes in often, she's silent the rest of the time. It's still not nearly as strong as I suspect considering her soul is somehow within me. I can only assume it'll get worse the closer I get to the end. I'm not sure how I feel about that.

I look out the window, out over the high society ladies and gentlemen going about their business, unaware of the rising turmoil around them. Most of them don't even know the creatures that exist, happy in their ignorance. I used to be just like that, so naïve, so weak. They have no idea that I could destroy their world, that there will be a war between angels and demons, between the other lower creatures of the world most never know about, that me picking no side might be detrimental to their survival.

Jealousy slams into me. I envy them for their naivety. How dare they be able to walk the street without a care in the world? How dare they not see the struggles I face and reach out to help? I'm not sure what I expect. They don't care about anything unless it's sensationalized. The only reason they're interested in my deaths is because of the rumors surrounding them. It makes for great tea conversation.

I wish I could go back to that. I wish I could simply enjoy my life, the freedom I'd fought for. I want it badly. I can simply fix my monster, erase my darkness, and it'll all go away. Not my men. I don't want them to leave.

Will they stay if I'm no longer some powerful reincarnation?

That thought makes me hesitate. They claim to love me, but would they really if I was no longer a tool? If they leave, will I be okay to continue my life of normalcy without them?

If I destroy myself, will they still remain?

I suddenly understand why Henry experiments on himself rather than others. The only thing we can control is ourselves. It's a terrible form of freedom, a horrible decision that no one can take from you. It's your body, no one else's. Therefore, I can do as I please to it. I can kill my monster. I can stop the destruction of the world.

This is a terrible idea, Mena. I do not advise you continue.

The voice is less panicked than I would assume considering it's her I'm trying to kill. After all, if I can kill Lilith's soul, I'll no longer be her reincarnation. I'll only be Philomena Seagraves again.

When Athan turns away, I pull the small bottle from my pocket. It's still warm to the touch, as if it generates its own heat. While he peers out the window at the passersby, I pull the cork and tip the bottle's contents into the half cup of tea remaining before me. Anyone looking on would assume I'm only adding a touch of liquor to my tea, a normal thing among the high society. No one will question what I'm doing.

I hide the bottle back in my pocket when Athan turns back to me, his eyes bright despite what I've just done. He no longer looks uncertain about our connection, and because of it, I hesitate to drink from my teacup. Here he is, overcoming his pain and guilt, and here I am, wallowing in it. Still, there's more at stake for me if I fail than there is for a reaper repaying his sins. If I fail in this, I will destroy everything I've ever cared about.

"We have not heard from The Masked Guild for a while," Athan comments. "Do you think they have given up?"

His words are a cold reminder than I'm a target, a tool everyone wants, and with this tool remaining inside me, I will never know a moment of peace again.

I lift the teacup to my lips. There's no smell from it, as if I never added anything at all. "No," I answer. "I do not think they'll give up so easily." And then I take a sip of the tea.

There's no taste either. It simply tastes like my normal Earl Grey. So I down the rest of the tea to make sure I don't miss any drops of it, to make sure it will work if it's going to. Athan continues to talk, completely at ease despite everything we're facing. A few minutes later, my stomach burns with the concoction, but I keep my mask in place even as I press my hand against my stomach.

Meanwhile, Athan brings up the weather.

Either this potion I've taken will cure me or it'll kill me. Either option is probably a better outcome than what may transpire otherwise. For a second, I regret taking the potion, only because of my men. I'm an idiot, but I can't reveal what I've done. It had not worked on Henry, so perhaps it will not have any effect on me either.

I'll be fine. I'll be fine. I'll be fine, I repeat over and over again in my mind.

Sure, you will, the voice replies. *Sure, you will, Mother of Monsters.*

79
MENA

I'm wrong. I'm so utterly wrong.

The first day after I took the potion, my stomach burns with the fire of a thousand suns. It feels as if it eats away at me, as if the fire is an eternal sun in my gut. I tell no one. I ask for no help. I'm able to continue through my motions even if I can barely eat anything. Every time I fill my stomach, my body revolts against it, the pain increasing out of spite. A rash begins to appear along my stomach, right where my pocket had hidden the bottle, which is easy enough to hide from the others. I pretend exhaustion and retire early, insisting I need the rest and nothing else. They don't need to see the spreading rash that grows to encompass my lower stomach and hip.

On the second day, I'm unable to eat or drink anything at all. I can't keep it down, so I tuck food into my skirts to make everyone think I'm eating. My tea has been poured into the nearest plants and they now wilt with the increase in flavored water. I suffer a coughing fit into a kerchief only to pull it away and discover blood. I quickly fold it up and tuck it back into my pocket. No one can see it. If Otto smells the blood, he must assume it's from my mostly healed neck wound or from my monthly cycle. He does not ask. I do not tell. The rash has spread up my sternum and along my breasts. It has spread down my hip and along my thigh, a bright red blemish that begins to itch horribly. My insides scream at me in anger, demanding I fix whatever I broke, but I don't know how. I don't know how.

By the third day, I can no longer hide my sickness. My skin is glowing, but it has sunken in, giving me more of a ghostly appearance. They would have noticed the change right away had I been able to stand and go downstairs. As it is, I could not even bring myself out of my bed to pretend I'm healthy any longer. It's Mrs. Kingsley who comes into my room and finds me so. She panics, but when she tries to come closer to me, I hold up my weak hand and stop her.

"No. Don't. I could get you sick," I rasp, my throat raw and bleeding. I'm coughing up a considerable amount of blood and though I know what it's from, I'd prefer Mrs. Kingsley to think it consumption rather than my own doing.

She backs up, her eyes wide as she takes me in. "What can I do to help?"

"Could you tell the others to stay away please? I don't want them to see me like this."

She nods and disappears, but I should have known they would not listen to her. The first to burst into my room is Hu, his eyes wide and worried. His form flickers with his emotion, as if he can't quite contain himself at the sight of me. When he gets a good look at my appearance, the fear in his eyes is strong enough to make me regret my decision. Here I had chastised him for making a huge decision without me and I've done the same.

Otto is right behind him, his eyes wild with worry. He comes over to me immediately, uncaring about what ails me, unafraid despite the scent of blood in the air. If it were a true sickness, it would not harm him, immortal as he is. As a matter of fact, it should not hurt any of them.

Athan comes in a few seconds later, his eyes finding me in the bed and his brows furrowing. "What happened?" he asks. "Are you ill?"

The rash has climbed my breast and covered my neck. It's red and cracked, terrible looking, and itchy, but I don't have the strength to itch it. Even now as I lay here, what little strength I have is fading.

Henry is the last to come in, his frown deep. I don't offer an explanation as he sits on the bed and begins checking me over. I let him, not speaking as he finds every detail. His eyes focus on the kerchief beside my bed stained with blood and the small droplets on my pillow.

"I don't understand," Henry murmurs. "You were fine only a few days ago. I noticed you weren't eating much yesterday, but I assumed it was just you being peckish."

"She can barely move now," Athan growls. "What sickness moves so quickly?"

"Smallpox?" Otto asks.

Henry shakes his head. "This is not smallpox. The rash is not the same as the small pocket marks that come with it."

"Consumption?" Athan asks. "I have seen many souls who have died of consumption."

Henry frowns and glances at the kerchief. "Some of the symptoms are the same but it takes far longer to get to this level and Mena was fine only a day or two before."

Their worry is what has me speaking up. Each of them beats themselves up for not noticing my sickness despite my capability to hide it the past three days, but Henry is right. This is no normal sickness.

"I did it," I rasp, and immediately descend into a coughing fit. I reach for the kerchief, but Henry offers up his own clean one and holds it to my lips carefully. When the coughs subside and he pulls it away, it's stained with bright spots of red.

"What do you mean, you did it?" Henry asks gently, his eyes on mine. The others come closer to hear my answer.

"Your potion," I croak. I gesture to the bedside table, to the drawer there.

Henry frowns and reaches for the drawer. When he opens it and sees the empty bottle nestled inside, his eyes widen.

"Mena!" he gasps, pulling the bottle out. "What have you done?"

The others clearly don't understand yet, but they will.

"I wanted to be normal again," I rasped. "I took it before realizing what a foolish decision I've made."

"What's happened?" Otto asks. "I don't understand."

Henry bows his head to the bed in dismay even as he holds up the bottle for the others to see.

"Is that your elixir?" Athan asks, coming forward to take the bottle.

"No," Henry chokes out. "No, it's a potion I made to kill Hyde."

Athan freezes. "To kill Hyde?"

"It failed," Henry continues. "It did nothing, but the concoction has radium in it and with such a highly concentrated dose—"

Hu snatches the bottle from Athan's hand. "You fed this to Mena?"

"No," I rasp. "No, I took it of my own free will."

Hu frowns, his anger abating at my words. "I do not understand."

"It was foolish," I whisper. "If it cures me, you would all leave. I'll be nothing special. If it kills me, then I'll have lost you all regardless." I look down at my withering body. "And of course, it's working to some extent."

"It's *killing* you," Henry growls. "Mena, how could you be so careless?"

I blink at the tears suddenly in my eyes. Henry is angry. Understandably so. I'd stolen from him and risked my life for a chance at normalcy again. Though he should be the one to understand my reasoning, there is unbearable anger in his gaze. I turn my head away, unable to look him in the eyes.

"You did the same when you tried to kill Hyde. I only thought it could cure me when it did not you," I whisper.

Henry straightens and stands, beginning to pace along the length of my rooms. The bed sinks when Athan takes a seat near me, his eyes sad. "We are not here because of what you are, Mena. Sure, we may have appeared originally because of such, but we stay because of you."

I turn toward him, my tears rolling down my cheeks. He reaches forward and wipes them from my face. "Why would you? I'm only human."

He smiles. "Because you looked at my darkness and sat with me there."

Hu takes a seat on the other side of the bed. "Because you are the cosmos and carry those stars in your eyes, in your heart, and despite what I am, you do not shy from my divinity."

"Because you take all my sins and wash them away. Because when I look at you, I see beauty and kindness and intelligence. Because you make me smile with your small quips and cleverness," Otto adds as he takes a seat on the bed, too.

But Henry remains standing and pacing, his head in his hands. "I've killed you. Oh god, I've killed the woman I love. Of course, I don't deserve you. Of course, this is my punishment."

"Henry," I call, my voice weak. When he doesn't immediately hear me, I try again despite the pain it causes. "Henry..."

He turns to look at me, sees my state, and immediately comes forward to take my hand. "I'm so sorry, I—"

"No," I croak. "No, this is my own doing. Do not blame yourself."

"I'm a failure. I couldn't kill the monster in me. All I can do is kill those I care about," he moans, pressing his forehead against my knuckles.

"You are brilliant," I murmur. "You are not a failure and Hyde is not one of your failures."

His face twists, but he doesn't reply, choosing to allow me the space to rest rather than argue.

I settle deeper into my bedding and rest, surrounded by my men, my mouth filled with the metallic taste of blood, my body too weak to pull them any closer. They remain near me, never leaving for long, never allowing me to be alone.

As I fade.

As I die.

80
OTTO

We watch Mena fade away before us, her body growing weaker and weaker with each passing hour. I do not pretend to know much about science. I had once dabbled in it, curious if there was a cure for vampirism just as Henry tries to cure his monster, but I had dismissed it. Eventually, I came to terms with what I am, accepted it, and decided that any good I was capable of was still within me rather I was a vampire or not. Of course, I spent many years after that thinking I was all evil and had spread my violence like a newborn vampire, but eventually, it caught up with me and I could view myself in a softer light again.

Henry is not able to do the same, and his disdain has infected Mena.

She had watched him try to kill his monster and thought to do the same.

When I was first turned, so violently and abruptly, it took me years to figure things out, to calm down enough to assess my desires and become what I am. Hu has always been a god, has always known what he is. Athan died and woke up as a reaper, knowing and accepting he had to atone for his sins. But Henry and Mena, they were both thrown into this abruptly. Henry because of a failed experiment. Mena because of no choice of her own. Both struggle just as I did, and we have not helped them adjust. We are failing them with our inaction.

I pray it's not too late to fix that.

Henry has shouldered most of the guilt, his eyes haunted as he watches Mena fade away. He tears at his hair, scratches at his skin, desperate to help but knowing he can't. Radiation. There is no cure for radiation poisoning. Though little is still known about this sickness, the results are always the same.

Death.

Henry did not die because Hyde makes him somewhat of an immortal. But Mena? Until her seventh death, she's as mortal as any human. The remnants of the bite wound on her neck are still healing and serve as a reminder of her mortality. She's so very fragile until she isn't.

And Henry had not even noticed his missing potion in the first place.

Part of me blames the doctor for the pain Mena now suffers. What temptation must it have been as he spoke about killing his monster, about being normal again. What yearning Mena must have felt to have an uncomplicated life, to not be chased down by creatures of the night, her home destroyed.

Part of me fears this death will be permanent.

There are only two deaths left, Envy and Sloth. I can't fathom how this death fits into either option and so I fear Mena will fall asleep and never wake up. If that's the case, then Henry will have to live with that, his monster, and the reminder that he had killed the woman he cares for. Even if it was not him who directly fed her the poison, his hand is stained with blood.

Then again, a healer's hands are always the most stained.

I'm lying on the bed next to Mena now. Her skin is sunken and blemished by the rash. Her eyes are clouded and broken as she takes rattling breath after rattling breath. The others are scattered around the room. Henry scribbles furiously in his journal, trying to find a cure despite knowing there are none. Hu and Athan are watching Mena closely, their eyes riveted to the slowing rise and fall of her chest. She has not been awake in hours now, her body too exhausted to keep her eyes open, but she curls into my side, as if seeking me out despite her weakness. It's why I keep her close. If this is the only comfort I can offer her, then so be it.

I look down at her face, at her cracked lips and stringy hair, and take note of how beautiful she still is. Here, cursed with sickness, her soul still shines bright. Most would look at her and see a monster. I look at her and see redemption, resurrection, bliss.

She has to survive this. She must. I cannot fathom a world without her in it.

As I watch her closely, her chest rises and falls one last time. There's no other breath. Her body stills and the silence in the room is deafening.

Survive. Survive. *You must survive!*

Sixth Death

I watch the birds soar on wings,
So free, so bright, so pretty.
So I climbed the stairs, stepped on the edge,
and gave myself to envy.

81
MENA

I blink open my eyes to the sunshine streaming in through the window, the haze of it cutting through the dust particles in the air and creating a scene out of a painting. It's a strange way to awake, my mouth still tasting of blood after my body faded, after I'd successfully killed myself. Regrettably of course. I'm not buried this time, at least. Climbing from a grave for a second time would be even more traumatic than the first time, if only because it would mean that I was dead for a long time, long enough for them to question if I would ever wake again.

At first, everything is hazy as I blink, as I become aware of my mortality, but when it comes into focus, I realize I'm not alone.

As I blink, I see Otto, Athan, Hu, and Henry hovering over me. I watch them all take an audible sigh of relief at my movement, as I start to shuffle in the bed. Their eyes are haunted, desperate, worried. If the sun is shining, I do not know how long I've remained dead, but I can only guess it was at least a day. The day had been cloudy and dreary when I'd gone.

This death could have been permanent. I could have never woken up again. I'd nearly made a monumental mistake in taking

Henry's potion, in not telling them my plans and taking action myself. Tears fill my eyes at the near loss, at the possibility that I could have left them forever, that I could have left that pain behind because of my foolishness. How silly of me to want to be normal again when I have them. How horrible of me to make that decision alone.

"Mena," Otto breathes. "I was starting to worry you would never wake up."

"How long?" I croak. My voice is still raw though it feels as if it's from disuse rather than the potion as before.

"Two days," Henry supplies helpfully, but he doesn't meet my eyes. He remains looking down and away, as if afraid of what he might find. "Now that you're awake, I must return to my work."

"Wait! Henry!" I cry, but he's already gone out the door, running away.

"Don't worry about him," Athan murmurs. "He'll come around. He's been wearing his guilt like a coat this entire time."

"But he did not cause this," I say. Otto looks away at my words, as if not wanting me to see the blame in his eyes for the doctor. I see it anyways. I see it in Athan's and Hu's eyes as well. "I took the potion. It was my fault."

"And yet he made it," Hu counters. "He had it there easy to take, a temptation like no other for someone desperate to be normal again. He did not even notice one was missing after you were in his room."

My face twists. "Do not blame Henry," I rasp. "I made my own decision. I made the mistake. Not him."

Otto glances at me. "If he does not accept who he is, he will get someone else killed, Mena. We're all monsters in our own ways, and if he does not accept his, either it will be at his cost or someone else's."

I know what he speaks is truth. I'd watched Henry take the potion without any hesitation and lately, he has held Hyde down completely, even refusing to transform when needed. He has power at his disposal he refuses to use any longer. And I had fallen into the same trap. I'd gone round and round in my mind until I'd convinced myself it was necessary to rid my body of a monster.

But I am Philomena Seagraves. A prophecy does not change who I am even if I carry someone else with me. I can still be good. I can still keep the world safe.

The men deserve to pay.

"There are bad people in this world," I say out loud, "but I am not one of them."

The others think I'm talking to them and not the voice in my head, but the message comes across either way.

"Of course, you're not," Athan murmurs.

Hu moves closer and takes my hand. "We're here for you, Mena. I know this must be difficult but—" He looks down at our joined hands in confusion, his words cutting off abruptly.

I do the same, following his gaze. There's a tingling in my fingers that I don't notice until he calls attention to it. My heart is swollen with the love in the room, with the worry for Henry, and without realizing, my powers have begun to leak out. This one, I don't recognize. I have never felt this flavor.

"Envy," Hu murmurs, and then winces as my power flares brightly. "Mena, release me."

I try to let go of his hand, but I can't and panic. I jerk, my strength returned after my awakening. "I can't!" I cry, pulling harder.

Athan and Otto stand and move to help, but Hu stops them. "No, do not touch her," he growls. "It appears our dear Mena has developed the skill of power absorption and thievery."

"What?" I gasp, trying to separate our hands. "What does that mean?"

Hu meets my eyes. "It means you're stealing my power, Mena."

Horror fills me and I wrench harder, trying to free him before I harm him further. "How do I stop it?"

"Relax," Otto commands. "Deep breaths. Slowly let them out until you feel calm. The more you panic, the stronger the pull may be."

I do as he says, forcing myself to take long lingering breaths. I close my eyes, focusing on the strange tingling in my fingers. Breathe in. Breathe out. Repeat. Slowly, I feel the power ebb, stronger with Hu's divinity within it, until I'm able to snatch my hand back.

Hu rolls his shoulders and grins. "My, what a gift, Mena," he purrs. "I wonder how that will feel when you're sucking my cock."

My face reddens. "Did I hurt you?"

"Of course not. I'm a god. A little sip off the top will not hurt me." He glances at the others. "I would be careful with the reaper and the vampire however."

I wince but nod. "I'll work on it."

I remember feeling weak and helpless, like my body was giving up on me. I feel completely fine now. The wounds I'd suffered in the vampire fight are completely healed now, not a single scar left as a memory this time. I'm whole, so when I try to stand, it's with ease, the cosmos I'd sipped from Hu bright in my chest. The feeling is addictive, effervescent, and I can't help but want more despite the danger it poses. I have to get a handle on that power quickly, so I don't accidentally hurt someone I care for.

I barely have time to step off the final step in the staircase when the ground shakes beneath our feet, a sound coming from the front of the house. Boom! Boom! Boom! I grab at the banister, my eyes wide as the sound continues in a rhythmic, constant beat. The chandelier above us sways with the force.

"What the devil is that?" I ask, careful not to cling to Otto at my side. It's best I be careful until I know how to control my new power. "An earthquake?"

"I do not know," Otto replies.

Athan steps in front of us. "We will investigate."

Together, minus Henry, we pull the steel front door open and get a look at what's outside.

A man, or... a man-shaped being, stands there. He's dressed in a pristine white suit, so perfectly tailored, high society would be proud. Where his head should be, there are only thousands of eyes looking and blinking at us. At his back flutter so many wings there would never be a way to count them, each of them as pristine and white as his suit. He glows brightly, terrifyingly, and inspires a horror inside me that I've never known. The sound had come from a great flaming sword he stabs into the cobblestone over and over again, a call, a warning. And someone I recognize from Lilith's memories.

Lilith hisses in my mind, angry, disgusted, at the sight of the creature before us.

"Archangel," Otto whispers, staring with wide eyes at the thing. "I've never seen one."

Hu is the one to bare his teeth and step forward. "Michael. What are you doing here?"

The eyes narrow as one, making my skin crawl. No being should have so many eyes. "The last I saw of you, great dreamer, you were trapped beneath the seas."

Hu growls. "Things change."

"Indeed." Those eyes focus on me, and I cling to Otto despite my worry about my new power, tempted to hide from the archangel's perception. "Blasphemous Mother, I come bearing a message on this day."

I tilt up my chin despite my fear. "What is your message, archangel?"

Despite him not having a mouth, I feel as if he's smiling at me, the emotion so full of malice, I know it's not out of joy, but out of cruelty. "You have three days," he declares. "Either die by my hand or by your own. That is your choice."

And then his wings snap out and he shoots into the sky, leaving us to stare at the large hole his sword had left behind in the cobblestone street. Yet another explanation I'll need to provide when the neighbors come asking.

I narrow my eyes after him, annoyed at the sudden takeoff. "What a prick," I growl. "I'm starting to really dislike angels."

Hu snorts. "You and me both. But Michael is no lower angel. He's the Creator's right hand, and if he says he will return in three days, he will. We better be prepared."

Sighing, I turn back to the door. "Fantastic. Just what we needed."

Hu studies me closely. "I could kill you—"

"With Sloth?" Otto growls. "No, best to formulate a plan before causing any trouble."

"Can we at least have tea first?" I grumble. "Tea before archangels and death."

Athan laughs. "Tea before archangels and death sounds perfect."

82
MENA

We spend the next couple of days practicing the new powers I possess and making sure I'm as prepared as I can be. As it turns out, I can steal power simply with touch, but I can also siphon from someone from a few feet away if I focus hard enough. It takes a lot of effort and willpower, but I'm capable of it.

Once I've figured out my newest power and practiced my others, the conversations turn to how I could die by sloth. The conversations go around in circles, going nowhere, as we all think of ways to kill me by lazy means. I have no ideas other than sitting for long hours and wasting away, but that's not fast enough. We need something that will kill me quickly and efficiently and it has to be perfectly tied with sloth or we risk my actual permanent death.

There is only a matter of twenty-six hours before Michael returns and somehow, I'm not looking forward to his company. The archangel terrifies me, but he's also not unfamiliar. He has played a part in my memories, the archangel who brutally beat Lilith within an inch of her life and who intended for her to drown in the ocean before she found herself in Hu's city. The voice in my mind has been strangely quiet after this death, not in fear, but because she wants to say so much, nothing will come. I know she thinks me capable of destroying the world, wants me to, but that's not my intention. If I have my way, I'll end this all without bloodshed.

Taking a break from the lessons and discussions, I find myself in my back garden to have tea. The day is not sunny, but at least it's not cold and dreary. The wind only has a small bite of chill, but I still find myself with a blanket over my lap to keep my warmth. The clouds keep the sunlight at bay, but also the rain thankfully. I'd prefer warm days to take my tea in the back garden, but I'll take what I can get.

The gargoyles are stone on the roof, great assets at night, but useless during the day. Their watching eyes always make me feel strange knowing they'll remember watching me drink my tea when they wake up. I'm not supposed to be alone, so after a few moments of sitting outside, Henry appears.

I blink in surprise as he steps out as he hasn't spent much time with me since my last death. He has remained in his room, riddled with guilt no matter what I've tried telling him. He comes out with his own teacup and takes a seat at the small table.

"Hello," I murmur, glancing at him from the corner of my eyes.

"Good morning," he replies, taking a sip of his teacup as if there is nothing amiss between us.

We fall into tense silence. I allow it to continue for a few minutes before I sigh in annoyance and turn toward him. "This is ridiculous. Henry, it was not your fault."

He glances at me and looks away. "It was. Even indirectly. I've been so insistent on my own cure, I did not think how it must sound to someone else also wanting a cure."

"I no longer want a cure," I declare. "This is who I am. I accept it. Despite what I carry, I am still Philomena Seagraves, just as you are still Henry Jekyll."

"But I am not just Henry Jekyll," he murmurs. "I am also Edward Hyde."

"And I am also Lilith," I point out. "It matters not, Henry. They are a part of us, but only a part. They do not control every outcome."

He frowns into his teacup. "You forgive me so easily..."

"There's nothing to forgive," I argue. "I took the bottle. I chose to drink it. Blaming you would be like blaming the bartender for my drunkenness."

He snorts. "I suppose you're right. But the bartender is still the supplier."

I shrug. "It is not your fault no matter how you look at it. There is nothing to forgive."

He runs his fingers along the edge of the teacup. "The others would disagree."

Sighing, I reach for his hand, but he slides it from the table, hesitant to touch me. I know it's because of his own insecurities, but my mind says it's because he's afraid of my new power, that he's afraid I'll hurt him. It hits me in the chest in a way I do not expect, and I take a shuddering breath in as I return my hand to my lap. Henry, seeing my reaction, looks longingly toward me, but doesn't reach out. The distance between us is great as we both fall into silence, a chasm that cannot possibly be traversed so soon.

"Perhaps my problem is that I see Hyde as the other side of you, as part of you," I whisper, not daring to look at him. "And you see yourself as a failure. You do not wish to admit that Hyde is you, that he is the darker parts of you. Just as I had trouble accepting the darkness within me."

He doesn't speak, only listening to my words.

"Killing Hyde will be killing the side of you who fails, the side that is brutal and sometimes cruel. Killing him will be killing a piece of your soul," I rasp. "I will love you regardless, whether missing pieces or whole, but just know..." I meet his eyes then, "... I do not see Hyde as a curse, but as a blessing."

He swallowed hard and opens his mouth to speak. I hover in anticipation, needing to hear what he's going to say, needing to hear his apology and his admittance that I'm right.

He never gets the chance.

BOOM!

The garden wall explodes in front of us, bricks raining down around us in chunks. I lift my arms to protect my eyes, the pieces slamming into me before I can do much more than gasp. Dust hovers in the air, and my ears ring from the force of whatever attacked the wall. Henry tips backward in his chair as a large piece hits him in the chest and he scrambles to return to his feet, shoving the chair away, his chest heaving in confusion.

I stand as the pieces settle, the dust heavy in the air, as creatures I recognize begin to step through the gaping wall.

Victoria's monsters.

There are at least a dozen of them streaming in through the hole they created. I throw out my arm, pushing my power toward them, but these creatures are not alive, not in the same sense as I am. They're undead and powerful. My power does nothing but bounce off them and fade into the air.

"Henry!" I shriek as one of the monsters grabs me. "Henry! Your elixir!"

Henry is on his feet now. No doubt the others are rushing out at the commotion, but they won't be here in time. It's up to Henry. He reaches for his hip, and I think, for a moment, he's going to grab the elixir bottle he always carries. If he transforms into Hyde, he'll be able to stop this. He'll buy us time for the others to come help. But when he pulls his hand away, I find a pistol in his hand rather than the bottle I know.

My heart sinks.

Henry points the pistol at the nearest Frankie and pulls the trigger. His aim is impeccable, his many years hunting with his father a blessing if we were in the forest. The boom makes my ears ring even as the Frankie who holds me begins to drag me away. The Frankie Henry shoots doesn't react to the hole now in its sternum, right where it's heart should be. It continues to come after him, and with great strength, it wraps giant hands around Henry's throat and throws him backward toward the house. He slams against the wall, his head hitting with an audible crack, and begins to slide down it, out cold. A trail of blood follows his collapse down the stone wall.

"Henry!" I cry, trying to rush toward him, but I'm lifted into the air and thrown over a shoulder despite my best efforts. I kick and scream and fight but it does no good to these inhuman creatures who no longer feel. My powers are useless against soulless bodies. "Henry!"

My shriek is ear piercing, but I can do nothing more as I'm carried away from my home quickly. I hear the others burst out, trying to figure out what happened, but we move so fast, they fade before they can discern where I've gone. When I continue to scream for them, the sound echoing around us, I suffer a blow to my head from who knows where, and I know no more.

I come to, freezing, my body shivering with the cold seeping in through my dress. My head aches fiercely, my pulse beating behind my skull, and I press my hand to the rising bump there in hopes of stopping it. It fails, but it does ease minutely, enough that I can peer around me and see my surroundings. Details come into focus slowly. Furniture around me, muted light from the gas lanterns, metal bars enclosing me. I tense, realizing quickly I'm not in a room at all, but in a cage decorated like a room.

Metal bars surround me, the space large enough I suppose. It does not feel like the matchbox sizing of what a prison provides. It's furnished with better furniture than I would expect for a prison, a sofa, a small bed, but still there is only a bucket to relieve myself rather than a toilet.

Frankies line the room outside my cage, but they're not alone. I recognize the woman and the humans among them as I've seen them before.

"Victoria Frankenstein," I muse, getting to my feet despite the pounding in my skull. "I was wondering when the Masked Guild would make their appearance again."

She smiles and holds out her arms like a circus ringleader. "Surprise. Welcome to our headquarters, Miss Seagraves. I apologize for having to resort to such violence to bring you here."

"You don't mean that," I grunt, rubbing my skull. "You fully intended to resort to violence."

She shrugs. "I have a role to play just as you do. And your role is here."

As if her words reawaken the time frame, my eyes widen. "How long have I been here?"

"A matter of hours," she replies, narrowing her eyes. "Why?"

Which means if the others don't find me within twenty-three hours, Michael will.

"You don't realize what you've done," I warn. "You cannot keep me here."

Victoria smiles. "Actually, we can keep you here as long as we would like, at the Queen's orders. Clearly, you're not as strong as you think you are if my Frankies were able to take you with your protectors hovering around you." At my expression, she scowls. "It's for your own good. We can protect you and the world will be—"

"You're all going to die!" I spit. "You cannot possibly protect me from what's coming."

"Sure we are," Victoria laughs and the masked humans around her join in. "We'll make you as comfortable as possible, Mena. If you should need anything, just ask."

"Freedom," I growl, wrapping my hands around the bars. "I desire freedom."

Victoria tilts her head. "Anything but that."

And then she turns and leaves the room, her men following behind her. The Frankies remain, ominous sentinels with no emotion that unnerve me with their hollow, haunted eyes. I reach out with my power again, but find nothing, no awareness, no souls. What monstrosities did Victoria make? What horrors?

Desperate and terrified, I settle into my cage to wait.
For my men or for the archangel.
I know not which will reach me first.

83
JEKYLL

Wake up, Henry! HENRY, WAKE UP!

The voice echoes like mine used to in the mountains. I'd been so enamored with the science behind it. My one trip to the Swiss Alps flickers in my memory, the memory of me screaming into the mountains and my voice ricocheting back to me over and over again. The scream rolled into another and another until the mountains were full of my scream, and each time the sound came back, it was more haunted than before, until the mountains were full of my ghosts. It had been therapeutic in some ways, to scream so loudly and to have it echoed back to me. In some ways, it had been sobering. The scream that came back was different somehow, as if from another creature, more tortured, more anguished.

Stop reminiscing and wake up, you idiot!

The voice is clearly agitated, anger coating every word. Not an echo at all.

Of course, I'm angry. You lost her! You lost our Mena because of your foolish fear! Wake the fuck up and go get her!

Mena? I've lost Mena. I start to shift under those words, trying to drag myself up from the depths of unconsciousness. It takes long seconds to push through it, like I'm swimming through a pool of molasses. There's a strange pop as I pull and then I'm blinking open my eyes. The day is the same, the clouds offering coverage that keep the sun at bay. But the garden I'd been sitting in with Mena, having such a terrible discussion in, has been destroyed. There's a gaping hole in the stone wall before me, pieces of bricks littering the carpet of grass. The table and chairs have been overturned and smashed. The carefully planted garden Mena had taken the time to tend to is a mess, plants pulled up and kicked over, many of them stomped on.

"What. . ." I press a hand to my aching head and find wetness on the back of it. I pull my fingers away and see the red of my blood. Despite the ache and the evidence of injury, there's no longer any wound. Hyde heals me. He always does.

The pop was your skull repairing itself, Hyde snarls. *You would have died if not for me, but it would not have been a problem had you let me protect her!*

The door of the house crashes open and the others tumble out. Hu, Otto, and Athan are a few seconds too late. No doubt they ran as soon as they heard Mena screaming, but. . .

Mena!

I struggle to my feet, slipping on the wet stone. It takes me a second to realize the wetness is from me, from where my blood dripped down the wall. Hyde is right. If not for him, I would be dead right now. That I can clearly see even as I stumble in my own blood, as I brace myself against the wall before facing the others.

Fucking traitor, Hyde sneers in my head. *You let them take her because of your fear. If she dies, it's on your conscience, no others.*

My chest squeezes at his words and I realize he's right again. I hadn't wanted to transform. I had not wanted to give in and let Hyde take the reins. I'd chosen a weapon incapable of hurting the beasts instead, though I had not known that. I should have suspected, but I had not thought past anything but my fear of the monster inside me.

"Where is she?" Hu demands, turning in circles. His eyes focus on me and the blood staining the area around me. He does not seem concerned by the sheer amount of it, only narrowing his eyes on me further as I attempt to right myself. "Where is Mena?" There's an urgency in his voice that heightens my own panic, that forces me to realize the true mistake I've made.

"The Masked Guild took her," I admit, wincing at the pain in my skull that comes with talking. "Victoria's monsters came through the wall and—"

Otto appears before me, moving so fast, I cannot track it until he's right before me, menace on his face. It's twisted so savagely, I take a stumbling step back and slam into the wall for a second time, true fear in my heart for the monster he hides inside him. "Why didn't you transform?" he snarls in my face.

"I. . . I. . ." No words will come. I can't force them out past the rapid beating of my heart, past the panic in my soul.

It's no less than you deserve, Hyde snarls.

"You let them take her?" Athan growls, his form flickering between his human one and his skeleton. I have not often seen him flicker, his control ironclad. The fact he does so tells me everything I need to know about how he feels for Mena, how they all feel.

"You hesitated and let them take her," Hu spits, his arms crossing over his chest. Hu has always been a large and imposing character, but here, being looked at with such disdain, it makes me recoil. His power snaps out like a warning and I wish there was a way to get away from it.

"I am not that beast—"

"You are!" Hu snarls. "You have always been Hyde! The elixir did not create him, you imbecile!"

His anger is palpable and terrifying. I do not want to face these men. I do not want to face their anger and disappointment in me. Still, I whisper, "What do you mean?" because they hold themselves back for Mena's sake, because they will not kill me and risk Mena's wrath.

What a coward, Hyde hisses. *Relying on Mena to protect you.*

Hu's face twists with annoyance, his frustration clear at my question. "Hyde has always been inside of you. The elixir gave him the platform, allowed him to speak, but it did not create him. He is you. You are him! Refusing to give him control only puts Mena and you in danger!" He slams his fist against the damaged stone wall and more pieces shatter away. "And now she's at their mercy!"

Athan points his finger at me. "You better hope they don't hurt her," he warns. "You better hope she does not suffer at their hands. Because if she does, you will suffer at mine."

"And mine," Hu adds.

Otto simply glares at me.

"I'm... I'm sorry," I rasp. "I did not know—"

"For a scientist and a doctor, you're far less perceptive than I'd hoped," Otto spits. "So convinced Hyde is a beast, you don't even realize that you're a monster, too."

His words slam into me, unravel me at the seams. "Must I be a monster?"

"We're all monsters," Otto scowls. "I have killed more people in my lifetime than I care to admit. Athan is the literal embodiment of death. Hu is an arrogant god that drives humans insane who dare to look at him. Do you think a regular doctor could hold a flame to that? Do you think you would be so in love with Mena if your monstrosity did not match her own?"

Hu steps forward then, his face softening at the stricken look on mine. "A monster does not equal evil, Henry. Therein lies your confusion."

"What makes a monster monstrous then?" I ask, straightening. "If not an evil nature."

Athan's face twists into a pained expression. "Being willing to burn the world for the ones you love, uncaring who else is hurt because of it."

I meet his eyes, making sure he knows I mean my words. "I'm willing to die for Mena."

The Grim Reaper tilts his head. "Is that because you care so much for her, or because you care so little for yourself?"

I open my mouth, but no answer comes out. There's no answer to give because I do not know it.

Because we care so much for her, Hyde whispers. *But also because you fear yourself.*

"Is it true that you have always been a part of me?" I ask him, my fingers clenching into fists. "Have I been fighting myself all along?"

Silence and then...

I have always been here, Henry. We are one. Your elixir gave me the power to speak, to take control, to heal, to repair your arm, but it did not create me.

"Why did you never tell me?"

Must I explain myself to myself? he asks. *You would never have listened.*

I hesitate. "It will not be easy to accept you after so long of denying you," I whisper.

Then we worry about that later. For now, we go get our Mena.

I nod and meet the eyes of the others. "Okay," I croak. "My mistakes have put us in danger so close to Michael's arrival. You can punish me later for my foolishness, but for now, we go get Mena and we dispose of anyone who gets in our way."

Hu grins. "And to think you thought yourself less monstrous than us."

I pull a bottle from my hip, my eyes lingering on the small, ornate bottle, as if even unconsciously, I decorated Hyde's existence as something other. I hesitate for three seconds, staring at the bottle I've spent so long trying to avoid.

For Mena, Hyde murmurs. *You do this for her.*

I nod solemnly. "For Mena," I repeat, and toss the elixir back, giving control over to Hyde.

My body stretches and pulls, the feeling strange after so long of denying him this. I expand, and then my consciousness takes a backseat to Hyde as my limbs respond to him instead of me. I rush inside and shove more bottles into my pocket so I have plenty of potion for what's to come, for the fight we must face.

Hyde grins. "Let's go get our Mena," he purrs. "And we'll destroy any who attempt to stop us."

And then together, as one for the first time in weeks, we go hunting...

84
MENA

It's difficult to keep time in the cage. They do not bless me with a clock and there are no windows, so I can only guess at how long I've been here. It feels like forever, but likely, it has only been a day. I have not slept nor have I eaten the food they bring in despite it being gourmet concoctions I never expected. I don't trust them not to tamper with it. My men are taking far longer than I'd expected to come find me and part of me fears they'll leave me here. A silly fear really. There's no way they would abandon me and the thought is merely from my insecurities. They have already proven their love and loyalty. There are only obstacles in their way that they must overcome to find me.

Henry's face flashes in my mind again, the image of him slamming against the wall and sliding down. I hope he's okay. I hope he's not punishing himself too much. I hope the others did not string him up by his toes for refusing to let Hyde out.

The Frankies move around the room like lumbering stones. None of them seem to know what to do other than guard me, but to them, that does not mean much. Some of them trail in and out. Only about six of them remain at a time, their emotionless and lifeless eyes focused on my position in the cage. It makes it difficult to bother relieving myself, but ultimately, my bladder demands release and I'm never more thankful for my skirts than I am then.

"Do any of you speak?" I ask after some time. I'm looking at the nearest Frankie, but none of them answer. They don't even react to my voice. "Do you remember who you were before you became these... things?"

No answer, but I'm not sure I expected one. These creatures were stitched together from the dead, their bodies a mix of terrible grey parts put together to form one being. Some of them appear whole, as if all the parts were from one person, but others, their bodies are a terrible masterpiece of brutality, a mixture of parts that don't match. Their faces are human, but they have clearly been modified heavily with strange science and metal. Whatever Victoria Frankenstein did to these poor people, they're no longer who they once were. I only hope their souls are long gone from this plane so they cannot witness this.

Which makes me suddenly aware that there are no phantoms in this room.

I have not been in a room where there was not at least a single phantom in a long while. They often linger around in the background, sometimes popping in, sometimes passing through, but they're always there. Here, in this cage and this room, there are no phantoms. As if they cannot walk here. As if they're purposely kept out. I would have asked them questions about this place otherwise so I suppose that's why they're using something to keep them out.

"This is ridiculous," I murmur to myself as I pace around the cage. Victoria has not returned yet, her business keeping her away, and despite my warning about what's coming, she does not seem to care. I'm not worried about my men, even if they may come crashing through these walls and leave destruction in their wake. I'm worried about still being in this cage when Michael shows back up. I'm worried to be at his mercy, mortal and unprepared.

I'm so wrapped up in my musings that when there's a crash from outside the room, beyond the door, followed by a scream, it takes me a few seconds to register that something is happening. I tilt my head curiously, confused as I listen, trying to figure out just what's going on. More screams follow the first, screams of terror and pain, and then the sounds of metal clashing against metal echoes. The Frankies remain, their eyes on me, despite the roar of their brethren outside.

"Aren't you going to go help them?" I ask, gesturing toward the door.

No response. Of course, no response.

I jerk at the bars, annoyed when they don't simply give away beneath my hands. Which is silly. I should not be surprised that I do not suddenly have the strength of twenty men. It is a fact of the matter. I do not magically have super strength or the ability to push through steel bars. Tiny symbols glow with my touch along them. I don't know what they are, only that I recognize the things as some sort of protection, like the mixture Tallulah made. Though I wear the pouch around my neck still to protect against the witches, it does nothing for these symbols so I'm not sure if they're of the witches or something else. I don't recognize them or what they mean, so they do not benefit me.

The sounds of fighting grow louder outside the door, grunts of pain and screams of fury echoing, and still the Frankies do not move. Not until the fight spills inside this room.

The door slams open and clangs against the wall so suddenly, I jump. I'm trapped in this box, completely sealed in, but it does not prevent the demons from spilling inside and rushing toward me. The protection wards glow bright on the bars as the demons bounce off, too enraged and feral to focus on actually breaking them or finding a better way in. They rush toward the Frankies guarding me, and finally the creatures move. I watch with wide eyes as hordes of demons spill inside, as they swarm the room and attack, but they have only a moment of control before more creatures come rushing inside. Apparently, we're having a full-blown party.

This time, I take a step back from the bars of the cage, not wanting to be near enough to grab. The lower angels who flood in behind the demons screech in unholy terror, their many eyes and many wings only making the image ever more horrifying as they throw themselves at the demons.

"She is ours!" they scream, ripping at the demons, to which the demons respond with spitting and curses and claims that I belong to them instead.

They tear at each other, fighting over me like dogs over meat. There's nothing I can do locked in my cage as I am. I only hope they forget to focus on me completely, that they kill each other and leave me here for my men to find. At least the bars keep them all out, even if it keeps me caged.

When the vampires and witches come flooding in, I blink. This has grown... ridiculous. I don't even know how to react at this point. How is it that everyone but my men seem to know where I am? The members of the Masked Guild are mixed into the crowd, fighting, until this room and around my cage is surrounded with violence, until there is no space where there is not a creature. All because of me. All in an attempt to control me.

I cross my arms in annoyance. "You're all idiots," I grumble, but no one hears me. How could they when they're so focused on tearing each other to shreds? I may be the reason they're here, but they certainly don't expect any input from me.

The Frankies go down quicker than I expect. The demons and angels rip at them, but it's the witches who fell most of them, their savagery pushing them to leap on their backs and cut off their heads. Apparently, the creatures can survive a gunshot, but not their head coming off. One witch sets a Frankie on fire and it lets out an unholy scream that makes me cover my ears. Fire and no head. The concoction to destroy one of Victoria's creations, apparently.

The demons and angels are mostly focused on each other, a war as old as time, the kind that the Bible writes about. The witches and vampires get caught in the crosshairs often, fighting anyone who comes too close. The Masked Guild members simply fire at anything that moves, assuming everyone is an enemy, assuming no one is on the right side.

They're not wrong.

When a gargoyle comes flying in from the doorway, I rush to the edge of the bars again. "Asikor!" I cry, even though he has already seen me.

Behind him fly the others who distract the fighting while Asikor comes to the door of my cage. The roar that breaks the air behind them makes my heart freeze in my chest. Not in fear, but in excitement.

Hyde bursts through the door, slamming those in front of him out of the way, his savage snarl filled with all his worry and his need to find me. Hu, Otto, and Athan follow behind as they join Asikor at my cage, the other monsters too distracted to notice their actions.

"You came!" I cry, rushing forward.

"Of course we came, little void," Hu declares.

"Our apologies for taking so long," Otto grunts as he holds off the demons who take notice and think to attack. He makes quick work of them surprisingly, as if he's done this before.

Hyde meets my eyes. "We do not have long, Mena. Michael will be back at any moment."

"And Henry?" I ask.

Hyde grins. "Henry would like me to wax poetry and grovel at your feet as we apologize. Later, I plan to kneel before you and worship you until you accept his apology."

My body tightens despite the circumstances. "Can you get me out of here?"

Athan studies the wards. "Witch wards. Mostly protection, but a few containment ones as well." He turns to look behind him, reaching out to snatch up one of the witches sprinting past. "You. Break these wards."

She spits at him. "Fuck off, reaper!"

He rolls his eyes. "Break the wards and the Mother of Monsters will grant you a favor."

Her eyes widen and she nods frantically. "Yes, Yes, I will. Let me down, reaper. Let me down."

He meets my eyes, telling me that he had been lying, but the witch doesn't seem to realize that. I watch as she severs the symbols one by one, muttering under her breath as she undoes whatever had been sealing me in. The gargoyles keep the demons and lower angels busy, barreling through their ranks like the soldiers they are. It must be night for them to be here. I can't even remark on what time of day it may be so that's the only sign I have to go on.

The witch claps. "Done! Now grant me my—"

Before she can finish her sentence, Athan grabs her and tosses her into the fray. She lands near a particularly savage demon who immediately stabs a spear up through her jaw. I stare in horror as her eyes pop open in surprise before the demon rips out the spear and she drops to the floor to be trampled by the others. Athan doesn't seem to be affected by the sight, but I am. My stomach roils even as Hu jerks the door of my cage open with strength I often forget he has, strength that would have come in handy for me. He reaches in and jerks me out of the cage with rough hands, urgency in his movements. A bite of pain throbs from his touch, but I don't complain. We're in a hurry, and there are worse things to worry about.

"Come, little void. Let's get out of here," he growls, his image flickering dangerously.

I cling to him, preparing to run through the fighting, but before I can follow his lead and the others, strong arms wrap around me from behind. I don't know where he came from, or how he appeared behind me, but the arms are iron clad. No matter how I jerk against them, I can't free myself.

"Come now, Lilith. Did you think my warning was a lie?" The words are whispered in my ear, like a lover would, but I don't shiver because of that. I shiver in fear.

Michael.

I jerk harder in his hold, trying my hardest to free myself, but his wings flare as I look over my shoulder up into his thousand eyes.

Hu turns, sees who holds me, and throws himself at me before it's too late. His fingers clutch onto my petticoats just as Michael shoots up into the air at a speed that makes me nauseous.

The screams of Hyde, Otto, and Athan follow after us, but none are so loud as my own.

85
MENA

We burst through the ceiling, sending debris raining down on the fighting below us. My scream is shrill as we rise too fast, as Hu's weight pulls at my skirts. I pray that his fingers don't slip, or that my dress doesn't tear. I look down at him to see the worry in his eyes, but he holds on strong as he dangles beneath me. Desperation keeps us connected. If he drops, he will not die, but the chances of him finding me again before it's too late are slim. Michael intends to kill me, and I know he means the threat. Of all Lilith's memories, the one where this archangel beats her within an inch of her life is the clearest.

Filthy feathered monster, Lilith whispers in my mind, and I don't argue. This creature, Michael, is far more terrifying than any other.

He flies us only a few blocks, clearly not thinking this will take so long that the others can follow fast enough to save me. He drops us when he flies over a nearby building, too high for humans, but I'm no longer all human even if I'm still mortal. We fall through the air, Hu and I, until we slam into the gravel on the roof. The stones bite into my skin, tear it open, make me bleed, but my bones blessedly remain whole. My skirts fly around me, covering my head, but I throw them off quickly and drag myself to my feet despite the blood beginning to trickle from my wounds. Hu retches himself up beside me, his human form gone to be replaced by his natural form, all black wings and tentacles and feral anger. Somehow, he appears larger than he is, this brutal monstrous god. Sometimes I forget how imposing he is. Now, with his great wings and the tentacles on his face, he looks every inch the monster I know him to be.

At least I'm not alone if I should die here.

Michael lands before us on his many wings, his eyes narrowing on the defensive stance we take. I have no weapons but the power inside me and I coax it out, encourage it to be at the ready, even if it may not work on an archangel. When Michael starts to laugh, I straighten in annoyance, my eyes narrowed on him.

"What a sight the two of you make," he chuckles. "A failure god and an incomplete reincarnation."

Fuck him, Lilith snarls. *Tell him that.*

I narrow my eyes further on the archangel, but my mind is taking in the surface we stand on as quickly as possible. A trick Otto had taught me. Always know your space. Always know your exits. I do not know what building this is, but it isn't a tall one. Six stories at most. There is not much here, and there's nothing to use against this monster, but my weapons are inside of me now. I coax my power forward as it dances around my feet, encourage to reach out toward Michael, knowing it might not affect him as I hope, but that it could aide me in some way. After all, affecting his emotions with my power isn't my only tool. I also possess the power of illusion and siphoning power now.

"Lilith sends her regards," I tell him my chin high, and his laughing abruptly stops.

I can feel his anger. It cuts through the air like God's wrath. Hu, at my side, doesn't say a word. Instead, he remains beside me, the protector, prepared to fight.

"*Lilith*," he snarls. The bitterness in the word puts me on edge. "I hope the bitch has been enjoying Hell."

"Did you tell her that as you hurt her?" I ask, tilting up my chin. "Did it make you feel better to beat a human so badly, she could not see through her swollen eyes or breath for her broken ribs?"

Michael has no mouth I can see, but I can feel him bare his teeth. How strange to feel emotions from a being with so little to show emotion with.

"My only regret is that I did not kill her by my own hand," Michael spits. "I will not make the same mistake twice."

He storms forward, intent on killing me, but Hu leaps before me, my protector, prepared to fight this archangel. Michael takes one look at his snarling face and his feathered wings slice out. A glint of metal flickers at the ends and only as they slice through Hu's stomach do I realize they're blades. Hu grunts and is thrown to the side, his momentum sending him crashing over the edge, injured. My heart leaps in my chest in fear, but I remember quickly that Hu has wings, that he's a god and cannot die so easily.

"What is your failure god going to do to me?" Michael snarls. "I am the Creator's favorite."

I don't back down from his approach, standing my ground despite my fear. I will not let him see it. I will not cower before him.

That's my girl, Lilith purrs. *We will show this motherfucker how women fight.*

"My understanding is the Morningstar earned that title," I say with a raised brow. "You were just the second best option."

His anger slams against me with his fist to my jaw. I grunt in pain as his hit sends me sliding on my spine backward in the gravel, the stone biting further into my skin, embedding in it. My power surprisingly snaps out and halts my trajectory before I can go tumbling over the edge, as if it's opaque enough to do so, something I had not known possible. I bare my own teeth at the archangel as I claw my way back to my feet, my dress billowing around me with the wind that suddenly swirls around us. The clouds turn dark above me, signaling the coming rain, but I don't back down. I cannot.

"It appears you are not as immune to feelings as you think you are, archangel," I point out. "Jealousy is a potent drug. And it means you're no better than us humans."

Michael roars his anger and takes a step toward me. I don't move. Instead, I hold up my hands at him, my power sizzling in my veins, power Lilith gifted me with. I don't know what I intend to do, only that I need to do something. This power was not gifted to me for sport. It has a purpose, and right now, that purpose is to stop this archangel from killing me.

You are strong, Lilith whispers. *No man nor angel will control you. Your freedom is your own.*

"Yes," I breathe. "My freedom is my own."

Michael laughs as I speak out loud. "Freedom is life's great lie, Lilith. What are you going to do to me? Hit me?" He laughs again. "You are no threat to an archangel as powerful as me."

Hit him, Lilith whispers. *Teach him a lesson about angry women.*

Michael rushes forward and I wrench my arm back, the power building in my fist. When I slam it against Michael's chest as he nears, all of my weight behind the hit, he surprisingly flies backward a few feet, his boots sliding in the gravel. His eyes all blink in surprise the same as mine do.

Behind me, I hear Hu's wings and with a wave of my hand, my power of illusion begins to weave, taking advantage of his surprise at my strength. I straighten and bare my teeth at him. "My name is not Lilith," I sneer. "It's Philomena Seagraves." I throw my middle finger up at him, something I've never done to another being, but Michael deserves it. He really does. "And fuck you! From both Lilith and me."

I turn and sprint toward the edge of the building even as Michael roars his anger. He shoots forward, but he doesn't come after me. He flies toward the illusion of me I left behind, her dress flaring around her as she dives out of his way. In his anger, he doesn't even realize she flickers, or that he should have been able to grab me, but his hand passes through the edge of her dress. Arrogance is always a weakness. Ego will be his downfall.

I leap off the edge of the building, having full faith in my monster as I land in Hu's arms. He'd read my thoughts, knew precisely where he needed to be as he flew up the building on large black wings prepared to catch me. My illusion still spins, keeping Michael busy for precious minutes as it quickly saps my strength. We won't have long, but Hu seems to understand the urgency with which we need to move. He flies on swift wings, the buildings around us blurring as he shoots further and further away, as he pushes himself to his limits. He's a god, but he is not all powerful. His powers are very specific, and none but flight will help us right now.

No matter how far we go, no matter how fast we fly, I hear Michael's roars of fury behind us. They follow us like the storm, the clouds rolling with darkness. When the rain begins to fall around us, I barely feel it. When my strength runs out and I know the illusion gives away, I collapse into Hu's arms, exhausted.

The roar of a tricked archangel echoes through the heavens above.

86
MENA

We can't go home. Michael would easily follow us there as he already knows where it is. We do not know how he knew my position at the Masked Guild, but we have to assume he can track me in some way even if I hope he only followed the commotion. Which means we cannot go anywhere predictable or easily followed.

Apparently, the others already knew this and planned for it, Hu reaching out with his mind to inform them of our escape. We fly for another ten minutes at a speed that makes my stomach roil, shooting through London and the storm that haunts it, before Hu lands us in the warehouse district. He shifts into his human form once again so the humans walking the streets don't notice. Not that I think any of them will. The majority of people here have hollow eyes and the stumbling step of those having drunk too much ale or suffered too much life.

"Where are we?" I ask, looking around as he sets me on my feet. I'm still tired from the push of power, but I'm aware enough to know this is not a place I've ever been.

When Otto, Athan, and Henry appear from the darkness, I nearly jump out of my skin, clutching at Hu before I realize it's them. They appear like phantoms from the shadows, even as the real phantoms trail along the cobblestones around us. These phantoms are more forlorn here, sadness and grief stronger as they yearn for some sense of relief that they will never find on this plane.

"We must hurry up the last death," Otto says by way of greeting. "Sloth is the only one remaining and the longer it takes to complete, the more vulnerable you are."

My heart kicks at the thought of dying one final time, but I nod. This time, they're including me in the decision, like they did with the fifth, and I will not be afraid. "And I suppose you all have already figured out how to make that happen?"

Henry reaches forward and takes my hand, an apology in his eyes that we do not have the time to discuss now, but I accept it all the same. "Sloth is defined as a reluctance to work or make an effort, or laziness."

"Correct," I reply. "And how does one die of laziness?"

"It's not the laziness part we focus on," Otto counters. "It's the reluctance to work or make an effort."

Athan points to the warehouse. "And who makes less an effort than those caught in the clutches of addiction, than those floating in the bliss of a high?"

I blink. "Drugs?"

"Opium," Henry corrects. "This warehouse behind us is an opium den. We would have preferred a higher class one, but this is our best option to remain unseen by Michael while we accomplish our endeavors."

"My death," I murmur, looking down at my hands. "Will it hurt?"

"On the contrary, most opium users describe a sense of euphoria," he replies, glancing toward the door. "And you will not be alone."

For a moment, I linger. I know that it's necessary if we're to survive this. Whatever it means to be at full power is required for this war. I have no other option. I cannot simply disappear and expect this to end. We'll be hunted to the ends of the world unless I stop this. And Michael will never stop and I cannot stop him as I am. It's personal for him after Lilith survived and put her plan in motion. The Creator can't suffer that failure. And Michael will refuse to take that failure home.

I tilt up my chin. "Alright."

"Alright?" Otto clarifies. "We do this?"

Nodding, I take his hand. "Yes. We do this and take care of Michael. Then, we take care of the rest of them."

On my other side, Hu slides his fingers into mine, offering comfort. Athan and Henry take up positions in front of and behind us, so that when we step inside the dim warehouse, I'm protected on all sides.

I'm not sure what I expect, but the lush dim building is not it. There are walls preventing us from seeing into the back, but the front is decorated in black and dark green, the smell of tobacco strong in the air. There's a man behind a counter before us, and when we come inside, he immediately straightens.

"A private room, please," Otto demands before tossing a bag of coins on the desk.

The man's eyes widen as he snatches the gold and stands. "Of course. Right this way gentlemen and lady."

He leads us to the back where the sickly-sweet scent of tobacco and smoldering resins are stronger, so thick, it makes me nauseous with them. The walls are decorated in the same deep green and black all throughout the den. As we pass doorways, I see a variety of people within the rooms. Some of them simply sit and stare unseeing into the distance, witnessing something no one else is. A few of the rooms contain tangled bodies and soft moans of pleasure as they dive into their high. Some are empty, devoid of anything but lonely walls and the lingering scent of addiction. We walk until the man stops at a large empty room and gestures for us to step inside.

"All of your requirements are presented on the table. If there is anything else you should need, simply ring the bell and someone will be here promptly to tend to your needs," the man says. When we step inside, he closes the door. A private room where we can't be witnessed. A private room meant for those of higher class it seems judging by the décor.

I take in the room before us, studying every detail. If this is where I'm to die for a final time, I want to burn it into my memory. There is a large cushion in the center of the room, large enough for us all to rest on like a bed. There's a table against the opposite wall laden with needles and pipes and all manner of items I don't recognize. I assume it's for our opium use.

"How does this work?" I ask, turning toward Henry. "Do we smoke?"

He shakes his head. "That would take too long. We need something direct that can give you a large dose all at once." He presses his hand to my cheek. "Would you like to know the symptoms, or would you prefer not to know what's coming?"

"Tell me," I rasp, needing it all broken down to ease my anxiety.

He nods in understanding. "I'll inject you with opium, a large enough amount to cause overdose for someone of your size. You will feel your heart rate slow at first and you'll enter a sense of euphoria. When it becomes too much for your body to maintain, your symptoms will become slow breathing and general unresponsiveness. You'll float away, your heart stopping, respiratory failure, until you lose consciousness completely." He clears his throat. "And then you will succumb to... well, death."

Taking a deep breath, I wrap my fingers in his. "Thank you for your honesty. It grounds me." I can always rely in Henry to tell me the scientific steps of something like this, even if they're difficult to hear.

"The gargoyles are here," Hu declares suddenly, his eyes unfocused. "They've taken up position on the roof. Michael still has not found us, but there's no telling how long that will remain truth."

His special sight, and the all-knowing power, comes in handy now when so many are searching for us.

"We don't have much time," I rasp. "Let us proceed."

"You're certain?" Athan asks. "We can find another way."

I smile gently at him. "I'm no longer afraid of the monster I may become, Athan. This is necessary and I understand that. We do it now so that we stand a better chance in this war."

He nods before carefully helping me onto the cushion. He eases me into the center of it and I relax onto my back, staring up at the ceiling broken up by metal beams. He doesn't bother removing my clothing or making it more comfortable, but he does gently remove my shoes. My bare feet wiggle as I watch Henry move along the table, getting the instruments ready.

"You'll still be Philomena Seagraves," Athan tells me as he climbs onto the cushion beside me.

I nod. "I will still be Philomena Seagraves."

"You will not be alone," Otto adds as he climbs onto the cushion by my feet.

"I will not be alone," I repeat like a mantra.

"We all love you," Hu adds as he takes up residence near my head. "As you love us."

I smile despite my nervousness. "You all love me, just as I love you."

Henry comes forward with a syringe and climbs onto the cushion on my right side. "You are not evil," he says. "You are the brightness in the dark."

"The cosmos in the stars," Hu adds.

"The beauty in the pain," Athan murmurs.

"The perfection in worship," Otto whispers, leaning down to press a kiss against my forehead.

"And you are not alone," Henry repeats before gently grabbing my arm. He ties a rubber strip around my upper arm tightly. The rubber pinches at my skin, but I don't focus on it. I focus on them, on their presence.

"I am not alone," I repeat. "I am not alone."

You are not alone, Lilith whispers in my mind.

The prick of the needle is barely felt with the tight band while Henry moves quickly. For a few seconds, I feel nothing but the release of his band and the return of my blood to my arm. The bite of pain from the needle is what filters through my mind first, the remnants of where he'd administered the shot before pressing his thumb tightly against the entry point. And then a warmth travels up my arm from that point and covers my body like a blanket. My eyes focus on the ceiling above me, on the drip, drip, drip of water somewhere nearby. My body grows heavy and then light, sinking into the cushion so deeply, I feel as if I could never get out, and then feeling as if I'm floating into the stars. My head lolls back as hands stroke along my body, grounding me, offering strength and encouragement.

"I love you," I whisper, speaking to all of them.

Someone whispers beside me and I can only make out a few words. "Archangel... closer..."

And then Hyde is beside me, stroking my arm, cooing into my ear. "Float into the ether, butterfly. Let yourself fall away."

"My monster," I rasp, my lungs beginning to burn. The edges of my vision begin to close in. I can't focus on Hyde, can't see him, but I know he's here. I know they're all here. "My monsters."

"Your monsters," Hyde agrees. "We're here for you, butterfly. You are not alone."

And then my lungs ease, my heart rate loud in my ears as the beats slow to an agonizing drudge. It aches, but it's not painful as I float away. As I float into the cosmos with my monsters at my side. They curl against me, holding me close, even as I float away. The darkness closes in on me as my body buzzes with euphoria I've never felt before, as my body gives in to the large dose of opium.

See you on the other side, Mena, Lilith whispers. *Prepare yourself.*

And then she disappears, too, leaving me to float among the stars, into space, and eventually, into all-encompassing darkness...

87
OTTO

She fades away and her heart stops. The blood in her veins stops flowing and her chest no longer rises. I stare at her despite the approaching danger, waiting, desperate. There's no immediate gasp of breath. There are no jerks of consciousness. Mena does not move, her skin taking on a bluish color in the dim light.

I pray that we did not make a mistake, not to any particular god, but into the universe. There are no longer any gods I trust with something so profound, except for maybe the one sitting near me, eagerly waiting for her to wake up as the rest of us are.

"How close is he?" I ask, glancing at Hu in worry.

"Perhaps eight minutes away," Hu answers. "He's following the pulse of her power, and her death has only made it easier, though being among so many may help give us more time."

That's true. Each time Mena dies, we can feel it, and now, it's stronger than even I expected. With her final death, a ripple echoes out into the world, drawing every creature, every monster, to our location. In eight minutes time, this opium den will be overrun with horrors. Those too doped out to notice will suffer, a detail I had left out for Mena, but there is nothing to be done. If we fail, the whole world could die, and Mena is determined to keep that from happening.

"We protect her until she wakes up," I say, lifting myself from the cushion and rolling my shoulders. "No one gets close."

Athan stands and shifts, revealing his skeletal figure. The black cloak he wears dances around his feet as he swings his scythe around to his front. His empty eyes somehow still show his emotions. Determination. Love. Desperation.

Hu shifts so quickly I barely notice it. His large black wings rise from his shoulders, his monstrous face peering back at me. Of the four of us, he's the largest, his height making him nearly touch the ceiling.

Hyde is already ready, Henry within him to help. He stands, his grey skin and demonic appearance eager for violence and determined to protect Mena until she wakes. We have no way of knowing how long this will take so we do what we must.

For as long as we're able.

"No one gets close," Hyde repeats. He strokes his fingers along Mena's still face before straightening and taking up position at her head.

"Five minutes," Hu warns. "The gargoyles are at the ready." He blinks. "The remainder of the Masked Guild are surrounding the building, but... they're not coming after us."

"That's because we're here to help," Victoria Frankenstein declares as she opens the door. "We acknowledge we were wrong, and there are far worse things than a woman with the powers of Lilith."

I sneer at her. "You flip sides so easily."

"It's self-preservation," Victoria says with a shrug. "Nothing personal. I've simply decided Mena doesn't want to destroy the world. But that creature coming after her, he does. And that's not okay with us."

The temptation to throttle her, to rip her throat out, is strong, but it's Athan who touches my shoulder to calm me. "We could use their help."

Eventually, I nod. "Nothing touches her while she sleeps," I growl.

"Understood," and then she disappears, leaving us to stare after her in disbelief.

"Humans will not help us much," Hu warns. "But perhaps, they can prolong Michael's approach."

I shrug. "I don't care what they do," I say honestly. "I don't care if they die. Only Mena matters."

We wait, at the ready, with Mena lying as still as the dead behind us.

"He's here," Hu says, just as the ceiling above us rips away.

Seventh Death

Languid.
Float into the salty sea.
The water carries you away
and then under like a lover.
This is the price you pay for love,
To offer yourself up for destruction,
To lie in wait for your demise.
Fade...
Fade...
Fade...

88

MENA

"Are you certain you would like to make this deal, Lilith?" a man asks. This man is beautiful though twisted in such a way that tells me someone once harmed him. He shines so brightly I have to squint as I stare at him. His radiance speaks of holy divinity, but his twisted features seem as if they were meant to detract from that. They don't. Instead, the twisted wings at his back, no longer capable of flight, the scars across his face, make him only more beautiful.

"You've asked me that three times, Luci," Lilith growls, her brilliant red hair reflecting the man's glow from the depth. "Of course I'm certain."

The man, Luci, shakes his head. "You won't be yourself any longer. She will be you. She will have the powers you afford her. You will not be in control."

"I know that," Lilith rasps.

"And you're okay with this?" he asks, genuine concern in his eyes. "Once accepted, this cannot be undone. Your immortality will die with you even if your soul remains."

Lilith glances at Luci, her eyes bright. She does not flinch from his light as I do. She does not cower before The Morningstar.

"No woman should ever have to suffer what I did," she whispers. "If not me, then her. She'll make sure that happens."

"You're so certain?" Luci asks. "You know nothing about her."

"I am certain in my choice in soul," Lilith nods. "I know the heart of women, and I can feel her strength in hers."

Luci takes her hand. "You'll die."

"A sacrifice I'm willing to make," she tells him. "Thank you, Luci, for everything."

He nods his acceptance and takes her hand, placing it on a small glowing orb before her. It seems familiar, as if that orb is a part of me.

Or as if it is me.

She closes her eyes, and the soul grows bright gold, so bright, I have to look away.

Lilith's voice whispers in my mind, an echo, a promise.

Be strong, little destroyer. Bring down every man who dares to silence us. Bring down every beast who binds our wrists with chains and command we be happy with it.

Bring them all down.

Every. Last. One. Of them.

I blink open my eyes to chaos. Complete and utter chaos.

The ceiling above me is gone and the sky is filled with lesser angels and gargoyles. Around us, screams rent the air, from monsters and humans alike. My final death has called every creature to this location, has made it easy for them to find us. Those humans unfortunate enough to be in the opium den barely notice as they breathe their last breath, as demons and angels fight around them.

My heart hurts for them, for this unnecessary pain that fills the skies. The darkness is here, all around us, sticking to every surface and painting it black. Within me, that same darkness moves like molasses, oozing through my body, but it does not feel evil. It feels...powerful.

Athan turns in his reaper form as he fights back enemies and sees me sitting up. Relief flickers in his eyes before he offers a skeletal hand out toward me. I wrap mine in his without hesitation, allowing him to help me stand. "Welcome back," he grunts before pressing a quick kiss against my lips, a strange feeling when he's nothing but bone and hardness. I can still taste the sweetness of overdose there, of the opium that had flowed through my blood, the remnants of my final death.

I will die no more.

Immortally oozes through my veins. Lilith's immortality. She gifted it to me, knowing that I could take a stand when she could not, knowing that my power would grow greater than hers. It feels strange as I stand, as I shed the knowledge of what I once was and accept what I am. Around us, monsters fight to get close, to kill me or take me. There are a few I don't recognize, creatures I have yet to learn about, but there are many I do. Demons, angels, witches, werewolves, humans. They all fight, each for their own interest, each for their own gain.

The powers come easily now to my fingertips, my mind buzzing with awareness. It's simple now, as if dying the final time unlocks every ability within me. The power of manipulation, of control, echoes in my body with newness, and when I reach out my hand toward the nearest demon, he freezes and begins to dance at my encouragement, as if he can't help himself. As if I am his puppeteer.

The roof is gone and the dark stormy sky above us mists in warning. Rain will soon follow again, but as the lightning streaks across the sky, it is not the clouds I focus on. It's the archangel who hovers there, his eyes fierce, a great flaming sword in his hands as he zeroes in on my position, as he finally finds me in the chaos.

"Lilith, you bitch!" he snarls. "You traitorous fucking whore!"

I tilt my head, taking him in even as my men keep me safe from harm. I do not fear him. I do not cower or run or worry. I am certain of what I am. Of who I am. And I'm still myself even if I'm more powerful now.

I smile up at him, and he falters, the first sign of fear. "Yes," I say, my body humming with power. "Bitch and whore, forsaken and demon." My smile widens and he blinks in surprise. "But I'll always be Lilith," I purr. "Never Eve."

And then before my men can stop me, before I can understand what I'm doing, I shoot into the air on invisible wings, aiming right for the archangel who dared to punish a woman for the crime of wanting freedom.

I will have my freedom.

We all will...

89
ATHAN

She's beautiful. She always has been, but as she rises from her seventh death, her power swirling around her and no fear in her eyes, there's an otherworldly beauty about her now. She's still Mena, still our Mena, but in her eyes, the fires of every woman who has ever been wronged, abused, silenced, flickers. In her chest are the screams of their anguish, their pain, their yearning for freedom.

As she stands and does not bother putting her shoes back on, her dress swirling around her feet, her hair dancing across her shoulders, I can't help but wonder if this magnificent creature could truly love me back. Brilliant as she is, she makes the world tremble at her existence.

And I am only a lonely Grim Reaper.

Maybe it's as simple as this moment. Maybe the world has always been meant for this. When she steps into this being she truly is, the world does not burn like the prophecy warns. It's capable of it, sure, but it doesn't have to. Perhaps, rather than flames, it only means the brilliance of Mena glowing more brightly with the light she brings can change the world.

And oh, how she shines.

Even when Michael appears overhead, his face twisted in anger and murderous intent, Mena does not faulter. She looks up at him as he sneers hateful words toward a woman who has done nothing to deserve them. Whether you consider Mena as Lilith or herself, she is underserving of so much hatred for simply rebelling against the Creator's decisions. Free will is supposed to be his manifesto, but clearly, that has always been a lie, just as much else has.

The demons fighting around us hesitate as Mena's glow begins to radiate, their eyes on the Mother of Demons as she faces off against Michael, the archangel they all hate. The Morningstar cannot step foot here just as the Creator cannot, but the demons seem to recognize the power in her eyes.

Before us, without anyone else noticing, there's a slight shift in the demon's attacks. Despite their original intent to destroy the lower angels and take Mena, they stop attacking us and focus only on the angels now. Their eyes remain on Mena as they keep the lower angels away from her and our little group. I don't know if they've fully switched sides or if they've only now realized this is a fight between us and this archangel instead, but I'm grateful for the reprieve.

"Lilith, you bitch!" Michael screams overhead, his voice thick with fury. "You traitorous fucking whore!"

My spine straightens. He dares to speak to my Mena that way? My heart-soul?

I snarl, prepared to launch myself at him, but it's Mena's reaction that halts me.

She smiles and it's the most brilliant smile I've ever seen. Michael even pauses at the look, fear flashing in his eyes for the first time. Good. He should fear her. He should fear her forgiveness.

"Yes. Bitch and whore. Forsaken and demon," she says, her smile widening. "But I'll always be Lilith," Mena purrs. "Never Eve."

And before I can stop her, before I can know what she intends to do, she lifts into the air on wings she does not possess, and launches herself at the Creator's most powerful archangel.

90
MENA

The power that courses through my body is liquid heat, as gentle as the touch of a lover. It gives me wings, both literally and figuratively, and though no feathered appendages spring from my back, I can feel their ghostly existence there. When I lift into the air, I don't question it. Henry would propose some hypothesis about manipulation of the air or something else deep and science-like, but I embrace the unknown. I am Philomena Seagraves and I carry the weight of Lilith in my soul, of the first wife of Adam who rebelled against Heaven and her creator. I bear witness to her heart.

Michael flies backward as I shoot toward him, the fear flickering so fast again, I almost miss it, but he gathers his training, remembers his role, and lifts his sword. The knowledge of the sword filters in through my mind as if I've always known it, Lilith supplying me with the important information. Angelic swords are potent and capable of killing most creatures. It will not matter that I'm immortal if that sword touches me. It's an immortal killer.

I dodge to the right before that sword can touch me, the flames cold where I expect heat as they brush past me. Michael's thousand wings flare bright, the blades flashing in the stormy sky above, and I can see why people would worship the angels. How terrifying must it have been the first time someone witnessed this monster. How must they have quivered before him as he walked past, treating them like rodents, meant to be used and nothing more.

If these angels, this terrible archangel, were born by The Great Creator, I dread to ever face that cruel god and what terrible horror he must possess.

"You will kneel before the Creator and beg his forgiveness," Michael snarls as he swings the blade after me, missing my thigh by mere inches.

I bare my teeth as I pull the small dagger from my skirts, the one Hu had tucked away in my pocket before I'd succumbed to the opium. "The Creator will have to ask my forgiveness if he ever shows his face. His sins far outnumber my own!"

Michael does not like that. What angel would?

"You know nothing!" he spits, his wings flaring as he launches toward me.

"I know what you have is not freedom, and that I yearn for it," I murmur. But explaining freedom to an angel is like teaching poetry to fish. Useless and disappointing.

My power leaks out of me, infecting those beneath me without meaning to. Every power I've gathered over my deaths falls like water, uncontrolled, easy. I don't stop it. I listen to the screams of monsters beneath me as things begin to change, as the tide of war takes another tone. I have not taken part in the worst of it, but my role is more important. Things cannot change while the Creator's monsters roam and hunt. I cannot allow this archangel to live if I am to stop this war before it truly spreads.

Beneath me, I can see each of my monsters moving through the crowd, fighting. There are so many lesser angels, their wings create a strange piece of art as they move, as they brutally cut down any being who stands in their way. The humans, those of the Masked Guild, seem to be on our side now, but they cannot stand strong against so many powerful beings. Their numbers suffer even as I catch sight of Victoria Frankenstein and her many monsters holding ground. The gargoyles are in the fray, fighting with their stone claws and savage teeth. Few witches and werewolves remain, their numbers dwindling in the face of bigger monsters. The demons neither come after my men, nor help them, their focus on the angels.

And my men. Oh, my monsters! Each of them is as beautiful as the power inside me. They work as a unit even as their attention dances to me and where I fight. None of them come to my aid, trusting that I know what I'm doing, but worried for me nonetheless. Athan is in his full reaper form, his great skeletal body slashing his scythe through angel after angel, tearing down any creature who appears malicious. Hyde moves alongside him, his beastly roar echoing in the world around us. Otto is beautiful as he slices and tears, blood flowing down his chest like a badge of honor. And Hu, Hu is wearing his true form, and he does not contain it. Those beings who come close crumple before him. He has no need to slash and cut. Most creatures who look upon him fall to the ground, clutching at their minds as they scream. Only when a few of the angels seem immune to his power does he start to cut a path through them, his great bat-like wings slicing just as his blade does.

The fight is brutal, but none more so than the one I take part in.

While the angels are a problem, while this is all terrible, Michael is the true problem here. He comes to finish the task he once failed, and he intends to finish it here in the skies above London. He will fail. I refuse to accept any other option.

Michael brings down his sword with the intent to cleave me in two, but I raise my small blade to meet his large one. The dagger is so small, it shouldn't be able to do much of anything at all, but it does. The angelic blade sings as it crashes into my blade and holds there, the fire cold as it brushes my knuckles. It does not come closer, stopped by my simple, tiny dagger. Michael screams in anger at my strength, but he's forgotten one fact.

It is not only my strength I possess. I now carry Lilith's. I carry the strength of every woman who has been silenced by the Creator, who has had agony shoved down their throat to keep them quiet. Just as I did. Just as every woman has experienced. We are all Lilith. We are all capable of monstrous rebellion.

We only have to remember the savagery we carry in our hearts.

My power leaks from me and brushes against Michael, and for the first time, I see it affect him. He twitches, his strength faltering for a moment as his expression changes to one of unbearable sadness. He shoves it away quickly, fighting it, but I am a force to be reckoned with now.

"How does it feel?" I ask him as I hold his sword at bay. "To know you're not God's favorite?"

His face twists. "I am his chosen one."

"His second pick," I counter. "Only because the Morningstar was cast out. It does not count when you're chosen by default."

That makes him truly angry, and with his anger, comes a slip in his barriers. I grin and shove my power into him with everything I've got. He stumbles in the air, his wings collapsing briefly. His face twists with sadness, with horror, his body growing heavy with it. When he slowly starts to pull back his sword, he realizes what's happening and pushes harder against me until it becomes a struggle between powers rather than physical strength.

"My will is stronger than yours," I tell him as he fights. "You're held back by your creator's cruelty. I am held back by nothing."

Around us, illusions begin to spin, scenes from my memories, the Garden and the snake, the visage of Michael staring hungrily at Eve as she takes the apple.

"You wanted us to fail, didn't you?" I accuse. "You wanted Eve to take that apple. And above all, you wanted her for yourself, but she was for Adam." I tilt my head as I shove my power harder at him. "How does it feel to be nothing more than a sword?"

It's a small exaggeration. I do not actually know if Michael wanted Eve, but when his face twists with pain from unrequited love, I realize this archangel has as many sins as his creator. He's only been pretending to be clean and holy.

He shoves his power at me. I can tell it's meant to burn my flesh from my bones, but instead, my body begins to sip from the power, absorbing it, stealing it, and his eyes widen in surprise and horror. The power of an archangel, a great terrible trembling power, dances in my veins, and for the first time, I feel the cruelty I'm capable of. I want to kill, to teach a lesson, to draw angelic blood and dance in it, to smear it across my brow like a warning.

"What a pretty angel you make," I coo, sipping at his power. He can't draw away, can't pull back, my power holding him in place, this archangel who underestimated me. "Did it feel good to nearly kill Lilith? Did you yearn to do more?"

"Lilith was a traitor!" he spits, his face twisted with fear. "A terrible creation, just as you are."

"Yes," I agree. "Every being the Creator has made is terrible. The humans who consume and fight, who kill the very earth they live on. The vampires with their thirst for blood. The angels with their thirst for violence. The werewolves and the witches, driven by their darkness and the moon. The gargoyles and their curse to walk only at night. There is no good unless we make it." I lean in, getting close to his angelic fire. "The Creator does not make us good. He makes us evil, creates us with sin no matter his claim not to, and we are still good despite it." I growl at the archangel so determined to kill me he had not realized he's just as much a monster. *"We are still good despite it!"*

"Ants," Michael spits. "Playthings."

"Yes," I nod. "Angry ants. Angry playthings. Powerful ones." I lean closer. He's frozen in place, my power holding him despite his desperate attempts to get away. "And we are tired of being played with." I press a kiss against his cheek. "Lilith asks for your blood, archangel."

"Then give it to her," he spits. "If you're so powerful, prove yourself."

I smile, and lean back. "I am not an archangel." I release him from my powers, and he drops in the air at the sudden withdrawal. "Tell your Creator to stop this war. Play messenger and withdraw your mission."

"Never!" he shouts, rushing me despite my show of mercy. I gave the archangel a choice and he chose wrong. Again. So overcome by his blind loyalty, he cannot stop to think about how he's a pawn just as we are. He cannot fathom that he has been betrayed as we all have been since the beginning.

Because I gave him a choice of mercy he did not take, he takes my choice away. I cannot allow the archangel to cut me down. I cannot allow him to win.

I raise my dagger as Michael brings his burning sword down above me. The scream on his lips is full of pain and anger, of the truth leaking into his mind that he refuses to see. All he sees is a woman who dared defy him twice, who dared win twice, and so he can see nothing else.

My dagger slides into his sternum, the tip of it coated with the cosmic stars that make up my ancient mate. It slides in with ease, cutting through the angel's flesh easily. When he stops, his eyes wide in horror as he feels true physical pain for the first time, I twist the blade.

My power caresses him, strokes along the wound, cruelty dancing in my blood as his power seeps into mine. I take his sword from him, my fingers closing around the great hilt belonging to the Archangel of War. He doesn't put up a fight, frozen as he is, his eyes wild and desperate like a cornered animal.

"Shh," I coo as I twist the dagger, making him gasp in pain. "Don't worry, Michael. I forgive you." My lips twist with savagery. "But Lilith? Lilith does not."

I jerk the blade from his chest and slide it back into my pocket, listening to it clatter to the ground beneath us. On instinct, I punch my fist through the wound left behind by my blade, digging my nails in, using my newfound strength at that of the archangel I stole from to do so. My hand bursts through his ribcage, his eyes wide in horror as I wrap my fingers around his heart.

"And Lilith wants you to bleed," I say before yanking that heart from his chest.

He gasps as I hold it before him, his still beating heart in my hand. Interesting that he still bleeds like me, that his blood is as red as mine. And yet he is in no way human, this creature of a thousand eyes and a thousand wings. Still, he bleeds for his sins and those of his Creator. He will pay the price.

Without waiting for him to heal or to gather his wits, I take the angelic blade, his blade, the fire burning bright along the edge, and I shove it through the gaping hole I left behind. He screams, his body bowing backward as the flames crawl along his body, engulfing him. I watch the flames, enraptured, as the archangel burns by his own fire, as it claims him and crawls along his many wings. He begins to fall, just as the Morningstar did so long ago, and when he slams into the ground below, still burning, those fighting leap away in surprise and horror. I slowly descend, landing before the funeral pyre of an archangel come to bring pain. The destruction I could cause now tempts me. No being could stop me if I give into this thirst.

Darkness whispering in my soul, the temptation to draw more blood strong, I look out of the creatures and roll my shoulders. "Who else would like to control me?" I ask.

A warning. A dare.

I narrow my eyes when no one steps forward. "Who else would like to make me bleed?"

91
MENA

The fighting comes to a screeching halt around me. They stare at the burning carcass of an archangel at my feet as the angelic flames consume him. The sight makes me happy, makes me want to do the same to the other angels watching me and taking halting steps back. They look between the burning body and the woman who felled an archangel, afraid, uncertain.

Their fear makes my toes curl.

I want them to fear me. I want them to worship me. I want them to kneel.

Tilting up my chin, I take in the creatures around me, their expressions of horror and interest, their desire to make me their queen and their weapon.

This is not you, Mena, Lilith whispers in my mind. *Listen to your heart.*

My heart is dark and deadly. My heart wants to see the world burn.

No, Lilith counters. *You are Philomena Seagraves. You are loved by four monstrous men. You are not alone.*

I hesitate. The darkness pauses long enough for me to search them out, to find them easing forward, their eyes on the archangel dead at my feet, on the blood dripping down my dress and coating my arm. I make a terrible visage, I'm certain. Is this the power they expected? Is this what they wanted?

Hyde is covered in blood, his claws stained with it where he had ripped our enemies to shreds. Though it's Hyde in control, it's still Henry's eyes I look into. It's still Henry. My Henry. My mad scientist. Both monster and man.

Blood runs down Otto's chest, his beautiful clothing torn and stained. His eyes are bright with feral battle, but within those eyes is also his love for me. My vampire king.

Athan appears in his human form now, his scythe still in his hands. He's watching me closely, with worry in his eyes, not because of what I might do, but because of what I might regret after all of this should I lose myself in the darkness. He fears for my soul, my grim reaper. My kind death.

The monstrous god who stands beside them makes many withdraw in fear, but not me. His huge wings, his imposing size, his terrible face that drives you easily to madness, I do not fear his cosmos. I revel in it, wrap myself in his stars like a shawl. He calls me his void, but he is my cosmos, and there are no stars without the darkness surrounding them.

Looking at them grounds me, makes me realize how close I am to losing myself in this taste of power. I could be powerful. I could bring this world to its knees. I could destroy it if I want to.

But that's not who I am.

I take a deep breath and look out at the creatures watching me with fear. I meet their eyes, make sure they can see me, make sure they can feel my emotions through my power. And then my power withdraws back into myself, hiding away, so I do not influence them one way or the other.

"You have all come here for a purpose," I say into their heavy silence. The crackle of angelic flames punctuates my words, making them heavier. "To capture me. To kill me. To control me." My eyes dance over to the gargoyles. "To help me." I jerk the angelic blade from the carcass of Michael and the flames go out abruptly. His body crumbles into dust and swirls upon the cobblestones, carried away by the wind and washed away by the mist still raining down and soaking me to my core. The creatures closest to me take a step back at my hefting of the sword. "But I will not be a toy. I will not be a pawn. I will not be a prisoner." I point my sword toward the crowd. "I will not be weak or afraid. I will not be exploited or harmed." I bare my teeth. "And I will not destroy the world I live in, but I will change it."

Victoria Frankenstein steps forward, her expression purposely blank. "But the power—"

"Is not yours," I declare, meeting her eyes. "There will be no more fighting. Those who do so will die by my hand."

To make my point, my power brushes out along everyone again, touches them, makes it known what I can do. They each feel the horror and fear I elicit in them, making them quiver. Surprisingly, Victoria does not cower at the brush of power, nor does she tremble. Her eyes only take in my stance, before she barely bows her head in understanding, relinquishing her endeavors. The rest of the monsters minus the angels around me do the same, their heads bowing in respect, accepting my command.

My power blasts out across the world at their acceptance, a message going out to all creatures, to all monsters, my warning.

"Women will not be subservient. They are equals. We are equals." I narrow my eyes. "They will not be harmed or silenced. They will not be abused by man's hands. If they are, the perpetrators will answer to the Mother of Monsters," I hiss. "I will always be Lilith, never Eve."

The warning blasts brutally outward, my back bowing with the pressure, as every monster receives my message. It wakes every creature sleeping, commands them to hunt the terrible men who repress women, and in it, I hear the prophecy.

I will destroy the world as we know it. I was never meant to destroy the world completely, only change it, destroy what has been done and remake it new.

The lesser angels run first, their horror at watching one of their own, an archangel, die bright in their eyes. They disappear so fast, it's difficult to know if they took to the air or turned to ash. The werewolves and vampires taking part fade into the darkness, bowing their respect at my power, giving into the urge to claim me. The witches have suffered great loss and so the few that remain simply bow their heads in respect and run away, hiding in the streets of London, blending in as human. The demons gather around, watching me.

"Mother of Demons," one of the nearest ones say. He bows his head. "You have earned your freedom. The Morningstar sends his regards to you, and his love to Lilith."

Because he had loved her. He had sacrificed for her plan as well.

I bow my head just barely at him before they too disappear back to where they came from, leaving my men and what remain of Victoria's in the small square. We leave a massacre here, in the middle of the warehouse district, evidence of a battle fought and won.

Victoria tilts her head, her bright eyes strange in the low light. Though the mist soaks her the same as I, she still looks regal, even as her hair plasters around her face. "You are not what I expected, Philomena Seagraves."

I meet her eyes. "Is that such a terrible thing?"

Her smile is gentle, a juxtaposition to the cruelty I know she's capable of. Her monsters are a testament to that. "No. No, it's not." She gestures to her monsters and the few remaining humans. "I hope there is no more trouble inside London from you. We'll be watching."

"You are not a god," I tell her as she turns away. "You do not get to decide fate."

She freezes, her shoulders tense, before she looks at me over one. The smile she wears is sad but also terrible, a flicker of knowledge no human being should possess. "We are all our own gods, Mena. Remember that."

And then she too leaves, so that it is only me and my monsters. They watch me for a moment, uncertain, before they rush forward, their arms wrapping around me, unafraid of the new power in my soul. They do not care about the savagery I nearly lost myself to. Their touch is what keeps the darkness away now, keeps it controlled. It bleeds, but it does not consume.

It does not consume...

I am Philomena Seagraves, and I am free...

92
MENA

Winter has fully arrived in London, the chill air coming with the taste of snow and the scent of coal. The streets are yet to turn to ice, but the cobblestones are cold to the touch, a promise that they will soon be frozen. No matter how many layers I wear, the chill still seeps into my skin like a kiss, like a reminder that I am still human even if I am immortal.

I am immortal.

Just as my men will live forever, so, too, will I. We have as many lifetimes as we could ever want in front of us. We can go wherever we wish, do whatever we desire, love until we are overflowing with the emotion. There is no limit to what we can do, what I can do, where we can go, and the world changes with that knowledge.

Here in London, the tides have turned. Women are starting to gather together, demanding rights and many other things. The change will not be instantaneous, but it will happen. When men fail to heed my warning, their blood scents the air the same as the snow does. The monsters and creatures of the world keep them in check, allowed to be monstrous at my behest.

And no one comes for me.

The angels no longer appear, as if they're afraid of me. The Creator sends no one else, and I hope that he shakes in fear at the mention of my name. The demons appear every so often, but they do not hurt me. They keep to the Morningstar's promise and give me the freedom I seek.

Today, we stroll through the streets of London, the cool air kissing our cheeks. I hold the arms of Henry and Athan. Otto and Hu take up residence beside them, so that we're one unit travelling together. No one questions our relationship out loud, though there are the rare whispers I catch. The high society has never taken well to oddities, but I'm so well-known now in my uniqueness, no one dares question my actions. Rumors fly, some more insane than others, but I find I almost like the hesitation I see in their eyes when they see me. I certainly enjoy the jealousy. No matter how I hold back the darkness, it leaks in sometimes in moments of weakness, and I shudder in pleasure at the at the way the high society envies me. The temptation to throw a party and let them watch our debauchery is strong, but I restrain myself.

For now.

We have no destination in mind, only out for a brisk walk so that I can take in the winter air. There's something about the coming frost that relaxes me now, as if the winter is a reminder that even nature must die for it to bloom again. As I have seven times.

Gluttony, greed, pride, wrath, lust, envy, and sloth. Each death terrible. Each is a reminder of the chaos I'm capable of should I choose. Each speaks of my humanity, even if my mortality is no longer in play.

Most do not approach us as we walk, preferring to keep their distance and talk. Some view me as a bad omen, death following in my wake. It's true that for each death I returned from, another followed in my wake when I came back to life. It's a detail I feel immense guilt over, but one I cannot control. Athan assured me that the deaths would have been quick regardless, that their time was just around the corner, and I only sped it up a miniscule amount, but I still carry that guilt. Just as I carry the guilt for the lives lost during the battle, even if they had all come for me with malice.

"Mena!" someone calls, and I turn to take in the woman approaching us. She's alone, her husband in the distance talking to another gentleman about some business I assume. I recognize her from society, a young bride with intelligent eyes. I attended her wedding at her invitation only two seasons prior.

"Missus Williams. What a pleasant surprise," I reply, and I mean it genuinely. I have not attended many gatherings for the last few months, not after the battle that had painted the warehouse district red. It had been too much to be around so many, so I stayed away. I only regret that I have not spoken to Missus Williams sooner.

"Oh, you know you can call me Ellie. We're much closer than that." She smiles brightly at me, one of the more genuine women of high society. She's a rare breed and it's no wonder her husband fell madly in love with her. "I heard you were caught in that nasty explosion over in the warehouse district, yet here you look as pristine as the last time I saw you. You're positively glowing."

I smile despite the reminder that we'd had to set a fire to cover up the remnants of the battle. Humanity is not ready to know about the monsters in their midst and there had been too many bodies there that would have revealed the secret. It had been difficult to make the decision, but it had been necessary. An explosion is an easy cover up when compared to the alternative.

"Such a strange occurrence," I agree. "I am alive and well as you can see, but I do keep finding myself caught in strange events. I'm sure you heard there was a sink hole beneath my home?"

"I did, indeed," Ellie nods. "I was so worried, but when I came to check on you a few days later, your house lady informed me you were out. Mrs. Kingsley is such a kind soul. What I wouldn't give to steal her from you," she teases, knowing full well it would never happen. "Anyways, I heard you sold your businesses as well. Is that true?"

"Indeed. It seemed a good time to retire, what with death on my heels and all," I laugh. The rumors have been many, but they're entertaining at least.

The sound that leaves Ellie's throat is nothing short of a tinkering laugh, her amusement palpable. "Will you be coming to Miss Farrow's ball in a few days' time?"

"Sadly, I will no longer be in town," I reply, glancing at the others with a smile. They're listening raptly, allowing me to make my acquaintance without interruption. "We're taking an extended holiday. The city is too busy for my tastes these days and I've often wished to see more of the world."

"Pity," Ellie muses. "My husband has suddenly allowed me to take over some of the business affairs and I would have loved to pick your brain." She smiles brightly at me. "I do hope your holiday is lovely and when you come back to London, call on me. You shall tell me all about your adventures."

I lean in and hug her. She blinks in surprise for a moment before returning the embrace. "Good luck with your business," I say into her shoulder. "And if you ever need help from me, anything at all, send a letter in the post addressed to my name. No address. It'll reach me."

When I pull away, she's looking at me curiously, but still she continues to smile. "Good evening, Mena," she dips and then does the same to my men. "Gentlemen, I expect you'll take care of Mena for me."

Hu grins. "We will take the best care possible of our sweet Mena." When he winks, implying just how well they take care of me, Ellie flushes and clears her throat.

"Good," she says, and then she shoots a look toward me, one full of coyness and amusement. "Safe travels, Mena."

And then she leaves us, returning to her husband as he finishes up his business.

"You play the part well," Hu muses, his eyes bright in the dim light. His own powers are dimmed down, my illusion over him strong, so that no one goes mad we don't intend to. It has helped to combine our powers so.

"Of what?" I ask, tilting my head.

"Mysterious lady," Otto answers with a grin. "You're still the talk of the town and it's been months since all the happenings."

Athan rolls his eyes at Otto. "It's difficult to forget the destruction we left behind."

"Indeed," Henry adds, laughing, his smile bright and easy. In his eyes, Hyde dances, both merged as one in a far easier dance than they'd had before. He had indeed waxed poetic and apologized while Hyde begged his forgiveness on his knees after the war. It's a memory I will cherish for years to come. "It's a wonder we were never called in for questioning."

We continue our stroll down the street, happy in each other's presence, content, safe, and free.

"So, where to now?" Henry asks. "The pyramids of Giza? The plains of Africa?"

"Anywhere," I reply. "Everywhere. As long as we're together."

"Together," Athan agrees.

We join hands, all of us, each as in love as the others, content to explore our new lives. We are one, a unit, and we will travel the earth together, lifetime after lifetime, and we will love.

We will *love*.

Until the world we know ends...

...and the next one begins...

EPILOGUE
MENA

TEN YEARS LATER

We left London and never returned. The city I grew up in had become too much, too potent for someone who feels emotions so easily. My powers, though less used now, are still strong, and often times, it leaks out of me without my intention. So, after tying up loose ends, we had left and started our adventures across the globe.

We've seen the world. I've stood at the base of the pyramids in Egypt and marveled at their beauty. I've watched wild horses in the great plains of the States. I've helped protect rhinos from poachers in Africa, lending my hand where I was able.

I have loved my monsters in every place, on every continent, in every way.

Now, we've settled in Hu's city, now an island in the Pacific off the path of most trade routes. R'yhel, where he was once imprisoned and where we now call home is a beautiful island, a tiny city we have slowly made our own. It's remote enough that we rarely get visitors, but those still wondering about the Mother of Monsters find their way here every so often.

Some still dare to hunt me, but they fail each time. I prefer this quiet life, enjoying my men, lounging about and enjoying my freedom to do as I please. Athan still attends to his duties, his grim reaper repentance still necessary. There's no telling when he will complete them, and when that time comes, we will face what happens together. Henry has his own lab set up here where he experiments and creates without worry of consequences. Every now and then, he creates something monstrous we must take care of, but sometimes, it's as simple as the little dog that glows with a thousand stars in my lap. I've named him Cosmo. Otto is happy to lounge around in luxury, happy to be at my side any moment he's able, spending time reading or painting or any numerous hobbies he's picked up. Hu busies himself with whatever he wants, whether it's to build another house or stand on the beach naked while a ship goes by. Every so often, he hears the prayers of humans and makes an appearance to cause chaos, but for the most part, he remains here, happy and content.

Mrs. Kingsley visits every so often when Hu retrieves her. She now lives in the grand house I once owned in the country with her husband and her growing family, as well as with the retired racehorse named Morningstar I'd once rescued from my own foolishness. I had signed it all over to her, had made sure her family was set up for generations. One day, as she ages, I will have to live without her in my life, but I will watch over her children and her children's children. She knows and understands what I am and is grateful her bloodline will be taken care of, their own guardian angel.

It's been years and I'm happy, so far removed from the hell we'd left behind that it's impossible to be anything else. We suffer the rare sight of angels on this island, but they usually fly away in fright from the woman who killed an archangel. I receive a card from The Masked Guild, every so often, always signed by Victoria. There's never anything but an update on London, on the advancement of women, and I appreciate it. The last card was a few months ago, and there has been no update since.

London is no longer my city. It is no longer my home. Home is where my monsters are, where they wait for me with open arms, where they love me.

But London still speaks about the Autumn of 1901 and Philomena Seagraves, the lady with the reaper on her heels, the woman who cheated death over and over again. But it's easy to put that out of my mind, to return to this happiness I know will never change. The darkness may dance at my heels, but I am good. I will remain that way. I will never change.

After all, if you hear no evil, if you speak no evil, if you see no evil.

. .

...then there will be no evil...

Until the day that all must change.

ABOUT KENDRA MORENO

Kendra Moreno is secretly a spy but when she's not dealing in secrets and espionage, you can find her writing her latest adventure. She lives in Texas where the summer days will make you melt, and southern charm comes free with every meal. She's a recovering Road Rager (kind of) and slowly overcoming her Star Wars addiction (nope!), and she definitely didn't pass on her addiction to her son (she did). She has one hellhound named Mayhem who got tired of guarding the Gates of Hell and now guards her home against monsters. She's a geek, a mother, a scuba diver, a tyrannosaurus rex, and a wordsmith who sometimes switches out her pen for a sword.

If you see Kendra on the streets, don't worry: you can distract her with talks about Kylo Ren or Loki.
#LokiLives #BringBackBenSolo

To find out more about Kendra, you can check her out on her website or join her
Facebook group, Kendra's World of Wonder.
Sign up for Kendra's Newsletter:
https://mailchi.mp/feb46d2b29ad/babbleandquill

facebook.com/AuthorKendraMoreno
x.com/KendramorenoA
instagram.com/kendramorenoauthor
bookbub.com/authors/kendra-moreno

ALSO BY KENDRA

SONS OF WONDERLAND

Book 1 - Mad as a Hatter

Book 2 - Late as a Rabbit

Book 3 - Feral as a Cat

Companion novel - Cruel as a Queen

DAUGHTERS OF NEVERLAND

Book 1 - Vicious as a Darling

Book 2 - Fierce As A Tiger Lily

Book 3 - Wicked As A Pixie

Companion Novel - Monstrous As A Croc

THE HEIRS OF OZ

Book 1 - Heartless as a Tin Man

Book 2 - Empty as a Scarecrow

Book 3 - Cowardly as a Lion

Companion Novel - Vengeful as a Beauty

THE LORDS OF GRIMM

Book 1 - Cunning as a Trickster

Book 2 - Bitter as a Captain

Book 3 - Twisted as a Princess

Companion Novel - Hateful as a Sister

THE KEEPERS OF ENCHANTMENT

Book 1 - Charming as a Killer

Book 2 - Ethereal as a Swan

Book 3 - Tricky as a Thief

Prey Island

Book 1 - Prey Island

Book 2 - Predator Point

Clockwork Almanac

Book 1 - Clockwork Butterfly

Book 2 - Clockwork Octopus

The Valhalla Mechanism

Book 1 - Gears of Mischief

Book 2 - Gears of Thunder

Book 3 - Gears of Ragnarök

Race Games

Book 1 - Blood and Honey

Book 2 - Teeth and Wings

Book 3 - Jewels and Feathers

Book 3 - Fur and Claws

Stand-alones

Treble Maker

Pharaoh-mones

Philomena And The Seven Deaths

CO-WRITES

with K.A Knight

Stolen Trophy

Fractured Shadows

<u>Shadowed Heart</u>

Burn Me

with K.A Knight and Poppy Woods

Shipwreck Souls

The Horror Emporium

with Poppy Woods

The Blooming Courts

Book 1 - Resurrect

Book 2 - Sprout

Book 3 - Flourish

Book 4 - Emerge

Book 5 - Blossom

The Dinoverse

(Shared universe with Poppy Woods)

Book 1 – Dances with Raptors by Poppy Woods

Book 2 – Rexes & Robbers by Kendra Moreno

Head Case: A Dark Twist on a Classic

FIND AN ERROR?

Please email this information to thenuttyformatter1@gmail.com:

- *the author name*
- *title of the book*
- *screenshot of the error*
- *suggested correction*

Made in the USA
Coppell, TX
19 January 2026

68472357R00330